MAMA'S
BOY

MAMA'S BOY

Charles King

POCKET BOOKS

New York   London   Toronto   Sydney   Tokyo   Singapore

POCKET BOOKS, a division of Simon & Schuster Inc.
1230 Avenue of the Americas, New York, NY 10020

Copyright © 1992 by Charles King

King, Charles, 1934–
Mama's boy / Charles King.
p.   cm.
ISBN: 0-671-74469-0 : $20.00
I. Title.
PS3561.I4736M36 1992
813'.54—dc20   91-30575
                           CIP

First Pocket Books hardcover printing April 1992

10 9 8 7 6 5 4 3 2 1

POCKET and colophon are registered trademarks of
Simon & Schuster Inc.

Printed in the U.S.A.

To Katharine

· 1 ·

While the Harrow family of Skokie, Illinois, were all down on the floor in front of the linen closet, whooping and laughing, the man who had come to kill them was getting off a plane at O'Hare.

He strode briskly but without haste down the crowded concourse. Clean-shaven; dark suit neatly cut; regulation tan trench coat of the American business class over his arm: the everybody nobody would remember.

As he passed a trash can he casually tossed away the two paperbacks he had been reading on the plane. One was in Maltese Arabic, the other in Israeli Hebrew. Both were translations of the same book: Jane Austen's *Pride and Prejudice.*

He stepped into a men's room and locked himself in a toilet stall.

Suddenly free to hurry, he stripped to his underwear. He unzipped his carry-on bag, spilling out dirty jeans, a worn bomber jacket, and a blond hairpiece streaked with gray. He balanced a makeup mirror on the toilet paper dispenser and went to work with practiced haste. In five minutes he switched clichés—businessman to aging hippie, complete with a scraggly little beard.

He grimaced briefly at his reflection in the mirror. There was something ridiculous about disguises; most ridiculous of all was that they worked so well. Whatever people said, they didn't care about strangers. They took a glance, saw stereotypes, averages, what they expected to see. Sad, really, how little misdirection it took to make the magic trick come off.

The man rapidly folded his businessman's clothes and shoved them in his bag, which he checked in a locker on the concourse.

In his wallet were the driver's license and credit cards of a man who

1

did not exist. These were not mere flash-alias documents, but a fully backstopped *dead baby*: a paper identity built up from an actual birth certificate.

The woman at the car rental desk told him to "have a nice day in the Chicagoland Area." He promised he would.

"It's going to be a chicken!" Roger Harrow said. He brandished a black Pentel over a blank drawing pad. "Look right here. It's definitely about to become—" He collapsed into helpless laughter. His wife Mandy had a gasping, intaking way of laughing—now she practically strangled. Five-year-old Alexander gave a piercing squeal of delight. Even Jill, their usually quiet eight-year-old, had the giggles.

They were sprawled in front of the open door to the linen closet on the second-floor landing.

They had been trying for ten minutes; now they were getting silly.

"Maybe he's scared 'cause all of us are here," Jill said. She looked grave for a moment, then broke up again.

"Try one last time," Mandy said.

"Once more into the breach, dear hearts," Roger said. He clambered up on all fours, his open cardigan sweater hanging down. "Winstonnn . . ." he crooned, "Winston Churchill . . ."

He crawled into the linen closet, holding the drawing pad and Pentel ahead of him. "Remember Squibble? Remember how much fun you had, playing Squibble when Uncle Jake was here? Don't you want to play Squibble now?"

At the back of the closet, in the large space below the bottom shelf behind a cedar chest, crouched a little black boy. He was kneeling on a mattress—this was his bed. Beside him was a single toy—a stuffed English policeman doll. He took the proffered pad and pen, held them politely for a moment, then handed them back.

"No use," Roger said. He backed out of the closet and stood up. The fun, such as it had been, was abruptly over.

"How did Jake get him to play?" Mandy asked. "Maybe we should call him and ask."

"You think he could tell us? Jake is good with kids because he's like a kid himself." He paused, aware that his frustration was making him unfair. "It's just a gift he has. He's always been better with kids than me." It hurt Roger to say that. He was not only a father, he was also a teacher in a local progressive school, a man who had devoted his life to the cultivation of children. Jake was his younger brother, with no children of his own, working as a cop in New York, playing at cops and robbers instead of doing serious work. But fair was fair. Jake was better with kids, so Roger forced himself to say so.

Seeing he was upset, Mandy hugged him. "It takes time," she said.

"We'll reach the boy," he agreed with a confidence he didn't feel. This had been going on for two months now. When would the breakthrough come? He pushed his doubts away. If they were kind enough —good enough—Winston would come around.

Goodness. Roger and Mandy believed in that most of all. Roger had quit a lucrative job at a big Chicago charity so he could spend more time with the children. Mandy was active in the Skokie Green party trying to save Mother Earth. Collecting signatures, putting up posters, making fiercely sincere speeches to disappointing turnouts. Sometimes it seemed she *was* the Skokie Green party.

But it wasn't enough to fight for abstractions such as peace and ecology and justice. You also had to save the world one child at a time.

Winston was that child; they had adopted him. Not that they couldn't have had more children of their own—they intended to. But right now, they wanted to provide a home for a child of the Third World.

Winston wasn't cooperating. He had been born in a tiny ramshackle village on the Caribbean island of Trinidad, on a green hillside halfway to the sun. He had been hauled northward, tragedy by tragedy, along a human chain of hard-pressed women. Finally, alone and defenseless, his good old bad luck had run out on him. Now he found himself in a house full of endlessly smiling and generous people who were always giving him food or trying to play with him. It was too much—he had stopped talking in protest. Instead he sat in the back of his linen closet, with big eyes, ate whatever they gave him, and darted out only to go to the bathroom.

Even though Alexander was "just about the same age, why they could be *brothers*," Winston never ventured out to play with him. He wasn't becoming "a true member of the family."

Another couple would have dragged him out of the closet, made him eat at the table and sleep in the comfortable bed they had provided. Not Roger and Mandy. To them, force was never justified. Especially not with children. They felt that, like the Third World itself, Winston had a right to follow his own path of development.

"I want to play Squibble!" Alexander shouted. He grabbed the pad roughly away from his father. Some fathers might not have tolerated that, but Roger only smiled. He was always pleased at a show of vitality from his children; he delighted in playing games with them.

As if to show his superiority to Winston, Alexander worked indus-

3

triously for several minutes, carefully producing a stack of parallel curves, which he clearly regarded as insoluble.

He grinned with triumph. "Do that one!" he challenged.

Roger held it aloft and groaned theatrically. "Too hard!"

"Gottcha! Gottcha!" Alexander chanted.

"Oh, wait a minute!" Roger rapidly sketched a profile that converted the curves into the feather headdress of an Indian chief.

"Well," said Alexander, recovering quickly, "you got *that* right."

The man who had come to kill the Harrow family drifted toward them over cracked secondary roads, in no hurry. It was a warm Thursday afternoon in mid-April. The sky was blue, the suburban hedges already green. Some trees were still bare or budding, but most already showed a complement of small leaves. They hung over the flat landscape like green mist.

He stopped at the post office in Skokie and picked up a large parcel wrapped in brown paper from general delivery. The package had been sent to the false name on his ID. Although he was right-handed, he signed for it with his left, a carefully practiced scrawl nothing like his real signature.

The Harrow's house had been built before the Civil War and had once been a station on the Underground Railroad. Unlike its modern neighbors, it was oriented toward the road, not the backyard, with the kitchen in the rear and the living room in the front; sometimes passing trucks drowned out the TV.

There had once even been a front porch, but it had rotted so badly that last year Roger had replaced it with a cinder block stair up to the front door. He had also put on a new roof, but the place still looked dowdy.

There were nearby houses on three sides, but the lots to the north were still vacant. The area had been laid out for a subdivision in the late twenties, then abandoned in the Depression. You could still see rusted fireplugs and crumbling sidewalks among the brown wreckage of last year's weeds.

Late that afternoon, the killer came down the old truck highway, doing about forty, his eyes scanning the far side of the road.

There. The battered mailbox with the name *Harrow* slapped on it in black paint, nailed to a tree stump at the end of the property.

He continued past and parked on a mud road behind a line of trees about half a mile to the north. It wasn't perfect—there were two houses across the road that might notice him parked there. But he had unobstructed sight-lines to the Harrow's home across the abandoned subdivision.

In the raking light of the setting sun, his eye caught the sparkle of broken glass—the neighbors had been using the lot as a dump. Disgusting. Some people had no respect for the law.

He unwrapped the parcel from the post office. It held two steel boxes.

The first steel box contained electronic equipment: an instrument faced with dials and knobs that he clamped under the dash magnetically, a device shaped like a toy rifle that he lashed to the sun visor, and a wireless earpiece containing a receiver, amplifier, loudspeaker, and built-in power supply, which disappeared completely into his ear canal. The whole setup was a laser listening device that would allow him to hear the voices in the Harrow house half a mile away by reading tiny vibrations in the windows. The laser beam was infrared: there would be no telltale dot of light on the windowpane.

The remaining box he stowed carefully under the car seat.

He cranked down the side window, positioned the listening device, and clicked it on. The machine was a marvel. It could dig the human voice out of surrounding noise with unerring accuracy—the laser beam was the least of it. Its beating heart was a computer that knew the resonances of every kind of wood, of copper vs. aluminum, and plaster vs. plasterboard, that from sound alone could distinguish center-hall Colonial from Cape Cod cottage, and well built from shoddy. In microseconds the CPU constructed a sonic model of the target house, down to the gaps beneath the doors, the quarter-inch camber of the basement floor, the number of spoons in the kitchen drawers, and computed the house's harmonics, its bass notes, tremolos, and falsettos. Now the machine knew how the house roared in the wind, creaked as it warmed and cooled, rattled in sympathy with passing trucks. The machine carpentered a virtual house, singing the same song—but phase-shifted by ARN circuits so that they canceled the sounds of the actual house and left silence. Any unpredictable noises were rolled off with a recording studio's worth of equalizers, frequency notch filters, and formant filters. The entire house had become transparent to his ear.

He immediately had to turn down the volume; the Harrows were having dinner. They chattered, laughed, even broke into song. Nothing had changed, daddy Roger was still master of the revels, turning everything into a game: here's how we mash our potatoes, let's see who finishes their peas first; they were obviously having a wonderful time.

The windows of the old house throbbed like membranes, modulating the beam of coherent light. The listening man might as well have been sitting at the table with them.

5

At one point, Roger told Alexander, "Come on now, finish your Venus." The listening man nodded. He knew that *Venus* was short for *Venus's flytrap,* and was their private word for salad. The Harrows were still using their elaborate family language. Potatoes were *clouds,* vegetables were *crocodiles, lions, kangaroos*—any wild animal. He was puzzled briefly when Roger complimented Mandy on the tender *steel-belted radials.* Ah, yes—steel-belted radial *tires. Tires* were meat. *Steel-belted radials*—a new coinage. Well, all languages evolve and change; who knew that better than he?

The April night was coming on; the world turned grainy black-and-white like a newspaper photograph. Lights glowed in the windows of the houses across the road and to the south of the Harrows.

A truck rumbled by, rattling the windows, wildly overmodulating his laser beam. An automatic digital audio-processor in the box under the dash choked off the surge of sound, sparing his eardrum.

In the abandoned subdivision, a man walked his dog on a spool leash—the unconnected fire hydrants at least served one function. The listening man slid down below the level of the car door, but the walker and his dog never came near.

After dinner, the family played a game called Up Jenkins. Something about guessing which hand held the coin. Little Alexander was especially good at it—every time he won, he would squeal, and the needle on the listening man's dash would jump.

It was hard to hold back.

Control yourself. Wait until the world is asleep.

He had bought the bomber jacket from an old-clothes store on West Broadway in New York. It stank of stale tobacco. He found the smell unpleasant—he didn't smoke. His false beard itched—he resisted the temptation to strip it off. Many hours remained before his final costume change. He folded his arms and slumped down in his seat, a dinner guest who had arrived too early.

Although it was an hour later in New York City, Roger's brother, Jake Harrow, was still at work. He was negotiating to buy a quarter of a million dollars worth of snort.

The venue was not consonant with the grandeur of the transaction. It was the basement of an abandoned building in Manhattan's Clinton section. A few blocks away, yuppies gobbled tofu burgers in fern bars, chattering about wheat futures and the co-op market. But here the floor was of hard-packed earth. The back was open to a fenced yard full of bricks and broken glass. A fire flared fitfully in an old steel drum against the chill of the night.

A single twenty-five watt bulb dangled on a cord above a battered card table. Five men watched Jake Harrow drop bits of powder into a row of test tubes in a wooden frame, like a kid doing experiments with a home chemistry set. One was Jake's associate in the buy, a powerfully built man calling himself Marchiselli. The sellers were led by a well-respected dealer in abusables, Noble Tang, said to have connections right to the top in Queens Road Central. With him was a motionless young black man with a fade haircut and a Brooks Brothers suit, called Ice, a white man with jumpy eyes called Rocca, and a wired young Hispanic man called Bumpus, who hip-hopped around the basement like a devil-chaser on the Fourth of July.

Jake squinted at the powder as it sifted downward in the oily reagent, like white flakes falling on a tiny house in a snow-dome paperweight.

Rocca had Tang over by the fire barrel and was whispering urgently in his ear. Jake was aware that something was rapidly going wrong.

"You sure?" he heard Tang ask. Very bad words, under the circumstances.

Yes, yes, Rocca was sure.

In a loud voice, Tang said, "Problem!"

Before Tang got to the "r" in "problem," Bumpus and Ice had their weapons out, designer stuff, very stylish. Christ, Jake thought, when was the last time he'd seen anybody in this business with a simple, old-fashioned revolver? He looked up, careful not to make any sudden motions.

"Put your hands on the back of your neck," Tang said. "Both of you. That's right."

Jake tried to sound puzzled. "What's this about, gentlemen?"

But Rocca was pointing a bony finger, not at him, but at his partner. "Your name ain't Marchiselli."

The temperature was dropping toward absolute zero. Something was sucking all the air out of Jake's lungs.

"What is it then, asshole?" the former Marchiselli asked. Brilliant.

Rocca said, "Your name is Gatto and you're a cop."

"This is crap. We're here to make a buy."

Rocca's eyes blinked rapidly. "You went to Christ the King High School in Queens. You played right guard on the football team. Your old man was a cop. You told everybody you were going to be a cop. And you did it. Everybody in the neighborhood knew that."

"I look like somebody you knew in high school? Give me a break!"

"I was two years behind you. I remember you. Your first name was Matteo, or some shit. They called you 'Meatball.' Meatball Gatto."

"Hey, Tang, this guy's nuts! You're not—"

7

"Shut up," Tang interrupted. "Denials aren't enough. You'd better have proof you're not the police—proof that will satisfy me. Or the consequences will be severe."

Jake stared at the barrels of the machine pistols. Ice's gun was as steady as if it were locked in a vise. Bumpus's wobbled with eagerness. These guys were ready to blow Gatto and him away if they so much as breathed funny.

Jake grinned. "Okay, you've made us. We're both cops."

"Hey, you *fuck!*" Gatto shouted.

"What's the use?" Jake asked him. "Game's up. No way we can scam them now."

"Thank you for your candor," Tang said. "But I'm afraid it won't buy you much leniency. This is very serious."

"It's worse than you think," Jake said cheerfully. "I'm wearing a wire."

Gatto's eyes bulged in disbelief at Jake's words. Even Tang looked nonplussed for a moment. Then he turned to the two young men with the machine pistols. "Give me thirty seconds to clear the building, then kill them. Rocca, clean up here." He started up the stairs to the lobby.

Jake whistled after him as if he were a dog. "Yo, asshole! You can't kill us."

Tang paused. "Why not?" he asked. The speed of Jake's revelations had apparently unnerved him enough to listen.

"Because somewhere within a ten-block radius, a big Nagra reel-to-reel is twirling like a merry-go-round, recording our every word."

Rocca yelled, "You ain't selling us no wolf ticket!"

"Shut up Rocca," Tang said without taking his eyes off Jake.

Jake grinned. "If we don't emerge from this building in a few minutes—your order to dispose of us is on tape."

"So what?" Tang said. "Somebody's voice on a tape."

"Yours. We have your voice print."

"It'll never go in court. Inadmissible evidence."

"Don't get technical on me. Forget court. We're cops, remember? We're talking cop killers here. Officer down, shit like that. Makes other cops irritable."

"You think you can scare me?"

"Not in a million years. Just stating facts."

"A risk I'll have to accept."

"Why? Nothing has happened here."

"You were buying!"

"We *talked* a deal. Millions do that daily. But the deal was to *go down*, as we say, somewhere else, sometime else. There are no drugs *here*—oh, a little, a taste for your friends, but we wouldn't run a measly buy-and-bust on a man of your stature. And there's no money here, either—not in the sense of actual *money*. All the essential ingredients of a *deal* are missing. What we've been having is a party."

"Which means?"

"You're madder than hell at us. It's not nice to fool Noble Tang. You'd love to waste us. Ah, but you didn't get to the top by indulging your whims, now did you. Think. You got lucky. You caught us early—before anything indictable happened. Why turn a headache into an upset stomach? Do you really want thirty-two thousand peace officers down your throat?"

"You're saying I should let you just walk out of here?"

"We walk, you walk, everybody walks."

Tang thought for a moment. "Ah, but what if you're not wearing a wire, after all?"

"Want to see it?"

"Keep your hands up, please. Rocca, check him out."

Warily, Rocca walked up to Jake. Bumpus jitterbugged to the side, so Rocca wouldn't be between them. Ice never moved, too cool to care about Rocca. Rocca was visibly shaking. He obviously didn't relish being anywhere near the line of fire.

"Where?" Rocca asked Jake.

"In my underpants."

"Fuck you."

"No really."

"Check his crotch, Rocca," Tang said. "If he wants to die for a stupid joke, that's his business."

Head averted, Rocca plastered his hand against the front of Jake's pants.

Jake said, "Oh, darling, I'll give you just twenty minutes to stop that."

Rocca jumped his hand from spot to spot, hoping for a direct hit.

Jake said loudly, "If we're shot, the perpetrators are: One, Hector Colon, street name Bumpus . . ."

Bumpus began to tremble. His teeth chattered loudly. Sweat exploded from his hairline and streamed down his face. "I blow you foockin head off, man!"

". . . male Hispanic, five foot ten, small mustache, black mole over left eye . . ." Jake went on.

The tip of Bumpus's gun jerked up and froze its aim, like a penis at the moment of inevitability. Meatball Gatto was swaying with fear. "Jake—shut the fuck up!" he screamed.

Rocca's hand froze in one position on Jake's fly.

"You're on mike, Rocca—sing a few bars. You know *Volare?*"

Rocca jerked upright. "It's there, it's there! The fucker is wired!"

"Whip it off me," Jake said. "Show the man."

"That's enough!" Tang said. He sprinted for the stairs. "Leave them. Let's get out of here."

A few minutes later, Jake and Gatto were driving away in their un-marked car. Jake had to take the wheel; Gatto's hands were shaking too badly.

As Jake pulled away from the curb Gatto shouted, "What the fuck are you *doin'!* When did you lay on a wire? Why didn't you tell me? I'm your *partner*, for Christ's sake!"

Jake fought a grin. "Come on, Meatball—that would take all the fun out of it. Don't you like these little surprises? That's what keeps our marriage fresh."

"You can't pull this shit! I'm going to Captain Cowen!"

"You were the one they made, remember? Why didn't you check with me before you went to high school with Rocca? You know how I worry about you hanging out with evil companions."

"You fuck! I don't care if you did just save my life! I'll file a formal complaint. I'll have your ass!"

Jake broke up and pounded the wheel with his fist. "I did it! I did it! This is the best! Thank you, God! Thank you for this night!"

"What's so fuckin funny?"

"There was never any wire."

"Don't jerk me around; I can't take no more of your bullshit!"

"When Rocca was pawing at my groin, you know what he was feeling?"

"If you say you had a hard-on—"

"A gun."

"You had a piece in your *crotch?*"

"Nobody grabs you there, even in a street search. They're embarrassed to, and besides, most guys won't carry a gun there anyway—they're scared they'll make a mistake and blow off their Johnson."

"But Rocca was feeling you up for about a week. How could he mistake a gun for a microphone?"

"What's a microphone feel like? Through two layers of cloth? There's all different kinds. I had him *thinking* microphone. He's scared, he's embarrassed, he feels a metal object where one shouldn't be. Bingo! It's a microphone."

"There was really no microphone? But you were trying to get Rocca to take it off you to show Tang."

"Hey, if you don't buy your own bullshit, who will?"

"What if Rocca had gone ahead and unzipped your fly?"

"I would have pulled out the gun and used him as a shield."

"Oh, yeah, like they care about Rocca."

"Lucky I didn't have to try it, huh?"

"Fuckin A. It would have been your pecker pistol against two Mack tens."

"Hey, I talked our way out, didn't I?"

Gatto stared out the windshield at the floodlit fountain in Columbus Circle.

"Why did you have to ride Bumpus like that? The guy was so beamed-up he was ready to blow us all away, Tang included."

"Yeah, but it was good, man; it was right for that moment. Couldn't you feel it? I was flying, I could do no wrong."

"It's that fuckin mouth of yours!" Gatto shouted with surprising vehemence. "You let it run away with you."

"There's something about machine pistols jammed in my face that stimulates my conversation. Like a bracing cup of English Breakfast tea."

The lights of Tavern on the Green floated past on their right, blazing in the New York night like a boy's dream of success.

Gatto studied Jake's face in the brightness as if seeing him for the first time. "It ever occur to you—maybe you're having a little bit too *much* fun?"

Jake sniffed the air. "Yo, Meatball—I smell something in here. You didn't by any chance shit yourself?"

Jake's brother Roger and his wife Mandy put the kids to bed, and were alone together at last. They read for a while, then went upstairs.

Although he could have heard well enough with the beam on a downstairs window, the listening killer went to the trouble of adjusting the angle of the laser to read their bedroom window directly. Words of love, cries of pleasure—low so the children couldn't hear. It was very difficult for the waiting man not to go in right then.

After a time the only sound was of breathing. And the faint groaning of boards—the old house complained to itself even when there was no wind.

Friends often said that Roger and Mandy "lived in a hug." They had fallen asleep folded in each other's arms. Only gradually did they separate, matching their movements like synchronized swimmers, careful to protect each other's sleep.

11

High above, the Big Dipper wheeled through an hour of time.

It was the darkest part of the night, when dreams are short and never remembered, when sleep stops the ears, and no one is listening for danger. From downstairs came the faint sounds: a click, a thump, and then soft footsteps, like the coming of Santa Claus.

·2·

Rape! Rape! Rape! Rape!

She tried to scream the word, but no sound came out. The man bore down on her, his great paw stopping her mouth and nose. Why didn't Jake save her? *Where was Jake?*

Sally Harrow woke up gasping for air.

Early morning sunshine streamed through the bedroom window of her little house in Queens. Jake was in bed with her, still asleep, his broad back a wall protecting her from a world full of rapists.

Just looking at him calmed her immediately. Thank God for Jake! He made it possible for her to live a normal life. If she had to go somewhere out of the neighborhood, he would drive her. He never demanded she go on her own, never embarrassed her. He covered up for her with other people, always found an excuse for her. Best of all, she never had to ask him. He had radar. He knew.

Sally's fears had begun two years earlier, when she was a senior at Princeton.

She had been on a date in Manhattan with a Princeton football player—a huge, powerful boy-man called Bo. No one said no to Bo. Not his nanny, nor his mummy, nor his trust officer. Bo's idea of fun was to throw a party in a suite at the Plaza Hotel and rip out the toilets with his bare hands.

Bo believed that drinking made him more attractive to women, and by the end of this particular evening, he had become so adorable he was overturning trash baskets and shouting curses at passing cars.

None of the passing cars pulled over. Bo was six-five, two hundred fifty pounds, without an ounce of fat on him. His tree-trunk legs, steroidally pumped, stretched his tuxedo pants tight as jeans.

13

Sally wasn't worried. Bo looked dangerous, but he was just being his usual charming self. People loved to tell "Bo stories." Bo loved to tell "Bo stories."

Bo had parked in a lot west of the theater district. As they reached his BMW, Bo decided to give her the full benefit of his glorious manhood.

He shoved her down on the seat and pawed under her dress. Sally had a moment of disbelief. Bo was a joke. Jokes don't rape you. She clamped her legs shut. He doubled up his cantaloupe-size fist and clubbed her in the face.

She saw stars, tasted blood, felt her legs being wrenched apart. She was as helpless as a calf in a slaughterhouse; Bo's biceps were thicker than her thighs. She felt his hand, heard her panty hose ripping, felt something butting against her vagina. It was impossible, she knew, but his penis felt red-hot like a poker. She was being torn apart, burned open.

The lot was dimly lighted, and they were at the far end of it. There was no one around, no one to hear. She knew it was useless to scream.

But she must have screamed anyway because Jake heard her. He wasn't on patrol; his car just happened to be parked in the same lot. No uniform, no badge—he was off duty, out on a date himself. She remembered seeing his face through the windshield—could it have really been like that?—the streetlight behind his head, his hair glowing like a halo, wearing a trim blue suit, Lochinvar come out of the west.

Jake tapped Bo on the shoulder. "Don't look now," he said, "but I think your fly is open."

Bo roared his primal rage and backed out of the car. His big pink penis wobbled as he stuffed it back into his pants like a salami into a duffel bag. He rushed Jake, ready to sack him for a twenty-yard loss. She still remembered him towering over Jake like a grizzly, his huge fists clenched.

And then it was over. She never saw what Jake did. Neither did Bo. But abruptly Bo was flat on the asphalt, gagging on sushi, badly in need of dental work.

That beating was the only punishment Bo got. Strings were pulled, money was flexed, Princeton rallied round. Sally's father was Professor August Payden, known as Popsy to the Princeton community. Department heads got to Popsy, Popsy got to her, she dropped the charges. Bo even apologized, sort of. Sorry I tore your panty hose, ha ha. Youthful indiscretion, won't happen again, no harm done.

At first it seemed no harm had been done. While everybody was yelling at her not to ruin Bo's life, Sally was fine.

Not that people didn't try to help her. The phone rang off the hook with information and suggestions. Like any high-powered academic community, Princeton had more rape crisis centers and women's support groups than coffee shops and Laundromats. But Sally said she had better things to do than sit around crying in her beer with a bunch of traumatized teenagers. Nan Payden, her mother, agreed, pointing out that people in her family solved their problems by pulling up their socks and getting on with it. Several of Nan's women friends suggested psychotherapy—not exactly a radical idea for a professor's daughter who has just been sexually abused in a parking lot. Popsy was outraged at the idea. As a philosopher he could prove that Freud's metapsychology was logically flawed. Besides, he'd be damned if he'd spend his hard-inherited money on some witch doctor.

The thing to do was forget about it. But she found it curiously hard to do.

She began to berate herself for going out with Bo in the first place. She had known perfectly well that he got violent when he was drunk. Why hadn't she been more careful? Why had she exposed herself to the risk?

Then a generalized, unspecific fear began to seep into her soul like damp into a basement. The nightmares began. Night after night she woke up gasping, trying to get enough air to scream for help.

She tried talking to Nan about it and was told to stop coddling herself. What did she expect if she insisted on morbidly dwelling, etc.? In short, the fear was her own fault. Sally felt she had no one to turn to. She stopped dating. Men terrified her. Bus drivers, countermen, any man she didn't know. Strangers in the street. Even in Princeton. If jokes like Bo could turn on you, where were you safe?

Only one man could protect her. The policeman who had saved her. She became obsessed with him. His likeness was burned into her memory. She had only to close her eyes to see him: the face in the windshield coming to save her. It wasn't only what he had done, but the way he had done it. "Don't look now, but I think your fly is open," he had said to Bo. The *style* of him, the insouciance. Just thinking about him excited her. She couldn't believe it—a policeman, a cop was the biggest turn-on she had ever met. She couldn't help it—the man was hot!

She called him up, asked to see him. At first, angry that she had dropped the charges against Bo, he refused. She kept on, bugging him every night on the phone, hanging around the precinct, coming on to him right in front of the desk sergeant.

She had her work cut out for her. He was a swinging single, living in a Manhattan apartment with black furniture, three blenders, and a

15

quilted mover's pad for a bedspread. He figured her as just another cop-groupie looking to lick the blood off his sap glove and hop a ride on his nightstick, an overprivileged rich-bitch, chippying around with danger before settling down with a corporate lawyer.

He'd hung up the phone on her, bawled her out, told her to get lost, but she'd bounced back as if she were spring-loaded.

Finally she'd enticed him to her parents' house in Princeton, one weekend when her parents were away. As soon as they were in the door, she was on him like a starving cougar, kissing and moaning and pawing at his fly.

Only she pawed from the wrong side and got the barrel of his crotch gun.

"Umm, so hard," she moaned in his mouth.

"That's nothing." He moved her hand over.

She felt, gave a little yell, and jumped back.

"You've got two—two—!"

"Wait'll you see the condom," he said, and fell out laughing.

Then he showed her the gun and told her it was a twenty-two, which sounded like a BB gun to her, and she thought it was cute, and she laughed and they started hugging and kissing and undressing each other. He tossed the gun on the couch, and while he was stripping his undershirt over his head, she picked up the cute gun, pointed it at the wall, and pretended to pull the trigger, with just a bit too much enthusiasm.

Bang!

From the other side of the wall, *Crash!*

He swore, and they both streaked into the kitchen naked as jaybirds. The cute bullet had gone clean through the wall, traversed the kitchen, and penetrated a wall cabinet. Sally couldn't look. Jake peered into the cabinet. All he saw were little bitty white shards.

"Looks to me like your mom's best china."

"Not her *Spode?* Oh, my God. She'll die. That was her *mother's* Spode, and her *mother's* mother's Spode. It's been in her family since Charlemagne. Is it *badly* damaged?"

Jake nodded his head woefully. "De Spode explode."

She started to laugh. He started to laugh. They couldn't stop laughing. And wham! they were making love, and they couldn't stop doing that either, from one end of the house to the other, all weekend long, like two people trapped in a Spanish-fly joke, so hot they couldn't stop to eat the Chinese and Italian meals they kept ordering in, so hot they couldn't finish showering and did it standing up in the stall, her feet braced on the insides of his calves, slipping and sliding and sudsing and kissing and chewing each other.

Three weeks later, they were married.

Popsy, a philosopher of ethics and author of a seminal book called *Ethics Engaged*, was furious when his daughter married beneath her station to a mere policeman. Sally was so disgusted by his hypocrisy that she turned against all academics and the academic life itself. Against Jake's advice, she dropped out of Princeton in her last semester. She had *him*, she insisted.

Besides, she was going to be a writer, and writers didn't need degrees. Hadn't she won the Solent Prize—the prestigious literary award—for one of her short stories? As a writer she could stay home and still have a career.

Jake would supply the material. He was a gold mine of hilarious, bizarre, and tragic stories. He was a legend, the original Mr. Cool Moves—every cop in the department told Jake Harrow anecdotes. Hey! There was her title right there: *Cool Moves*. She would transmute them into literature, place them in their setting and background, bring out the social and moral significance, make literature out of them—the way Dostoevski had turned a sordid tabloid murder into *Crime and Punishment*. She would call her hero Detective *Raskol*—after *Raskolnikov*, Dostoevski's tormented hero. He was the murderer, not the policeman, but so what? And *Raskol* had a nice echo of *rascal*, which Jake was a bit of. Perfect.

They bought a little house in Queens, all Jake could swing on his salary. The place was a fifth the size of Popsy's stately home in Princeton, where she had grown up, but she loved that it was small, contained, everyday, safe. A house like a million others, a house into which she could disappear.

Sally hadn't conquered the fear, merely hidden out from it. She was still terrified—especially of the city, the wild uncontrolled urban turf where Jake ranged so fearlessly.

She could barely nerve herself to walk in the immediate neighborhood, even though she knew it was actually quite safe. It was still the old Queens, full of ethnic strivers: cops, accountants, school teachers. No projects, no high-rises, just single-family homes—neat chicken coops with concrete-bunker driveways and crew-cut lawns and above-ground swimming pools in the fenced backyards. The budget version of the American Dream.

She had decorated the house to make it rapist-proof. But last night one had broken in anyway, into her cozy room with the yellow walls and the lace throw on the vanity and the flower pattern on the coverlet. There was no way to stop them—you can't hang chintz curtains on your memory.

Hmmm. Can't hang chintz curtains on your memory. Not a bad line. Where's my notebook?

"Did I tell you—I got another rejection slip yesterday for my *Cool Moves* proposal? A form letter. They suggested I get an agent," Sally said.

Jake was in uniform—he was getting a medal today. Sally was also dressed for the ceremony; her light spring dress concealed and revealed her high, perfect breasts and long, shapely legs. Jake could hardly concentrate on his eggs with sun-dried tomatoes. "Don't get discouraged, babe. These things take time."

"The publishers only look at stuff from agents, and the agents only handle published authors. It's catch-22."

Jake took a swallow of coffee. "Maybe that article in the writer's magazine was true—nobody trusts first-time writers enough to buy a few chapters and an outline. Maybe you're going to have to write the whole thing."

"But that'll take another year—and then I could find out nobody's interested."

"Watch it, kiddo—that's my life you're talking about."

"It hurts to wait a month and then find out they didn't even read what you sent them."

Jake walked to the stove and spooned another helping of eggs on his plate from the frying pan. "Hey, listen to what happened last night. This is the wildest yet."

He told her all about his little adventure with Noble Tang. She listened with sharp-eyed intensity to every word, laughing in all the right places, really *getting it*. God, he was lucky! Most cops' wives didn't want to know about this stuff—Sally was writing a book about it.

"So I'm not the only one who gets confused by your BB gun."

"Twenty-two."

"Whatever. Are you wearing it now?"

"Not to the medal ceremony."

"Bet you are. Bet you never take it off."

Jake stood up. "Only one way to find out."

Sally pressed her soft young body against him, gently rolling her pelvis. "Umm, feels more like a forty-five Magnum to me."

"Oh, shit. I just remembered. I can't be late this morning. Captain Cowen wants me in his car."

She kissed him and stroked his face. "You should have thought of that before you reminded me of the night de Spode explode, honey-tiger."

"You're right," he said. "To hell with Cowen. There's gotta be time for this."

•3•

"You said *what?* Stop it! You're killing me! Gatto, tell me he's bullshitting!"

Captain Douglas Cowen wiped tears of laughter on his sleeve. Jake was telling him about the Noble Tang caper and had him nearly helpless.

Gatto said sourly, "It's a lot funnier now than it was at the time."

"You had to not be there," Jake said.

That remark set Cowen off again, wheezing with laughter.

The three men were in the backseat of a cruiser headed downtown.

"Go! Go!" Cowen shouted to the driver. "Run the light! Turn on the siren! Can't keep the mayor waiting, can we?"

In the New York Police Department, Medal Day comes but once a year.

For the third consecutive year, Jake was being decorated for valor.

He had a drawer full of other awards—plaques from the Centurion Society and the New York's Finest Foundation—but this was the big one, the department's own military-style ceremony on Police Plaza, with medals, not plaques, and speeches from the mayor and the commissioner.

The ceremony was open to the public and the television cameras. That accounted for the eager smile on Captain Cowen's face. He saw his job as PR and Jake Harrow's medal was great PR for the precinct.

Captain Cowen loved the precinct the way a rocket loves its launching pad. He had higher ambitions—political ones—and the society marriage to prove it. He had the looks for it too: tall and sullenly handsome. Perfect casting for high office; he could have been right off the old "B" lot at Warners.

21

Gatto was miserable. No medal for him. He was going to the ceremony only because he was Jake's new partner.

He hated being in the back of the police cruiser, sandwiched between Cowen and Harrow like the third wheel on a date, riding the transmission hump with his ham hands on his legs sweating the crease out of his pants. Harrow of course was firing away like a verbal machine gun. The guy could talk to anyone, Gatto thought. Even a snake like Cowen.

Gatto hated Cowen. The arrogant son-of-a-bitch with his uptown wife and Italian suits and razor-cut hair was like no cop Gatto had ever seen. He was political the way DAs are political, not captains. He was plugged in way upstairs, beyond Manhattan North, beyond the commissioner. He was a user; he wanted big things. Anybody who got in his way got run over. Even his own men. *Especially* his own men.

Gatto had been caught cooping, snoring away on a cot in a basement, wearing his PJ's—the whole shot. Internal affairs had jammed his old partner, and the guy had snitched on him. The previous captain would have let him off with a warning, but not Cowen. No, Cowen had threatened to lift his badge and only relented after Gatto had agreed to partner with young Jake Harrow.

Worse, Cowen had him under a goddamn microscope. He couldn't fart without it going into his service jacket and becoming part of his permanent record. His career was dangling by a thread. He had to play everything Harrow's way.

That was why Cowen had done it. Any other partner would have been able to slow Harrow down.

As far as Gatto was concerned, being a cop was a civil service job. The name of the game was pension. Now, with only a few years to go, he was suddenly partnered with a hard-on who wanted to arrest the world.

Harrow would go anywhere, do anything, say anything. If somebody was stealing horses, Harrow would put the two of them in a horse suit and wait in the barn.

And guess who would get to play the horse's south end.

New York City Police Headquarters hunkers behind the Municipal Building, wedged between Park Row and the approaches to the Brooklyn Bridge. Surrounded by a rich jumble of architectural styles, it has no style of its own: it looks like the headquarters building of a soap company. Near a thruway off-ramp. In Ohio.

Its plaza is built over six lanes of traffic; the kind of place where trees grow out of metal grids. It is dominated by a Rosenthal metal sculpture that looks like outsize ammo drums from the old Thompson submachine gun.

Today, the sun shone brightly on Police Plaza. The Brooklyn Bridge traffic thrummed softly in the distance, a big sad musical instrument. The wind whipped bits of paper high into the air, like the souls of departed cops.

Everyone wore his uniform for Medal Day, sucked in his gut, stood at attention, tried to look sharp and military. For one day, the police department was an army.

The commissioner announced that eight cops had been killed in undercover drug busts this year. But that was no reason to stop the drug busts, and he wasn't going to stop them. That would be giving in to the drug lords. We are in a war, and we are going to win it.

The mayor made his speech, bouncing the word *valor* off the surrounding buildings. Inevitably, he said these cops were "the finest of the Finest." He also said they were "the best we have."

Many of the medals were posthumous. Widows wept, kids snuffled, Captain Cowen pulled his grim-yet-resolute face in case the TV cameras were on him.

To end on an upbeat, they saved Jake's medal for last. He had earned it throwing a crowd-control grenade in a room where five people were being held hostage, creating the cover for a SWAT team rappelling from the roof to smash in through the windows.

Cowen took the microphone, looking super-sharp as always. Rumor had it his uniforms were tailor-made. He had somehow wangled the right to tell the story. He ruined it of course, making it heroic and leaving out the cool moves. According to him Jake had used a TV set as a shield to fight his way into the room.

Actually, as Jake remembered, the thing started as a fuck-up. The hostage takers had demanded the TV. He had lugged it up four tenement flights with a flash-and-smoke grenade hooked inside his left sleeve, hoping to get into the room. But the hostage takers must have smelled a rat. One of them came out to take the set away from him in the hall —a big blond guy wearing some kind of funky cameraman's jacket with lots of slanty zippers and hidden pockets.

As Jake reached the top step he saw the guy running toward him, cocking his sawed-off shotgun.

Jake would never forget the sound of that shotgun being cocked; it had tightened his scrotum like walking into a January sea. He had flung both hands high, letting go of the set. The guy couldn't help but lean over to watch that beautiful twenty-seven-inch Sony crash, bash, and trash itself all the way down to the next landing. As Jake had stepped

23

past him he'd seen that the back of his jacket had ventilation mesh. Piece of cake to hook the grenade into that.

"Don't shoot!"

"You dropped the set! You dropped the fuckin set!"

"What are you worried about? It's still under warranty."

"Okay, smart ass. You just became a hostage. Hands behind your head. Move!"

Somebody nudged him. Cowen had finished talking. Jake's name had been called.

Sally watched proudly as he marched up to the dais; Hizzoner draped the ribbon around his neck and pumped his hand.

She was thinking that in her book she had done a much better job of telling that story than Captain Cowen had.

For a moment she had the fantasy of receiving an award herself—the National Book Award. She imagined it as a cross between the New York Police medal ceremony and the Academy Awards. She stood on a platform in a long décolleté blue gown and said, "I want to thank my husband and my agent and my editor for believing in me. But most of all, I want to thank my father, Popsy Payden, for acting like such a jerk about my marriage to a policeman. It was his pigheaded arrogance that led me to drop out of school and get off to a fast start with my writing. I also want to thank my lily-livered mother for caving in to him every chance she . . ."

Out of the corner of her eye she saw a man in a brown suit pop out of police headquarters and charge across the plaza. Heedless of the solemn occasion, he jumped up on the dais, passed directly in front of the mayor, and ran straight at Jake.

The lobby of New York City Police Headquarters is a cross between a subway station and an airline terminal: a Friskem gate and package X-ray for visitors, turnstiles for cops. Behind the turnstiles stands a monumental statue of a police officer in an old-fashioned uniform protecting a boy with one hand, gripping a furled flag in the other. Plainly an anachronism, left over from the old headquarters, the old days, when cops were neighborhood heroes, not an army of occupation.

The man in the brown suit had told Jake only that he had a phone call that couldn't wait. Together they burst through the turnstiles and hurried to a private office in the rear of the ground floor, where Jake was left alone.

Like the building, the office could have belonged to a soap company. The furniture was anonymous gray fabric and brushed steel. The desk was snowed under by statistical reports to a depth of two feet—the only indication of police work was that the reports referred to "offenders" rather than "consumers." Vertical blinds screened out the details of the day, allowing only a uniform white light to filter through.

There was a phone on the desk's return. The receiver was off the hook. Jake picked it up.

"Hello."

"Detective Harrow?" A hard man's voice, with something restraining the hardness.

"Yes."

"I'm Lieutenant Rourke. Tom Rourke. Skokie, Illinois."

"Yes?"

"You have a brother Roger?"

"What happened to Roger?" Jake had made a few calls like this himself. The news was never good.

"I'm sorry to have to tell you this. Last night your brother killed his entire family and then shot himself."

Harrow registered the words but had trouble extracting their meaning.

"Shot."

"They're dead, Detective Harrow, the whole family."

"Roger too?"

"All dead. I'm sorry."

Harrow said nothing. It was all he could do to hold the receiver to his ear.

Rourke said, "The bus driver from Mr. Harrow's school found them early this morning. Since Mr. Harrow teaches there, and both children are students, she found it strange when nobody responded to her honk, so she went to the back door and began knocking and calling. The next-door neighbor heard her. She has a key. The two of them went into the house to investigate."

Jake suddenly had to sit down. "You're telling me Roger murdered his wife and kids? And then committed suicide?"

"I'm sorry."

Jake stared at the desk in front of him without seeing it. His mind slipped in and out of focus like a defective camera.

Finally he said, "You want to run it down for me?"

"I can call back later if that would be—"

"Thanks, but I'd rather have it now."

"Sure. Okay." He began to read. "Uh, wife and children tied with clothesline, gagged with pillowcases, death by stabbing. Weapon appears to be steak knife, recovered from scene. Father's posture, head-wound consistent with death by suicide. Weapon, automatic pistol, also recovered."

Jake suddenly shouted, "No, it's a mistake. He couldn't—" He paused, got control, started again. "It couldn't have been Roger. He could never have *stabbed*—"

"I'm sorry, Detective Harrow, but there's no other way of looking at the facts. According to all the people we've interviewed, your brother and his wife didn't have an enemy in the world. There was money and other valuable property in the house, untouched. The condition of Roger Harrow's wound is consistent with—"

"Could Roger have been tied up and gagged too?"

"No, no. As I told you, when we found him, Roger—"

"Not when you found him, earlier?"

"I'm not following you."

"Could someone have tied Roger up and then untied him again after he was shot. As a way of making it look like suicide."

"I doubt it."

"Did you check for ligature marks, rope burns, bruises on his neck?"

"He looked clean to me."

"Looked *clean*? We're talking about a human being, not a car!"

"I understand that. That's why I called you."

"What time did this happen?"

"Probably sometime after midnight. Everyone was in pajamas or nightgowns when found."

"You don't have a more precise time of death than that?"

"Well it didn't happen this morning. They'd been dead awhile when we got there."

"Didn't the neighbors hear anything?"

"No."

"Nobody heard the gunshot?"

"The house is on a highway. It's easy to mistake a gunshot for a truck backfiring."

"What kind of gun?"

"An old thirty-eight-caliber Smith and Wesson automatic."

"Roger never mentioned to me that he owned a gun. He was a pacifist."

"Maybe that's *why* he never mentioned it."

"When did he buy it?"

"Probably quite a while ago. It's an old piece."

"Probably? You don't have anything on it?"

"We didn't see any reason to make a big deal out of it."

"You're going to have to check it out. I don't believe he owned a gun."

"This isn't New York. Most of the men around here keep a gun in

26

the house for protection." Rourke's tone was hardening, becoming more cop-to-cop, as if to say: *C'mon, Detective, you know better than to give me this civilian shit.*

"How did he—do it? To himself."

"In the mouth."

"No way."

"It's the surest."

"Yeah, right," Jake said. "Cops do that—deep throat. Never the side of the head—they know bullets can be deflected by the skull. Roger didn't think about stuff like that."

Rourke ground on, heavy as a road grader. "I'm not telling you what he thought about; I'm telling you what we found."

"Okay, which hand did he use?" Suicides almost always use the dominant hand. Roger was left-handed. Jake used to kid him that's why his politics were left.

Paper sounds. Rourke was paging through the report.

"The left."

"Oh. What about the hair-and-fibers people? Did they find anything they couldn't explain?"

"We saw no reason to call them in."

"Sounds like you saw no reason to do much of an investigation at all. If you had, you would have found out my brother didn't do it."

"He did it. He left a note."

"Saying?"

Paper sounds. " 'I can no longer live in a world that permits so much suffering.' "

"You're sure it's Roger's handwriting?"

"I'm sure."

"A handwriting expert looked at it?"

"I checked it against a memo he was drafting for the school. It's the same."

"*You* checked it? That proves nothing! I could probably fake Roger's hand well enough to fool you too, given a few days practice. That's why we have handwriting experts."

"Look, I'm calling you to tell you personal bad news, not to ask for advice. I've been trying to be a little kind here, to maybe spare your feelings until you're over the first shock. When you know the whole story, you'll agree with our—"

"Maybe you better tell me the whole story right now, because it looks to me like you guys were so damn sure Roger did it, you didn't bother investigating at all."

"I was there, you weren't. I saw things—"

27

"I don't care what you saw. I want a full-dress investigation: forensics, ballistics, hair-and-fiber, bloodstains, latent prints. The real thing, Rourke, not slam-bam-thank-you-ma'am."

Rourke digested that. Then he said, "Ever made one of these bad-news calls, Harrow? Let me tell you, they can be a bitch. Some people want to kill the messenger, they're screaming and cursing and blaming you, but see—there's an unwritten rule—you can't hang up. You can't add insult to injury. Now, you keep on like this, I'm gonna break that old unwritten rule, *capeesh?* And you can call back and discuss this with a desk guy who wasn't even there and is reading off somebody else's notes."

"Yeah, yeah, all right."

"You want to hear any more about how your relatives died, you ask your questions nice and polite. I don't care how bereaved you are; I don't need this chicken shit second-guessing."

After a while, Jake asked, "Where were the bodies?"

"All in the upstairs bedroom. Roger Harrow was sitting in a chair, Amanda was on the bed, both children were on the floor."

"Both?"

"Jill, female, aged eight. Alexander, male, aged five."

"What about Winston?"

"They had another kid?"

"Adopted. A little black boy."

"I didn't see any— Hold on." More paper sounds. "No mention of any other child."

"He hides. Winston hides most of the time. In the back of the linen closet across from the master bedroom."

Rourke's voice rose in pitch, lost its gravel. "The house was searched thoroughly. We couldn't have missed him."

"Lieutenant Rourke, would you send somebody over to Roger's house right away? Tell them to look—"

"Second-floor linen closet. Yes. Stay by that phone. I'll go myself." He clicked off the line.

Jake put his face in his hands.

Finally he got it together and picked up the phone, intending to call his father. Instead, he sat without moving, his mind swirling with memories of Roger and Mandy and Jill and Alexander. The ceremony was ending. The sound of applause drifted through the window, but Jake didn't hear it.

The phone was making strange noises. He hung it up. What had he been doing? Oh, yes, his father. He picked up the phone again.

Jake's mother had died when he was five. Joe Harrow lived in a trailer camp with his new wife. He had no phone, it was always a hassle to reach him. Jake called the trailer camp office. They said they'd try to locate him and have him call back.

Sally came in, looking scared and upset. Obviously Brown Suit had given her the news. They clung to each other.

The phone rang. The trailer camp people had known exactly where to look for Joe Harrow. Jake could smell whiskey breath through a thousand miles of fiber-optic telephone line. It took the old man a while to understand about Roger.

When he finally did, his first question was, "Who gets the house?"

"I don't know. Dad, are you coming to the funeral?"

"I'll see. I got important business down here."

"Good-bye, Dad."

Time passed, Jake had no idea how much.

Finally, the phone rang.

"Harrow?"

"You found him?"

"Where you said, way in the back of the closet. In the space behind a cedar chest. He sure knows how to hide—he was wrapped up in a sheet like a mummy. It's not surprising that nobody noticed him. You really can't criticize . . ."

Rourke trailed off, sounding upset and oddly distracted, as if he were involved in another problem.

Jake stumbled over his question, afraid to hear more bad news. "How—? I mean, is he—?"

"What? Alive? Oh, yeah. Winston's alive all right."

·4·

The next day was Saturday. Wet and windy all over the Midwest. It was still morning when Jake's rented car topped a small rise and he saw his brother's place ahead.

The old house stubbornly refused to blend with the neat tract houses nearby. It had survived from another era, the holdout house that had never been sold to the developer. It was battered and rundown, too close to the road, and exposed to weedy fields on the north side. Despite the closeness of its neighbors, the house seemed vulnerable and isolated, like an old man waiting alone at a bus shelter.

The Skokie spring lagged slightly behind the New York one; the tree in the yard with the swing dangling from it was just coming into bud. Three police cruisers jammed the driveway; a panel truck rutted the weedy lawn. Half-a-dozen uniforms and lab coats huddled around the coffee urn on the panel truck's tailgate.

Jake parked on the far side of the highway and trotted across, vaulting the yellow police ribbon that cordoned off the crime scene. He was underdressed for the cool weather in a thin polo shirt, but he didn't notice. He was thinking about what he might find inside.

Two men erupted from the lead cruiser and hustled to intercept him. Both were tall, but there was a sixty-pound difference in their weights.

The heavy one was Lieutenant Tom Rourke of the Skokie police. His face belonged on a post office wall: if you see this man, do not take any action yourself, but call the authorities immediately. His voice had sounded rasping and fiftyish on the phone, but in the flesh he looked at least ten years younger than that, with coarse hair the color of road tar on a hot day. Up close, Jake could see flecks of bloody toilet paper

31

clinging to his jawline. His skin was raw and battered looking; he probably shaved twice a day to reduce his thuggish look.

As they shook hands, Jake asked, "How's Winston?"

Rourke frowned and looked uneasy. "Fine, fine. You'll see him right after we leave here, okay? Meet Dr. Motley. He's the head of the forensic unit."

Motley came across as a cold fish, a thin lipless type who had spent his life squinting at bloodstains and washing his hands. He wore a green bow tie. He gave Jake a narrow, pro forma smile and pumped his hand once, European style. His skin was as cool and dry as a snake's.

Rourke seemed eager to control the agenda. "Lookit," he said briskly, "I think the best way to proceed is this. First I'll take you through our original reconstruction of the events. Then Motley will explain what he plans to do. Okay?"

"Fine," Jake said.

Rourke opened a small, blue spiral notebook and stared at his notes. "Detective Harrow, I— It's just that—I hope you understand that yesterday's call was to give you the bare facts. I withheld certain details, because—well, that was my judgment at that time. Now I'm going to give you the full story, but first I have a question."

"Yeah?"

"To your knowledge, did your brother take drugs?"

"Hold on. We both know damn well that Roger didn't murder his family. Winston being alive proves it. Whoever killed Roger's family didn't know Winston was there. Which means it couldn't have been Roger."

"Why won't you just answer the question? Did he take drugs?"

"What the hell is this? Are you still looking for some way to pin this on Roger? Because if you are, this drug thing is a pretty cheap trick."

"There's a lot more to it than that. We have reason to believe that whoever did this may have been under the influence of drugs. So it's my duty to ask you if your brother took drugs."

"No, not in the sense you mean. An occasional joint with his jug wine." Jake remembered that Popsy Payden had once dismissed Roger and Mandy as "jug-wine radicals," and he had to hammer down a spike of anger at his father-in-law.

"What's occasional?"

"Once a month, if that. To celebrate something nice. Why do you think the killer took drugs?"

Rourke looked embarrassed. "Sometimes it's hard to distinguish the effects of drugs from extreme rage."

"Maybe you better tell me what this is all about."

Rourke nodded. He was clearly nervous. "I'll start at the beginning. With our original reconstruction. But don't get upset if I say things about your brother you don't like. This was the way we saw things yesterday."

Jake looked at the sky. "Get on with it."

Rourke cleared his throat. "Okay, well, the way we figured it, the trouble started sometime after the family was in bed. Everyone was in pajamas or nightgowns when found. Our people fixed the actual deaths somewhere between midnight and three A.M. Friday morning."

"They were guessing," Motley said.

"We theorized that your—Roger Harrow and his wife, Amanda, had a fight in their bedroom. He, uh, struck her, and consequently she started making noise, leading him to gag her with a pillowcase and tie her up with clothesline.

"After that, we weren't too sure about the sequence, but the sound of the fight probably woke the two children, and they began to call out or make noise or something. So he went into their rooms, tied and gagged them, and dragged them to the front bedroom. At least, the pillowcases used to gag them were from their own rooms. After that both children appear to have been . . . sodomized and at some point he got a steak knife, probably from the kitchen, and began to mutilate them."

"All right, stop," Jake said. He turned his back on them and walked a few yards away.

The three men stood quietly in the misty morning air.

One of the tailgate crowd told a joke. Like sparks from kindling, the laughter flew up and was gone.

Finally, without turning around, Jake asked, "How mutilate . . . ?"

"He stabbed them repeatedly. All over their bodies."

"Jill and Alexander?"

"Amanda too. When all three were dead, he sat in a chair, wrote his note, and shot himself." He snapped shut his notebook, relieved to be finished.

Motley said, "Tell him the rest."

Rourke sighed. "He—whoever did this—before he cut their throats —he did a lot of work on—he slashed their faces."

"Their faces."

"I've never seen anything quite like it," Motley said. "There's no pattern or form to the wounds, except that each one starts with a fairly deep puncture. They're so many of them, so close together, they're

33

impossible to count. I'd say he was in some kind of frenzy when he did it. See for yourself." He proffered Jake some Polaroid photographs of the murder scene.

"That's why I asked about the drugs," Rourke said helpfully.

Jake studied the pictures, his face working in spite of a strong effort of control. "You asked about my *brother*. Whether my *brother* took drugs. Roger didn't do this! What the hell are you out to prove?"

Rourke put his big, pink raw hand on Jake's shoulder. "Take it easy, Harrow, okay? We still have to catch the guy."

Motley said, "If this was done by an outsider, it would be pretty hard for him not to leave some trace of himself. Somebody may have put up a struggle along the way—maybe Roger or Amanda managed to cut him, or hit him with something that would cause bleeding, maybe one of the kids bit him—my team and I will crawl the likely routes, looking for orphan bloodstains. Of course we'll do the hair-and-fiber work you wanted. Maybe he washed up before leaving. I'll scrape the sinks, pull the traps from the drains—take prints from the toilet handles. Even the careful ones will take off their gloves to pee, then flush the toilet from habit before they put them on again. We've got the valuables vouchered yesterday, and of course the steak knife. Even if he wore gloves, we might get lucky with the laser and pick up a print.

"And then there are the lab workups on the victims. If one of them so much as scratched our friend, we'll get enough from under the fingernail to blood-type him, which right there could clear your brother."

Jake listened to this recital with mounting impatience. "Sounds good to me. Let's get going. How come everybody's standing around?"

Motley shrugged and looked at the ground.

Rourke took a deep breath. "Before we do anything, we need a little help from you."

Jake gave him a hard sideways glance, suddenly wary. "Help doing what?"

"This boy Winston. There's no point dragging him into the case. He's got enough problems without a lot of publicity. It's not like he was really your brother's kid—he was only adopted a couple of months. What do you say we leave him out of it?"

"Leave him out how? He was there."

"But who knows that?"

"Say again?"

"I was alone when I found him. I smuggled him out without anyone seeing."

"What's the point? Sooner or later—"

"Not necessarily. If you keep your mouth shut, we can make it stick he wasn't there the night of the murder."

"I don't believe this! Where the hell was he supposed to have been?"

"I cut a deal with the head of the adoption agency, Mrs. Appleby. She's going to say he was with them the night of the killings."

"The *adoption agency* is in on this?"

"They placed one of their kids with a mass murderer. It's in their interest to play down the danger as much as possible."

"And you expect me to go along with this?"

"I'm trying to protect the boy. A thing like this could follow him the rest of his life."

"Yeah, yeah, like you care about his life. Don't give me this crap," Jake said. "What do you think, I just got out of the academy?"

"I told you he wouldn't buy it," Motley said.

Rourke vigorously rubbed the back of his neck. "Look, Harrow, I know it's your brother and all, but try to be a cop again for a minute."

Motley groaned. "Why don't you stop trying to jerk him off and just tell him what happened?"

Rourke looked sullen. "The lady bus driver who found the bodies—after she called us she called her friends. We got here half a step ahead of 'Eyewitness News.' Maybe you New York guys are used to slaughter, but we were shook by what we found in there. We're all standing around deep breathing, trying to keep down breakfast. The press is camped out in the driveway. Meanwhile the phone is jangling every two minutes with captains and mayors and shit. I'm getting major pressure to make a statement. You know what that means? America is a monarchy, my friend, and the media is king. They want answers. That's an order. If you don't have them—well, it's not only defendants who are tried and convicted in the newspapers. Okay, we thought we knew what we had—I mean, family dead of stab wounds, bloody knife on floor, dead dad in chair, gun in lap, note beside him—it was all laid out like the Hollywood Wax Museum.

"So I blew it. I made an official statement to the TV cameras. I committed the department in front of the media."

"Before you called me? That was delicate of you."

"Frankly, the feelings of next of kin were not on my mind at that point. Anyway, I go back to headquarters. I call you. I come running out here again. I find Winston. We missed an entire human being! A small one, I grant you, but bigger than a fingerprint."

"You made a mistake. So what?"

"Mistake! Hey, when you got four dead bodies, there are no

35

mistakes—only career-ending fuck-ups!'' Rourke yelled. ''I had to do something!''

Jake said, ''This is pathetic, you know that?''

''It's my career. I know it's hard for you to give a shit—''

''It's not the way it happened.''

''So what? What *difference* does it make?''

''Winston's being left alive is proof my brother didn't do it!''

''It's not proof! He was new to the family—there's a million reasons your brother might have spared him. His being left alive is just a piece of interesting evidence. No more.''

''Evidence you want to destroy.''

''I destroyed nothing! I know the truth. If we need Winston to have been there, we can always establish that he was.''

''Oh, this I want to hear.''

''I can always say we found Winston at the scene, but kept it a secret. We gave the 'dad slays' story to the media to buy time. You know— investigate other leads, lull the real killer, whatever.''

''Got it all figured out, haven't you.''

''Except for you. I need you to cooperate.''

''I'm not going to lie.''

''I'm not going to lie,'' Rourke mimicked. He rubbed the back of his neck again. ''You're one of those guys, aren't you.''

''What guys?''

''Yesterday, when I called you, they said you were getting a medal. You're one of those guys who gets medals and doesn't tell lies.''

''That's right.''

''Okay, then it's hardball time. See Motley here? See his guys and gals in the lab coats? See the Skokie blues? They're all ready to start looking for your murderer. Or not. Depending.''

''Maybe I should call your captain and tell him the whole story, including this conversation.''

''That's why you took the early flight from New York, to make sure I wind up as a floorwalker at Marshall Field's? Go ahead, bust my ass. That's not going to convince the captain to reopen this investigation. So a crazed father didn't get around to killing a recently adopted kid. So what? Maybe he couldn't find him either.''

''I'll make a stink. I'll embarrass him into reopening the case.''

''I sincerely doubt it. But let's say you do. This is Saturday. Bad day to reach people. Sunday's worse. And then schedules have to be re-arranged. By the time all the wheels have rolled—you'll be lucky to have anything up and running by Wednesday. What do you think, Motley?''

"Wednesday's optimistic. I'd say Monday of the following week. By then you'll be reading tea leaves. There'll be nothing left. A murder is like a sinking ship. You've got to get the clues off quickly or it disappears forever beneath the waves.

"We've already lost our chance to pinpoint the sequence of murders. Body temperature can give you the time of death, but you've got to catch it early. In twenty-four hours it falls to the level of the environment. It's gone. We've got four stone-cold bodies. See, dying doesn't happen all in a moment; it's a process. Death has a life of its own. Bruises can fade in a few days. Stab wounds can seal with clotted blood. Fluid can pool in the tissue and create new bruises that weren't there originally. It's now or never. Frankly, Harrow, I'm you're only shot."

Rourke nodded. "There's nothing like a ten-day wait to sharpen up the neighbors' memories. You want to first start asking bus drivers and cabbies about suspicious passengers a couple weeks from now? When do you want us to fine-tooth that vacant lot? Now? Or after more April showers have brought May flowers? Your call."

Jake had never lied about police work in his life. He fully expected himself to tell Rourke to go to hell.

Instead, he heard himself say, "I'll do it your way."

It was noon before Motley finished. While his people loaded their cardboard boxes of samples and equipment into the panel truck, he came over to the cruiser where Jake and Rourke waited.

"Anything jump out at you?" Jake asked.

"An unreasonable amount of blood. More like a building collapse than a murder. He must have kept them alive for quite a while, working on them." Motley smiled thinly. "I won't have to write QNS on this report." QNS meant "Quantity Not Sufficient"—a little forensic humor. "Your brother smoke these?" In a small clamp, he held the butt of a black cigarette.

Rourke said, "Sadowski left that. One of my guys. He smokes Gauloises at murder scenes. Gets the smell of death out of his nose."

"A cop smokes Gauloises?" Motley said.

"That's so we'll know it's his and won't mix it up with the evidence."

Jake thought, *No wonder Rourke has problems.* He kept it to himself. For better or worse, he was on the guy's team now.

"How do you think he got in?" Jake asked.

"Don't know. There's nothing under the windows. I've taken out the locks for microscopic analysis. I replaced them with padlocks. Here's a key, if you want a look."

Jake was about to ask another question, but Motley held up his hand.

"If I leave now, I may be able to get the lab started on most of this stuff today. We'll be working all weekend."

"When will we have your report?" Jake asked.

"I'm shooting for Monday, late morning."

"That's after the funeral."

"It's also the land speed record. We're talking double golden overtime on this one."

Jake pushed through the back door into the kitchen.

Someone had done the dishes. Mandy? Or the police? The oilcloth place mats on the kitchen table had been wiped down and shone in the pearly light from the windows. As always, there were too many plants for Jake's taste—Mandy liked jungles. Plants dangled from ropes, lined windows, sat in pots on countertops. Although their caretaker was dead, they were still thriving with heartless vitality. She must have watered them the day she died.

Jake made a circuit of the room. He picked up a faint whiff of gas from the leaky old stove. All the drawers by the sink were pulled open. One held a plastic tray with dividers: forks, soup spoons, steak knives. Three steak knives. The one they found in the bedroom would make four. Jake picked up one of the remaining knives and studied its brass fittings and dishwasher-bleached wooden handle. In spite of the cruel serrated edge, it seemed too small, too flimsy, to qualify as a murder weapon.

He dropped the knife back in the tray, elbowed the drawer shut, and walked to the front of the house. He passed by the stairs. He wasn't quite ready to go up yet.

Without people in it, the living room seemed even shabbier than he remembered it; he and Sally had been sitting on these spavined chairs and butt-sprung couch just a few weeks before. When Roger and Mandy had married, they had bought everything from the Salvation Army, and never changed it: political furniture. The television was a prehistoric black-and-white model, soldered to the educational channel. Even the darkest corner harbored plants—he always wondered how they survived with so little light. The ficus tree by the window was too big for the room—it threatened to break through the ceiling. On the wall behind the couch, an OXFAM poster of a black child, starving, scrawny, arms outstretched. The child's screaming mouth was a wide oval, like a begging bowl. He looked a little like Winston. Posters for liberal causes had always been Roger's idea of living room art.

With a rueful smile, Jake remembered how during the last visit Roger had tried, as he always did, to draw him into a political argument. That time it was the death penalty. Roger took the position that murder was an insane act, therefore all murderers were insane, therefore they should be treated, not punished.

Jake had agreed, laughing. He couldn't take such discussions seriously—they were kid stuff; they belonged in college bull-sessions. Life was a matter of tactics, not grand strategies. "What now?" was the question, not "Whither mankind?"

Jake's attitude had irritated Roger but never touched the deep love he bore for his brother. Nothing could interfere with that. They had been through too much together. In childhood it had been the two of them against the world.

Jake remembered his early childhood as a golden age, when the family had all lived together and been happy. He had been especially close to his dad. They were always roughhousing; Joe had called him Little Feisty.

But when Jake was five, and Roger six, their mother had died.

Joe had taken them to live with Aunt Freezie—who was not their aunt at all, but a "special friend" of Joe's. Still, it was a family of sorts, and Aunt Freezie was kind to him. But after a time, Joe had decided to leave and to hand the boys off to different relatives, separating them.

Jake still remembered the scene of his father's blue Chevy driving away with Roger in the backseat as the worst moment of his life.

Roger and he were reunited the next year, but they never lived with their father again. He shipped them around among a large circle of distant relatives and old girlfriends and dropped in for an occasional cameo shot.

Joe had been a welder. He liked to travel, and his union card was his magic carpet. He was always about to settle down and go into business for himself.

"A restaurant with a difference—football! Stars' pictures on the walls, football food names: Goalpost Goulash. T.D. Tacos. Long-Bomb Burgers. And get this—Hash-mark Hash with a two-minute warning! We'll call the place Harrow's Huddle. I got the location picked out, even lined up a chef—the man has dancing wrists on the grill. You boys will wait table on weekends and in the summer—you'll make a fortune in tips. And the best part is—we'll all be together, a team."

Jake had learned early not to ask what happened to Harrow's Hardware Heaven, the surefire scheme from the previous visit.

Jake and Roger had tried to be each other's parents. Roger the careful planner, Jake the battler, scared of nothing. They had always slept in the same room, played together, shared their secrets. Although Roger was a year older, almost from the beginning Jake was the better athlete.

When they had lived at Aunt Freezie's—Jake couldn't have been more than six—he had saved his big brother from drowning in a lake. The triumph of that day had never quite left him. It had glowed inside him like a pilot light, the feeling of being good and strong and useful. Sometimes he thought it was why he had become a cop.

If only I had been around on Thursday night, Jake thought.

He went up the stairs.

At the top was a small pedestal table with a red night-light.

There was a sign on Jill's door: Beware of Unicorn. The walls were plastered with fierce-looking posters for English rock groups. She had painted a rainbow on the ceiling and down the wall. At the end of the rainbow was an empty bed. The bed was messy, but there was no sign of a struggle. No blood on the floor, nothing broken or overturned.

Alexander's room had a large carton of wrestling action figures in the middle of the floor. The hulks and brutes and musclemen looked macho and tough, but they had been no better protection than Jill's unicorn.

Apparently, Roger and Mandy had allowed Alexander to draw on the wall with crayon—there was a childish mural beside his bed.

His bed was like Jill's—messy, but not torn up.

There was another bed in the room, small, neatly made up, apparently for Winston if he had ever wanted it.

Jake retraced his steps past the head of the stairs to the parental bedroom. He noted the linen closet was directly across the hall. Winston's mattress was still inside. The door would have been left open, for air. The killer must have passed directly through Winston's line of sight several times. The boy must have been awake—nobody could sleep through something like that. The bedroom light would have been on. Even without it, there was the hall night-light. Winston had occupied a ringside seat. He must have gotten a good look at the killer.

In the parental bedroom itself, the first thing that hit him was the smell. The murders had occurred on Thursday night, but even now, on Saturday, the rusted-iron reek of blood was strong.

Blood splashed and swirled and stippled the walls, almost to shoulder height; the work of an abstract expressionist with a palette predominantly red. He blinked, trying to find the room he remembered, now so vigorously redecorated in its new color.

He walked over to a balding easy chair and studied the single red blot—like a color Rorschach—on the headrest. It reminded Jake of a fat red spider. *Here's where he made Roger sit while he wrote his note.*

He paced around the room for a few minutes, remembering Motley's Polaroid photographs, trying to be objective, struggling to study the bloodstains like a geologist reading rock strata in a canyon.

These slide marks on the rug and baseboard—that's where he sodomized and slashed little Alexander. He walked to the bed and pointed to a low red sunrise on its side. *This is where he raped and face-stabbed Jill.*

The sheets were stiff with gouts of dried blood on Mandy's side of the bed. Innocent Mandy—who was always watering her little indoor jungle, who let her kids draw on the walls and thought she could save the world—the killer had rushed at her with his prick and his steak knife. . . .

The suicide note said: "I can no longer live in a world that permits so much suffering." Roger could never have committed suicide; it wasn't in his repertoire; he would have considered it irresponsible, cowardly, socially retrograde. But if he had committed suicide, that would have been his note.

The killer was smart, all right, but he'd depended on the police buying the suicide scenario and not carrying out a heavy-duty forensic number. He'd thrown too wild a party here. There was no way he was going to escape Motley's tweezers.

And he had missed the boy in the closet. Winston had seen him and might be able to identify him.

Jake looked at the bloodstained walls.

We will meet, you and I.

Soon.

On the way out, Jake paused by the sink in the kitchen and took a steak knife from the drawer.

He studied it, turning the blade this way and that, watching the sawteeth sparkle in the cloudy brightness of noon.

He lifted the flap of his right-hand jacket pocket and dropped in the knife.

· 5 ·

The Appleby Agency occupied its own building, a neat three-floor structure of blond stone and glass brick, way out on Western Avenue in an area of weedy lots and black-windowed bars.

There was a small reception area, but no one was at the desk. Jake followed his ears to a noisy playroom where twenty or so kids, mostly toddlers and kindergarten age, played noisily on a bare wooden floor, under the care of several teenagers. The air reeked of full diapers.

A two-year-old Chinese girl immediately ran to Jake and handed him a dead spider.

"Thanks a lot." He inspected it closely and smiled at her. "Say, this is a good one. I'm saving this for later." He put it in his pocket.

She banged her hands together with glee and toddled off to find something else to submit for his approval.

One of the teenagers directed Jake to Mrs. Appleby's office.

Mrs. Appleby herself was a large pink woman, with a perpetually worried look. When Jake stuck his head into her office unannounced, she looked up and screamed.

It took him a moment to understand. Then he said, "I'm *Jake* Harrow—the brother."

"I'm so sorry." She put her hand over her mouth. "It's just that—the family resemblance—"

"That's okay. Where's Winston?"

"Mr. Harrow, I have some very good news for you. The Appleby Agency stands ready to take Winston off your hands. I have the dis-adoption papers all ready."

Jake looked blank.

She rushed into what sounded like a prepared speech. "So many

43

people have false ideas about our work. They see all outplacement situations as cruel or neglectful. The media like to seize on the rare abuses and sensationalize them. Sells papers. It's especially unfair to a private agency like ours. Our foster homes are carefully selected and continuously monitored for—"

Jake cut her short. "Sounds like the best thing for him."

"You weren't planning to take him?" She looked as if she would pass out with relief.

"To *keep?* The idea hadn't occurred to me. Frankly, I was so shaken up by what happened, I haven't been able to think about next steps."

"Yes, of course. I should have offered my condolences for your loss. What a terrible . . . thing."

"Thank you."

"We'll require your wife's signature too, of course. Have you discussed this with Sally at all?"

"You know her name?"

She patted a manila folder on the desk in front of her. "From the file."

"Ah. Tell you what. Give me the papers. Sally's flying in tomorrow for the funeral; we'll sign them and stick them in the mail."

Mrs. Appleby handed him the papers with a big smile. "I'm so pleased you see it our way. You're absolutely doing the best thing for all concerned. Can you find your way out?"

"I'd still like to see him."

Her smile faded. "May I ask what for?"

"I need to question him."

"About what?"

"Mrs. Appleby, we both know where he really was on Thursday night."

"He doesn't speak."

"He wasn't always that way."

"He hasn't said a word since he came back here. It's a waste of your time."

"I've got to try. He could be an important witness."

She jumped as if shocked. *"You mean in court?"*

"It all depends on what we find."

"Lieutenant Rourke told me the case was solved."

"It wasn't."

"Oh, dear. I'd hate to see the poor little tyke dragged through a court case."

"Don't get upset. It probably won't be necessary. Now, please, if I could just have a few minutes with him . . ."

44

She led him up a flight of stairs to a long hallway with an impossibly large number of doors, like a row of lockers. Some stood open revealing neat rooms hardly more than a cot wide.

"We put him back in his old room. Familiarity is so important after—in these cases."

She rapped briskly on door sixteen.

"Winston Churchill? You've got a visitor." Jake noticed she used his first and middle names but didn't add *Harrow*. In her mind the dis-adoption papers were already signed.

She opened the door. The little boy with the big man's name was sitting on the side of his cot, staring straight ahead, not fidgeting, not moving a muscle, as if he were afraid that the slightest movement might get him hurt.

His toys were lined up neatly on the shelves at the foot of the bed, obviously untouched.

Jake dropped to one knee. "Yo Winston, how ya doing?" he said.

No reaction.

"You remember me. I'm your uncle Jake, the Squibble man."

Winston's eyes widened slightly, that was all.

Mrs. Appleby spread her hands in a gesture of hopelessness. "As I said, you're wasting your time."

"Wow, look at these great toys. Which one's your favorite? Can you point it out to me?"

The boy didn't move.

"Remember the Constable? You had such fun with him," Mrs. Appleby said. She took a stuffed doll in an English policeman's uniform from the shelf and shoved it into Winston's hands. He made no effort to hold on; it dropped to the floor.

"You see?" Mrs. Appleby said. "That's what I was trying to tell you. That Constable doll was what psychologists call his *transitional object*. You know, like that blanket Linus drags around in the 'Peanuts' comic? He slept with it, took it everywhere with him. Now he doesn't even recognize it."

"If I could be alone with him," Jake said.

"As you wish. I'll be in my office."

Jake closed the door. He squatted in front of Winston, so they were eye to eye.

"I know you're scared. You saw some awful stuff. You don't want to talk about it; I don't blame you. But see, you gotta talk. I need your help. You gotta tell me what happened. Will you do that? Will you help your unca Jake?"

Winston stared gravely ahead.

"Please? I'm on my knees, kiddo. Pretty please? Pizza please with sausages and peppers on it?"

Nothing.

"Say yes. Just say yes. Or say no. Or say boola boola bandersnatch. Say something."

Silence.

"Okay, okay, you don't want to talk, you don't have to talk. It's up to you. This is Liberty Hall. All you gotta do is nod your head up and down, up and down for *yes*. And shake your head side to side, side to side for *no*. How's that for simple? Will you do it?"

Winston turned his face to the side and looked at the foot of the bed.

Jake picked up the fallen toy and held it in front of Winston's face.

"If you won't tell me, how about telling the Constable? He's your old pal. You can tell him."

A long wait. Jake's left knee began to ache dully. Then slowly, slowly the boy's hand floated out and settled on the Constable's cap. Gradually the fingers curled, held, gripped. Winston took the doll from Jake and hugged it to him.

"I bet the Constable is happy to be with his—"

The boy slid off the bed, opened the door, and walked out.

"Where you going?" Jake jumped up, both knees crackling, and followed.

Winston strode briskly down the hall, past the head of the stairs, the Constable clutched to his chest.

"Don't leave yet. We've got things—"

Winston walked straight into the bathroom at the end of the hall.

"Oops, sorry," Jake said. "See you back at the room." He turned around and walked the other way.

Flush! Flush! Flush!

Jake turned back. The bathroom door was wide open. He went in. Winston was pumping furiously on the toilet's foot-flusher with both hands.

Staring up from the water, spinning, tumbling, bumping the sides, too big to go down, was the Constable.

·6·

That evening, in central New Jersey, Professor Julian Lamb arrived at a party. As he rang the bell he found it hard to suppress a smile. This evening was going to be excruciatingly boring—a pleasant prospect.

It was one of the best things about Wren College: you were not in the fast lane. More like the exact-change lane. Wren was a catchall college for students who hadn't gotten into either of their first two choices. It was at the top of no one's list, first in nobody's mind.

And that, Lamb thought to himself with a glow of satisfaction, made it a better place for him than Harvard.

Just then the door was flung open by the great Harvardian himself, Osbert Orpington. Orpington had left Harvard to become the dean of Wren College and had never quite recovered from the shock. He lived at Wren like Napoleon at St. Helena, surrounded by memorabilia and remorse.

"Julian! My dear boy, you made it! I'm so glad!" Orpington embraced him as if he had crossed the Libyan desert to get there, not just the quadrangle. The hug was a bit too tight and a beat too long, but Lamb endured it. Orpington was vital to him, the one man he could never cross, even in the smallest things.

Orpington finally unclasped him, eyes misty with joy. "Dear boy! Please, help yourself. There is food, there is drink, there is good conversation!"

Two out of three ain't bad, Lamb thought to himself, and pushed into the crowded room.

Orpington's living room resembled the common room at the Harvard Faculty Club, only more so. Overhead were great hand-hewn beams, blackened by decades of roaring fires in the great fireplace. Hors

47

d'oeuvres rode to glory atop oaken tables. The wallpaper leapt with hunting scenes. Lamplight rippled warmly in the wiggly, nineteenth-century windowpanes of the leaded casements. Windowpanes through which one viewed, unfortunately, not Harvard Yard but the Wren Quad in all its resplendent mediocrity.

Of course, all around were Harvard chairs, Harvard lamps, Harvard glasses. Copies of *Harvard Magazine* fanned out on the coffee table like a winning hand at poker. Every little breeze seemed to whisper VE RI TAS. When Orpington jogged, he wore a Harvard sweatshirt and a billed cap that should have said John Deere but instead said John Harvard. He even sported that unthinkable, greasy-grind, math-major object, a Harvard ring.

Lamb was the youngest professor in the room. He had been at Wren less than a year. Slender and wiry, with boyish good looks that were almost pretty, he had fluttered the dovecote (or was it wrencote?) of younger academic women and senior girls when he first arrived, but he was so aloof they had gradually backed off.

But he always attended the faculty parties. He felt it was important he be seen there. He wanted to be an unremarkable part of Wren, a fixture.

As he eased patiently through the crush toward the liquor table, all around him he could hear them chattering away—always with transparent dismay at their own greatness. At Wren, the opposite of speaking wasn't listening; it was waiting to speak. A room full of ancient mariners, loaded to the lips, smiling and nodding, fiercely impatient to fire for effect.

"Phone ringing off the hook with speaking engagements, must learn to say no."

"The publisher seems to think my book could be quite a blockbuster—more faith in it than I do."

"Frankly, I found it hard to think about Melville with all that camera makeup on—and the interviewer's questions were pretty elementary, but well, it was only Channel Forty-five, on cable, for God's sake; I never thought anyone would see it, but the response was amazing . . ."

"I told them, I said, 'You know it *is* possible to have a conference on semiotics without me. It *can* be done.'"

Lamb reached the liquor table. He snagged a glass of white wine. Lamb enjoyed alcohol but drank very little of it—it made him less alert. This glass was less a drink than his timekeeper for the evening. He would nurse it carefully, taking only the smallest of sips. When it was empty, he would know it was time to leave. So much less obvious than constantly checking his watch.

He noticed a jump in the decibel level. Someone important had just arrived. He craned his neck and saw, just inside the door, a tall, beautiful, extravagantly dressed woman.

He felt a lingering hand on his elbow. It was Dean Orpington. "Come come, dear boy—meet Jessica."

Oh, yes, now Lamb remembered—this would be the honored guest for whom Orpington was giving the party: Jessica Thorne, the new writer-in-residence.

Jessica Thorne was a publicist's dream of a writer: tall and raven-haired and beautiful. Ten years before, while still in her twenties, she had produced a blockbuster best-seller called *Malibu Fire Sale.* It had been an instinctive book, written out of her own experience, wild, sloppy, full of emotional excess and purple prose. She had never been able to repeat its success. Since then her books had enjoyed better reviews and shrinking sales. As she learned her craft and honed her skills, she made the long slide from Johnny Carson to Dean Orpington.

Lamb let himself be dragged into her presence. He had to admit she was attractive. But that outfit! He decided that as her notoriety diminished, she must have tried to compensate by overdressing. Tonight she was wearing fire-engine-red Wellington boots and a pathetically exhibitionistic black jumpsuit quirked out with designer details in velvet and leopard skin. Her great mane of black hair blasted upward like the Eniwetok H-bomb. It was weaponry perhaps appropriate to the fierce sexual-literary wars of New York, but here at Wren, where L. L. Bean was avant-garde and men bragged about the longevity of their Harris Tweed jackets, she stood out like a fugitive from "Star Trek."

As they were being introduced he resisted the impulse to ask if her phaser was set on *stun,* muttered a few pleasantries, and moved on.

Others pushed in eagerly to meet her, to bask in her celebrity, however reduced. Here at Wren she was still a name, a name, a droppable name. The faculty buzzed around her, busily collecting quotes for their next dinner party. "As I said to Jessica Thorne, dear Jessica; as Jessica said to *me.*"

Lamb circulated, forcing himself to be social, but he stayed away from the big, hilarious circle around Jessica Thorne. He wound up at the mercy of a historian named Rountree, a loudmouth in a belt-buckle string tie. Rountree was a professor of ancient history who was really interested only in the history of himself and his family. Rountree told him in detail, with footnotes, how many miles he had driven each day of his vacation and the food preferences of each of his children. Lamb successfully resisted the temptation to take notes.

He leaned against the wall and pretended to listen, occasionally moistening his lips with wine. The only good thing about Rountree was that he never asked a question that wasn't rhetorical. You could keep him rolling without actually having to say anything, reinforcing him with nods and grunts.

Aeons passed. Nineveh fell. Alexander the Great sacked Arbela. Lamb's clothes went out of style. Finally, his glass was empty. Duty done, mission accomplished—he could safely make his getaway.

As he edged toward the door he saw Dean Orpington bearing down on him brandishing a bottle of plonk, the goodly host, generous as a Rothschild with the Chilean Riesling. "Empty glass? Can't have that."

Reluctantly, Lamb let him pour.

"Julian, I crave a small boon of you," Orpington said.

"Of course."

"Jessica wants to leave now. I'm stowing her in Jowett for the time being. Would you be so kind as to walk her over? She's had perhaps a few too many. I wouldn't want her falling in a hole."

"What hole?"

"Oh, God, didn't you notice? The grounds keeper and his merry men have been digging up the quad again. It's the only thing this jerkwater knows how to do well. They would spot Harvard two trowels and a Weedwacker and beat them at landscape gardening. Still, I wish they'd wait until summer."

"I'm happy to walk her over," Lamb lied. "But why me? Every man at this party would be delighted to do it. And quite a few of the women."

"Don't be naughty. She asked for you."

"Really? I haven't said two words to her since you introduced us."

"Perhaps she regards you as a challenge, dear boy."

Lamb fidgeted in the hall while she broke away from her admirers. Nervously, he knocked back the wine without thinking about it.

She burst through the door like the sun. "God, I'm exhausted," she said. She didn't look it to him.

She clasped his arm tightly. They walked across the campus together in the dark of the April night. Lamb smelled boxwood and loam and the sweetish smell of the alcohol on her breath. He also smelled her not so subtle but puissant perfume. It excited him, stirred up memories he couldn't quite locate.

He guided his charge to the left of the lily pond in the center of the quad, past statuary, arbors, and trellises. She pressed her body against his, whether from booze or intimacy, he couldn't tell. When he tried to disengage, she gripped his arm harder and clung to him.

"I hear you're a linguist," she said.

"That's right."

"Ummm. Sounds good to me."

Lamb surprised himself by laughing out loud. He felt slightly out of control, but he wasn't worried.

"I'm glad somebody in this backwater has a sense of humor!" she said.

"Frankly, I'm not sure what I was laughing at."

"Yes you are. A smutty innuendo from the formerly famous Jessica Thorne."

"Still pretty famous."

"That's what my publisher keeps saying. And *while* Jessica Thorne is still pretty famous, how about writing *Malibu Fire Sale Two* and *Malibu Fire Sale the Next Generation* and *Malibu Fire Sale Nine Meets Terminator Ten* starring Arnold Schwarzenegger."

"I didn't mean—"

"My real name isn't even Thorne, you know. I'm Jessica Nyeburg, your basic Jewish princess from Great Neck. Thorne sounded terrific to me ten years ago—classy yet phallic—and now I'm stuck with it. *Thorne*—it sounds like I write bodice-rippers. Actually it sounds like a pseudonym for Nyeburg. Accent on *pseudo*. I wish I was Nyeburg again; it's got some *kishkas* to it."

"Why not change back?"

"My agent would feed my tits to a wolf. Thorne is already a property. My whole life is a property. You think I like dressing up like Liberace? I've gotta be Jessica Thorne every minute. I'm trapped inside a cartoon, like Pee Wee Herman."

At Jowett he tried to get away, but she insisted on giving him a drink. Before he knew it, he was sitting on her couch, being served yet another glass of wine.

She sat opposite him, sipping from her own glass, watching him across the rim, her eyes never leaving his face.

"Orpington told me all about you," she said.

"All good I hope."

"Too good. He was telling me how he hired you over the objections of the trustees. He said they couldn't understand why Wren needed a specialist in middle eastern languages when most of the student body considers German too exotic for normal humans."

Lamb shrugged and smiled. "I pay my way."

"He told me you carry the strangest course load on the eastern seaboard. He said you teach medieval Persian to one dreamy Iranian girl, Arabic to a bright but disturbed transfer student from Yale, Israeli Hebrew to a few would-be kibbutznics from New York, and fourth-year French to half the senior class."

"Sounds like I'm going to be in your next book."

"That depends."

She took another sip of wine. "So tell me—what's the story? What's a bright boy like you doing in a dump like this?"

"What makes you think I'm bright?" Lamb tried to keep the question light, but he could feel the paranoia pushing through. He didn't like this line of questioning.

"Don't be coy. Orpington tells me you're some kind of language supergenius."

"Orpington's the dean. It's his job to talk up the faculty."

"They need more than talking up—nothing wrong with those bozos that reincarnation wouldn't cure. Orpington himself is Valium with legs. When we shook, my hand fell asleep. His name should be *Dorkington*."

Lamb smiled in spite of himself. "Don't you think you're being a little rough on—"

"Don't play innocent. I saw you with the *zhlub* in the string tie."

"He's quite a good . . ." Lamb trailed off. He couldn't think of anything Rountree was good at.

"God, you were bored! He had you in deep meditation. Your heart stopped three times." She giggled.

"I didn't notice you watching me."

"I can check out a room without being obvious about it. Comes from having been married twice."

"You're looking for number three?"

"No, no, just a big handsome hunk who looks like he'd be good in bed. My next husband will be an older man who dotes on me. With very deep pockets *kine-ahora*."

Lamb didn't like the trend of the conversation; he tried to change it. "Interesting expression, *kine-ahora*. It comes from—"

Jessica Thorne continued to stare at him. "I know, Flatbush Avenue. To tell the truth, I didn't get you in here to play Scrabble."

Briskly, she set down her wineglass. She rose, walked around the coffee table, and plopped on the couch beside him. "You know *kine-ahora*; you must know *tokhes-on-the-table*."

Lamb could think of nothing to say. He kept his eyes to the front.

When he finally glanced at her, she raised her eyebrows and shifted her body toward him until they were touching.

He heard her sigh, saw her agile fingers dance down the front of her jumpsuit, unlocking the buttons. No bra. Her breasts thrust outward, the nipples hard.

Now that he was looking into her soft brown eyes, it seemed impossible to stop. Her perfume burned his face, filled his nostrils. Her face seemed to float in the air, surrounded by darkness. She strobed toward him, heartbeat by heartbeat.

His excitement was intense. Deep yearnings from other places, other times racked his body. So great was the power of his need, he lost his grip on what was real. He seemed to be in two places at once, looking at two different women.

The left side of Jessica's face changed, softened, yielded its tan to a delicate porcelain whiteness. The green of the sea flowed into her left eye like the tide. Her hair flamed to red above it, leaving the right side midnight black. He was seeing two faces that were one face, unified by the overwhelming force of his desire.

The mouth was different on each side, but it spoke as one mouth. "Come on, Julian," it said, "make me feel good." The divided face wore a single pleading expression.

He thought, *Somewhere in this apartment there are pillowcases, twine, sharp knives.*

She put her arms around him. He felt her heat, the force of her breathing.

No! Not on campus! I promised myself, never here! This is my bolt-hole, my base, my safe house. The place I come back to. I have to keep it separate!

He jumped up. His throat was thick with saliva. His heart was hammering. He started for the door.

"Oh, no, please don't go." Jessica jumped up, clutching her jumpsuit in an effort to hide her breasts. "I'm sorry, maybe I went too fast, okay? I'm not used to nice guys."

He blundered through the door and into the areaway. She followed him, talking a blue streak. "I didn't mean to slap the cakes on you. I got carried away. You're the best guy I've met in a long time. I'll slow down; we'll be fine. Don't worry about getting it up, I can be sensitive, I can listen, I've got toys."

He glanced back. Her face was still divided, her hair still split in color punk-style. He started to run.

She shouted after him, "Whatever you want to do, I'll like it."

Don't bet on it, Lamb thought, as he raced into the night.

· 7 ·

The funeral was on Monday. Saturday night on the phone, Sally mustered her best don't-worry-about-me voice and told Jake of course she'd fly out. He was her husband, these were her in-laws, it was only a two-hour flight. She would just have to force herself. Don't think about it, just do it!

Sunday afternoon she began to pack and couldn't find the black shoes she was planning to wear at the funeral. "Where are they? Damn it to hell, where are they?" she screamed. "What's the matter with me, I can't even find my shoes! I can't do anything!" She burst into tears and threw herself on the bed. She lay there until she stopped crying. It finally occurred to her to look under the bed; there were the shoes, grinning at her like two big mouths. She thought: *It's lucky I didn't have an out-of-body experience just now—that little crying act would have looked pretty feeble even to me.* She swallowed a Valium and somehow managed to finish packing.

Her friend Tina drove her to the airport. After she left, Sally was fine. The Valium swaddled her nerves like a blanket of peace.

She was early. She strolled into a concourse bookstore and asked for "true crime that's also literary."

The saleswoman suggested *In Cold Blood.* Sally had read it. A young businessman buying gum took a book from his briefcase and handed it to her. "Try this," he said. "It's very powerful—wonderfully written. Go ahead, keep it; I've finished it." He smiled at her, his eyes dancing.

Sally knew that smile. She thanked him and moved off before he could ask her if she came here often.

She boarded the plane and settled into the aisle seat she had so carefully requested. A plump middle-aged woman fidgeted in the window seat, her face pale, her eyes bulging. Her routine was: inspect boarding pass, tug her earring, brush lint from jacket, sigh, inspect boarding pass, etc.

Feeling superior in her Valium swaddling, Sally looked at the book she had been given: *Singing in My Chains*, Mel Haney's letters from prison. With an introduction by Humphry Shaw. Humphry Shaw. She knew that name. He was one of the few literary writers left in America who could both scale the best-seller list and command the respect of the quarterlies. These letters had been written to him. Their literary quality had so impressed Shaw, he'd gotten Haney out of jail.

That's what Cool Moves *needs, Sally thought. A famous writer to talk it up at the publishing houses. Why not Shaw himself? He's interested in crime literature. He helped Haney; maybe he'll help me. I'll write him a letter . . .*

The plane moved. She clutched the armrest. Her Valium blanket scooted away. An ice cube of fear slapped her on the back of the neck and began to melt and trickle down her spine.

Read. Stay calm. She read the same sentence four times, then stuffed *Singing in My Chains* into the seat pocket in front of her.

Breathe deeply and slowly. You're going to make it. Everything is going to be all right.

The plump lady was facing straight ahead, eyes shut. Past her head, in the far distance, Sally saw the towers of Manhattan do-si-do as the plane came about.

The sound of the engines deepened to a powerful roar. The plane thrust forward, picking up speed. The acceleration vector pinned her against the seat back.

"I've got to get out," Sally said, as evenly as she could.

Without opening her eyes, the plump lady said, "We can't get out now, dear, the plane is taking off."

Clumsy with panic, Sally fumbled at her seat belt. "I can't stand it! I can't stand it!"

Her seat companion didn't open her eyes but said with merciless lucidity, "We're already past the go/no-go point."

Sally wasn't listening. "Out! I've got to get out."

"I have something to help you, dear," the plump woman said. Still without opening her eyes, she pulled a half-pint of vodka out of her cleavage. "I usually drink this myself, but I think you need it more than I do."

Sally snatched the bottle and took a pull. The liquor burned, her throat contracted, vodka gurgled into her lungs, she coughed violently, flopping back and forth. The woman pounded her back.

Her coughing came under control. She glanced out the window, and saw the whole of Manhattan Island falling away beneath them. They were two miles up and climbing. She felt like someone had plunked a hot water bottle into her stomach.

"Isn't that better?" the plump lady asked. She opened her eyes just long enough to give Sally a conspiratorial wink.

Sally took another pull of vodka. "Much," she said.

She killed the bottle over New York State, knocked back two miniatures from the drinks trolley, and enjoyed the full complement of fine wines with her gourmet in-flight dinner of Velcro au jus, bath sponge, and mistletoe.

The next thing she knew, the plump lady was crooning, "We're at O'Hare, dear. Time to wake up."

Sally groaned. Her face felt as if she were wearing a mud pack. Her head had forgotten its proper size and was systematically running through all the possibilities. She could hardly stand up—her body's entire supply of blood seemed to have pooled in her feet.

Her carry-on bag was tightly wedged under the seat; she broke a nail clawing it loose. She ducked under the carry strap and tottered to an upright position. Outlaw leprechauns had stolen the bag's contents while she had slept and repacked it with paving bricks. She struggled into the aisle and inched past the galley module toward the distant exit door in lockstep with the rest of the passengers.

She lurched past the captain. He smiled and told her to have a nice day in the Chicagoland area. She stumbled up the ramp. Ahead she saw Jake, beckoning her urgently. What was his hurry? She tried to walk faster but found she couldn't. It was strangely crowded in her immediate area.

"Mrs. Harrow. How did you feel when you learned your brother-in-law had killed his family?"

Reporters, cameras, microphones surrounded her. A balding man with a Minicam walked recklessly backward in front of her, matching her step for step, his lens two feet from her face. "Mrs. Harrow! Mrs. Harrow! How did you *feel*? How did you *feel*?"

Popsy always said, "When invention flags, it's permissible to tell the truth."

"Numb!" Sally shouted, as she stumbled toward her husband. *"Numb!"*

* * *

Four flower-draped coffins in a row at the front of the Community Church: Roger, Amanda, Jill, Alexander.

"We bring nothing with us into the world, and it is certain we take nothing out," the Reverend Dr. Ewald intoned.

His words seemed especially true that morning. Roger and Mandy had always had hundreds of friends, but few were there at the end. The manner of their death seemed to have tainted them retroactively, wiping out the good things they had done. As the minister counterfeited his way through the eulogy, even the resolute few who had come looked away, as if they shared a guilty secret.

Later, at All Souls Cemetery, Roger was the last to be buried. All the words had been spoken. The coffin hung suspended over its dark hole. It was late morning. The sky was gray, the faintest of drizzles sifted down. In the far distance, a freight train mumbled forlornly, passing by on the old Chicago belt line.

Roger began his final descent. The hydraulic mechanism hummed discreetly. The ropes creaked in protest as the box began to move.

Sally squeezed Jake's arm in sympathy. His face was like a slab of stone, wet with rain but not with tears.

Behind them in the trees, a whiskey-soaked voice profaned the silence. "They want to bury my beautiful boy."

Jake kissed his fingertips. "Perfect timing," he said.

An old man in a cheap madras jacket and blue wash pants staggered into the circle of mourners. His bald pate was fringed by drugstore-black hair and was so sunburned it glowed even in the pale light.

He stumbled straight to the edge of the grave and stepped boldly on top of the coffin. He swayed for a minute, arms flapping, then bent his knees and eased down like a landing albatross, stretching himself full length. He looked straight up into the rain, giving a good imitation of a sacerdotal monument.

"You'll have to bury me with him, ya bastards!" he screamed.

Somebody stopped the motor. The coffin swayed. The lid was more rounded than Joe had realized, and he had to clamp the sides with his arms and legs to keep from sliding off.

Jake applauded at derisory half speed: Clap . . . clap . . . clap. "You're showing me something here. And I thought I was a hard player!"

Dr. Ewald said, "He's not himself."

"Could have fooled me."

"Be kind, Jacob," Ewald said. "It's your father's way of grieving."

"Then let's leave him alone with his grief." Jake strolled back toward the parked limousines. Sally followed him. The rest of the mourners stirred uncertainly and then gradually began to disperse. Finally, with no more to milk from the moment, Joe Harrow hopped nimbly off the coffin lid and trotted after the retreating group.

Everyone was invited back to the rectory. The small funeral party melted away even further to a few close friends of Roger and Mandy's, eating Sara Lee pound cake and making small talk in the living room.

Joe Harrow balanced his napkin on his knee and ate his cake as daintily as anyone, rattling on to Sally as if he hadn't done a thing out of the ordinary at the cemetery.

Jake listened to the chitchat for a decent interval, then went into the minister's study and got Rourke on the phone.

"I just got Motley's report. I'll give you the bottom line first," Rourke said briskly. "The bottom line is there's nothing. No evidence of any kind that another man was there. Not a hair, not a fingernail, not a drop of blood."

"What about semen?"

"Semen in Amanda's vagina. Roger's."

"They must have made love before the killer got there."

"It's so simple once it's explained."

"What about the kids?"

"No semen."

"The killer must have worn a condom. Would a suicidal murderer have bothered to do that?"

"Maybe. We had a suicide in Morton Grove last month who went for a tooth extraction just beforehand."

"Crazy things happen. That doesn't make them plausible."

"So maybe he didn't cum. Maybe he used a broom handle. Lookit, you don't prove things that way. Nothing is nothing."

"No sign that Roger might have been tied up?"

"Not a mark on him, except for the bullet wound. No bruises from a gag, no ligature marks from a rope. He wasn't hit on the head, punched in the face, throttled, anything like that. And not one but two hand-writing experts swear he wrote the suicide note."

"I don't get it. How could that be?"

"Meanwhile, my guys searched the whole area, including that vacant lot next door. They interviewed the whole neighborhood, everybody at your brother's school and in the Green party. Nothing. They located all the bus drivers on lines he might have walked in from. Ditto the cab companies. Nothing."

"Were you able to trace the gun?"

"Forget it—somebody filed down the numbers long ago. Your brother didn't have it legally; there's no record of purchase or permit, but that's not particularly unusual. Could have been picked up in a private sale. Maybe at a gun show, or—"

"Roger didn't go to gun shows!"

"And none of his friends did either? Jesus, there are a million hand-guns floating around. Don't start up about the damn gun again."

"All right. What's your next step?"

"We've got a few people to talk to still. We'll keep our eyes open—something may turn up."

"You're closing the case."

"You got something specific you want me to do?"

"If you really believed a family murderer was loose around here, you wouldn't ask me that."

"You're right. I'm sorry about your relatives, Jake, I truly am."

By the time Jake got back to the living room, the mourners were gone. Sally was trying to hold a desultory conversation with Ewald. Joe Harrow was stumbling around the room, clutching an empty sherry bottle, haranguing empty chairs.

"I raised them boys; they owe me something! That house belongs to me now. Roger ain't going to use it no more; that's for damn sure!"

He paused in front of an ornate book stand in the corner of the room, leaned forward carefully to avoid hitting his pants, and puked his breakfast into the gutter of the book.

Ewald rushed forward in a panic and began blotting the pages with his clerical sleeve. The pitch of his voice had ascended a full octave. "This is *Incunabula*—Cranmer's Great Bible from the reign of Henry the Eighth. He *vomited* all over it!"

Jake said, "It's just his way of grieving."

·8·

"Oh, Detective Harrow—come in. And you must be Sally Harrow."
Mrs. Appleby shook their hands and waved them to chairs in her office.
Sally sat down. Jake remained standing.

Mrs. Appleby withdrew behind her desk. "You folks needn't have
delivered the papers yourself. The mail would have been quick
enough."

"I'm afraid there'll be a slight delay," Jake said. "I need to take Winston home with me for a while."

She tensed. "Oh, dear. I was afraid of that."

"I just want him for a short time."

"I'm sorry, but it's not possible."

"Two weeks at most. No longer."

"You're not going to take that boy."

"We have a legal right to him!" Jake flared.

"You may have legal rights. I have Winston."

"Not for long, you don't." He jumped to his feet and strode out of
her office. Sally followed him into the hall, but he waved her back.
"Stay. Keep an eye on her."

He mounted the stairs to the second floor and tapped on the door of
room sixteen. "It's Uncle Jake. Hope you're decent, cause I'm coming
in."

He opened the door.

"Are you my new daddy?"

A little white girl about four years old was sitting on the bed in a
blue party dress. She held out her arms to him.

He checked the number on the door. Sixteen. No mistake.

"Your new daddy will be here soon," he said. The shelves were lined

61

with different toys; Winston's were gone. He checked the dresser drawers. Little girl's clothes.

"What's your name?"

"Camille."

"That's my favorite name."

She giggled.

"Hey, Camille—how long have you lived in this room?"

"Since yesterday."

"Truly? You slept in this bed last night?"

She nodded.

"What room were you in before that?"

"The blue one."

"And can you tell me what number the blue room was?"

"Uh huh." She nodded vigorously.

"What number?"

"Twenty-seven and it's up the stairs."

"Very good, Camille. You are a smart girl."

She giggled.

"Hey, Camille, do you know somebody named Winston?"

"Uh huh."

"Can you show me where he is?"

"Uh huh." She sat without moving.

"Could you do it now?"

She carefully slid off the bed, bustled to the toy shelves, and brought him back a teddy bear.

"Nice try," Jake said. "I'm looking for another Winnie."

Mrs. Appleby was sitting at her desk, glaring at Sally, her pink arms folded tightly beneath her bosom, her mouth set in a determined line.

"All right, where is he?" Jake asked quietly.

"Where you'll never find him."

"You can't do this! Winston's all I've got left. He's my only chance to solve this case."

"The case is closed."

"Where did you get that idea?"

She brushed a nonexistent fly away from her face. "Do you think for a minute I would have removed that child if the case were still open?"

"But you moved Winston yesterday."

"*Who told you that?*" she flared. "*Who's been talking to you?*"

"Don't start firing your staff. I got it from Camille."

"Camille? Who's Camille?"

"The child in Winston's old room."

"Oh." Mrs. Appleby looked blank.

"She said you took Winston away yesterday. How did you know to do that? The case wasn't closed until this morning."

She looked at him levelly. "That's what Lieutenant Rourke told you."

"But the forensic report didn't come in until this morning. How could he . . . ?"

She sniffed. "I've spent years building my relationships with the police."

"I get it," he said. "The forensic came in yesterday. The case was closed yesterday too. Rourke delayed telling me to give you time to hide Winston."

"Whatever I did, it was to protect that child."

"You're also protecting the real murderer, have you thought about that?"

"Your brother was the real murderer. The boy sensed it, you know. He stopped speaking before the murders. Long before. He saw it coming. He felt how dangerous your brother was. Children pick up these things."

"I don't have to prove my brother's innocence to you. That child was legally adopted. I'm next of kin. The law says he's mine unless I go through a formal procedure of disadoption. You're legally bound to tell me where he is."

Her face turned from pink to fiery red. "Your brother tricked me into giving him a child for adoption. He was clever—many psychopaths are—but you know who would have gotten the blame. We could have lost our reputation, even our license. A lifetime of public service, down the drain. But through the mercy of God we were kept out of it. Now you want to open everything up again, drag us through the mud. Because you won't accept the truth of what your brother did. Well, I don't care how many lawsuits you mount; you're not getting that boy!"

• 9 •

Jake paced the departure area at O'Hare. Sally had gone to get them both coffee. A loudspeaker voice announced that the "boarding process" was about to begin. Jake snapped his fingers and walked rapidly to the row of pay phones on the wall.

He dialed the Appleby Agency and asked for the billing department. He was connected to someone called Cindy.

"Hi, Cindy? This is Officer Fashonado of the Skokie police. We talked before, remember?"

Fashonado, said quickly and sloppily, was Jake's favorite phone alias. Like the Stealth bomber, it slid through the mind's radar without a trace.

"Umm, yes?" Cindy said noncommittally. She didn't want to present herself to the world as the kind of person who forgot important phone conversations.

"Now that the Harrow case is closed, we've got to devoucher all the evidential materials, you understand? So we've got this box of clothing that belongs to this boy Winston Harrow?"

The loudspeaker boomed out a set of boarding row-numbers.

"Hold it down, you guys!" Jake yelled. Into the phone he said, "Sorry Cindy, you know how noisy these squad rooms can get. Anyhow, Lieutenant Rourke says you folks have relocated him to another venue, so I need the forwarding address."

"We're not supposed to give out that information, okay?" Cindy said.

"Of course not. But this is the police."

"I'm terribly sorry, but Mrs. Appleby said absolutely no exceptions. You want to talk to her?"

"No, I guess not. A rule is a rule. Gee, that's too bad! We'll have to

65

throw it all out. We got no place to store it here. Breaks my heart; it's nice stuff. There's even a winter coat. I hate to think of the poor little guy freezing his buns."

"Just a mo, okay? I want to talk to somebody, okay?" She put him on hold. He was treated to twelve bars of "Breaking Up Is Hard to Do." Sally was motioning him urgently from the boarding line—their row had been called. He waved her off.

Cindy came back on the line. "Okay, now listen, okay. Mrs. Appleby went home; she had this headache? I'm not supposed to do this, okay. Will you promise to keep this under your hat?"

"What Mrs. A doesn't know won't hurt her. I've seen her with her knickers in a twist."

"Tell me about it!" Cindy said. "Winston's at—get this—Halcyon Hills, okay? Isn't that, like, totally amazing?"

"Halcyon Hills! You're putting me on!"

"Cross my heart. I wouldn't kid you, Officer Fush . . . Fash . . . Officer."

"Hey, I really appreciate this. Thanks to you a little boy will be warm next winter. Cindy—you're okay!"

Jake flipped intently through the Chicago phone book as Sally came running up.

"It's last call," she said nervously. "We'll miss—"

"We're staying here. I found out where they stashed Winston."

"You did? Just now? Jake, you're a genius."

"Except it doesn't seem to be in any of these damn phone books."

Sally grabbed the Des Plaines book. "I'll help. What should I look for?"

"Some place called Halcyon Hills."

She blinked. "The bin?"

"The what?"

"There's a loony bin called Halcyon Hills."

"Near Chicago?"

"It's where North Shore money goes to flip out. One of those places with designer straitjackets? Is this my massage or my shock treatment? You wear leotards to group therapy because it's right before your aerobics class. First cry, then sweat. You've lost your marbles, might as well lose your cellulite too. *Dahling*, you look *mahvlous*, schizophrenia has really firmed your neck."

It was Jake's turn to blink. "You know all about it!"

"Nan's best friend from Miss Hewitt's Clahsses spent a year there. She wrote every day—brilliant letters, really funny. Popsy used to read them aloud at parties. People would wet their pants laughing. Then she drank Lysol, poor thing. Popsy never forgave her."

Halcyon Hills was north of Chicago, tucked in among the forest preserves and music festivals on the Fox River. Screened from the road by phalanxes of trees, it looked more like an exclusive country club than a mental hospital.

It was just before four when Jake steered their second rental car of the day up the long sweep of the gravel drive toward the main building. The day was still cold and drizzly. He passed a row of automobiles, all Mercedes or better, beneath a sign that said Staff Only.

The smell of newly cut grass wafted in his car window. From somewhere out of sight, yells and splashing proclaimed a swimming pool.

"Swimming in April?" Jake said. "They *are* crazy."

"They swim year-round," Sally said. "They've got one of those indoor-outdoor pools. I told you, the place is a spa."

He crunched to a stop near the front portico.

"So where's the valet parking?"

"Wait'll you see the head honcho's office. Nan's school chum described it as 'what God would do if he had money.' "

The young woman at the front desk did not wear starched whites, but she still projected an unmistakable air of medical authority.

Jake told her, "We're looking for one of your patients."

"We prefer to say 'guests,' " she corrected him without smiling. Firm but fair.

On the card she gave him to fill out, Jake put down his relationship to Winston as "uncle."

The woman's face tightened when she read Winston's name on the card.

"I'm sorry, sir, there's no one here by that name."

"Yes there is," Jake said. He showed her his badge.

"You claim on the card you're his uncle," she said reproachfully, as if catching him in a lie would make him go away.

"I'm that too."

"And I'm his aunt," Sally said sweetly.

"But he's a—I mean, you're—" The receptionist looked bewildered, then angry. "I'm going to have to call Dr. Smoak."

Sally said, "Smoaky the Bear. He's the guy who owns this place. How it all comes flooding back."

The receptionist stared at her flintily as she punched some buttons on her desk phone. "Linda? This is front. Tell him there's a couple here looking for W.H. I know, but one's a detective. A police detective. Harrow. Yes, he put down *uncle*."

A moment later two burly young men dressed in tennis outfits burst out of the side door as if they were hot-wired and ushered Jake and Sally into Smoak's office. They said Smoak would be along shortly and remained watchfully by the door, as if afraid Jake might take the opportunity to rifle the Queen Anne desk.

"You could bowl in here," he said.

"Didn't I tell you?" Sally said, looking around. "Oriental rugs, leather-topped tables—Are we talking unexampled magnificence here or what? This is Popsy's kind of stuff. He'd kill for an office like this."

Perhaps twenty paintings covered the walls, hung two and three high in the old European fashion. Sally peered closely at one of them. "Jake, come here! I think this is *real*."

"Very real. Nice outdoor atmosphere. I like it."

"No, I mean it's the original painting, not a reproduction. It's a Sisley. It is extraordinary. He was known as the 'poet of the riverbanks.' "

"Worth how much?"

"Oh, God, who knows anymore? Millions probably."

Jake went on to the next painting. "Now, this one I'm not crazy about."

"It's a Seurat. It's real too. I think they're all real."

"A lot of money?"

"Forget it. He's got the GNP of Portugal hanging on his wall."

"Who's the most famous art dealer of all time?"

"I don't know. Duveen, I guess. He sold a lot of old masters to J. P. Morgan. Why do you ask?"

Dr. Smoak walked into the room. He could have been an upmarket television evangelist: tall, tanned, and handsome, his white hair coiffed to perfection. "Ah, Detective and Mrs. Harrow. Sorry to keep you waiting. Sit down, please."

Sally sat. As he had done at the Appleby Agency, Jake stayed on his feet. The doctor watched them with an expression of wise sympathy. "*Don't worry*," his look seemed to say. "*We'll get to the bottom of your problem.*"

"Would either of you like coffee?" For all his show of politeness, he hadn't asked the two burly young men to leave the room.

"Thanks, but we won't be staying that long," Jake said. "We're just here to pick up Winston and be on our way."

Smoak steepled his fingers on the gleaming rosewood of his desk. "Winston is exhibiting traumatic aphasia." He pronounced the words deliberately, the world-famous psychiatrist announcing his diagnosis, slamming the door on all argument.

"Or maybe he's just scared shitless."

"Speechless, Detective. He does not speak. Serious business."

"I think I can get something out of him."

"When he flushed that doll down the toilet, he was sending you a very strong message that he did not want to talk to you."

"I can handle the rejection."

"It doesn't strike you as significant that the doll he flushed was a policeman?"

"That's my problem, not yours. I only want him for a week or two, and then I'll give him back to Mrs. Appleby."

"Why must you interrupt this child's life for a case that has been officially closed?"

"That's why I have to take him. He's all I have left."

"You're trying to solve this all on your own? A sort of personal crusade?"

"Crusade? You make it sound like I'm harboring some kind of grandiose delusion. What would you prescribe for me, Doc? Maybe a judicious blend of psychotherapy and lithium?"

Smoak smiled an unruffled smile. "There's really no need to get defensive."

"Not for me there isn't."

"You think I should be defensive?"

"Game's up, Jim. You and Appleby hid the kid. We found him. We're leaving with him."

"In my judgment, that's not in the best interest of the child."

"Duly noted. Now take us to him."

"No."

"Does the word kidnapping mean anything to you?"

"I hear it all the time. Not everyone is here by choice. And where substantial money is involved, our malcontents can often recruit greedy relatives, ambulance-chasing lawyers, or other opportunists to make trouble. Halcyon Hills retains excellent legal counsel. I doubt any attorney you could afford would stand a chance. But even if you won, one thing I can absolutely guarantee you: my people would get so many court postponements, Winston would be shaving by the time you got him. Since you admit you only want him for a short period anyway—what's the point?"

Jake was standing behind Sally's chair, his hands on her shoulders. He pressed down gently—an unmistakable Don't move.

"Guess you beat me, huh, Doc?"

"You persist in seeing this as a game. I assure you, I never play games. But if you consider the boy some kind of trophy, then yes, I keep him, not you."

Jake jammed his hands deep into his pockets and strolled idly around the office. He paused at the Sisley. "Ah, Sisley. The poet of the river-banks. I've always admired his atmosphere."

Smoak couldn't resist a supercilious smile. "I wasn't aware they taught art appreciation at the police academy."

"They do, but they're ambivalent about it—the art gallery is also the shooting gallery."

The doctor frowned. "Is that a joke?"

Jake held out his thumb at arm's length and studied the next painting. "Truth to tell, I've never really warmed to Seurat. Too much studio, too much thought. I prefer the improvisation of the moment. Still, it must have set you back a bundle too. As Duveen said when he met J. P. Morgan, 'I'll show you mine if you'll show me yours.' "

"Mrs. Harrow, your husband's speech is becoming quite inappropriate. Is he on drugs?"

"Nah, he just likes paintin's," Sally said in her best Brooklyn accent.

"Halcyon Hills," Jake said. "The place that gets to charge triple because it's so discreet, so far from the madding media. And then a big blabbermouth spoils everything. You know, if I had a superego, it would tear me to pieces."

Smoak stiffened. "You're not my patient. I don't have to listen to your word salad. Especially when it's insulting."

"See, what I'm going to do, Doc—I'm going to take your golden goose out in the yard and stomp it."

"If that's a threat, I don't follow it."

"So modest. And you gave me the idea yourself. You're right, taking you to court for kidnapping—that's playing on your field. But obstruction of justice in a big, bloody, headline murder case—now we're talking. I'm not taking you to court; I'm taking you to the Chicago *Tribune* and the 'Eyewitness News.' I'm naming you along with Rourke and Appleby, as coconspirators to hide the fact that Winston witnessed a murder."

"Who would listen to you? A New York policeman with a crackpot theory."

Jake strolled easily toward Smoak's desk. "Ah, ah, ah, don't forget—I'm the brother. I spent yesterday fighting off reporters. They're in a feeding frenzy, biting their own dorsal fins. You can't smother a story like this with a few well-placed phone calls; not when you got a guy ripping and raping whole families. You want reporters swarming over this place like ants on chocolate cake? You want television cameras zooming into the faces of your Winnetka weirdos and Kenilworth crazies? You want reporters with major hair standing in front of Halcyon Hills, speculating into a Minicam? 'And still the question haunts us: Why did Dr. Smoak suppress the evidence of a multiple murder? Greed? Perhaps. Overweening ambition? Possibly. Temporary insanity? Could be. Or did the handsome little black boy know about certain practices at this home for the wacky wealthy that Smoak wanted to hide? Only time will tell. This is Brad Fashonado at the Mansion of Mad Millionaires, Halcyon Hills. Back to you, Anneka.' "

"You lied to the media. You're involved in the coverup too," Smoak said. "Have you thought how that will play with your superiors back in New York?"

"I'm the whistle-blower. I'll get off."

"But you lied on a criminal case. You're a cop—it's worse for you. This could destroy your career."

Jake put both fists on Smoak's desk and leaned over him.

"Want to know something? I don't give a rosy fuck. My relatives were butchered like hogs in a yard. You're a psychiatrist. Figure it out."

"You can't threaten me!" Smoak shouted shrilly.

The men in the doorway started forward. Jake wheeled to meet them. "Throw me out. I haven't got all day; I've got to get to a phone booth. Don't just stand there like bumps on a log. Honestly, it's so hard to get competent help these days."

They'd had enough experience with violent people not to like Jake's loose movements and vigilant eyes. They separated, splitting wide and angling in warily.

"Stop!" Smoak shouted, jumping up. "All right! Take him! Take him!" He flung a room key at Jake, who caught it deftly. "You goddamn storm trooper! You barge in here, talking crazy, threatening me; you think you can get away with anything. Son of a bitch! You're worse than the criminals."

"Thank you, Doctor," Jake said without apparent irony. "I appreciate your trust."

Smoak gaped. He looked from Jake to Sally to the two young orderlies, who now looked totally confused.

In a quiet voice he said, "I don't suppose that a week or two with you will pose a significant risk to the boy's mental stability. One might even consider it as a form of milieu therapy."

71

"I knew you'd see it my way, Doc," Jake said. "Aren't things simple once they're explained?"

Winston made no sign he remembered Jake. He acted like a frightened little robot. Buckling him into the backseat of the rented car, Jake had the feeling that whatever posture he arranged the boy in, Winston would maintain it all the way to O'Hare. He didn't look back as they drove away from Halcyon Hills.

"You were astounding!" Sally said. "I couldn't believe what was coming out of your mouth." She was scribbling madly in her notebook. "What a chapter this is going to make! A famous psychiatrist, with a whole building full of people on his side, and you beat him hollow! How could you stay so cool? Weren't you scared when those two orderlies came at you?"

"Why? It was all over by then. He was scared to death."

"*Really*? When did you know you had him?"

"When I said Sisley was the poet of the riverbanks. You gave me the line yourself."

Sally hit the notebook with her pencil and looked over at him. "*Poet of the riverbanks*? That's what did it?"

"The lithium/psychotherapy bit didn't work, a cop could have a relative on lithium. But *poet of the riverbanks*. Whoa! Killer line. Takes no prisoners. Death from above."

"Obviously, I just don't understand the first thing about how a cool move works. I had no idea why you were even talking about art at a time like that."

"Neither did he."

"You wanted to confuse him? That was the idea?"

Jake shook his head and smiled. "He thought he could file me in his filing cabinet. Under *D*. 'Ah, Detective. Sit down, Detective. Coffee, Detective?' He thought he could squat in his shell and laugh. But *poet of the riverbanks* pried his clam just enough to get the fork in. So I forked him. Never let them think they know who you are."

As she scribbled "Never let them think they know who you are" in her notebook, Sally asked, "By the way, who are you?"

Jake shrugged. "Beats the shit out of me."

On the late flight to New York, Jake took the middle seat, while Sally white-knuckled it on the aisle. At the smallest bounce her hand dive-bombed Jake's arm and gripped it like an eagle's talon. Winston sat by the dark window, staring straight ahead, looking more and more unhappy, but making not a sound. The plane was over Lake Erie before Jake noticed how scrunched up his face was getting.

"You're going to have to turn my arm loose, honey, I think we've got a little emergency here." He opened Winston's seat belt and his own.

"What emergency? *What?*"

"Our friend hasn't been to the bathroom since we left Halcyon Hills—and God knows how long before that."

Walking Winston down to the head, he could see he was near bursting. The poor kid had been just sitting there, holding it in, afraid to move a muscle.

They arrived home around eleven o'clock. Jake dragged a cot into the upstairs hall and made it up invitingly with fresh sheets and pillowcases while Winston watched warily.

"This is for you, kiddo. I'll put it anywhere you want." He took the boy's hand and led him on a short tour of the second floor. "You can have the guest room all to yourself. That could be fun, huh? Or you can sleep in here, with Aunt Sally and me."

Winston kept his eyes on the floor.

Jake sighed and opened the door to the hall closet. "Or, if you really want to, I can put the mattress on the floor, and you can sleep in here. Now, which one will it be?"

Without raising his head, Winston pointed at the closet.

"Hey—one thing you gotta admit," Jake told him, "I'm easy to get along with."

Winston gave no sign he heard the remark.

Jake went downstairs. Sally was sprawled on the couch, sipping a glass of wine, tapped out from the trip.

Jake slumped down beside her and put his face in his hands. "Maybe this is all a big mistake. He's more frightened now than he was at Mrs. Appleby's. I'm beginning to feel like a child abuser for wanting him to sleep in a bed. This is the kid who's going to tell me all about last Thursday night?"

Sally patted his hand. "He used to talk. He will again. What do you want to bet, he'll be driving you nuts before you know it?"

"I hope. Maybe talking's not his thing. Maybe he just—"

"What's the matter?"

"I just had a far-out thought. You know how stutterers can sing without stuttering?"

"Uh huh. It's a left-brain, right-brain thing, I think. So what?"

"If Winston won't talk, maybe I can get him to sing."

· 10 ·

Julian Lamb, professor of languages at Wren College, had gone by many different names during his lifetime.

His original name, the one he was given at his birth in 1960, was Evan Highland.

In 1970, when Evan was ten, he was awakened by his mother creeping into his bed.

He was used to her stealing quietly into his room during the night. He would occasionally wake to find her staring down at him in the faint light from the hallway. Whenever that happened she would kiss him, say, "Go to sleep now," and tiptoe out.

Tonight was different. She was cuddling against his rounded back, breathing harshly. He didn't know what to do, so he pretended to be asleep.

After a few minutes, she began to stroke his shoulder, very gently. Her touch made him feel sick in an odd way he had never experienced before, but he kept his eyes closed, hoping she would go away.

Her hand wandered down his body, patting and stroking, and crawled through the elastic top of his pajamas. In spite of himself, he tensed violently and grabbed her wrist.

"Don't," he said.

"I love you so much," she said. She tried pushing her hand down, but he was already too strong for her.

"No!" he said.

"You're my darling, my only darling. I've given you everything. You're mine. I have a right."

"Mom, please—"

"I just want to touch you. I washed you there when you were little—"

"No!"

She struggled violently and started crying. "My husband's dead," she wailed. "It's not *fair*."

Evan could think of nothing to say, but he continued to fight her off.

"You're breaking my wrist!" she screamed in his ear. "*You're hurting your mother!*"

Instantly, Evan let go. Her hand softly clasped his penis.

"Husband," she crooned, drawing out the word.

They lay like that for what seemed to him like an hour.

Gently, her hand began to slide up and down.

Evan clamped his eyes shut so tightly he saw flashes of light. He could hardly breathe.

He felt his mother's weight shift and knew that she was inserting her other hand between her own legs. She began to move rhythmically against him.

She chanted: "Marital, *sexual* . . . marital, *sexual* . . . marital, *sexual* . . ."

She continued to stroke him, her hand like rippling silk on his skin. He felt an electric wire buzzing in the pit of his stomach, thrilling and nauseating him at the same time. His penis began to stiffen.

Still stroking him, she pushed down the covers and turned him on his back. She spread his legs wide apart and knelt between them. His body was floppy as a rag doll. There seemed nothing he could do to resist. He saw her head, a black balloon in the dim light, bob down as she kissed his erection.

"My darling, my little *husband*."

She took his left hand and slid a man's plain wedding band on the third finger. It was too big; she closed his hand so it wouldn't fall off.

Evan thought, *It can't be my father's. He crashed in the jungle. His wedding ring was lost with him.*

"With this ring, I thee wet," she said.

She took his penis in her mouth.

That summer, Claire Highland crept into her son's bed three more times. Then she stopped doing it. Neither of them ever spoke of it again.

1972

"You little sneak!" his mother screamed. "What were you doing going through my things?"

Evan was crying. He was also looking her straight in the eye. He would not back down. In his hand was a sheet of carbon paper.

"It's a letter to my father!"

They had no secrets from each other—his mother always said that. But sometimes she would lock her bedroom door, and he would hear her mumbling agitatedly as she typed a letter—followed by clicks and bangs as she locked the carbon copy safely away in her white one-drawer filing cabinet—followed by the slam of the front door as she hand-carried the letter to the corner postbox.

When he heard the slam, he would bolt into her room, hoping she might have left the cabinet key on the desk. She never did, but today she had failed to tear up the carbon paper.

He had fished it out of the wastebasket beside his mother's desk, smoothed it out, and held it up to the light. She had used a fresh sheet—it had been easy to read.

"You know perfectly well your father's dead!" she shouted.

"Then how come you're asking him for money?"

"Give me that!" She tore the carbon paper from his hand and balled it up. "Your father died before you were born!" she screamed, as if destroying the letter made it so.

The parlor was small and hot and untidy, cluttered with cut flowers and porcelain bric-a-brac. His mother had made it into a shrine to the memory of Walter Highland, young eagle, fearless airman who had crashed to his death in the jungles of Southeast Asia in the uneasy years before the Gulf of Tonkin.

He smiled from under crossed sabers in wedding pictures on the piano, waved from the tarmac of the Kennedy-era TansonNhut in a snapshot on the mantel, looked solemnly into the Asian wild blue yonder in a portrait photo on the wall. Sacred relics were displayed everywhere: scarves, hats, even boots.

Evan had always been a willing acolyte in this religion. The sky over his bed was thick with model planes of his father's era: Phantoms, Thunderchiefs, Intruders, B-52s, Herculeses, and Huey helicopters. But pride of place was given to a rare solid model of the Voodoo recon-naissance plane his father had flown on his final mission.

"You said we'd never lie to each other!" Evan shouted.

His mother's face turned splotchy, and her eyes seemed to dance in their sockets. "I don't like sneaks, and I don't like spies!" she screamed. "Swear you won't spy on me again, Evan!"

"But what about my father? *What about my father?*"

Fluttering like an unsteady moth, she stumbled toward him and slapped his face. It was the first time she had ever struck him. It was unthinkable. To both of them.

She fell into a chair and buried her face in her hands, sobbing. Evan turned and brushed through the beaded curtains into the hall. He ran out of the house.

He trundled his bike off the rickety front porch and rode off through the stifling heat.

It wasn't until he was half a mile away that he realized where he was going.

The letter had been typed in neat business form, with his father's address over the salutation. Walter Highland lived only five miles away, in the town of Malcolm.

He was going to visit his father.

Even though Malcolm was nearby, few people from Evan's hometown of Selvage ever went there. The two towns were on different railroad lines. In those years, all the connections between towns grew along those rail lines, like beanstalks on a trellis.

Selvage and Malcolm seemed to stand back to back, facing into different space-time continuums. To get to Malcolm, Evan had to cross an undefined area of dumps and cemeteries, peddling along empty back roads, their pavements heaved and broken by hot weather, darting across roaring highways, edging truck farms, walking his bike through the tall grass under marching power pylons.

As he traveled Evan worked things out in his head. This deception must be his mother's idea. When his dad had asked for the divorce, she must have made an ultimatum—his father had been forced to agree never to see his own son again. She wanted to keep him all to herself.

But now he was coming—of his own volition, his own will. How his dad would embrace him! A dad! He would have a dad! Like he always did in his dreams!

He found his father's house in the most well-off subdivision of Malcolm. It was a big center-hall Colonial, surrounded by lawn and trees. Compared to the shabby little box where he lived with his mother, it seemed to Evan like a mansion.

His own name was on the mailbox: Highland. He was home at last.

A big green Buick was parked on the street in front of the house. A man was sitting in the car. As Evan dismounted from his bike the man motioned him curtly to come over. Evan knew instantly that it was his father.

"Get in. I want to talk to you."

Evan got in the car. There was no embrace. His father didn't even shake hands.

The car smelled faintly of cigars. Evan perched on the big seat and stared. This was the man in the pictures, all right, but different. Not just older. The man in the pictures had an open, friendly face. This man's face was cement. His eyes were cold as hailstones. Evan couldn't meet them. His gaze kept sliding down to his father's shirt. He noticed there was a little alligator there and wondered what it meant.

"Claire warned me you might be coming. Took you long enough."

Evan didn't know what to say to that. He studied the alligator.

"You can't come here. Do you understand? I don't want to see you."

"But I'm your son."

"That's all in the past. Forget about that."

"But what about—"

"I don't want you coming around here, interfering with my new— with my family."

"But, Dad . . ."

"Don't call me that."

"But aren't you? *Aren't you my dad?*"

"Look, my marriage to your mother—it was all a mistake. She was a mistake. You were a mistake. Understand?"

"Okay, so you hate her," Evan said. "Does that mean you have to hate me?"

"It's not a matter of hating her. She's got a screw loose."

"That's a lie," Evan said loyally but without much conviction.

"Why do you suppose she was fired from the high school? I'm telling you, she's not all there. She couldn't support herself in the real world for one minute. What do you think, there's money in giving a few music lessons? Don't make me laugh. I'm the one who supports you."

Evan remembered that the carbon paper letter had been all about money. Money for a new roof, new gutters—he began to choke.

His father went on relentlessly. "I said you were a mistake. But I'm not like some men. I pay for my mistakes. I've paid through the nose all these years. Who do you think bought that house you live in? Who do you think foots the bill for your food and your clothes? Not that wacked-out mother of yours, I'll tell you that."

"Thank you, Dad."

His father gave him a startled look. "What the hell's the matter with you? I'm not asking for your thanks, for God's sake. I'm trying to tell you we have a deal, your mother and me. The deal is, I send you money, and you two stay off my back."

"But can't I see you just once in a while? I won't bother anybody."

His father turned and glared at him. "Listen, you. If I ever see you around here again, I'll cut your mother's checks off for good. You got that? Then she'll be in an institution where she belongs. And so will you."

Evan began to sob, loud and heartbroken.

The cement face hardened even more. The hailstone eyes narrowed. "Oh, boohoo—she's turned you into a regular little fairy, I see. How the hell could you be any son of mine? You're just like her."

Evan forced himself to stop crying. "I'm thirsty," he said with as much dignity as he could muster. "I need a drink of water before I ride back."

"Use the hose on the lawn," his father said. "I don't want you in my house."

When he arrived home that night, his mother had already gone to bed.

The next morning she was quite composed. When he tried to tell her what had happened, she seemed not to hear. He soon gave up—he knew she couldn't tolerate very much reality. There was some truth in what his father had said—she was . . . fragile. She couldn't protect him. He had to protect her.

After that she talked about his father as she always had—as if he were long dead. He never contradicted her.

A week later he took his mother's opera glasses and cycled to Malcolm. It was getting dark as he arrived. He hid his bike in the woods behind his father's house, climbed a tree, and watched the lighted windows for several hours through the opera glasses. All he got were glimpses, tantalizing moments of a rich, complex life being lived within the house. But it was enough to bring him back.

The Walter Highland family became Evan's obsession.

He began spying on them regularly. Some nights he would creep up to the foundation of the house and strain to hear the voices inside. Some days he would watch them from a distance with the opera glasses. He stole letters from their postbox, steamed them open, read them, and returned them, carefully reglued.

Bit by bit, he pieced together their lives.

There was Walter himself, the father Evan should have had. Evan eventually worked out that the young eagle really had crashed. But he had not been killed. His plane hadn't even been in the air. He had piled into another plane while taxiing. After that he had left the air force and now sold stocks and bonds.

Evan had been born while his father was in Asia. Within six months of the flyer's return, with Evan only a year old, Walter walked out on his wife and child.

Evan found it hard to reconcile the loving, tender family man with the cold bastard in the Buick who had threatened his mother's financial survival if Evan didn't stay away.

Then there was five-year-old Walt, Jr. Junior! He had to name him Junior! As if to rub it in. And three-year-old Liza. And Marilyn Highland, the second wife, ten years younger than her husband, a striking redhead with pearly white skin and huge green eyes.

They were living the life he should have had. They had stolen it. He watched by the hour while his father taught little Walt, Jr., to ride a bicycle, patiently running alongside, holding the bike, letting it go, steadying it again when Junior wobbled. No one had done that for Evan. He had been forced to learn by the skinned-knee method. Alone.

But the most painful thing of all to him was the secret family language.

He discovered it one hot night, lying on his stomach in the soft loam by the foundation of the house. From the open window of the dark children's bedroom he heard a strange falsetto croon, "*Zazali . . . Eeorjun . . . elelho!*" It was Walter Highland, speaking a secret family language he called "Pushme-Pullyou, where the words run sideways."

In the next few days, Evan figured out how to construct the words and learned to recognize the often-used ones. Liza was *Zazali*. Junior was *Eeorjun*. Hello was *elelho*. Good was *ogdodo*, bad *adadba*. Mother Marilyn was *Linlinma*. Walter Highland was called *Terterwall*. But he was always discussed as if he weren't there. He would lie on the floor in the dark, speak in falsetto, and call himself *Tumtumbobo*.

The children believed in Tumtumbobo. They told him things they would never say to either of their parents in the daytime. They even complained to him about Terterwall and Linlinma. Tumtumbobo would sympathize with them and take their side.

The language seemed to be a secret between Highland and his children. Marilyn never mentioned it. It was taboo outside the bedroom. Once Evan overheard Junior say that he wanted to stay up and watch TV because he wasn't *eepsilee*.

"I don't know what that word means," his father had said rather sternly.

"It means *sleepy*."

"Then say *sleepy*. We don't allow baby talk around here."

81

Night after night, Evan lay against the foundation of the Highland home and listened to the soft voices with the strange words drift out the open window above him.

They were so intimate. It was a torment to him. But somehow he couldn't stop listening.

With the coming of fall and cooler nights, the Highlands began closing their bedroom windows. Evan could no longer hear them at night, but he could still watch.

One night, Evan was in the woods behind their house, high in a tree, watching the house through a new pair of field glasses he had bought by doing yard work.

He was excited by how close everything looked through the big lenses. He watched the children being put to bed, the light being turned off. A minute later, he watched Walter return to their room, and knew he was about to transform himself into Tumtumbobo.

Feeling bitterly excluded, Evan was about to shinny down the tree and bike back to Selvage. But then he saw the light come on in the parental bedroom. For once, the blinds hadn't been pulled. He watched Marilyn walk into the bedroom after a shower. Her naked body, still slightly moist, glistened in the warm lamplight. She removed her shower cap and shook out her red hair, picked up a towel and, in no hurry, began to dry herself. Her image danced in the lenses from the heartbeat in his hand.

The bedroom door opened and his father entered—as Tumtumbobo. He was walking on his knees, only his head protruding above the windowsill.

Marilyn crossed in front of the windows and sat in a chair. The angle was bad for Evan—most of her body was below the sill and the window jamb cut her in half vertically. Even when he leaned to the right as far as possible, he could see only the left side of her face and a bit of her left shoulder. Tumtumbobo was kneeling on the floor in front of her, the top of his head appearing and disappearing as he moved his mouth from breast to breast. She didn't look down at him, she looked out the window, upright and unmoving. After a time, his head worked downward and disappeared from Evan's view below the line of the windowsill.

At that moment, Evan felt an intense burst of pleasure. Tumtumbobo was still there, but out of sight. Evan was alone with Linlinma. She was looking at *him*.

He pushed his eyes against the lenses of his field glasses, straining to get closer. He could see the green of her eye, the red of her hair, the prim set of her mouth.

Her half-face moved through the window and floated toward him like the surviving fragment of a beautiful statue, high above the dark lawn. She was coming to him, drawn by the power of his gaze. She loved only him. Closer, closer. He drowned in the green of her eye.

The eye fluttered and closed. Her lips softly parted.

"Oh, Linlinma," he whispered. "I ovovlee ououyu. Vanvanlee ovovlees Linlinma."

He clung to the tree with one hand, the field glasses in the other, trembling harder and harder, until his own eyes closed, his own mouth opened, and he climaxed with his father's wife. In his father's tree.

Speaking his father's secret language.

1984

"But it's *crazy!* It's *crazy!* What can I say to you that will change your mind?" Professor Osbert Orpington was almost crying.

"I'm afraid there's nothing you can say, Ozzie. My mind's made up," said Evan Highland.

Evan was sitting in the office of his thesis adviser near the Lampoon Building. It was late June. Outside the streets around Harvard Square lay abandoned in the sunlight. Too late for the regular students, too early for the summer school.

"But you're wasting yourself," Orpington said agitatedly. "You mastered Arabic in six weeks. Even Friedrich Engels broke his pick on Arabic. I've never seen anyone with your gift for languages."

"That's what the CIA is interested in—my languages."

"Where did you get that? From a matchbook cover? 'Good at languages? Join the CIA and see the world.' You're a Harvard Ph.D., for Christ's sweet sake. You have a great career in front of you. You don't need this!"

"I want to do more than just study languages."

"Yes, but you're not a spy; you're an academic, a translator of genius. You could be the next Bob Howard."

"I've thought long and hard—"

"All right, you don't like Harvard. Too many old bulls in the way. Hell's bells, I can understand that. I myself will probably be moving on one of these days. But don't leave academia. You can write your own ticket!"

"It's what I want to do."

"I don't believe that. Not for a minute! How did this start? How did they get their hooks into you?"

"Oh, I suppose you could say they've been courting me for years. This man, Cal Ordway, would show up in town maybe twice a year and take me to dinner. No pressure, just pleasant conversation."

"What did you have to talk about with a CIA recruiter? Why did you go?"

"I don't know—I suppose I thought it might have something to do with all the federal scholarships I kept getting."

"Evan, Evan! You didn't need them! There's always money for a student like you. I would have gone to bat for you. How could you let them bully you like that?"

"Nobody bullied me. Ordway never mentioned the scholarships. I was just being careful. Anyway, it was my only chance to eat in three-star restaurants."

Orpington banged his desk. "Money! That's how they got you, isn't it! What did you offer you?"

"Nothing that unusual."

Orpington's eyes narrowed. "They aren't taking care of your mother, are they?"

"They've offered to pay for a psychiatrically trained person to be in the house twenty-four hours a day."

"There must be some other way. Can't your father contribute?"

"That's blood from a stone, as you well know. Anyway, he hasn't got this kind of money—do you know what this kind of full-time professional help costs on the open market? We're talking about hundreds of thousands of dollars a year."

"Evan—you can't build your life around your mother's mental problems."

"I can't put her in an institution, Ozzie. It would kill her."

"She's telling you that, but it may not be true. A lot of people—"

"Claire is not a lot of people! She's my mother and she wants to stay in her home. Now, I don't want to discuss this anymore!"

"Don't do this to yourself! The CIA is a mug's game if ever there was one!"

Evan stood up and extended his hand. "Good-bye, Ozzie."

Orpington didn't move. Evan was surprised to see there were tears in his eyes.

"All right, but just one more thing. If things don't work out in the CIA—I'm not trying to jinx you or anything—but if they don't—look me up. Wherever I am, I'll get you in. Promise me you'll do that."

"I promise, Ozzie." Evan was touched. He hadn't realized the impact he had made on Orpington. And it was a nice offer too.

Not that he'd ever need it.

· 11 ·

The next morning after breakfast, Jake drove to Planet O' Toys on Queens Boulevard and bought a child's tape player with a sing-along microphone shaped like a banana.

When he got home, he realized he'd neglected to buy cassettes. He found Sally in the kitchen, reading *The Village Voice*.

"Jake! Humphry Shaw is speaking in Manhattan on Friday night."

"Who?"

"The writer! The one who might help me with publishers? I told you about him on the way out to Halcyon Hills. I was going to write to him—now I can ask him in person."

"That's great. Listen, do you have any cassettes with songs a young kid might like?"

"I'll go look." She jumped up and started toward the living room. "If I can get Tina to take me in, would you mind staying home alone with Winston that night?"

"Sure, no problem. Maybe by then I'll have him talking."

Together they rummaged through several cardboard cartons full of old tapes gathering dust since they had bought the CD. The only kiddie tape they could find was a relic of Sally's days as a camp counselor: *Let's All Howl at the Moon with the Two Gitt Brothers* featuring songs like "Skip to My Lou" and "Clementine."

Jake bounded up the stairs and swung the closet door wide open. "Yo, Winston. I got something terrific for you."

Winston had buried himself in the rear of the closet, wedged against the water turn-off handle for the hall bathroom. He stared up at Jake, big-eyed.

85

"Look at this! Your own private music machine. It plays all kinds of great stuff."

Jake squatted and duck-walked into the closet. He dangled the tape player in front of Winston. It was made to look like a lunch bucket, arsenic green, decorated with singing cats.

With sweeping finger gestures, Jake demonstrated how to push the *play* button.

Two adenoidal male voices warbled mournfully:

> He's got the whole world in His hands,
> He's got the whole world in His hands,
> He's got the whole world in His hands,
> He's got the whole world in His hands.

Jake pushed the *off* button. "That button turns it off. On. Off. Got it? Now, if you like a song and you want to hear it again, just hit *off*. Then *rewind*—see this goes backwards—and you can hear the same song again."

Winston continued to stare.

Jake handed him the player. "Here you go, all yours."

Winston took it politely and handed it back.

"Keep it, keep it! It's for you," Jake said. "Break my heart if you won't take it." He handed it to Winston again. This time the boy hung on to it, but his eyes stayed on Jake.

Jake snatched it back. "Just a second! I forgot the best part. You see this professional-style microphone? It allows you to actually sing along. Well, of course you can do that anyway, but with this amazing microphone, your voice is broadcast right through the speaker. You are actually howlin' at the moon with the two Gitt brothers. It's a dream come true!"

Jake jumped to his feet enthusiastically. "Ever catch them boys at a hog-calling contest or a tractor pull? You didn't? Gee, too bad. They could tear you up pretty good."

He flung out his arm like an emcee. "And here they are, just a'strummin' and a'singin', just a'pickin' and a'grinnin' for your listenin' pleasure—the two Gitt brothers and Jake."

Jake started "He's Got the Whole World in His Hands" again, this time in sing-along mode. Eyes crossed reverently over the banana microphone, he joined the Gitts in song, tossing in hound dog howls, scratching himself and occasionally high-stepping with an imaginary partner.

Winston's eyes followed every move, but without the slightest flicker of emotion. When "He's Got the Whole World in His Hands" ended, he watched gravely while Jake showed him how the sing-along feature worked. He accepted the machine again without handing it back, his eyes on Jake.

Jake walked by the closet many times during the rest of the day and evening.

Silence.

· 12 ·

It was the day Mandy came home from the hospital with baby Alexander, the magical day, with the excitement and the bustle, and the house full of Jill's signs, "Welcome home, Mom!"

Five-year-old Jill greeted her mother at the kitchen door, wearing her Wonder Woman cape and bracelets.

"How come you're Wonder Woman today?" Mandy asked.

"I gotta protect the new baby. I love him, but there's lots of bad people out there who want to get rid of him!"

Mandy handed the baby to Roger and swept Jill into her arms. "Don't worry, darling, Mommy loves you just as much as ever."

"Really? You really do?"

It was perfect, it was wonderful, one of the best scenes he had, good clear audio, nicely framed below the button-sized camera installed in the kitchen ceiling. Julian Lamb clawed at himself, his eyes glued to the television screen. But his body would not respond.

"No!" he said aloud. "Not yet!" It was impossible—he couldn't be burned out on the Harrows already. The Leith and Giles tapes had lasted two weeks after the murders. Sturluson almost that long. It was only a week since Skokie. What was happening to him?

Try something else. He took the channel changer off the back of the couch, where he was lying, and fast-forwarded, looking for another scene, something different to start his motor. He watched part of Alexander's first birthday, usually infallible. It did nothing for him. He ran through an especially clear lovemaking scene between Roger and Mandy: a hot summer night with moonlight streaming through the open window. He had been masturbating to that scene for years, but now his penis hung dead.

Angrily he punched the rewind, admitting defeat. A year in the life of the Harrow family whirled backward in fast motion, taunting him like a broken promise. Unable to watch, Lamb toggled out of VCR into TV. A late-night talk show blasted into his living room; its audio level much higher than his videotape.

The apartments around his own housed Wren faculty who had already tucked in for the night. His loud TV would probably disturb them, but Lamb, usually careful to remain inconspicuous, was too tense to worry about that now.

He was impotent, even in fantasy. From their shelves, his erudite books mocked him in twelve languages.

After April fifteenth, Wren College arbitrarily stopped heating its buildings to save money. The April night was chill, and Lamb was naked. But he trembled, not from cold, but from thwarted sexuality. He had to have his orgasm! *Had to!*

If he went to bed without one now, he would have a wet dream. He hated those dreams. Sometimes in those dreams the roles were reversed. Sometimes—

The Harrows had failed him. All right. He would go to the next family. The Reneckers. He promised himself he would make the Reneckers' tape last him an extra long time—at least a month—before he enjoyed the Reneckers themselves, the flesh-and-blood Reneckers.

Still naked, he walked quickly to the locked steel filing cabinet in the bedroom closet, where he kept his file of videotapes.

The cabinet was jammed—hundreds of tapes. He pawed through them, too frenzied for a systematic search. Most of them were worthless to him. Routine families that did nothing for him erotically. Why did he keep them at all? It would be safer to throw them away. But somehow he couldn't do that. They were his lifework, years of surveillance, years of watching people who didn't know his electronic eyes were on them. He had taken big risks to copy these tapes, to keep for himself what only his masters were supposed to have.

And they represented more than work and risk. Although the newest of them were little more than three years old, they belonged to a time of his life he could never go back to—his few brief years of comparatively innocent surveillance. Before all the killing.

But the speed of the Harrow burnout was worrying. The tapes were losing their erotic power. What he wanted sooner each time was the direct experience. The real thing.

From that point of view, the cupboard was almost bare. Only two families left out of all these hundreds who met his specifications. Only two families worth . . . experiencing directly. Renecker and Grant. He seemed to be rushing toward the awful moment when they were both gone. What then?

He pushed the question away and scanned the labels on the tapes. He spotted Grant. For the first time that day, he began to get excited. The Grants were warm, caring people, deeply committed to the welfare of animals, especially endangered species. Their family language was a glorious mixture of wild-animal sounds—wonderful for expressing emotion. The wife even looked like Marilyn Highland—*Linlinma*.

He hadn't pleasured himself with the Grant video in several years. He had been saving the best for last. But now he couldn't resist taking their tape. He felt another burr of worry—he was breaking his predetermined order, his discipline had slipped another small notch. But he knew it was too late. His excitement over the Grants had passed the point of no return. They had earned the honor of being next.

The poor Reneckers would just have to wait.

· 13 ·

Sally sat on the floor in front of the linen closet and talked to Winston.

"Mr. Churchill, did you know us grownups could be scared of things too? That's right. I'm just like you. You're scared to leave that closet; I'm scared to leave the neighborhood. Like tomorrow night, there's this talk I want to hear, but I'm afraid to go by myself. So I had to ask my pal Tina to go with me."

Winston watched her intently. She wasn't sure how much he was picking up. "I know this is a lot to ask, but I wonder if you could help me out—being that we're fellow sufferers and all. Jake has disappeared; I don't know where he's gone. I'm lonely. Will you do me a big favor and keep me company while I do the breakfast dishes? You don't have to, but I'd really appreciate it."

She stood up. To her delight, he did too and trotted ahead of her down the stairs.

He sat politely at the kitchen table and watched her tidy up. Whenever she said something, he looked at her. His face was impassive, but he seemed to understand a lot of what she was saying.

A car motor died in front of the house. She stepped into the living room and looked out the window. Jake was getting out of the red Mustang, carrying a black box. She went back to the kitchen. "Jake's back. You can keep us both comp—"

Winston had vanished.

She hurried upstairs. He was back in his closet.

How had he done that? The stairs were at the front of the house. He must have followed her out of the kitchen, darted past her when she went to the window, and run up the stairs before she turned around.

And he had done it quietly too. She hadn't heard a sound. It was slightly unnerving.

"Thanks for helping me not be lonely. You're a good boy, Winston. And a fast runner too."

She stepped back, then leaned in again. "Was that a smile I saw? Did you smile, Mr. Churchill?"

Winston shook his head.

"Okay, if you didn't smile, you didn't."

Winston looked at her, now obviously trying to control his mouth. He clapped his hands over his face. Sally patted his shoulder. "The two of us, we just can't help it. No matter what we do, we like each other. Ain't it awful?"

Jake was on compassionate leave, but that morning he had gone into the precinct house and borrowed Detective Vitulano's Identi-Kit.

Technically, Vitulano wasn't supposed to lend it. Using the Identi-Kit was a priestly craft, reserved for those who had taken a special course at John Jay. But Detective Vitulano knew what had happened to Jake's brother; he grumbled but acquiesced.

Jake had to promise to be careful with it. Yes, yes, he knew these transparencies were irreplaceable. What did he want it for? He wouldn't say. He operated on a strict need-to-know basis where Winston was concerned.

Sally met him at the front door. "He's definitely loosening up," she said. "I asked him to sit in the kitchen while I did the dishes, and he came right along."

"No kidding! This may go a lot faster than I thought," Jake said. He stowed the Identi-Kit in the bedroom and took a slow walk along the upstairs hall.

After a few back-and-forths, he leaned into Winston's closet and extended his hand. "Shake, pardner." Obediently, Winston reached up and took the first finger. Jake yelled, "Ow!" as if his finger were being crushed. Startled, Winston let go and pulled back, but Jake followed, holding contact and lurching forward as if Winston were dragging him into the closet by sheer force. Pretending to use all his strength, Jake yanked his hand back and blew on the finger. "What a grip! What power! What a man!" He grinned broadly at Winston and walked away as if he had other things to do.

Jake wandered around the second floor, whistling and singing for a few minutes, then returned to the closet and repeated the show.

The third time he came by, Winston already had his hand out, his face unsmiling but intent. When Jake gave him his finger and yelled

"Ow!" Winston kept squeezing. "Ow! Ow! You're too strong for me! You're killing me! Have mercy!" Winston took his time letting go.

Jake jumped back into the hall, as if terrified of Winston's power. He dropped into a squat, grinned, and drawled in a John Wayne voice, "Well, ya beat me that time, but I bet ya couldn't do it again." He dangled his hand over his knee, first finger extended. Winston's eyes were glued to that finger. He crawled forward, out of his closet, and grabbed it.

As if trying to break free, Jake moved his hand back and forth, grunting with effort. "I'll show you who's stronger!"

Winston grabbed Jake's wrist with his free hand and stopped the movement. Jake gave a big grunt, as if trying to heave his weight against Winston's hold, and crashed sideways onto the floor. Winston's eyes widened with surprise, but he hung on gamely. They wrestled up and down the hall, Jake alternately struggling to free himself and begging for mercy. Winston quickly began to use all his strength—Jake was pleased to note he had quite a bit in his wiry little body in spite of his lack of activity.

Jake didn't want to spoil the game by actually breaking free. He went limp and snored loudly. Winston let go but didn't scamper back to the closet. He sat on the floor and watched Jake expectantly. Jake stood up, stretching and yawning as if from a good sleep. Suddenly, he snapped his fingers. "Ooops. I just remembered. I gotta go out in the yard. C'mon, you can help me." He turned and, without looking back, went down the stairs. When he got to the yard, Winston was behind him.

Jake always cut his own grass with a hand mower. The power mowers favored by his neighbors for their postage-stamp lawns seemed like ridiculous overkill to him, and hiring somebody else to do it he thought was sheer laziness. As a result, the grass was nearing jungle length—it obviously hadn't been a big priority this spring. Jake got out the mower and went to work. It occurred to him that he should have borrowed a toy mower from one of the neighbors, but Winston didn't seem to need it. He marched solemnly at Jake's side, up and down, never more than a foot away. Working together like that, they did the whole yard, finishing up in spite of a light rain.

They went in for lunch. Sally complimented the "men" on the fine job they had done.

After lunch, they had another wrestling match. By now, Winston was smiling openly.

The rain had turned heavy. No more yard work today.

Why not get him used to the Identi-Kit?

"I've got a great game. C'mon, let's go upstairs."

The bedroom was stifling. Jake raised the window, but it hardly helped. The rain drew long straight lines in the motionless air.

"This is nutty, wait'll you see . . ." Jake put the black Identi-Kit box on the bed. Winston watched him intently, not sure what was happening. Jake opened the box. Inside were files with labels such as "lips," "glasses," "mustaches," and "age lines." He pulled out several transparencies with charcoal line drawings on them. "Look at all these funny noses."

Winston took one, a tentative smile on his face.

He's into it. He's going to play.

"See, the fun part is you can put together all kinds of different faces."

Jake assembled a beetle-browed man with slack, heart-shaped lips and a square chin.

"Put the nose on him, let's see. Wow! He's funny. How about that nose there. Hey, he's really ugly. How'd you like to look like him?"

He's grinning; he's loving it.

"You're really good at this. I bet you couldn't do one all by yourself, though. That would be too hard."

Winston swiftly slapped together a face.

"Whoa! How'd you do that? Uh-oh—something's wrong here. Can you spot it? That's right! His glasses were upside-down. Boy, nothing gets past you."

Sweet Jesus—he's on a roll. Why wait? He might lose interest by tomorrow.

"Hey, Winston—it's really important for me to know what a certain person looks like. Would you help me—you know, pick out the right nose and eyes and everything to make a picture of him? Would you do that?"

Winston nodded eagerly.

"Remember when you lived with Jill and Alexander? Sure you do. Remember the last night you stayed there? A man came to your house late at night. A bad man who did bad things to Jill and Alexander and everybody. Let's call him *Mr. Bad News.* I know you saw him from the closet. Can you show me what he looked like?"

Winston shook his head violently. The cords on his neck stood out like guy wires. His eyes bulged with terror.

"Hey, it's okay. You don't have to do it now; we can try again tomorrow or—"

Winston snatched the Identi-Kit, darted to the open window, and flung it out. He arced around Jake and dashed out of the bedroom; the hall closet door opened, *slammed.*

Jake sat stunned on the bed, clenching and unclenching his fists.

He couldn't help himself, he felt like going after the kid and giving him a good spanking.

No, that's silly. I can't react like that. This is a traumatized child with all kinds of problems. I obviously went too fast with him. It's my fault, not his.

Jake stood up, took several deep breaths, and walked to the window.

On the newly cut grass below, expensive transparencies of disembodied ears and eyebrows sprawled forlornly in the pelting rain like scraps of an old circus poster.

Vitulano was going to have a coronary.

·14·

"*Dead Sea!*"

Sally jerked upright in bed. "*Someone's in the house!*"

"I'll look," Jake said, his bare feet already hitting the floor.

"It sounded near—in the hall," she said nervously, as he bolted across the room.

Jake flicked on the hall light. Winston crouched on the floor by the closet door, head back, staring up with sightless eyes. In a startlingly powerful baritone he repeated, "*Dead Sea!*"

Jake wanted to rush to him, but he restrained himself. Instead, he got down on the floor and crawled forward until he reached the boy.

Jake held out his finger in front of Winston's face.

"Shake, pardner."

Winston's eyes blinked rapidly. He gripped the finger. He looked at Jake and then around at the brightly lighted hall in a kind of wonderment.

"It's okay," Jake whispered. "You're safe."

Sally walked carefully down on the hall and stood over them. "What's the matter, Winston? Bad dream?"

He stared at her unblinkingly.

"I've got ice cream downstairs. Would you like some ice cream? Mm, nice and cold."

He continued to stare.

"You can sleep in our room," Jake said, still in a whisper. "I could move your bed in, no problem. How about it?"

He seemed to consider it, then shook his head.

"It's up to you." Jake stretched out on the floor. "Hey, this rug is pretty comfortable. Maybe I'll just catch a few winks right here." He yawned elaborately and closed his eyes.

A moment later he heard Winston go back into the closet.

Jake stood up and leaned into the closet. "You want me to leave the hall light on?"

Winston lay motionless, staring at the underside of the shelf above him.

"If you need me for anything, I'm right down the hall." Jake turned out the lights and went back to bed.

"He scared me half to death," Sally whispered.

"That was weird."

They lay in silence for a few minutes.

"Jake?"

"Uh huh."

"Suppose the killer found out—you know—that Winston saw him?"

"No way."

"You're sure?"

"Who'd spread it around? Rourke could lose his job. Mrs. Appleby could lose her agency. They've buried the truth ten feet deep. And I'm sure as hell not going to say anything."

"What about at work?"

"I didn't even tell poor Vitulano why I borrowed his Identi-Kit."

"Will you tell Captain Cowen?"

"Nobody."

"That's good."

"I'd never expose you or Winston to any danger."

"Of course you wouldn't. 'Night, darling."

For the next hour he lay on his back, looking into the darkness, pretending to be asleep. He had the feeling Sally was doing the same.

Then he heard music—so faint he thought at first it was playing only in his head. But the house was absolutely still, and after a time he knew the music was real:

> He's got you and me, brother, in His hands,
> He's got you and me, sister, in His hands,
> He's got you and me, brother, in His hands,
> He's got the whole world in His hands.
>
> He's got the night and the day in His hands,
> He's got the sun and the moon in His hands,
> He's got the night and the day in His hands,
> He's got the whole world in His hands.

· 15 ·

WhaNNGG—YaNNG—WeeEEEEEEEEEEop.

"Testing. Testing. One, two, three."

The loft belonged to a dance collective. You had to leave your shoes by the elevator and hunker, as comfortably as you could, on the highly polished wooden floor. Sally and Tina had arrived early, but the place was already so full they had to sit near the back by the windows.

Tina was Sally's only real pal in her Queens neighborhood. She was also married to a policeman. Tina admired Sally for her Princeton background, her correct way of speaking, her excellent mind. There were days—especially when another form-letter rejection slip rolled in—that Tina's opinion meant a lot to Sally.

Tina had jumped at the chance to accompany powerhouse Sally on her heroic trek into Manhattan to beard the literary lion in his den. She didn't know that without her company Sally would never have dared ride the subway.

It was night; they were eight stories up. Sally tried not to gawk at the light show outside the big loft windows: the fiery towers of midtown—Empire State, Chrysler, and a hundred other giants with numbers for names, the hellfire caldron of Times Square, the big avenues writhing north like neon anacondas.

Toto, we're not in Queens anymore. So long, push-up bras; hello, push-up sleeves. Although she would never have told her, Sally was a bit embarrassed by Tina's idea of dressing for a literary evening: angora sweater, navy skirt, imitation pearls, pale pink lipstick to match her sweater. Sally herself wore a wide-brimmed hat, a dusky purple silk blouse with a flowing scarf, and a long slinky skirt of deepest black.

In her bag she carried the manuscript of *Cool Moves*—well, two

101

chapters and an outline anyway—to give to Humphry Shaw. Would he take it? Would he love it? Would he do for her what he had done for Mel Haney—get her noticed, get her *in*? She struggled to keep her teeth from chattering.

A tall man in a black turtleneck hopped on the stage and gingerly tapped the microphone as if it had not already been tested. *Bonk.* "Is this on? Can you hear me? Good. Thank you all for coming. This is definitely the largest turnout we've ever had. By now most of you know—my name is Lorenzo Segura and I'm from the SoHo Samizdat. I want to welcome you to the seventh in our series of evenings titled 'Outlaw Voices.' We have a very special presentation ahead of us, but first I need to say a few brief words."

He described the work of the SoHo Samizdat. According to him, they were a ragged band of underground poets and scribblers fighting a fierce guerrilla war against a hostile establishment.

Sally glanced at the one-page program and was surprised to note the Outlaw Voices were sponsored by a laundry list of government arts councils, oil companies, banks, television networks, publishers, and private foundations.

Segura held aloft a book. "Tonight's presentation begins with this: *Singing in My Chains.* Mel Haney's letters from prison. Unfortunately, Mel himself can't be with us tonight." (Scattered laughter from the crowd, some hissing.) "Unless the attorney general grants him amnesty." This remark, evidently intended as a joke, backfired. There were boos and catcalls. Segura continued, unfazed.

"Luckily for us, there's someone else who can be with us. The man who wrote the introduction to *Singing in My Chains.* The man these prison letters were written *to.* The man instrumental in getting Mel Haney out of jail. I'm speaking, of course, of Humphry Shaw."

There was applause, but there was also some booing. When the noise had died down, a woman behind Sally shouted, "Murderer!" This set off others. "Shut up!" "Let him speak!"

Segura fought to control the audience. "Hold on! Listen to me! It's already six months since the night Mel Haney disappeared. In all that time Humphry Shaw has made no public statements on the issue—"

"Why not?" a man down front shouted.

"Anything he said would have been twisted by the media. You know the abuse he has had to take from the law-and-order crowd in the last six months. Not to speak of *The New York Times.* You know, the *Times* generally stays on cloud nine, far from reality, but every five years or so they discover the problem of evil and then—watch out! They've done an incredible kangaroo-court number on him. There was no way he could have spoken out."

"What about the Barker letter?" the man shouted.

"That was meant to be private. The family released it to the press; there was no way to stop them. I thought it was a moving letter."

"It was a cop-out!" the same man yelled. He sprang to his feet, an especially threatening action when everyone else was cross-legged on the floor.

Segura glared at him. "Excuse me, sir, maybe you missed your subway stop. You're not at Carl Sandburg night at Lincoln Center. The SoHo Samizdat is a forum for painful and unpopular and dangerous truths. We will not be silenced."

The man's shouted answer was drowned out by a cheer from the crowd.

Segura broke eye contact with his heckler and pleaded with the audience. "Humphry Shaw has come here tonight to give his side of a painful and humiliating story. That took a lot of courage. If you're not even going to listen to him, what is the point?"

A number of side arguments broke out around the hall. The people around the standing man shouted at him to sit down.

Segura leaned into the microphone. "I'm asking you—will you give him a fair hearing—without interruptions?"

Loud applause. Sally joined in. A chant of "*Humm-FREE, Humm-FREE*" went up. About ten people, the standing man among them, walked out. She looked around: the woman who had shouted "Murderer" was still there, sitting in the lotus position, staring hard at the floor.

Shaw waited for quiet. "Thank you, fans of the First Amendment. And now, I give you our greatest living American writer, Humphry Shaw."

The applause was heavy and sustained. Shaw came through a side door on cue, head down, a self-deprecating smile on his face. He was dressed like a Harvard undergraduate of the fifties, in tweed jacket and chinos. Sally recognized his old-young aristocrat's face from a dozen educational television shows but was surprised at how tall he was—well over six feet. His height didn't make him look stronger. The effect was of weediness, of a structural defect that might topple him at any minute. He looked like a big, thin rabbit. He took the microphone off the lectern and spoke without notes, slouched over the back of a chair with one foot resting on the seat—undefended, impromptu, a college senior holding forth at an all-night bull session.

He spoke with slow, careful precision. Sally thought he might be disguising a stutter and felt a rush of sympathy. She knew what it was like to hide a shameful fear from the world.

He told the story of *Singing in My Chains*. How one day, years ago, letters had begun arriving at his home from a man in a penitentiary—powerfully written, tormented letters, telling of a life spent in the hell behind bars. How he had tried to ignore them, asked himself over and over why Haney had selected *him*? Unlike the other writers of his generation, the Capotes and the Mailers, Shaw had never written about true crime or criminals.

Combing his hair with his hand prep-school style, searching almost painfully for the right words, he confessed winningly that he was a "bleeder" when it came to writing, that he found letter writing a chore and a distraction from what he thought of as his "real work."

But Haney had persisted. The letters had come in a steady stream, sometimes two a day, painstakingly printed in pencil, nine pages long, no margins. "My secular prayers," Haney had called them. After Shaw received his three hundredth unanswered prayer, he finally wrote back, asking why? Why *me*?

"Because you care about truth," Haney had answered.

Shaw had always stayed away from the chases and causes that had gripped other writers, but now, as if to atone for the private nature of his books, he made Mel Haney what, he ruefully told the audience, he called his "project *pro bono publico*."

He became Haney's editor, literary agent, and advocate. He oversaw the publication of *Singing in My Chains*. Eventually, he got Haney out of jail, remanded to Shaw's recognizance as his "private secretary."

"What I didn't know—couldn't possibly understand—was the terrible effect of prison on a young man like Mel. I, who had shepherded *Singing in My Chains* into print, who had written the introduction to it, had no real idea what it meant. He had been systematically driven mad, inflamed with hate and rage by a system that can only survive by locking up its bravest and most indomitable members.

"How could he function as a secretary? How could I have dreamed of such a thing? He'd been in prison so long, he didn't know how to dial a telephone." The audience gasped, more convinced of prison brutality by that detail than by a dozen whip marks.

He told them about "that night." He had been in New York for a speaking engagement, staying at the Pierre. Haney had a room down the hall. Two A.M. Shaw was awakened by wild pounding on his door. It was Haney, in an incredible state of excitement, covered with blood. He had been attacked by a gang of muggers. He'd taken the knife away from one of them—a large black man—and killed him with it. The gang knew him; they would certainly set the cops on him. With his record, he had no chance—he'd be back in the pen for the rest of his life. He had to escape, leave the city.

Shaw argued with him, but it was no use. Haney begged him to lend him money, swearing he would pay it back. Shaw ended by giving Haney five hundred dollars—all the cash he had on him—in return for a solemn promise to keep Shaw informed of his location.

The next day the police showed up with a very different story. No gang of muggers. Haney had killed—not a large man, but a small woman. He had brutally raped and repeatedly slashed a nurse named Megan Barker. There were witnesses. Several other nurses who had come home from a late party and caught him at it. They had been quick enough to lock him in the apartment and escape with their lives.

"I thought the cops were lying," Shaw said. "Trying to trick me into revealing Mel's whereabouts. Pigs is pigs, as we say." The audience chuckled appreciatively. Tina gave Sally the elbow. She was a policeman's wife, and she didn't appreciate that last remark. Neither did Sally, but she remembered what she was here for and kept her eyes front.

It soon became obvious it was Mel Haney who had lied. And, of course, he never kept his promise to contact Shaw or tell him where he was. He vanished, leaving Shaw to deal with the consequences.

Consequences there were. Shaw's involvement with Haney and the murder were headlined in New York. People who didn't even know Megan Barker cursed Shaw and spat at him in public. He received death threats and was warned not to attend the dead girl's memorial service. A woman kept calling his home for months, leaving the message, "Megan Barker is still dead," on his answering machine. A cabdriver recognized him and ordered him out of his cab on the dangerous Park Avenue ramp at Grand Central.

And now, a confession: for a time, Shaw had been angry at *Mel*. Not only for lying to him, but even, embarrassing to relate, for cheating him out of some money. A paltry five hundred dollars!

It had taken him a while to work it out. At first he tried to forgive Haney. Then he realized there was nothing to forgive. Megan and Mel *both* were victims of a sick society.

"It was society that killed Megan—as surely as if it had plunged the knife under her rib cage and twisted it."

Humphry Shaw straightened up from his crouch, eyes burning. "Dostoevski said . . ." Sally thought, *Dostoevski! He's going to love my Detective Raskol.* ". . . the best people in Russia are in jail. How much

105

more true in the cancerous culture of late-capitalist America! In a society that itself rests on a foundation of crime, there can be no
criminals—only freedom fighters. The so-called criminal justice system
is nothing but an instrument of class oppression. In fascist America,
all prisoners are political prisoners!''

The audience broke into heartfelt applause.

And now, because he had tried to change that sick system, society
had turned against him too. He, too, had become its victim. Not, of
course, that his sufferings compared in any way to those of Megan or
Mel. . . . Again, the disarmingly boyish gesture of combing his hair with
his hand, waving off well-meant pity.

"You came here tonight to hear what I had to say. I take full respon-
sibility for what happened. I have no excuses. If it makes you feel better
to blame me, to hate me, to boycott my books, to denounce me in the
supplements, be my guest.

"What happens to me hardly matters," he said. "It's Megan and Mel
I grieve for.'' Somehow, in his telling, Megan and Mel had become a
couple, tragically linked like Bonnie and Clyde or Frankie and Johnny.
"What a waste! What a tragic waste!''

A long, emotional silence followed by heartfelt applause. His triumph
was complete—even the woman who had shouted "murderer" joined
in, her eyes shining.

Sally unfolded her aching legs and stumbled to her feet.

Tina said, "You sure you want this cop-hater judging your book?''

"He's not a cop-hater.''

"Could have fooled me.''

"He's wrong about the criminal justice system, but not in any simple
way. He's written thrillers himself. He's a literary man, he sees everything in complex terms.''

"Cops are pigs. Crooks are beautiful losers. Very complex.''

"Look, he deals with true crime in a literary way, which is what I'm
trying to do. And he has a history of helping people. Who else would
you suggest I give my book to?''

"Okay, okay, I guess that 'pigs is pigs' crack caught me wrong. Go
for it, Sal. Good luck. I'll get our shoes, before someone else walks off
in them." She moved away.

Sally swayed, paralyzed with nerves. The crowd was already jam-
ming the exits. In the distance, she could hear the old freight elevator
clanking and booming with departing intelligentsia. She put her hand
into her bag and touched the manuscript of her story. Dared she approach Shaw after a triumph like that? Come on, Sally baby, can't stop
now. She took a deep breath and moved forward.

Well-wishers circled Shaw, jockeying for his attention. Sally lurked timidly on the fringe.

The crowd thinned. She closed in. *What to say? How to get his interest? I've read all your books? Who in this crowd hadn't? How to be different?* Up close, and without her shoes on, he looked ever taller and more remote.

Suddenly, like a gift from God, she had the answer. When her turn came, she said, "Mr. Shaw, I just want you to know that not all 'pigs is pigs.' I'm a policeman's wife [*never guess it from the clothes, right?*], and, frankly, I came here tonight feeling hostile to you [*a fib, but what the hell*]. Your explanation really turned me around."

"That's wonderful! Thank you for staying behind to tell me. Lorenzo, look here—I converted a policeman's wife tonight. How about *that!*"

Segura smiled thinly and looked at his watch.

"What do you think was my best argument? Was there a turning point for you?"

Sally played back her favorite bits from the speech. Shaw writhed with pleasure at every quote, as if being tickled.

"Are you sure you're a policeman's wife?" he asked. "You don't look like one. Not that there's anything wrong with being a policeman's wife. But you know who you remind me of? Virginia Woolf. Lorenzo, doesn't she look like the young Virginia Woolf?"

Segura pointed carelessly at Sally's blond hair. "Woolf was dark."

"Don't be so literal. I'm talking about her aspect, her attitude."

"The restaurant also has an attitude." Segura shoved his watch under Shaw's nose. "We're going to lose our table."

Sally thought, *Now or never.* "Funny you should compare me to Virginia Woolf. Actually, I've got a novel in progress. It's called *Cool Moves.* It's about good and evil with a really authentic police background."

"See there! I was right! Well, well. If you ever want an outside opinion, why don't you send it to me?"

"You'd critique it?"

"Delighted to. Tell you what—if I like it, would you mind if I pass it on to some editors I know?"

"That would be fantastic."

"You're sure? I wouldn't want to get your agent's nose out of joint."

"Not a problem."

"Good. Just send it to my publisher in care of me. It'll get there."

"We've got to move, Humpty," Segura said. "This place is hot—they hold reservations for no man. The pope waits twenty minutes at the bar."

107

"Actually, I happen to have a sample of my novel with me." She drew a manila envelope out of her bag.

"That's even better!" Shaw took it, beaming. He seemed reluctant to turn away.

She took her courage in her hands. "Maybe I could call you? After you've read it?"

He gave her a piercing look. "Tell you what—Lorenzo here is throwing a little get-together for me in a few weeks. We could discuss it there."

A party? Sally fought down her panic. She would have to travel to a strange place, deal with strange people. "That's very kind of you, but—"

"Lorenzo, give our Virginia Woolf one of those invitations, would you?"

"It's not necessary," Sally said. "I included a stamped, self-addressed envelope."

Segura zipped the invitation into her hand as if he were peeling off a C-note to be rid of her. "Now can we *go?*" he said, dragging Shaw with him.

"See you in a couple of weeks," Shaw said, backing away, her manuscript in his hand, his eyes drilling into hers. "Don't forget." He disappeared through the rear door with Segura and some other insiders.

"Yo, Virginia Woolf! I rescued our clodhoppers." Tina was standing behind her, a pair of shoes in each hand.

"He invited me to a party," Sally said numbly.

"Yeah, I heard. You may be Virginia, but you sure played him for a wolf."

"All I wanted was for him to read my manuscript."

Tina dropped the shoes, curved her body to the shape of an S, put her fingernail coyly to her teeth, and batted her eyes. "Maybe I could call you, huh, big guy? *After* you've read it, of course."

"I wasn't trying to come on to him, and I certainly didn't want to get invited to a party! How can I discuss my work with him in front of a lot of other people?"

"What's your problem? He promised to read it. He even said he might show it to some editors. You should be jumping up and down."

"I suppose."

"You suppose? Sally, this could be the turning point of your life."

·16·

The next morning, when Sally woke, Jake was already shaving. In order to talk to her, he was using the bedroom mirror, stepping into the adjoining bathroom only to rinse the razor. Sally watched him from the bed, not quite ready to venture into the day.

"It just hit me," he said. "I've been missing a bet. I broke through to Winston once, back at Roger's house. Remember how?"

"Nope," she mumbled. She preferred to drift toward wakefulness, floating slowly upward through layer upon layer of warm confusion before finally breaking surface into cold clarity. Jake, on the other hand, came up from sleep in a vertical climb, afterburners already lit, and instantly broke the sound barrier, asking questions, drawing distinctions, using subordinating conjunctions before she'd had coffee. It was horrible.

"I used that drawing game—Squibble."

"Uh huh."

"I'm going to try it again. Is there an art supply store on Queens Boulevard?"

"Urmf."

"Sally? Sal-lee."

"Oh. Good morning." She propped herself in a sitting position against the headboard. She blinked, sniffed, rubbed her face.

"Oh, I forgot to ask—how did it go last night?" Jake said. "Did what's-his-name take your book?"

"He's going to read it."

"That's great! Good for you!"

"He says if he likes it enough, he might even show it to some editors."

"Honey—that's tremendous! You're on your way!" Jake rushed to the bed and kissed her, getting shaving cream on her cheek. "What's the matter, why so glum?"

"He wants to give me his critique in person at a party."

"What's wrong with that? You'll have a chance to ask questions and explain what you were trying to do."

"Yes, but when I checked the calendar, I saw I've got something else that night."

"Like what—open-heart surgery? Cancel it. This is big stuff."

"It's the same night as Cowen's bash. Isn't that awful? The one night in the whole month I can't change."

Jake frowned. "What are you talking about? This is more important than Cowen's thing."

"That's sweet of you, but getting invited to Cowen's is your big political plumb. It's your chance to meet the top brass socially."

"I'll go by myself. I'll say you got sick the last minute. You can't pass this up."

"Oh, no, I couldn't sacrifice your career to something as chancy as this."

"Hey! Your career counts too."

Sally dropped her eyes. "Tell you what. I'll ask Tina if she can drive me. If she can, I'll go. Otherwise, I'll go to Cowen's with you. How's that?"

"Why should Tina's schedule decide your life? I'll drop you on my way to Cowen's and pick you up on the way back. Door-to-door service."

"I guess I'll go then."

Jake walked to the side of the bed and put his hand gently on her shoulder. "Last night was a turning point. Don't quit now."

She put her hand over his. "I won't, I promise."

Jake kissed her. "Now, this bigtime writer—he's obviously got great literary taste. Do we have any of his books around?"

"No, we don't," she said. "I'll get you one from the library." She had *Singing in My Chains* in her purse, but she decided not to mention that book to Jake. It was so anticop it embarrassed her.

Besides, Shaw had written only the introduction.

At noon Jake was sitting on the floor in the upstairs hallway. Beside him was a large white drawing pad and some marker pens. In his lap was a hot box of pizza just delivered by a nearby pizzeria.

Jake opened the box and let the savory odors waft out. "When the moon hitsa you eye like a big pizza pie," he sang enthusiastically. "Boy this looks good. Sausage-and-peppers, my favorite." Jake's favorite was pepperoni and mushroom. Sausage-and-peppers was someone else's favorite. Or so Roger had mentioned to him on his last visit.

Jake rubbed his hands together. "Ummm. I'm gonna eat this whole pizza all by myself. Nobody else can have any. Your aunt Sally wants some. She loves sausage-and-pepper pizza. She begged me for a slice. But I said, 'Sorry. This pizza is just for me.'

"I'll just take a nice big slice—hey, it doesn't want to come loose, it's hanging on to the rest of the pie, the cheese is so hot and stringy." He took a bite. "Mmmm! This is the best pizza I ever tasted."

Jake finished the slice, chewing noisily and commenting steadily on its deliciousness.

"This is great. Only one thing could make me happier. Some nice company. Somebody to sit out here in the hall with me. I'd give a lot for that. Why I'd even share this pizza.

"Mm, this slice is even better than the first one. It's just right, nice and hot. 'Scuse me, I shouldn't talk with my mouth full."

He chewed for a moment.

"Yo, Winston. I'll make a deal with you. You can have some pizza. But you have to eat it out here. None of this grabbing a piece and taking it back into the closet. And when you're finished, you got to sit out in the hall with me for a while and keep me company. Okay?"

Winston shot out of the closet door like a halfback running for daylight.

Jake patted the floor beside him. His eyes riveted to the pizza, Winston zoomed into position. Jake winkled out a slice and handed it over. Winston certainly loved his pizza. It was gone in a flash.

"Holy cow! You ate that whole slice *already?*"

Winston nodded, chewing intently.

"What did you do, inhale it?"

Winston swallowed and stared at the pie, his eyes full of expectancy.

"You don't want another slice?"

Nod.

"Gee, *another* slice. I hadn't counted on that. This pie is going fast."

Winston stared at the pie.

"I tell you what. There's something I like even more than pizza. A game called Squibble. Remember Squibble?"

A perfunctory nod. The kid's mind was on that second slice, so near and yet so far.

"We played it a couple times at—at your old house. Do you remember playing Squibble with me?"

Nod.

"If you'll play it with me, I'll let you have another slice. Okay?"

Nod-with-frown. He didn't seem to like this business of playing games to get food.

Jake held the pad in front of Winston and gently pushed a yellow Pentel into his hand.

Long pause. Somewhere in the house Sally was pecking away on a typewriter. The portable dishwasher splashed rinse water into the kitchen sink. His arm was starting to ache from holding out the pad.

"C'mon, champ, you can do it."

Winston swiped halfheartedly at the paper, almost as if he were trying to push it away with the Pentel.

"Ah ha! What's *this?*"

Jake thought, *Looks like an aimless row of feeble lines to me.*

He drew a big oval around the lines, added feet and a head. "Hey, look what you did. That's Big Bird!"

Winston stared at the pizza.

"This is fun!" Jake boomed. "Let's do a couple more. Try a blue marker."

Winston didn't wait this time. Jake turned his quick scribble into a blue rabbit.

They did several more. Winston's scribbles grew larger, but remained scribbles.

"Give me a hard one this time. Try to fool me."

Another scribble.

Jake tore it off the pad and tossed it away.

"I think you can do better than that. There are lots of ways you could really cross me up. Like remember in Skokie how you put that one little mark in one corner of the pad? You made me work that time. Remember how we laughed?"

Winston made a little mark in one corner of the pad.

Jake drew a line of migrating birds of which the little mark was the smallest and farthest away. The nearest bird was wearing a derby hat and smoking a cigar.

"How's that?"

He held it up for inspection. The boy stared through it with X-ray eyes at the pizza.

"Now do me another good one like that. Completely different, but just as hard. Can you do that?"

Another scribble.

"Aw, you're not really playing. How do you expect to get pizza if you don't really play?"

Winston gave Jake a startled look of purest betrayal.

"Okay, okay—we'll figure out something. Let me think. How can you redeem yourself? How can you—" He snapped his fingers. "Ah ha! Got it. Here's what we do. We play one more game. Only this time, we play it backwards. I start it, and you finish it off. Then you get the pizza. Okay?"

Winston looked confused, but he obviously liked that part at the end where he got pizza. He leaned forward to watch as Jake began to sketch with rapid strokes.

Daddy and mommy, boy and girl, standing all in a row. Behind them a tall rectangle with shelves. A bookcase? No, it has a door. It's a closet. Under the bottom shelf, another little boy with big eyes.

Jake handed over the marker. "Finish it off and it's pizza time."

Winston froze, marker in hand. He didn't seem to know where to begin, or what was expected of him.

"What's the problem? Oh, I see. You think it's already finished. It's not. I need to draw another man here. Trouble is, I don't know what his clothes looked like, or his hair, or anything. Can you help me?"

The boy didn't move.

"Okay, okay, I know it's hard. Give me the stuff a sec. Let's just say he was standing about here. Now, was he wearing boots, shoes, sneakers—what d'ya think? [Pause] Okay, we'll come back to that. Now, he must have had legs, right? Don't know how long, so I'll just rough in the middle part. And he probably had an arm some-where. Oh, and I know what was in his hand, he left it behind. It was a gun that looked like this." In spite of his excitement, Jake took a minute to make a detailed drawing of the automatic that had been found in Roger's lap. "Now where do you think his shoulder was? About here? Or—"

A thin black arm darted in front of him. Winston snatched the marker and flung himself on the drawing. He began to draw, not scribbling this time but moving the marker intently, heavily, straining to get it right.

It was only a moment—then he was through. He tore off the drawing, balled it up furiously, and threw it on the floor. He flung the marker against the wall, screamed a thin flat scream like a tortured animal, and fell to the floor, biting his hands. He screamed several more times, short piercing yelps, thrashing about blindly in terror.

Jake fell to his knees and pulled the struggling boy into his arms. "I'm sorry, I'm sorry. It's my fault. No more, I promise, no more. We'll have pizza, lots of pizza—"

Winston went limp. Jake continued hugging him, too mortified and stunned to move from the spot.

Sally appeared at the head of the stairs, looking scared.

113

"Was there an accident? Is he all right?"

"He'll be fine." Jake eased the boy to the floor, where he lay, glassy-eyed but conscious.

"What happened? It sounded like someone was killing—"

"Later. I'll tell you later."

Sally approached nervously, as if worried that Winston might scream again. When she saw the mess on the floor, her eyes widened: Winston had rolled over the remaining pizza, grinding it into the rug, and smearing his clothes with tomato sauce.

She stretched out her hand. "Winston, I think you could use a bath and some clean clothes. Come with me. Come on."

Politely but insistently, Winston freed himself from Jake's hug. He seemed completely in control of himself again. He took Sally's hand and the two of them went off toward the bathroom.

Jake stood up. He smelled pizza on his hands and his shirt—he could use a shower himself. He leaned against the wall, unsure of what to do next. His mind seemed to have shut down.

He heard water running in the bathtub. Sally came back, gave him a funny look, and began to clean up the mess on the floor. When she picked up the balled up remains of the drawing, Jake said, "That's what did it."

"This drawing set him off?"

"We were playing Squibble. I was trying to get him to draw the killer."

Sally unfolded it and smoothed it flat against the wall.

"Winston didn't draw this."

"I did."

"I thought you were playing Squibble."

"Sort of. I drew the killer's gun, and he was adding to it when he had that attack."

Sally nodded. "I think I'm beginning to understand. See how he extended your lines and made the whole barrel bigger and longer—now that I look at it, it's pretty Freudian."

"Freudian?"

"Well, if a gun is a phallic symbol, he's given this one a big erection. The poor kid must have been traumatized originally by the sight of that gun. So now he was trying to deal with the trauma by drawing the gun the way it appeared to him psychologically. Making it bigger, more dangerous, as a way of dealing . . ."

Jake stopped listening and stared at the drawing.

Sally was wrong. Winston hadn't made the gun bigger.

Instead, with passionate but unmistakable strokes of his pen, he had equipped it with a silencer.

· 17 ·

1988

Cal Ordway was at the wheel, preparing to come about; Evan Highland stood alertly in the cockpit, poised to crank the capstan as if this were the America's Cup.

Ordway grinned with enjoyment. He loved the slap of the spray on his face and the hard tug of the wheel against his hands. He was over fifty, with a shock of white hair, and deep furrows in the sun-cured leather of his face, but he could still do it all—swim the length of the pool and back underwater, rappel up a rock face, shoot a tight pattern with a Colt .45 at fifty feet.

It was spring. The day was clear, with a fair wind. *Blind Zoe* was nicely heeled over in the water, doing six and a half knots, thank you very much. Not bad for an old forty-footer.

Blind Zoe was rarely tied up. She usually swung at anchor off Cane Cove Plantation on the Georgia coast.

The plantation house was a tumbledown ruin, with a half-rotted pier running from the middle of the back lawn into the Atlantic. Ordway approved of its air of derelict magnificence; he disdained the Company's idea of a safe house: usually a tacky little apartment on Connecticut Avenue, mailbox stuffed with annual reports to make it look like someone lived there, a row of flowerpots on the windowsill for sending all-clear signals to the street. Good for a nooner, perhaps, but not much else. No one was fooled—not even the building superintendent.

No, this place was truly secret—even from the nosy fiscal clerks in the Company itself. Like everything in Cal Ordway's life these days, it was soft-filed.

Cane Cove Plantation itself was secure; trip wires crisscrossed the grass, motion sensors watched from the trees, cameras clicked in the weather-stained garden statuary; but Ordway preferred to hold all his most sensitive conversations on *Blind Zoe.*

Blind Zoe was an old-fashioned girl, with a wooden mast and no satellite navigation equipment—in fact, no electronics of any kind, not even a radio. That was more than a matter of style. Ordway knew that sensors could be made to send, speakers become listeners; he wanted nothing aboard that could be turned around on him. *Blind Zoe* was a blind zone and a far better one than the anechoic chambers and so-called cones of silence. To him, those places were sitting ducks. *Blind Zoe* was always moving, deep in the nap of the earth, surrounded by ocean waves that jumbled and blocked electromagnetic transmission. On a day like today, the wind helped too, whipping away their words.

Blind Zoe was swept for bugs every time she was used—once by a trusted technician, once by Ordway himself. He had been especially careful today—this conversation with Highland concerned the most sensitive operation he had ever worked on.

They came about. Evan joined him at the wheel. They sipped scalding coffee from mugs blazoned with the shield and dagger of the KGB—an old Langley joke.

"So, Evan—what's this nonsense about quitting Red Queen?"

"I want to go back into surveillance, Cal."

"That's hackwork—there's no comparison. You've got a chance here to do something really big."

"I've come to realize that surveillance is what I'm fitted for," he said doggedly.

"But you've just started—the training is only a month old. You're not giving it a chance."

Evan looked off to the horizon, stubbornly refusing to meet Ordway's gaze. "I can see it's not for me."

Ordway snorted. "Be serious! With your knowledge of languages, did you think you could stay in domestic surveillance forever?"

"Send me overseas, then. I'll work anywhere."

"I didn't spend three years recruiting you so you could spy on a bunch of third-rate security risks."

"Anything but Red Queen."

"Does it occur to you that I might see something more in you than you see in yourself?"

"You've always believed in me, Cal. I'm grateful. It's just that this time, I have to say no."

"Give it one more month. Will you do that for me?"

"I'm sorry. No."

"Sometimes in this life, you've got to roll the dice. You won't get an opportunity like this again."

Highland shrugged without answering.

"What is it? What's bothering you?" Ordway asked. "Is it that Red Queen is proactive? That we're hitting these men before they can commit their terrorist acts?"

"I'm sure they're—correctly selected."

"Then what's your problem?" Ordway exploded. "I don't have to tell you what the terrorists are doing to us—not just the U.S.—all the Western countries. They're distorting elections, toppling governments, ripping apart the social fabric. They've found the pressure point, the weak spot in an open society. Take a few hostages, and the TV cameras come. And once the cameras are there, the terrorists can talk right past the governments to the people. They can put a gun to a nation's head. You know what brought Jimmy Carter down? Four hundred nights of a network news report called 'America Held Hostage.' That's why everybody cuts deals with them—everybody!

"But they've got a weak spot too. No matter what they say, there are very few men who are truly eager to die. Being a terrorist is a dangerous business. And Red Queen will make it more dangerous."

"By killing potential terrorists."

"By killing real terrorists before they strike. Do you have a problem with that?"

"I don't—I . . . it's the killing. I'm not a killer. I'm a spook, I'm a snoop, I'm a spy. But I'm not a killer."

"Nobody's asking you to be. You're a surveillance man, the best we have. We have paras to do the killing."

"Then why all the weapons training—handguns, silencers, explosives?"

"Because—look, Red Queen isn't like anything else we've ever done. It's what the Brits call a one-off. We train you. We set you up in your phony businesses—all de novo, none of the usual Company shadow corporations or fronts. We give you your hit list, and then you're on your own. No reinforcements, no help, no contact with any of the Company's assets or proprietaries—no contact with me except in a grave emergency. You guys call all the shots. If you vote to stand down the operation, that's up to you."

"I still don't understand. If I'm not going to kill, why turn me into a killing machine?"

"Think it through. It's like a moon shot. Everybody's got to cover for everybody else. Everyone has several languages. The other men will learn surveillance, just like you learn explosives and weapons. Red

Queen will be a hologram, with the entire structure in each cell. Six men, six functions. Five men, six functions. Four men, still six functions. It doesn't mean we're asking you to be a killer. It means we're asking you to be ready, maybe once, if it comes to that."

"I don't know if I'll be able to do it. Kill."

The aft telltale fluttered; Ordway swung the wheel over hard, then brought it back; the woolly behaved itself again.

"Join the club. Nobody knows until they're in the situation. If we trust you, why can't you trust yourself?"

"Trust myself to what? Pull the trigger? What about afterwards? What about the rest of my life?"

"Will you at least talk to Greenspan?"

"A doctor who cures people of their inhibitions about murder? Isn't respect part of the therapeutic process?"

"Well, you'd better find some way to reconcile yourself to this. There's no alternative."

"Meaning?"

"It's Red Queen or nothing. You can't go back."

"It's like that, is it."

"I'm afraid so."

"I didn't expect this from you."

"From *me*? *You didn't expect this from me*? This isn't some kind of game. We've got to start all over—recruit a new man. You're delaying a major counterterrorist initiative by at least two months. Through your cowardice. Let's call things by their right names—*cowardice*. You're deserting under fire, Evan. If this were wartime, you'd be shot."

"Lucky for me it's not wartime."

Ordway dashed the remains of his coffee over the side. "It's the end of your career, the end of everything you've built."

"I can't kill."

"This hurts me too, you know. You're one of my people. This will be one hell of a black eye for me in the Company."

"I'm sorry, but I can't help that."

"If you don't care about me, what about your mother? This means the end of her free nursing care. Have you thought about that?"

"I haven't, no."

"Take a day."

"My mind's made up, Cal."

"Take a day to think about your mother."

"I'll take care of her somehow."

"It's a dangerous world."

"What's that supposed to mean?"

"You can't kill. Others can."

"Cal, if we weren't old friends, I might think you were threatening my mother. You're not threatening my mother."

"Ready at the capstan, we're coming about."

1989

Thump-THUMP! Thump-THUMP! Thump-THUMP!

Ronski was wearing a wire, and his heartbeat boomed in Highland's headset like distant thunder.

What the hell's the matter with him? Highland wondered. His heart had made no such racket at the dry run the night before. Of course, that had been in Piraeus, with grain sacks for guards, blanks in the guns, and a scarecrow in the bed.

Tonight they were in Jedda, the real thing—live ammunition, live guards.

Still, Ronski wasn't even in the house yet, and already his heart was rattling in his chest like small-arms fire. Ronski the hit man. Dapper Ronski, the shootist, the iceman, the professional. Could it be that now, at last, when it had really come down to it, when the dry runs were over and the body on the bed was alive, that Ronski was *panicking*?

Highland would soon find out. This was the team's first hit. Red Queen was about to lose her virginity.

It was one fifty-nine in the morning. The hot desert wind was blowing toward the Red Sea just a few miles away. The stars were big as planets; they blazed in the sky without twinkling.

Highland's van was parked across the street from the high wall surrounding the home of their target: a Saudi businessman, twenty-five years old, a graduate of MIT. His name was Ammed.

Ammed imported things. He had a big store in the souk selling Japanese electronics made in Taiwan and American refrigerators made in Italy.

Ammed was not a terrorist. His brother Omar was. A month ago, Omar had taken an American journalist hostage. Ammed was about to pay the price for that. If the journalist was not released after this, Ammed's father, the old sheik, would be next.

They had decided to kill Ammed in his house, at night, while he slept.

Ammed's compound was walled and thickly planted. The house itself was invisible from the street. Some weeks before, when no one was at home, Highland had broken in and done some interior decorating with video cameras the size of a spider's eye. In the process, he was startled to come across several bugs already in place, big clumsy microphones that a child should have been able to spot.

Worriedly, he had asked Sweep Carr if the microphones signaled danger. Officially, Red Queen had no leader, but everyone deferred to Carr as the senior man. "It's normal," Carr had told him. "Jedda is the bugging capital of the world."

For the next three weeks Highland had watched Ammed's homelife. It was mostly business entertaining. From one of his ceiling cameras, Highland could read the labels on the scotch bottles Ammed served to his American, Japanese, and Italian guests to prove he was thoroughly international and not bound by Muslim law.

His wife, who was Lebanese, was often in London or Paris on shopping trips, although she managed to call him every night—less from love than to check up on him. She needn't have worried. Ammed's only sexual sin seemed to be dirty jokes, which he told to the other businessmen in fluent American English.

Even when he wasn't talking to foreigners, Ammed had given Highland few chances to practice his Arabic. Ammed spoke English most of the time, as did his wife and all his friends. Arabic was for speaking to the servants. Occasionally Ammed would remark that he'd forgotten the Arabic word for something like *chair* or *bread*. From his tone, it was clear he was bragging.

Ammed hardly considered himself an Arab at all. He was furious with his brother for becoming a terrorist. Omar, he explained to his friends, had been named, not for Khayyám, but for Sharif. He thought he was a movie star. To him, Terrorist was a juicy role, with glamorous costumes and grand gestures. It made no sense to Ammed—it interfered with business. Because of his brother's self-dramatization, he had to install additional security systems, hire extra bodyguards.

The more Highland watched, the more disturbed he had become. "Aren't we killing the wrong man?" he had asked Sweep Carr. "Shouldn't we be hitting his brother?"

Carr had shaken his head. "That's a prescription for getting our hostage killed."

"But Ammed is just a businessman."

"Be glad of it. He buys a gun and buries it in a drawer instead of keeping it to hand. He hires guards and sticks their beds a mile away in the servants' wing. He installs an expensive alarm system designed to stop sneak thieves, not professionals. He thinks he's safe because he's spent a lot of money."

"I thought our job was to kill terrorists, not innocent people."

120

"This is how the KGB does it, my friend. You notice how few Russians get taken hostage."

"But I thought Red Queen—"

"Rule one: Never believe the intake briefing," Carr had said, and turned away.

Now, tired of listening to Ronski's heartbeat, Highland flipped some switches and began to monitor the bugs inside the house.

"Assassination is like farce," one of their instructors had taught them. "You must rehearse it to a metronome and do it to the beat." Highland was the metronome. He sat surrounded by small TV screens, picking up the cameras he had planted in the house. He wore a headset to listen to a dozen hidden microphones. He was in two-way communication with the other five men.

Forty seconds to go. Highland flipped switches, checking on the guards' quarters. Electronic eyes and ears testified the status had not changed—the four off-duty guards were asleep.

He toggled to the two on-duty men. They were in their places. The outside man was reading a book with a pencil flashlight he wasn't supposed to have. The inside one was sitting as usual on a chair at the foot of the stairs leading up to Ammed's bedroom, a Russian AK-47 assault rifle held across his lap.

In just a few seconds it would be time for the guards to change places.

He flipped to Ammed's bedroom. The target was snoring quietly, doubtless dreaming of Saudia stewardesses. He slept alone tonight; his wife was in Paris.

Even though he was working in the van, Highland pulled on his stocking mask. No one must ever see what any member of Red Queen looked like.

At exactly two A.M., Highland opened his mike to the man they called Houdini.

"Go," Highland said.

A moment later, a red condition light on the panel above him winked out. Houdini had disabled the alarm system. It was the clever-clever kind that sent an alarm to Jedda police headquarters if the obvious wires were snipped. Houdini had not snipped the obvious wires.

"Alarm off," Highland told everyone.

That was the signal for Carr to scale the front wall and race through the bushes toward the guard house.

Through the open mike, Highland heard a strangled half-yell, then silence. The tranquilizer dart was supposed to be painless and instantaneous. Obviously, it was neither.

"Guard down," Carr's voice crackled in his ear. He sounded cool, almost bored.

Highland's eyes were glued to the second guard on his center TV screen.

The man didn't move. He hadn't heard the cry.

Highland opened all the lines.

"Go."

Houdini sprinted for the front door. Borchard and Ronski scaled the front wall. Crowhurst climbed the rear wall to cover the back of the house, in case Ammed tried to escape that way.

Houdini silently picked the front door lock, an absurdly easy one for a man of his talents, then deliberately began to rattle the knob noisily.

Highland watched the second guard. The man looked up in surprise as he heard the noise at the front door.

"I forgot my key," Houdini shouted in Arabic. He had sounded more like the outside guard in the practice sessions, but the illusion was good enough.

Highland watched the guard slump irritably toward the door, yawning and stretching, his assault rifle held negligently under his arm like a baton.

When he was five feet away, Highland said, "Now."

Houdini kicked open the door, and Carr fired his tranquilizer gun point-blank.

This time it worked as advertised. The guard went down without a cry.

Houdini scooped up the guard's AK-47 and darted off across the lawn to cover the far side of the house. Carr took the guard's pistol and began tying his hands behind his back with a length of cord.

Borchard came up the path at a dead run and charged into the house. He was a big man, built like a linebacker, smart and brutal, the muscle of the team. Although he was twice Ronski's size, he had climbed the wall faster and outraced him to the house.

Once inside, Borchard slowed to a walk, slipping down the hall with his gun in a two-handed grip. As Ronski's backup, he was to wait at the foot of the stairs and cover for him if there was any problem getting out.

Highland flipped on Ronski's wire again. His heart was still pounding.

He picked Ronski up visually as he passed Sweep Carr by the front door. Having rolled the unconscious guard into the shadows, Carr was already in position outside the front door, waiting for Highland's signal to go inside. Carr's job was to be the last man on the scene, sweeping, making sure the target was dead, the cartridges gone, no sign of Red Queen left behind.

Click click click. Highland switched from camera to camera, tracking Ronski through the house. The hit man's image was clear even on the night scope, the face contorted with strain, his eyes bugging out of his head. He walked fast, foam soles silent on the thick rugs and expensive parquetry. He passed the waiting Borchard and mounted the stairs, his heart the only sound: *Thump-THUMP! Thump-THUMP!*

Highland jumped ahead of him. *Click.* Ammed's bedroom. The Microcam was on the center wall, showing the door and Ammed's sleeping form. The room was quite dark, but the infrared lens made Ammed glow with light like an Arabian saint. He was still snoring gently, unaware that anything was happening.

Ronski should have come through the door almost instantly, but there was an oddly long wait. Then the door opened. Ronski edged in.

Something was wrong. Ronski was supposed to spring to the bed and shoot Ammed at point-blank range with his silenced pistol. One bullet through the head. Instead, he stood in the doorway and slowly raised his gun in Weaver stance, like a marksman on a firing range.

Blam! Ronski fired at Ammed's sleeping form from the doorway.

There was no silencer on the gun! That was the wait in the hall—Ronski must have paused to unscrew it. In that confused instant, Highland understood why: a silenced gun is no longer automatic; the silencer swallows up the energy to work the mechanism; it must be hand-cocked before each shot. Ronski had lost his nerve; he couldn't shoot a man up close. He wanted to blaze away rapid-fire from the doorway.

Ammed jerked upright. *Blam!* Ronski fired again. Ammed bolted out of bed and lunged to his bureau. *Blam!* Ronski fired at him. Ammed fumbled an automatic out of his bureau drawer. *Blam!* Ronski shot again. Incredibly, Ronski the hit man, Ronski the shootist had fired four shots at Ammed's big body and missed completely!

Ammed spun around and fired one-handed. *Crack!* Ronski went down.

Christ! The first one, the by-the-book one! And already a broken play! Highland opened his mike. "Ronski down! Target still alive. Target has pistol!" That would start Borchard toward the bedroom. The house was still surrounded. There was no way Ammed could escape.

He could hear yelling. Ronski's thunderous shooting had roused the sleeping guards. This was getting messy. Ronski didn't seem to be breathing. They had to get him out. No Red Queen member could be left behind.

Ammed ran to the window, opened it, and climbed out. He wasn't supposed to do that! That wasn't in any of the contingency plans. He was on a high second floor. There was no balcony. His hands clung to the sill, then let go. He must have dropped to the flower beds below.

Nobody was covering that side of the house. The target was getting away!

Borchard burst into the room, vaulting Ronski's body and looking around wildly for the target.

Highland was the only man who knew what had happened. He made the decision.

"Get Ronski out," he told Borchard.

"Go left! Van side of the house," he said to Carr. "Target may be coming your way."

"Hold your position," he told Crowhurst. "Target may be approaching on your right."

He picked up the silenced Walther PPK he had never expected to use and jumped out of the van. The only way for Ammed to escape Carr and Crowhurst was to go directly to the wall.

Just as he was thinking that, he saw Ammed clamber over the garden wall and run wildly down the street away from the van. Highland sprinted after him.

Ammed was young and desperate, but Highland had just completed his training. He ran Ammed down in thirty yards.

Ammed heard the footfalls and twisted around. He had no gun! He must have dropped it while climbing the garden wall.

Ammed saw the PPK and stopped running, his chest heaving. He was wearing blue silk pajamas decorated with little British heraldic lions.

He sank to his knees. "Don't shoot! Don't shoot! I won't resist! I'll go quietly!" he said in Arabic.

All Highland could see were his eyes, liquid black and big with fear. Highland thought, *I've been watching this man for three weeks. I know him better than his father. Ronski couldn't shoot him; how can I?*

As if from a great distance, he heard a sound like *SHEW!* It was the Walther PPK, bellowing with strangled rage through the gag of its silencer. Ammed sprawled against the wall, the back of his head blown away. The light went out in his eyes, dulling them like a membrane.

Free of that gaze, unchained from those pleading eyes, Highland spun around and raced back toward the van.

Ronski was dead.

They had agreed that if anyone was killed, they would vote whether to stand down Red Queen.

Highland wasn't sure how he would vote. He felt that in some ways, the team was actually stronger without Ronski. It seemed absurd to stop after only one hit. But Ammed's eyes followed him in his dreams.

Highland's cover was as sales agent for a bareboat charter company working out of the Greek island of Spétsai. It was a small operation: no big party boats with phony rigging, no flotilla sailing. It had the further advantage that it had all the work it could use via word of mouth—there was little for Highland to do but muck around the boats, do a spot of crewing when a skipper wasn't too sure of himself, and bring in the odd suitcase full of spare parts from England.

Perhaps his most useful service was to accompany the skipper when he negotiated with Greeks, Arabs, Turks, Armenians, Maltese, Japanese, or Israelis. When they slipped into their native languages to discuss how they really felt about the deal, it never occurred to them that a smiling deckhand whose native tongue was American English would understand their every word.

Often there was nothing to do at all but loll at the nearby harbor café under a sign offering "Krep Suset" and read a book. The Brits who ran the charter had been well taken care of by Ordway; they never asked any questions.

The rest of Red Queen was spread around the nearby islands and the Peloponnesus, all within easy reach of the *Blue Dolphin* hydrofoil to Piraeus, the group's headquarters.

A week after the Jedda action, they met in a house outside Piraeus. Borchard, the backup hit man, voted to stop. Houdini joined him. Sweep Carr and Crowhurst voted to go on.

Everyone waited for Highland to break the tie, but he sat frozen, unwilling to speak. Finally, Borchard said that he would change his vote, but only if someone else would be hit man.

"I'll do it," Highland blurted out.

The others all looked at him, wondering. Had he been silent because he wasn't sure what he wanted to do? Or had he been holding out, trying to force Borchard to turn over the killing to him?

The one who wondered most was Highland himself.

That same night, across the Mediterranean in Beirut, an American journalist being held hostage by terrorists was left unguarded in a ground-floor room. After not hearing anyone move about in the heavily fortified house for more than three hours, the hostage finally screwed up his courage and "escaped" by opening the unlocked door and walking to freedom.

At the press conference, pale but beaming, he pledged to say a prayer of thanksgiving every day for the rest of his life.

"I see God's hand in this," he said. "There's just no other explanation."

· 18 ·

Winston had drawn the silencer for Jake on a Saturday. On Thursday morning of the following week, Captain Cowen sat alone in his office, looking lovingly at his own face.

Cowen's office was more like a corporate executive's than a police chief's: silver water carafe, Cross pens in a block of onyx, high-backed leather chair.

Manhattan detectives prided themselves on dressing better than Bronx detectives; but their ideal was Brooks Brothers: sober and lawyer-like. Cowen was in a different league entirely. Today, as usual, he was a walking picture-opportunity in his Gucci, his Pucci, his Fiorucci.

Some men keep a pint in the desk drawer. Cowen kept a mirror. He liked to sneak a peek between meetings, a little pick-me-up to help him through the day, a reminder that he was one hell of a hunk of political horseflesh, promotable, appointable—hell, *electable*, why not? With his demure wife Eden by his side. And ahead of him, kicking down doors. And behind him, scooping up the bills.

He was drinking in his reflection, imagining it on a poster for mayor: shirt-sleeves rolled, jacket over the shoulder, head held high, looking to a better day for *all* the people of New York: "Cowen. He cares."—when Jake stormed in and caught him slamming the desk drawer and hurriedly straightening up.

"What's with you Jake? You're not due back until next Monday. Compassionate leave is two weeks, remember? I insist you take it all. I don't want anybody at Manhattan North saying that I—"

"I've got something to show you."

"I'm sure it'll keep a few more days. Go home. I don't have the time anyway—I'm due at a police-dog retirement."

127

"A what?"

"Don't you know about this? When our police dogs get too old to work, we have this little ceremony to thank them for their years of service."

"You throw them a bone."

"What's so funny? Listen, it's good for department morale, and it builds bridges to the community. You'd be surprised at the interest it generates. We hold it in a playground; the whole neighborhood shows up."

"And the TV news too, I bet."

"Sure—it's animals, it's kids, it's cute, but it has its serious side too. We've never actually made it to the air, but I have hopes this year. Pray for a slow news day."

"Two minutes, that's all I ask." Jake placed a brown folder on Cowen's desk. "Last week I got a court order to have my brother's body exhumed."

"Jesus, why do a thing like that?"

"I had a hunch Skokie forensics missed something."

"Some hunch." Cowen looked down at the folder; it had an FBI logo on it. His eyes narrowed. He picked it up and slowly read aloud the legend at the bottom. " 'Dr. V. Singh. FBI Forensic Laboratories, Quantico, Virginia.' The Bureau examined your brother's corpse?"

He flipped open the report. The first exhibit showed a network of heavy black lines on a gray, oddly textured field.

"That's an electron micrograph," Jake said. "The forensic pathologist says it's a fragment of fiberglass screen from a homemade silencer. There was no silencer found at the scene."

"How do they know it was from a silencer? Maybe he was doing some shop work or something. Where did they find it? On the skin, in his hair—?"

Jake leaned over the page and put his finger down on the caption. "See where it says, '. . . fragments recovered from the temporal and parietal lobes . . .' His brain, Doug. They dug it out of his brain. My brother didn't commit suicide. He was murdered."

"My God." For a moment Cowen had the grace to be embarrassed, unsure whether to offer Jake congratulation or condolence. Then he rallied.

"That's the *Bureau's* conclusion?"

"They're exhuming more bodies on the strength of it."

"The rest of the family?"

"Other cases, other dads."

"I don't get it. On what basis?"

"The guy who murdered Rog's family was a calculated sadist. The bastard did things—no father behaves like that, not even when he's murdering his own family. The Bureau's computers can match cases on any variables you want. They fed it dads who supposedly murdered their families with extreme sexual cruelty and then committed suicide. The search went back ten years. There's never been anything like what was done to Rog's family—until recently. The computer spat out a cluster of similar cases all in the last six months."

"All Chicago area?"

"Nationwide."

Cowen whistled low in appreciation. "If they can tie all this together, we're talking about network news, CNN, the newsweeklies. Have they found anything yet?"

"About an hour ago they called me—silencer fragments in a corpse in Washington, D.C. A man named Albert Leith. Same kind of case. Family tortured, sodomized, dad supposedly a suicide. Happened last January. Looks like our boy did it. And that's only the first one out of the ground—they've got five more to go."

"They digging up any New York bodies?"

"No."

"Long Island? The tri-state area?" Cowen seemed to have forgotten all about the retiring police dogs.

"No. Listen, I want your permission to work with the Bureau on this. They're agreeable; they just want your signature on these forms." He shoved some papers in front of Cowen.

Cowen ignored the forms. His eyes were on Jake. "The FBI's not good enough? You have to work on it personally?"

"I want to be in on it."

"You wouldn't have some fantasy of maybe finding this guy on your own? This wouldn't be a revenge thing?"

"How long have you known me?"

"He killed your brother."

"I was the one who broke the goddamn silencer. This is my case. It belongs to me."

"Aren't you getting a little ahead of yourself? You may have called a good audible at the line of scrimmage, but you still take orders from the NYPD, not the other way around."

"What are you saying, Doug? You can't spare me? Because if you are, you can have my badge right now."

"That fast, huh? Chill out, amigo. I'm not saying you can't work on the case. But if it's as big as you say it is, I'm wondering if there might not be a role for the NYPD."

Jake looked suspicious. "What kind of role?"

"We work together with the Bureau all the time; we've got joint task forces on bank robbery, narcotics, terrorism, financial crime—you name it. We've got so many New York cops working at FBI headquarters, the commissioner calls it 'Two Police Plaza.' In fact—isn't that where your first partner works now? Rich Gimmler—I signed the forms myself."

"Yeah, right, Gimlet's down there. Listen, I don't know how you're going to turn this over to a joint task force. None of them specializes in—"

Cowen looked pleased with himself. "I'm not talking about the existing ones. I think we could get the Bureau to put one together ad hoc."

"A joint task force for one case?"

"If it's as big as you say it is, why not? As you point out, a New York detective handed it to them on a plate. You think they offered to let you work on it because they have a deep and abiding sense of fair play? You know too much—they're scared you'll second-guess them in the press. They need you, Jake."

"And you're going to make sure they need you too."

Cowen smiled blandly. "Don't be a hog. You'll get your blood. Let me have my ink."

·19·

"Dead Sea."

Winston couldn't breathe. He couldn't pull the air into his lungs. Too thick. Too . . . *red.* The red smell was everywhere. He remembered it.

The Constable was back.

Winston's eyes slowly opened. Everything was black, but the blackness had holes in it, like lighted snow. Big shadows moved on the wall like water.

He heard footsteps, echoing and full of doom. Each one sounded for a long time and had other sounds inside it—pleading voices, slamming doors, groans.

The Constable passed his closet. In the darkness his huge body loomed like a storm cloud. He was towing Jill behind him. She floated, stretched out flat in the air, the way people fly in comic books. Blood streamed down her face, and her mouth was gagged with a bloody rag. Winston wanted to shout to the Constable to stop hurting her, but she shook her head and raised her finger to her gag, warning him to be quiet.

The Constable vanished down the hall. Winston could breathe again, the fresh smell of laundry mixing with the fearsome red smell that was all around him.

A door opened, flinging a panel of light into the hall.

A moment later the Constable came running back. He opened Alexander's door and again thundered, *"Dead Sea."* It was a greeting, an order, a promise. Alexander screamed twice, and stopped. After a time the Constable passed by again, towing Alexander through the air. His head dangled in a funny way and his bottom was all bloody.

Soon there were more noises, thumps and crashes, and wet snapping sounds. And then there was a voice, talking and talking, sometimes like a man, sometimes like a child, sometimes like a parrot.

Silence.

Footsteps.

His turn had come. The door to his closet was flung wide. The huge figure towered over him.

"*Dead Sea.*"

Winston's fear grew so great it seemed to hurl him through space and time. He was suddenly running along the hallway, plunging down the stairs.

The Constable ran close behind him, grunting like a wild pig.

Winston burst through the front door of the house. But now he was not in Skokie, but on a beach in Trinidad. The sea rolled in to his right, moaning as it tugged at the land. Far ahead in the bright moonlight, a woman waved at him to hurry up.

He recognized his mother and raced toward her. She could protect him from the Constable.

Without looking back, she turned and disappeared into the dark forest of date palms. Why was she abandoning him? Where was she going?

He tried to shout to her to wait, but no sound came out of his throat, no matter how hard he tried.

He ran to where she had been standing, saw the path, and plunged into the trees. He flew through the woods at dizzying speed, but he could still hear the grunts of the Constable, crashing through the brush behind him.

The woods opened out into a beautiful meadow, bathed in moonlight. On the other side was a little white gate. His mother had gone through it and now faced him, beckoning him to her.

As he ran toward her a terrible conviction struck him that once he passed through that gate, he would always be the age he was now. He would never grow up. His whole future was the little stretch of path left between himself and his mother. She continued to beckon him, with gentle movements of her hand. He slowed, faltered, stopped running entirely.

Behind him he could hear the thunderous footsteps of the Constable, closer and closer. Winston's arms and legs lost all their strength, he couldn't breathe, his heart stopped beating. Pressure grew inside his skull until he felt his head was going to explode. The world was ending, rushing away from him. Huge shadows raced over the mountains.

The Constable's hands crashed down on his shoulders like the talons of a great bird.

·20·

Cowen had begun negotiating for a joint task force at a good time. The FBI had the bit in its teeth. All over the country, their legal staffs had rammed exhumation orders through the courts. As the body bags winged to Quantico, agents fanned out from local field offices, re-examining evidence, questioning hundreds of neighbors, relatives, and coworkers ignored at the time of the original deaths. The Bureau was convinced this was the case of the century; if the New York cops wanted a finder's fee, why not? It would keep Harrow from straying off the reservation.

"He's murdered four families. That we know of."

The speaker was Randall Brasswater, leader of the FBI contingent in the joint FBI/NYPD task force. Brasswater was a sharp-eyed man in a gray suit, with the nervously alert air of a bodyguard, as if he were always checking the roof line or listening to chattered warnings from a receiver in his ear.

He paused and looked around the crowded table. There were six FBI agents, plus three people from the Bureau's Behavioral Science Profiling Unit in Washington, plus Cowen, Harrow, and Gatto. "He's killed con-siderably more people than we've got in this room, a total of eighteen." He paused again. "Ten children."

They were on a high floor of the Federal Building in lower Manhattan. The window would have afforded a magnificent view of the Hudson River and New Jersey, but for the telephone company monolith directly to the west of it.

The room was uncomfortably quiet. These cops and FBI agents cus-tomarily dealt with extraordinary horror with flashes of callousness, cruel jokes at the expense of the dead. These inhuman cracks proved how human they were—they acted as if they didn't care so that they wouldn't care too much. It was part of being professional—they had a job to do, and as with surgeons, sympathy got in the way. But they couldn't crack wise or talk tough today—Jake Harrow sat at the table.

Brasswater cleared his throat. "Top line—don't bother to take notes; you'll get all this in the book, along with family photographs, relatives, neighbors, friends, a ton of addresses and phone numbers. We've been busy.

"January seventh, Washington, D.C. Leith, Albert and Claudette. Children: Martin, ten; Gelsie, eight; Parker, six. Albert was a financial adviser, very savvy, lots of politicians and senior bureaucrats as his clients. Had a reputation for keeping you on the side of the angels and still making you a pile. Apparently he had fantastic radar—his clients never bought stock in a staid old English bank, only to read in *The Washington Post* it secretly owned ranches that were burning down the Amazonian rain forest."

"February eighteenth, Los Angeles, California. Giles, Morton and Audrey. Three girls: Nodi, eight; Sandra, six; Francine, four. Morton Giles was a set designer, stage work mostly, some film. Audrey was a psychoanalyst with a number of patients and former patients in the movie business."

"March twenty-seventh, Beals, Colorado. Sturluson, Lyle and Marlene. Boy, Dwayne, seven; girl, Millicent, five. Lyle was an electrical engineer, Marlene a housewife who had been studying gemstones in order to open a shop with another woman." Brasswater smiled slightly. "Lyle Sturluson was a Rattler. The Rattlers are one of those survivalist groups who cache canned goods and guns to be ready for Armageddon. By all accounts he was slightly to the right of Attila the Hun."

"April twenty-seventh, Skokie, Illinois. Harrow, Roger and Amanda. Girl, Jill, eight; boy, Alexander, five. Roger taught in a progressive school; Amanda was head of the local Green party."

Brasswater looked up. "He's doing about one family a month."

"As often happens, the gaps between murders are getting shorter," said Dr. Josephson, the leader of the behavioral people. No suits for them: bow ties, pipes, and sweater vests. The resident intellectuals.

Josephson held up a one-page calendar of the year, with dates circled in red. "Leith to Giles was six weeks, Giles to Sturluson five weeks, Sturluson to Harrow exactly a month. If his next gap is three weeks, he could kill again as early as May tenth."

"Three days from now," one of the agents said quietly.

"Any idea what kind of family is at risk?" Cowen asked Brasswater.

"It's striking that the kids are all between five and ten years old. The families were similar in other ways too, educated, middle- to upper-middle class. And close-knit. In every case, the neighbors went out of their way to talk about how the family did everything together.

"But there seems to be no direct connection between them. When we picked up that Sturluson was an ultra-right-winger, we remembered that Amanda Harrow had been on the left and wondered if there might be some kind of political angle. But the Gileses weren't even registered to vote. And Leith had clients in both parties, so he stayed away from politics—bad for business."

"Anything more on the Rattlers?" Jake asked.

"Not at the moment," Brasswater said. "Of course, with a group like that, we're looking for a possible cult angle that ties to the other murders. Unfortunately, we haven't been able to interrogate any of Sturluson's fellow Rattlers. They're 'on maneuvers' somewhere in the mountains—you know, practicing how to shoot the neighbors when they come after those canned goods. Their leader—a guy named Chuell Vaughn—isn't due back for two weeks."

"So his next victims could be any close-knit family, anywhere in the country?" Cowen asked. "We've got nothing to go on at all?"

Brasswater looked out the window, checking the telephone monolith for snipers. "As they used to say in the KGB, 'Assassination is easy; it's making it look like suicide that's hard.' Think about it. He can't be seen going in. He can't be seen leaving. He can't cut the phone lines or nail the doors and windows shut. Yet he's got to break into a house full of people and force the dad to write a suicide note without leaving a mark on him—all without waking up anybody he can't immediately control. It's almost impossible—he's done it four times.

"He seems to leave nothing behind except bits of his silencers. From the fragments found in the bodies, they're obviously homemade. He probably makes a new one each time and destroys it afterwards. That way, if his premises are ever searched, there's nothing to find. Also, silencers are illegal just about everywhere. They're not like guns—homeowners don't buy silencers for protection. They're clearly a criminal specialty—hit-man gear. Even in the underground markets they're hard to buy without attracting attention."

"If he discards them after use, they have to go someplace," Jake said. "Have you checked the local dumps?"

Looking just slightly over Jake's head, Brasswater said, "We're doing that. In fact, we may have found something this morning. It just came in, too late to make the books."

Everybody stopped breathing so they could hear better. Brasswater said, "An eight-inch length of PVC tube, with what might be traces of fiberglass mat and resin. Crushed but still in one piece. It's on its way to Quantico right now by courier. If the fibers match, we may have something. He may have left a print or two somewhere on it while he was putting it together. It was out in the weather for three weeks, but our latent-print people can sometimes beat that. If we get lucky, we may get a hair or bit of skin. We only need a few cells for a positive DNA typing. And our chemical analysis is good enough now that we can probably specify not only the manufacturer but even the batch number for each of the components, which might enable us to pinpoint the sales outlet where he bought the stuff."

Cowen was growing restive under this recital of the Bureau's expertise. "What about the guns?" he asked. "How come nobody noticed they'd been silenced?"

Brasswater shrugged. "He taped the barrel, wrapped it in fiberglass, and used a hose clamp or something. When he was finished he stripped it. Maybe wiped it down with acetone. Anyway, nobody was looking for scratches. These were old, battered pieces. He probably bought them already sanitized—the serial numbers were rasped off years ago. They've been fired a lot, but not oiled or maintained—the kind of gun you find kicking around states where you can buy them in hardware stores. The only interesting thing is their similarity—he's probably got only one source. That's about it. Oh, and they're all automatics."

"No shit, Dick Tracy!" Gatto mumbled.

Brasswater stared at him. "What did you say?"

"Of course they're fuckin automatics. If you put a silencer on a revolver, the noise comes out at the gap between the cylinder and the barrel. You can't silence them."

"You must be a revolver then," Cowen snapped.

Brasswater smiled thinly and turned the meeting over to Dr. Josephson.

Josephson took his time stuffing his pipe, waiting until all eyes were on him. "We have a theory about the killer. I know that may sound odd to you all in the absence of any clues in the traditional sense, but we in the behavioral sciences unit have found the more bizarre the crime, the more we have to contribute. Ironically, weird killers are more predictable than the garden variety.

"Now, in this case we have a very definite dichotomy. On the one hand, he chooses families who live very far apart and seem to have no connection with each other. This is the pattern of a serial killer, who kills people he doesn't know. On the other hand, he slashes the faces —usually that's an indication that he knows the victim quite well.

"If you looked only at how carefully he covers his tracks—forced suicide notes, gloves, condoms, silencers—you'd swear he was a highly controlled man in his thirties. But if you look at the *way* he kills—the savage, almost insane violence—you'd place him much younger—early twenties."

"You're saying there are two killers here?" Brasswater said.

"That's right. Like the Hillside Strangler. They had a similar mix of impulsivity and planning."

Brasswater nodded. "That would sure help explain how they got away with faking four suicides. Two men can control a family a hell of a lot better than one."

"There's only one killer," Jake said.

"How can you be so sure?" Josephson asked. "Did you see something at your brother's house you haven't told us about?"

"My gut tells me it was one man."

"Your gut," Josephson repeated, as if Jake were a patient he was presenting at a psychiatric meeting. He leaned forward, his voice turning professionally warm and patronizing. "Now, Jake," he said, demoting him to first-name status, "I respect your streetwise intuition." Meaning he didn't. "Still, it must be very hard to maintain your objectivity, considering what happened to your brother. Are you able to entertain the idea that you're too close to this case to be completely objective?"

"Save your headshrinking for the killer," Jake said.

Under his breath Gatto said "Outstanding" loud enough to be heard around the table. Even some of the FBI men grinned.

Brasswater cleared his throat. "I'd like to read two documents. The first is a broadside to local police departments nationwide—we're going to need all the help we can get. The second is a joint FBI/NYPD press release."

Both documents contained the same meager information, simply naming the four confirmed families and ascribing their murder to the same assailant. The press release always mentioned the FBI and the NYPD together, as running a joint investigation. Brasswater and Cowen were mentioned by name.

"Where's the silencer? You didn't mention the silencer!" Cowen said.

"Of course not," Brasswater said. "That's his—or their—one mistake. If we tell them, they'll stop using it."

"But it's the link between the crimes!" Cowen said. It was also the link between the NYPD and the case—the triumph that had gotten them to this table. Now the FBI was burying it, robbing his department of the credit.

"And what happens when another family is murdered? How will we know whether or not to add them to the list?"

Cowen wasn't quitting. "But how are we going to convince anyone we've got a case? We need cooperation from local governments, from the *public*. What are we going to tell the *press*?"

"I wish we didn't have to tell the press anything—we're only putting out this much so the story won't leak out in a distorted way and create panic."

Cowen turned to Jake for help. "You made this case, Harrow. What do you think?"

"We can't show the killer our hole card."

Brasswater said, "Your own man agrees. It's settled then."

"Since when did he get a vote?" Cowen said. "I'm the captain."

The FBI agents were all grinning. The police were always pulling rank—it was something of a joke around FBI headquarters.

"We've discussed this enough," Brasswater said.

"I'll go over your head," Cowen warned.

"Better hurry," Brasswater said evenly. "This press release goes out today. With no mention of the silencer."

138

·21·

1990

Red Queen had killed six men since Jedda.

Five times, Highland pulled the trigger. The sixth was Crowhurst's operation, an explosive planted in a house a week before the target visited it. Highland had installed his camera in the middle of Crowhurst's bomb: in the hole of a semtex doughnut. The blast left no trace of the camera. Or of the target.

There were no more broken plays. Red Queen had become a band of brothers, fused by their common task, their common risk.

Cal Ordway was pleased. Especially with Highland. He let him know it in a number of small ways. In violation of all the rules, Highland was allowed to correspond regularly with his mother again.

Her letters were usually eight to ten pages long, single-spaced without margins, full of endless details of menus and clothing, but the content was unimportant. It was the fact of the letters that mattered. His mother was still cooking dinner and planting roses along the backyard fence, no matter how many men Red Queen killed.

And then Houdini was murdered.

The oldest trick in the book—a honey trap. Houdini had been alone in Athens. He had picked up a girl at the bar in the Hilton. Tall, striking, exotic-looking. Part black, part Oriental, the bartender thought. They had gone upstairs to a room and made love. Sometime during the night she had cut his throat.

Red Queen got no support, not even intelligence support, from Langley. They were completely deniable. They had been forced to live off the land. There was a terrorist supply network in Europe, dealing in weapons, electronics, information, services, even people—with fine impartiality. Red Queen was wired into it the same as Baader Meinhof or Al Fatah. It was perhaps through this network that whoever wanted Houdini killed had tracked him down.

The street ran two ways. Within a week Red Queen had located the woman. She was a high-priced call girl, apparently an independent contractor. She was now in Nice, staying in a big new hotel on the plage.

The trail ended there. No one could tell them who was behind the hit.

Two days later they met in the Piraeus safe house and had their first real argument since Ronski's death. Highland couldn't sit still; he seemed to be jumping out of his skin. He wanted to go after the girl, force her to tell who had ordered the hit, and then kill her.

Carr argued against it. Taking out the girl was a risk—what if she were part of a trap? And even if they got some names from her, what would they do with them? Go on a revenge mission? That meant more exposure, more danger, more chance of walking into a trap. It was a slippery slope. They were too close to the end. They should lie low for a while and then finish off the list.

"But what if one of the terrorist organizations has a line on us?" Highland asked hotly. "What if Houdini is only the first to be killed?"

"Then we'll know soon enough," Carr said. "Any course of action has risks. But we sure don't need more targets."

"And what about the girl?" Highland shouted. "She murdered Houdini in cold blood! You're going to let her get away with that?"

"The girl's a cutout, an independent," Carr said quietly. "She kills people for money. So what else is new? Assassinating her would be meaningless—blind revenge. It'll just expose our position even more."

"We can't let her get away with it!" Highland shouted. "What kind of message does that send to terrorists?"

"We're not a sovereign nation to be sending messages," Carr said. "We're a group that started with six members and now is down to four. We've got enough to do without going on vendettas."

Borchard and Crowhurst voted with Carr to do nothing.

Back on Spétsai, Highland paced the harbor area all night long, talking to himself, obsessively analyzing the branching possibilities like combinations in chess, until the elaborate arguments collapsed of their own weight. Carr was right. So what? Arguments were irrelevant. He was going to kill that woman. It was an inevitability, a fact he had known about himself for two days. It made no difference what the others thought. He would slip the leash. He would go after the girl alone.

He was on the hillside high above the town. The rim of the world began to lighten. The sea lay flat as a dance floor. A small wind flirted with the grass. Nothing moved in the town. Below him to the left, he could see into a half-constructed third floor that was being stacked on top of an old house in the nest-building way of the Greeks—room for the next generation.

Strange, he thought: he had slipped out of ordinary life when he joined the CIA, slipped out of the CIA when he joined Red Queen. Now he was slipping away even from the men of Red Queen. No one knew he was up here; he was the outsider; he was alone.

Ordinary life was like the town that slept below him: something he watched from a great height but could never join. So many marriage beds, so many couples sleeping in each other's arms.

At least now he had a woman too, waiting for him on another coast of this ancient sea.

A stroke of luck: the charter company had picked up an unusual bit of business. Three Wisconsin insurance agents, winners of a "Set Sale" contest, and their wives. One of the men had a yacht on Lake Michigan, but in these waters he preferred to let someone else do the serious sailing. The charter yachts were luxury boats equipped with hydraulic winches on the sails and anchor, satellite navigation equipment—the whole shot. Two men could easily handle the job. Highland went along as second man.

The insurance agents didn't much care where they went. Highland saw to it that they sailed to Nice.

They arrived one evening just as it was getting dark. As they entered the harbor, Highland slipped into the water and swam ashore, his clothes in a rubber pack on his back. The captain would forget about him when he filled out the form for the harbor police.

He took a room in the hotel where the assassin was staying. Not as Evan Highland, of course. Nor as any of his aliases. Ordway's people had taught him a lot about creating false identities. In the last year, he had learned still more. He would be untraceable.

As soon as he was in his room, he dialed her room and sent an electronic tone through the hotel system that converted her phone into an active microphone while on the hook.

He lay on his bed wearing an earphone and waited for her to come back to her room. By two A.M. he couldn't stand it anymore. He didn't care where she was; he had to get out. He went downstairs to the lobby.

Everything seemed strange to him now, even his own mind. Ordinarily, he was ice cold when he was on a job. Tonight he was tense, agitated, full of unfamiliar yearnings. He was killing with no plan, no dry run, no backup. He was an actor without a mark to hit or a script to remember.

Masses of paper scraps swirled through the lobby, as if a parade had passed through. An ugly little man with a push broom shoved the trash around, without seeming to get rid of it. The desk people looked tired but agitated. Highland waded through the ankle-deep scrap paper, feeling like he was going to jump out of his skin.

At one end of the lobby there was a railing around a flight of descending stairs. A party of chic young French men and women burst into the lobby and disappeared down them. The man with the broom grinned at Highland and gestured at the stairs. On impulse, Highland went after them.

He descended one flight, then another; he was twenty feet below the level of the Mediterranean. The walls were tiled and ugly—for a moment he thought he would end up at the *hommes.*

He went through a steel fire door into darkness and roaring music: a big discotheque, sweaty and crammed with bodies at two A.M.

He stood at the bar and drank Perrier at whisky prices, watching the crowd.

He decided to switch drinks and get his money's worth. He never drank while working, but now he wanted to—needed to. *Why the hell not?* he thought. Even God didn't know where he was.

Just as his drink came, he saw her. On the dance floor. Almost six feet tall, strikingly beautiful. In a flowing white caftan that set off her glowing light-brown skin, the exact shade of tan that white people dream of but can never quite achieve. The girl who killed Houdini.

When the music paused, she thanked her partner and came to the bar. She seemed to be alone. In fact, from the way she talked to the bartender, she was obviously working, hustling the place. She worked both sides of the street, selling love and death. *She's nothing but a whore,* Highland thought. *No cause, no commitment. This will be easy.*

He wedged himself in beside her and offered, in French, to buy her a drink.

"That would be charming," she said in English. "But you should know that I only drink expensive bottles of champagne."

He smiled as if money were no object. She nodded to the watching bartender.

Up close she was even more stunning. She wore a spice perfume that radiated from her dance-warmed body, bathing him in her sexuality. Her face was exquisite, a one-of-a-kind beauty that can haunt a man for the rest of his life. Which, Highland remembered, had been a very short time in Houdini's case.

The champagne was five hundred francs for a watered split. They chatted a bit, smiling and nodding at each other's lies. Highland gave her still another name and history from the one he was using at the hotel. She said her name was Tanaba and that her parents were diplomats who had met at the U.N. Her speech was affected and very strange. His linguist's ear parsed it as West-Coast American with a Vietnamese-French accent.

The music came back on. Earsplitting rock, the lyrics in English. The world music in the world language. Conversation became impossible. She pointed to the dance floor.

They danced. She pressed herself against him, her spice perfume softly wrapping him like mist. Except for those four times with his mother, Highland was a virgin, he had never had an erection in the same room with a woman. To his amazement he got one on the dance floor, a full-metal-jacket hard-on.

She began to kiss him, grind her pelvis against him, then pull back, in a teasing dance. The disco lights splashed over them, the roaring music swept them along like a river. His pleasure mounted toward delirium. Her exotically beautiful face—advancing to be kissed, retreating before he could savor the kiss—filled the world.

He was in a different state, on a different plane of existence. This moment of ecstasy bore no resemblance to the other moments of his life—except one.

The left side of her face began to change—the skin shading slowly to a tender, blue-veined white, the eye flooding with green, the hair igniting with red. He was looking into two faces—Marilyn Highland's and Tanaba's—fused into a single face. Twenty years fell away. Marilyn—his Linlinma—completed her flight from her bedroom to his tree. The two moments were one.

"I want to make love to you," he said thickly.

"I'd like that very much," she answered, the two-sided mouth forming a single smile.

Tanaba's price was two thousand francs. She knew it was a lot, but it was for all night. For everything. He nodded hastily and stuffed twenty-five hundred into her hand. They went up to her room.

As soon as she undressed, he showed her the gun in his ankle holster and tied her to the bed.

He began to interrogate her, his voice drugged with excitement.

She denied it all. He began to hurt her, crazily, enthusiastically, sometimes calling her Tanaba, sometimes Linlinma. When she broke, he was sorry. He wanted to go on hurting her.

Yes, she had killed Houdini. But it had not been her idea.

He forced himself to listen while she explained. Her parents had not been diplomats after all. She had been born in Vietnam. Her father had been a black GI. She had never seen him—it was doubtful he even knew she had been born. When the war ended, little girls like her were unpopular in Saigon. She felt she would have been killed or died on a boat in the South China Sea if an American sergeant named Thaddeus Minnick hadn't gotten her out.

Minnick had saved her life, brought her back to the states, fed her, educated her. Whatever she was—the fact that she was—she owed to him.

Sergeant Minnick was Major Minnick now. He was attached to Hellenikon—the big U.S. air base near Athens. She had killed Houdini for him.

She swore she didn't know who Minnick worked for. She didn't even know whether he had been paid for the hit; he had given her nothing. Highland knew there was more. He hurt her some more, taking his time, pacing himself so he wouldn't go too far. Toward dawn, she told him that Minnick got his orders from a woman with eye trouble. All she knew was her first name.

Zoe.

By ten o'clock the next morning, he was back aboard the charter boat, swinging at anchor in a cove many miles from Nice. He took a long cleansing swim, feeling better than he had in months, in spite of having been up all night. As he was sluicing salt off his skin in the luxurious freshwater shower in a well aft of the wheel, he noticed Julie, the younger of the two salesmen's wives, checking out his body. It was something women often did, and it usually made him nervous, but not this morning.

She smiled, aware he had caught her staring. "We missed you last night. The sardines in that little waterfront place were incredible! Where were you?"

"I had work to do."

"Work. I bet! You were partying."

"Something like that."

The hotel maid who found what was left of Tanaba had to be sedated to stop her screaming.

* * *

144

Highland lay on his belly in the tall saw grass beyond the end of Cane Cove plantation's frontage, just outside the ambit of its sensors, and watched *Blind Zoe* through binoculars.

For a long time, nothing happened. It was so quiet he could hear a bug-zapper hundreds of yards away on the plantation property, mindlessly killing everything that flew into it.

Around nine, a man appeared on deck. That would be the technician. He must have spent the night aboard. He took half an hour to sweep the boat for surveillance devices and then rowed to shore in the rubber dinghy.

He was met on the rotted old pier by Ordway and Minnick, who took the boat from him. Minnick was a short, powerfully built man in his late forties. He was in mufti, dressed for sailing in shorts and T-shirt. Minnick rowed them both out to *Blind Zoe*.

Highland watched as Ordway electronically reswept the boat on his own. He was, if anything, more painstaking than the technician had been, even checking out the dinghy.

Finally satisfied that there was no possibility of eavesdropping, the two men unfurled the sails and prepared to head for the open sea. Soon Ordway was at the wheel, and Minnick began to haul up the anchor.

As soon as he saw the anchor break the surface, Highland clapped on his earphones and began twiddling the dials of a small radio.

Hours earlier, long before dawn, Highland had swum out to *Blind Zoe*, breaststroking through the cool water so he wouldn't splash. Without touching the hull, he had eased his way forward to the anchor chain, taken a deep breath, and hauled himself down it. The anchor had been well-planted in the thick bottom mud; he had been forced to tug it back and forth to free it. His lungs burning, he had slid his hand along the shaft, wiped the muck from one of the flukes, and attached something that looked like a small lump of rust.

Now through his earphones, he could hear the thunderous rattling of the anchor chain as the anchor was dragged on deck.

"Don't just cleat it—tie it down!" Ordway shouted. Highland waited, fingers crossed, praying Minnick wouldn't knock the mini-microphone off the fluke of the anchor or position it badly for listening.

To his relief, the anchor was properly aligned. Nothing blocked the sound; the mike was highly directional; he easily heard Ordway's barked orders as the sails were set and the old boat began tacking out of the cove.

Sails flapped, ropes groaned, the capstan squeaked as Minnick turned the handle.

They were well out to sea before Ordway got down to business.

"I'm changing the order."

"But they're still all mine, aren't they? You're not thinking of farming some of it out?"

"God, you're suspicious. Of course they're still all yours. Red Queen belongs to you, I told you that at the beginning."

"Just checking."

"Watch out for the boom!" Ordway shouted. "You want your head knocked off?"

"I ought to know how to duck by now, working for you. You going to tell me about the target?"

The wind Bernoullied over the face of a sail, causing it to flap noisily. Highland lost Ordway's next few sentences. When the sail finally filled, he heard, ". . . a mama's boy. He didn't want any part of the killing, even as backup."

"So how'd you recruit him?"

"We jammed him. That's the problem. We've played out the string."

"Hold on. Jammed him how?"

"We threatened to kill his mama."

"That *worked*?"

"Better than we ever thought it would."

"I don't believe it."

"I have to credit Greenspan. He gave me an hour's lecture on ambivalence. Highland's hung up on his mother. Loves her and hates her. Supposedly, Red Queen would give him a chance to express both drives. The love would go toward protecting her, and the hate toward the targets. I was willing to try anything at the time. The guy is a genius at languages."

"You complain the Company is being ruined by bureaucracy and affirmative action and little men in green eyeshades. You're getting just like them—taking advice from psychologists. You're not hiring shoe salesmen, for Christ's sake."

"We weren't so far off about him. When our para got killed, he volunteered to be the hit man."

"Suddenly the vegetarian is hot to work in the meat department— that didn't raise any flags with you? You know, using these freaks always seems like a great idea for a while. But then something pushes them over the line, and you've got to pay the price. That's what's happening now, right?"

"No, as a matter of fact. It's just that we lost our lease. His mother was killed two months ago."

Evan knew that any outcry might be picked up by the Cane Cove sensors. He made no sound.

"She did something she shouldn't have?"

"Nothing like that. Just a crazy-lady grease fire. You know, talking to herself with sweeping gestures while frying a chop. Her nurse had stepped out to buy cigarettes."

Highland pushed his mouth into the dirt. The saw grass scraped his cheeks like a cheap razor. He tried to focus his mind on the distant, wind-whipped voices in his ears.

"The word-frequency boys have been faking her letters, but it's only a matter of time before he finds out."

"Oh, *that's* when his delicate love-hate balance goes out of whack. Who does he go after then? The other men in Red Queen? The U.S. president? You? Greenspan got anything to say about that?"

"You know psychologists. You can never pin them down to a prediction. But we can't take any chances. Highland's had a lot of training, and he's good at what he does."

"That's why I was thinking of using someone with a proven track record on this. Maybe Tanaba."

"Read the file. You can't use a honey trap on this man. He doesn't go for honey. Not any kind."

"Tanaba will come up with something. She's got more moves than a tight end."

"What is this, Thad? Who are you trying to kill—Highland or Tanaba?"

"Fuck you. Okay, maybe a little of both. She's getting too pushy for my taste."

"Wants to get paid, does she? Greedy bitch. Of course, if they're both killed, you get to keep her second payment."

"Her first one too, the way I play her."

"Forget it, stud. Tanaba is out. I want you to do this job yourself. Red Queen's next target is a bomb-maker named Kamad Bashir. Let Highland kill him, and then you kill Highland as he leaves the scene. I want it to look to the others like he died in the line of duty. I wouldn't want them figuring out that nobody is coming home."

"Plus you squeeze one last hit out of him."

Ordway seemed to find Minnick's remark funny. He laughed, then said, "Look on the bright side. Somebody might save you the trouble."

Kamad Bashir caught the last flight of the night from Hamburg into Heathrow. It was after midnight when he arrived at the safe house. He imagined Kentish Town as a district of low houses—at most three or four stories—and had worried about it the whole trip. In spite of his doctorate in electrical engineering from UCLA, he absolutely required a fifth-floor room for *chamza*. His kind of work demanded good luck and every favorable omen. Perhaps he would stay in a hotel.

As the cab turned into the street he relaxed. Jutting into the night sky above the row houses on either side of it, the safe house had a dormered fifth-floor room.

From a nearby van, Crowhurst watched Bashir alight from the cab. "Target arriving front," he said into the microphone.

Borchard, who had been watching the back, raced across the garden behind the row houses, burst through the rear door of the adjoining house, and started up the stairs, to position himself to go in after Highland if necessary. On the roof above him, Highland nodded to Carr, dragged his black stocking mask over his face, swung his feet into position on the safe house wall, and rappelled up toward the side dormer window of Bashir's attic room.

From a window across the street, Minnick tracked Highland's climb in the cross hairs of his gunsight, practicing for the return trip. He was behind a steel plate, aiming a rifle on a tripod. He knew the make and model of the Red Queen bulletproof vest—it had no chance against his .458 Winchester Magnum.

The Syrian woman who ran the safe house let Bashir in nervously, her eyes darting to his suitcase, obviously afraid he had plastique with him. He shook his head. "Tomorrow. In a drum marked 'Driller's Mud.' "

In a room off the hall, four young men played cards, assault rifles slung nonchalantly over the backs of their chairs. They watched him silently, trying to hide their interest in a man whose bombs had brought down three commercial jetliners.

After a few words with the Syrian woman, Bashir started up the stairs to his attic room.

Highland stepped through the window into the dark attic. He set his gun on the floor, kicked his shoes into the corners of the room, wrenched off his pants, and flung them against the wall. He stripped off his bulletproof vest and tossed it on the bed. He was now wearing only a black body stocking, with a climbing rope looped around his waist. Suddenly careful, he inserted a small silver tube into the material of the vest and tiptoed out of the room, opening and closing the door as gingerly as a chef checking a soufflé.

Bashir's footsteps thumped on the stairs below him. Highland padded down a flight and darted into the fourth-floor bathroom. With feverish haste, he lashed a rope to the radiator, levered up the window, rappelled down the back of the house, and sprinted away along the line of houses.

Bashir opened the door to his room. Through the open window he could see the softly winking lights of the British Telecom tower. What was that bulletproof vest doing on the bed? He had his own equipment; he didn't need help from these amateurs. He grabbed it, intending to throw it in the hall. But the material wasn't Kevlar; it was soft as putty; his fingers sank into it. And why so heavy? These small puzzlements were Bashir's last thoughts.

The impact of his hand shook the silver tube, activating the trembler switch, which triggered the C-4. The charge was an order of magnitude more than necessary to kill him. It took the top two floors off the house.

The next day, Minnick sent Highland's belt buckle and shoelaces and a few scraps from his black shirt and jeans to Cal Ordway via diplomatic pouch. It was all he could dig out of the wreckage.

Buzz! Buzz! Buzz!

Dean Osbert Orpington cringed as his secretary mercilessly demanded his attention.

"What *now?*" he groaned. He was afraid he knew. Wren, after raising a fat endowment by pledging to remain a bastion of women's education, had announced it would admit men. The lawsuits had caught the Wren trustees completely by surprise. They were flabbergasted that anyone —especially their own alumnae—would take them at their word. *Didn't they understand how much Mother Wren needed the money?*

Buzz! Buzz!

Why were they hounding *him!* He was only the dean, for God's sake! No one had asked his opinion. Like everything else in this ivy-slathered backwater, the decision had come down from that great geriatric ward in the sky where the president and the trustees remained permanently out to lunch.

Buzzzzzzzzzzz!

Orpington clutched his Harvard pencil cup for strength, obscuring VE and RI but not TAS. *For this I left Harvard? For this I traded Cambridge, Massachusetts, for the wilds of central Jersey? How could I have left an academic powerhouse for a school whose only boast is that it's an hour from Princeton? It's great to be a big fish in a little pond—but what if the pond is eutrophic?*

BZZZZZZZZZZ!

"Yes, Robert? For God's sake."

His secretary was coolly unruffled by his boss's anger. "There's a Dr. Julian Lamb to see you." *That little bitch Robert likes me to suffer,* Orpington thought.

"I don't know any Julian Lamb."

"He's here about a teaching job."

"I'm sorry. If he wants to see me he'll need an appoint—"

"Hello, Ozzie."

Barging in was strike two. Calling him "Ozzie," strike three.

"I can't see you now. You'll have to leave."

"Recognize me?"

Orpington ignored the proffered hand. "No, I don't."

"Good. Or I've wasted a lot of money on plastic surgery."

That voice! It was familiar. Orpington leaned across his desk, frowning, studying the face in front of him.

"I do know you, don't I. Who are you?"

"You were right about the CIA, Ozzie. It was a mug's game. In fact, I had to get a new mug to get out of it."

"My God—Evan!"

"No, Evan Highland was killed last month along with a certain terrorist who was blown up by his own bomb. Or, to translate it into the language appropriate to Wren, which I take to be Elizabethan English, 'Hoist by his own petard.' "

Dean Orpington turned pale. He searched the face of the man in front of him for signs of the brilliant student he had once, in his platonic, professorial way, loved.

"Blown up? But then you—aren't you—?"

"Evan Highland? He's dead and gone. I'm Julian Lamb. You promised him a job once; since he can't claim it, I was hoping you'd offer it to me."

·22·

What was that noise?

Suddenly awake, Winston strained to hear in the blackness.

He thought he had heard something—a click, a thump—just like the night the Constable came.

Was he in the house? Slipping through the first floor toward the stairs? Was he coming toward the closet, his eyes blazing with murder, like he did in the dreams?

Winston strained to hear until the silence hissed in his ears like a steam pipe.

Maybe he had dreamed the noise. Maybe the Constable wasn't here after all.

Another thump, louder, *closer.* The Constable was here. The Constable knew he was hiding in the closet. Quick! Get out! Run!

He scrambled over the stacks of sheets in front of him, shoved the door wide, and bolted into the hall.

Where could he go? He had to get out of the house, run away. But the Constable was coming up the stairs. There was no way out. Wait! The second-floor bathroom—he could jump out the window. Anything was better than the Constable with the blazing eyes.

Winston raced down the hall. From the shadows dead ahead sprang a huge dark silhouette. Winston skidded to a stop, slipped, fell, rolled over, jumped up, and ran madly back toward the stairs.

The Constable was right behind him! A powerful hand grabbed him, held him. He kicked and struggled to free himself, but it was no use. He was hauled off his feet, straight into the air. Click! The hall blasted his eyes with light.

A man's voice said, "Easy does it, kiddo. It's only your uncle Jake."

*   *   *

Winston kept struggling for a moment, his eyes wide with terror. Then he recognized Jake and stopped. Jake set him gently on his feet, but his knees buckled, so Jake scooped him up again and hugged him. His heart rattled like a machine gun, vibrating his whole body.

"You're safe. He's not here. I'm here. I'll protect you. I won't let him get you."

The boy did not hug back, but hung on tensely, his eyes shifting, his fear no longer out of control, but still strong.

"Let me show you something."

Jake carried him down to the kitchen and sat him on the sink. "See this shutter here on the kitchen window. It's supposed to be latched, so nobody can climb in from the garage roof. But it's loose. Let's watch."

Winston watched it bug-eyed. Soon the wind caught it—thump! He jumped, startled by the sound.

"That's what you heard. You thought Mr. Bad News was in the house, but it was only the shutter. Understand? Like a dummy, I forgot to lock it. That's where I was going when we ran into each other."

Winston's eyes widened, shifting from Jake to the shutter.

"I usually don't forget. Hey! Don't worry. From now on, I'll check it every night."

That was bright. I'm making it worse.

Jake fastened the shutter, carried Winston back upstairs, and set him on the floor. His knees didn't rubber this time, but he sat down immediately. Jake expected him to disappear into the closet, but he stayed in the hall, sitting against the wall, staring straight ahead.

"Want to sleep in our room tonight? You know you're welcome."

No reaction.

"How about listening to 'He's Got the Whole World in His Hands'? That makes you feel better, doesn't it?"

No reaction.

Jake eased himself down on the floor until he was lying full length on his stomach, chin on hands, looking into Winston's face from below.

"Guess you feel pretty hopeless, huh? Sooner or later Mr. Bad News will come to get you, and there's nothing a bozo like your uncle Jake can do about it. That's what you think, isn't it?"

Something, a flicker, passed over the boy's face.

"But maybe there's a way you could escape him by yourself. Let's see if we can figure it out. Okay? Now, pretend that I'm you."

Jake got on his hands and knees and crawled into the closet. He moved a stack of sheets out of his way and wedged himself under the bottom shelf.

Surprised, Winston watched him from the doorway.

"OW!" Jake pretended he had hurt himself on the cassette player. "That smarts.

"I'm asleep." He snored loudly, then jerked his head up. "Whoops! I just heard something. Sounds like old Mr. Bad News is rummaging around downstairs, looking for me. Maybe he doesn't know I'm here in this closet. Maybe if I'm quiet and don't move and make myself real small, he'll go away." Jake closed his eyes and scrunched down as far as he could under the shelf, hardly breathing.

He made his performance as comic as possible, but when he opened his eyes, Winston was staring at him intently, with no hint of a smile.

"That won't work. He knows I'm here someplace. He'll find me no matter where I hide. I've got to get out of the house. Only I've got to do it nice and quiet so he doesn't hear me. Now, before, when you did it, you pushed this door open. I heard that, way down the hall in the bedroom. That's no good. You've got to ease it open like this." He closed the door almost all the way, then slowly and silently pushed it open just wide enough to let him crawl out of the closet.

He looked up and down the hall. "Which way?" he whispered. "Can't jump out a window—too high. I've got to sneak down the stairs." He crawled rapidly down the hall. Winston crawled after him, tensely eager.

Jake suddenly stopped. "Sh! Hear that? This floorboard squeaks. Remember that. You're gonna have to learn where all the squeaky boards are and then practice until you can walk down this hall without a sound in total darkness."

Jake continued to the stairs. "The quietest way is to back down. That way, you can ease onto each step. Come on, do it with me."

Side-by-side they backed down the stairs. "That's right, doing good. Stay over next to the banister. If he's coming up the stairs, he might still miss you in the dark.

"Okay, we're at the front door. Uh-oh. Too much light from the street. We better slip out of the back."

Together, Jake and Winston crawled the length of the hall, across the kitchen floor, to the back door.

"You know how the lock works?" Jake whispered. "You release the button and turn. You do it. No, see, you have to push the button in until it pops out. Atta guy. Sh. Yipes, the door squeaks. I'll oil it tomorrow, I promise."

They stepped onto the landing. "Turn the knob when you close it, then slowly, slowly turn it back. No, no, don't just let go; you don't want that click. Try it again. . . . That's got it."

"Okay. By now, Mr. Bad News has figured out that you've slipped past him. He's going to burst through this door any time now. Show me what you do. Quick! I hear him coming!"

Winston ran down the steps, across the backyard, and through the gate. Jake watched until he was out of sight, then sprinted after him. He caught him ten yards down the gravel access road behind the house.

"Running away is no good," Jake said, no longer whispering. "He'll run after you and catch you like I just did."

They walked back to the house. Winston stamped down hard on any weeds that got in his way. He was frowning.

"You know what you've got to do? You've got to put a move on him. Let's see if we can figure out a cool move."

They stood in the dark backyard. Jake stroked his chin.

"See, what makes a move *cool* is doing something he wouldn't expect in a million years. Now, Mr. Bad News expects you to run away. So what if you don't? What if you stay here? But where can you hide? Huh." He stroked his chin again.

"I got it! You go *up!* He won't expect that. You stand on the lintel. You know what it is, a lintel? It's that little shelf over the door. You can't see; it's dark. Wait, let's get a little light on the subject, we don't want you breaking your neck."

Jake got a flashlight from the kitchen and beamed it above the door.

"See, here's the secret—people don't expect you to do stuff they couldn't possibly do. A grown man couldn't stand up there, the lintel's too narrow for his feet. So he won't even think about it.

"Can you shin up this column? Yeah, go ahead, show me. Atta guy! Piece of cake for a guy like you. Now step on the lintel. Hold on to that—right! Way ahead of me. Okay, just lie back on the slope, nice and—Where'd Winston go? Anybody see Winston? I got news for you—you are invisible. Old Mr. Bad News couldn't see you up there even if he looked—which he won't because he'll be hunting for you in the backyards. And it's comfortable, right? You could stay there all night. Let's see you get down now."

He came down quickly, all business now. The fearful look was gone.

Without being told, he shinned up the column again and scrambled onto the lintel. He made the trip in about half the time of his first attempt.

After three repetitions, he was working on a hot-dog finish, swinging his legs up from the column and landing on the lintel in push-up position.

Jake yawned elaborately. "I'm sorry, Winst, but I'm tapped out. Okay with you if we go to sleep now? We can practice some more tomorrow.

I'll time you—you may end up in the *Guinness Book of Records* for freestyle door climbing."

As they traversed the first floor Winston hung back, walking slowly, with downcast eyes.

For a moment, Jake worried the boy had slipped back into his despair. Then he understood.

Winston was carefully memorizing the squeaky boards.

·23·

He moved steadily but without haste down the crowded aisle of the airplane. Clean-shaven, dark suit neatly cut, regulation tan trench coat of the American business class over his arm: the everybody nobody would remember.

Julian Lamb settled in a window seat on the nonstop to Nashville. At Nashville he would pick up a connecting flight to Baton Rouge. And the Grant family.

The plane looked to be fully booked. A no-nonsense woman in a skirted suit took the aisle seat, opened her briefcase, and began to work. Good, no trouble there. Then an overweight man in a loud sport coat wedged himself into the middle seat, blubbering over into Lamb's space.

He was a heavy breather, with a perpetual dew line of sweat at the top of his forehead. He turned his head toward Lamb and said brightly, "Whew! Well, sir, how's it look? We gonna get off on time or what?"

Worse luck, a talker, Lamb thought. He grunted something noncommittal and closed his eyes, prepared to pantomime sleep. That way there would be less for the man to remember.

The man tried another conversation-starter with the woman on the aisle but had no better luck. Lamb heard the telltale rustle of a newspaper.

He pretended to sleep, but there was no chance he would drop off; he had never been so worked up in his life.

The Grants—it was their fault. Juleth looked like Linlinma. And then there was that language of theirs! The idea of making their own secret animal sounds to them, of seeing their confusion and fear as they realized *he knew!*

EEEAH! he screamed in the hot silence of his mind. *EEEAH!* was dolphin talk for "Let's play a game." The Grant family language had started as dolphin talk. *Dolphone*, they had called it. But soon other endangered species had muscled in, adding their own vocabulary. Dolphone had been enriched by whale words, turtle talk, puma patois, and rhino rap.

What he was doing was risky—he knew that. It was much too soon. The Grant tapes, supposed to last a month, had lasted only two weeks. Try as he might, he couldn't wait. Fantasy wasn't enough anymore. Masturbation left him unsatisfied, still hot, craving the real thing. The need to kill was exploding inside him, out of control.

To damp his mounting excitement, he slitted his eyes and stole a glance at the man in the checked sport coat. He was engrossed in *New York Newsday*. The headline screamed HE KILLS FAMILIES.

Lamb's eyes snapped open, and he read the subheads: "Fakes Notes to Blame Dad." "Death Toll 18."

"Mind if I borrow your paper for a minute?"

"I'm reading it now, but you can have—"

"I'll give it back."

Lamb snatched the paper away and began to page through it, looking for the main write-up. He didn't have far to look; it covered most of page three.

His eyes raced down the columns. *It was unbelievable.* The FBI had names, addresses, pictures!

Mistakes—he had prepared himself for mistakes, however bad. A bungled job, a clue left behind, he had always known he might have to deal with something like that.

But this was worse than he had ever imagined. Not just one family, but four families, all connected! Leith, Giles, Sturluson, Harrow. And no wrong ones, no confusion, no mix-ups! He hadn't just made a mistake or two. Something was wrong with his basic method! He was leaving a trail of bread crumbs from crime to crime, something they could trace. But *what*?

Could they follow it to Wren? To *him*?

Again and again, he went over the story. In vain. Information had been left out—essential information. They weren't telling all they knew. They had to have more to link the crimes. But how much more?

Enough to track him down?

The fat man was staring at him. "What's the matter, mister? You know some of the people?"

"Uh, no, I don't." Lamb tried to hand back the paper.

The man kept staring at him, as if memorizing his face. "I think you better keep it," he said cryptically.

Lamb's mind tumbled like a destabilized satellite. Did the FBI know about the Grant family? Could agents be waiting for him at their house? Had the postal authorities found the gun he'd mailed? Had they staked out general delivery in Baton Rouge? Or maybe they knew he was on this plane. Maybe when the airplane landed in Nashville, a team of FBI men would storm aboard and arrest him.

Maybe they were on the plane right now! When they opened his briefcase, they'd find his disguises!

Lamb looked up wildly, half expecting to see a line of FBI men striding down the aisle toward him.

Run, his mind screamed. *As soon as we land, jump on the next flight to anywhere. Get out now, before the circle closes. Don't go back to the college. By tonight I could be halfway around the world. I'll start over, create another new identity. I can always make money as a translator. I can work anywhere. They'd never trace me.*

Like smoke to a smoke alarm, his fear set off the voice of an old instructor in his head:

"Panic is the little brother of death. Slow down! Think!"

The paper was still on his lap. He tried to read it analytically, the way he was always counseling students to do. The story began, "The FBI revealed this morning . . ." It had been released *deliberately*. They must have known he'd read it and be warned. If they had enough to catch him, they would have arrested him first.

Was he one of several suspects? Had they put out the story to see which suspect would make a run for it? Was he being watched? Unlikely, he decided. Why would they go public if they had any real suspects?

No, it was more probable that they were desperate—trumpeting the case in the media in hopes that somebody would come forward with new information.

His identity was still holding. Wren was still safe. He still had a bolt hole.

Thank God he hadn't killed Jessica Thorne!

He leaned back in the seat and slowly let his breathing and heart rate return to normal.

No more families until he figured out what he was doing wrong. The Grants would have to wait, reprieved by *Newsday*.

Oddly, Lamb felt better than he had all week. The burning need to kill that had tormented him day and night was gone. An ice-water bath of fear had broken his fever. He could think clearly now. He knew what steps to take.

Continue to Baton Rouge, go to general delivery, pick up the gun and laser bug, and simply mail them back to New York. The risk is small; the bug irreplaceable. Teach your classes, go to faculty meetings, play the professorial role.

Meanwhile, get ready to run if you have to. You've already got the dead baby you made for this job; expand it: passport, gasoline credit cards, the works.

And watch the news. You never know what the FBI will tell you next.

No! That's what they want you to do—watch and wait, let them call the tune. They think they're dealing with an ordinary killer—smart maybe, but an outsider, somebody without experience, who doesn't know their forensic methods, their equipment, their thought processes, the limits of their expertise.

They've won today. You're standing down the Grants. But you can't go on just reacting. There has to be a way to get on top of this, control the agenda . . .

Hit back.

·24·

Early the following morning, Jake sat at his desk going over the FBI casebook from the meeting, forcing himself to look at family snapshots—beach games, barbecues, birthday parties—that were never meant for the scrutiny of hard-eyed men in distant cities.

Close-knit—that was the adjective Brasswater had applied to them. The photos were practically interchangeable. Harrow, Leith, Giles, Sturluson. Four identical loving families.

Except Sturluson. He was just a little different from the others. A survivalist, a gun owner, a Rattler. A man comfortable with violence. Jake kept coming back to him. The family pictures were the same as the others—all balloons, burgers, and birthday cakes. But in every photo you could see something else: a grenade in a case, a rifle on the wall, a T-shirt saying "Trespassers Welcome to Stay" over a picture of a tombstone.

Jake flipped a few pages, looking for the name of the head Rattler. Chuell Vaughn. He was on maneuvers, but maybe Mrs. Vaughn might be willing to talk. Without much hope, Jake phoned Vaughn's home in Beals, Colorado.

Someone picked up the phone and made a mouth-sound into it, vibrating the tongue on the roof of the mouth, imitating the sound of a rattlesnake. "R-R-R-R-R-R-R-R-Rattlers!" A man's voice. Was Vaughn home early?

"Chuell Vaughn?"

Vaughn had evidently been expecting someone else to call him at that time. He became guarded. "Who wants to know?"

"I'm Detective Harrow of the New York police. I want to ask you a few questions about Lyle Sturluson."

"Uh huh. Well, Detective Harrow, *sir*, let me explain something, *sir*. We don't talk to cops. So why don't you just go fuck yourself, okay?"

"Why are you stonewalling? Did you miss the story in the papers? Sturluson didn't kill himself—he was murdered."

"So what?"

"So don't you want to help find his killer?"

"Why the fuck should I?"

"For Christ's sake, Vaughn, he was a fellow Rattler."

"Don't try to stick us with him! We kicked him out two weeks before his death."

"Why did you kick him out?"

"I'm holding the phone to my ass—at the sound of the fart, start sniffin'!" The line clicked dead.

Jake looked up from the phone to see Meatball Gatto marching toward him, a big grin on his face. "You're gonna love this, buddy boy." He shoved a newspaper onto the desk, with a one-column story circled in red:

NY COP WHO BROKE FAMILY KILLER CASE
HAD VICTIM BROTHER

After a brief listing of Roger's family, the story explained Detective Jake Harrow worked under the supervision of Captain Douglas Cowen, necessitating the involvement of Captain Cowen's special New York City police task force with the FBI in "every phase of the investigation." There was a photograph of Detective Harrow standing beside Captain Cowen at the medal ceremony.

Gatto couldn't contain his delight. "Nobody goes around the Bureau's end like this! No-fuckin-body! They're gonna wire Cowen's balls to the floor and set fire to the room!"

"They're gonna have to stand in line," Jake said.

Cowen was on the phone when Jake barged into his office. He grinned and motioned Jake to a chair. Jake didn't sit down. When Cowen hung up, Jake waved the newspaper at him.

"What the hell do you think you're doing?"

"Making you a hero, among other things."

"Using me to grandstand for yourself."

"What goes around comes around. Maybe you'll think twice in the next meeting before you sell out the department." Cowen laced his hands behind his head and lolled back in his chair. "Randall Brasswater wasn't too crazy about that story either. That was him just now on the phone. Whew! He packs more wallop into words like *unprofessional behavior* than most guys deliver with *fuck you*."

"So why plant a story you know will piss him off?"

"Like we were playing together so nicely before, sharing our toys in the big sandbox."

"The investigation is just starting. You've trashed the joint task force before it had a chance to work."

"What was so goddamn *joint*? They screwed us out of our rightful credit. With your help, I might add. Their release reads like the Bureau made the case by digging up bodies at random. I had to get it on the record that one of our guys broke this thing open, even if I couldn't tell how. And I had to do it now—while the story's still front-page news."

"Is that all this case is to you? Publicity? This isn't one of your police-dog retirement parties. There's a guy out there butchering families."

"Right. And whatever the Bureau finds out about him, we'll be the last to know."

Jake flung the newspaper down on Cowen's desk, sending a Cross pen flying. "Yeah, well if that wasn't true before, it is now. This story of yours puts the nail in the coffin."

He stalked out.

"You should kiss my ass in Bergdorf's window," Cowen shouted after him. "I spelled your name right, I sent them your most flattering photo, and I didn't mention the silencer."

·25·

On the following Monday Julian Lamb drove slowly past a little wooded area, half a mile from Jake Harrow's house. It was as close as he needed to come.

Everything Harrow, or anyone else, had said in that house in the past two days was at the top of the big box elder tree encoded on a computer chip. The chip was inside his laser window-reader. He had taken quite a risk by hanging on to it from his old life, but like his tapes, he had found it impossible to surrender.

He touched a button. In a microsecond burst of transmission, the treetop computer chip downloaded two days of recording to a machine under his dash.

He waited until his gray Honda Prelude was skimming down the Grand Central Parkway to listen to the recording.

The window reader was voice-activated. No dead air.

A computer-generated voice quacked, "Saturday, May tenth. Six forty-nine A.M."

"MMM, honey-tiger. So good. Ohhhh, my honey-tiger." Bedsprings creaked, pillows thumped as they moved from position to position to position. Lamb cursed his window reader for not providing video.

Harrow called her *Sally*. Must have married her within the last three years. Mandy and Roger never mentioned her in the old days when he had them under regular surveillance.

A shower made white noise. A juicer chewed relentlessly through eight orange halves. Breakfast dishes clanked and scraped. Now a new name: *Winston*. Must be their little boy. He seemed to be sick in bed. Jake taking food to him. Upstairs. Jake talking to him, cajoling him, but no answer. Sore throat?

He had a radio by the bed. He listened to a lugubrious country western version of "He's Got the Whole World in His Hands." Not a radio, a cassette player—the song was repeated several times.

The house got quiet. Sally was tap-tapping away on a typewriter. Jake was clumping around.

Winston really liked "He's Got the Whole World in His Hands." He played it half a dozen times.

Sally made a number of phone calls hunting for a sitter. She and Jake were going out Thursday night.

Lamb's car rolled along the Grand Central, past LaGuardia, crossed the Triborough Bridge and the George Washington, as the bug stutter-stepped through the Harrow's weekend.

Winston seemed to be out of bed, following Jake around now. He chatted brightly away to the boy without getting any response, the way lonely people talk to their pets. Was Winston mute?

Voice-activated time flew.

"He's Got the Whole World in His Hands" again. And again. And *again*. Winston was obsessed with the damn song.

That evening Jake and Sally watched a rented movie on their VCR —*The Way We Were*. Lamb fast-forwarded past it. The movie seemed to have turned them on—more bouncing bedsprings and *honey-tigers*.

Sunday was a replay of Saturday. Hot and heavy early-bird special. Breakfast. Two dying-cow voices wailed. "He's Got the Whole World in——." Fast-forward. By the time it was Sunday afternoon on the Harrow tape, Lamb's Honda was well into New Jersey, rolling along the Garden State. Jake announced that someone called Gimlet would be coming over to discuss the case.

Gimlet arrived and immediately began to eat. Chips crunched, apples cracked, coffee slurped. Lamb visualized him as enormously fat.

Lamb's practiced ear picked up immediately that he and Jake were old and close friends. They shared jokes, memories, opinions.

Gimlet asked after several cops at the precinct. Lamb gathered that Harrow and Gimlet had been partners, but now Gimlet worked some-where else.

The conversation turned to the case. Harrow denounced Captain Cowen. "First he muscles in with this joint task force crap. Then he plants this damn puff-piece without Bureau approval. I had a nice informal thing going over there. Now Cowen gets in Brasswater's face with this bullshit. I've lost my access. I'm practically off the case."

"Take it easy, Jake. It's always like this when a task force sets up. I went through the same shit. It's the shotgun wedding of two different cultures. And let me tell you—us cops have more trouble with it than the Bureau guys. We're the ones with the ranks and uniforms. You know when my eyes first opened? When I called a field office in Miami to track some laundered money. Two minutes into the conversation, it hit me—they're talking to me like I'm Bureau. And I was. I mean, what do the titles matter? It's what you know, what you can do. Don't worry, it'll shake out."

"I can't wait. It's one case."

"I'm telling you, don't underestimate the Bureau."

"I want to set up a Dr Pepper."

"But it's your own investigation. I'm the outsider."

What's a Doctor Pepper? Lamb wondered.

"Brasswater's going to hold back the actionable stuff for his own guys. I just want an even break."

Doctor Pepper must be some kind of spying operation. Harrow needs a spy to find out what's happening? That damn newspaper story had credited Harrow with breaking the case. Lamb began to swear under his breath. Could he be bugging the wrong man? Maybe his window reader should be trained on Brasswater's house instead of Harrow's.

Gimlet wasn't happy. "Jesus, Jake, what do you want from me? I hardly know these guys. I'm supposed to hang around their office and pump them for information on a case I'm not even involved with?"

"You're there—in the halls, the labs, the cafeteria. You hear things."

"Okay, any elevator talk, you'll be the first to know. This is nuts. How do you know they're going to hold stuff back? Your meeting was only on Wednesday. You think they got all these hot leads since then?"

"What about the stuff they promised us in the meeting? Look, I'm not a forensics expert, but how long does it take to match up fiberglass fibers? Top priority, moon-project urgent?"

Lamb's face began to burn. *Fiberglass fibers.* He used fiberglass in his silencers. He made the nonsightable kind—they were quieter—so he machined an extra row of ports—it was Swiss cheese in there. Did the bullet's wake suck fiberglass out of all those carefully cut ports of his? Or did the shock wave rip fibers loose before the bullet reached the chamber? The bullet had to be subsonic or it couldn't be silenced! Whatever the ballistics, his silencers were putting out a fiberglass signature. That was the link!

How could he have known? He'd always used commercial silencers in Europe—the homemade ones were for emergencies. The Agency had taught him to make them by rote, a step-by-step procedure, like assembling model airplanes from a kit when he was a boy. It was part of the drill. Do every item on the checklist, and you were supposed to be invulnerable. And now the silencers had given him away!

Harrow was saying, "Brasswater was bragging to us in the meeting how fast they can identify this stuff. Quantico got it Wednesday; we still haven't heard, positive or negative."

"Really, they didn't send you the results?" Gimlet sounded embarrassed.

"Aw, shit. There we are!"

"Yeah, well, I did happen to see it. It was lying out on somebody's desk. Umm, all right, maybe they told me about it, but it was pure chance."

"So you know more than I do without even trying."

"Maybe you should ask Brasswater."

"Yeah, sure. Are you going to tell me the results, or do I wait a week for the interoffice mail?"

"Negative. It was nothing. Just a hunk of junk. Somebody got excited and thought tar was fiberglass resin."

There was more, but nothing worth hearing. The furniture warehouses and shopping malls were behind him now—he was in the open country. He let out his breath. All right. It was the silencers they were tracing. Now he knew. Now he could fix things.

He was bugging the right man after all.

·26·

The instant the bedside lamp came on, Bill Grant's eyes snapped open.

"Why are you here? What's happening?"

"*Shhh!* This is a robbery. Do as I say, nobody will get hurt. Do you understand?"

"Yes."

"Good. Now very gently. Wake up your wife."

"Jule, Jule, honey. Be very quiet. We're being robbed."

Juleth Grant blinked sleepily. Then she saw Lamb and his gun, enormous with its shiny commercial silencer. "Who's robbing us? *Him? He's* robbing us?"

Lamb put his finger to his lips. "*Shh.* Be quiet and nobody will be hurt. Understand? You must do exactly as I say, understand?"

Juleth said, "I understand," in a small, controlled voice.

"We don't want to wake the children, now do we?" Lamb said.

"No."

"Please leave them out of this," Bill said.

"Nothing will happen to them if you do exactly as I say."

"The safe is downstairs."

"In good time. Tear up the pillowcase and make a gag for your wife." Grant did so. Lamb handed him some clothesline. "Tie her hands and feet." Grant did that too, working quickly. His bald pate gleamed with sweat.

"That's good. Now sit in that chair." Grant scrambled out of the bed and did as he was told. He was wearing blue pajamas decorated with little sailboats. Although he was older and paler, he reminded Lamb strongly of Ammed. He had the same look in the eyes, full of fear and pleading. Lamb handed him a pad and pen. "Now, very quickly, write

169

these words: 'Nothing has meaning anymore. I'm taking the only way out.' "

Grant scribbled "Nothing." He stopped writing and stared up sharply at Lamb.

"*Quickly!* Write it. Then we'll go down to the safe together, and I'll leave."

Grant put the pencil to the paper again, as if to write, then suddenly lunged out of the chair. He drove his head into Lamb's stomach and clutched the wrist of his gun hand. *"The Family Killer's here! Kids! Run!"*

Lamb stumbled backward and ripped his gun hand free. His mind screamed, *It's got to look like suicide!* He shot Grant through the left side of his skull at the point where his hairline had once been. Both men crashed to the floor. Lamb heaved Grant's corpse off him and jumped up. In the hall he heard a door open and then another. Running footsteps. The kids were getting away!

Why hadn't he understood? Everything had changed. The whole world knew about him now.

He burst through the bedroom door. Eight-year-old Geraldine was just disappearing down the stairs. Rosa, ten, was behind her, scampering down the hall. Lamb raced after her, cocking his gun, and shot her in the back of the head as she reached the stairs.

He plunged down the steps, cocking his gun again. Take the silencer off and blaze away on automatic? No. Might wake the neighbors. He must have some time for Juleth.

At the bottom of the stairs he flicked on the lights and looked around wildly. Damn it! No Geraldine! He made a rapid circuit of the lower floor, turning on lights as he went, trying to be quiet, listening for a door or window being opened. If she got out of the house, he was in trouble.

There! A bulge in the dust ruffle of the living room couch. Geraldine's foot. He grabbed it—she screamed so loudly he almost let go. He yanked her out. Her white nightgown was smeared with the thick layer of dust under the couch. "Let me alone! Help! Help!" Screaming like a banshee. Pretty little thing—her fear excited him. He would have enjoyed screwing her as he slowly choked out her life, but he had no time, things were out of control. Still dragging her by the foot, he shot at her head, but she was writhing so violently the bullet missed entirely and buried itself in the couch. Cursing, he swung the screaming child clear of the floor and slammed her head against the wall, making a round crater in the plaster. She went limp. He flung her on the floor, cocked his gun, and jammed the barrel against her forehead. To his surprise, her eyes

170

opened, but the pupils had rolled up from brain damage, and all she showed were the whites. His gun went *SHEW*, and her open eyes filled with bloody tears.

Damn the little bitch and her screams! What if someone had heard her? Every minute he stayed in the house was a risk.

Juleth. He had been thinking of nothing else for weeks. Five minutes, he would take five minutes.

But wait—there was a third child, six-year-old Lincoln. Lamb charged up the stairs, cocking his gun as he ran. He flung open the door to Lincoln's room and snapped on the light. A freckled little boy was sitting up in the bed in his underwear, wide-eyed with fear.

When he saw Lamb, he shouted, "The man who kills families is here! Help my dad—"

Lamb shot him from the doorway. The bullet hit him in the mouth, knocking him back against the headboard with a dull thump. Crazy with excitement, Lamb raced down the hall into the parental bedroom.

The bed was empty!

A faint sound to his left. Most men would have turned only their heads to look. Lamb had been drilled endlessly by his CIA instructors to swivel the third eye—the gun barrel—with the other two. Juleth Grant rushed him from behind the door, brandishing a steam iron in both hands, and brought it straight down at his head. He pivoted and squeezed the trigger.

Nothing happened.

He'd forgotten to cock the gun.

He ducked backward off-balance and swiped upward with the big silencer, knocking the iron out of her hand. It spun sideways like a Frisbee and took a divot from the wall. She flung herself on him punching wildly, and trying to claw his eyes. She was amazingly strong, desperate; she wanted to kill him. She made no sound; all he heard was the rasp of her breathing. Still moving backward, he caught her arm and tripped over Bill Grant's body. They crashed to the floor, her on top. Lamb reversed the gun in his hand and began to hammer her head with the gun butt. She went limp on top of him, stunned.

He flung her off, jumped up, wrenched the bedding from the bed, heaved her on the bare mattress, and frenziedly tore the sheets into strips. He gagged her and quickly lashed her hands and feet to the four corners of the bed, spread-eagling her.

He filled the steam iron with water in the adjoining bathroom, plugged it in by the bedside, and left it on the floor to heat up.

Juleth's eyelids were fluttering. He made a series of high-pitched dolphin squeals, "EEEEAH, EEEEEEAH, EEEEEEEAH, EEEEAH!"

Juleth blinked and looked around in confusion.

"Party time! Or don't you speak Dolphone like I do?" he said.

Her eyes focused on him and slowly widened in horror.

She wore a watered-silk night shift. He grabbed it, ripped it, made her naked.

"*Grrrowlfy* said the cheetah, for he was a *predatow*."

He walked around the bed inspecting her. She was older than Lin-linma, older than he remembered her on the surveillance tapes, but she still had a dancer's body, tall, tight, and rangy.

"*AAAAOOO! AAAAOOO!*" he trumpeted. "Papa's gone to the ElumPHANT graveyard. So have Rosy and Gerri and Linckie. Poachers shot them for ivory. You Grants love endangered species—now you're an endangered species yourself. *AAAAAOOO!* I'm your big Elum-PHANT. Want to see my trunk?" He zipped down his fly and stripped a condom on his erect penis.

The steam iron began to sputter and hiss. "Listen. *HISSSS.* That's snake language for *hot love. HISSS. HISSSS.*"

He held the iron just above her left nipple, scorching it with steam. She made loud muffled noises behind her gag and twisted her body frantically to escape, the bones in her shoulders popping and dislocating.

"Give the snake a break. The steam iron was your idea, don't forget. You started it. Sauce for the gander, you silly goose. *HONK! HONK! HONK! HONK!*"

He loosened her gag. "Any last words before the Grants join the passenger pigeon?"

In a muffled voice she asked, "Why are you doing this?"

He yanked her gag tight again. In a high-pitched singsong he squawked, "Why are you doing this? *TURCLEW TURCLEW.* Why are you doing this? *ARKA ARKA NAR NAR NAR.* Why are you doing this?"

He hopped on the bed and knelt between her legs, holding the red-hot iron high, and whispered, "Just think of me as your reward for being happy."

·27·

When Jake Harrow was four, dad Joe had brought home a big round electric clock and hung it on the wall over the stove. It kept good time, but strangely, besides being a clock, it was also an advertisement for a soft drink. Jake had never seen such a clock in anybody else's house, but then nobody else had as smart a dad as he did. The clock proclaimed that Dr Pepper should be enjoyed twice each day, at eleven A.M. and again at four P.M.

At ten to eleven, Jake left the precinct house and walked toward Central Park. At Central Park West, he stopped at a public phone box and put his hand on the receiver without lifting it.

At exactly eleven o'clock it rang. Jake picked it up and said, "Dr Pepper."

Gimlet's voice said, "We may have another one."

"Oh, Christ. How sure are you?"

"We've got some heavy-duty slaughter. The lab hasn't come back yet on whether or not a homemade silencer was used." Gimlet's pay phone was on a noisy corner. Jake had to strain to hear over the hectic roar of traffic in downtown Manhattan.

"But otherwise the same?"

"Yes and no. Dad looks like a suicide, but there's no note. The kids were shot dead, but no torture, no rape. What's got everybody going is what he did to mom. Seared her front with a hot steam iron. Burned most of her skin off. Erased her face, crushed her skull, broke her arms."

Gimlet went on to describe each of the murders in detail.

Jake asked, "When did it happen?"

"In the wee hours of Tuesday morning. What do you think? Sound like your boy's playbook?"

173

"Beats me. Josephson said the wait between murders gets shorter each time; he predicted the next one would be around the tenth. Yesterday was the thirteenth. Whereabouts was this?"

"Baton Rouge, Louisiana."

"I better get down there while there's still something to see. Give me the rundown."

"Family name: Grant, William and Judith; girl, Rosa, ten; girl, Geraldine, eight; boy, Lincoln, six."

Gimlet went on to give the address. "If you happen to run into Brasswater, be sure not to give him my regards."

Jake called the precinct and told the desk sergeant he wasn't feeling well, then flagged down a cab on Central Park West and went home to Queens to pick up Winston. Jake felt bad about exposing the poor kid to another murder scene. Still, he was the only living witness. Who knew what he might notice?

Bounding up the stairs, Jake could hear "He's Got the Whole World in His Hands" playing in the closet. Sally had bought Winston an armload of kiddie cassettes, which he had dutifully played once each before going back to his favorite. Jake was getting very, very tired of hearing it.

He leaned in, shouting to be heard over the music.

"Come on out, Winst. We're taking a little trip."

Obediently, the boy grabbed his cassette player and started to leave the closet.

Jake took the player away from him, turned it off, and put it back in the closet. "Sorry, no music."

The boy gave him such a sorrowful look, Jake almost relented. "Don't worry—when we get back, the two Gitt brothers will be waiting. Right now they need to rest those golden tonsils."

The pilot's voice was warm with his knowledge that he was telling a surefire joke. "We are now arriving in Red Stick. Baton Rouge to y'all."

The passengers thought about it. Got it. Laughed. Surefire.

The late afternoon was hot and overcast. As Jake drove out of the airport in the rental car Winston started to close his window.

Jake, his nose sweetly minted by a Life Saver, said, "Hey, we don't turn on the air-conditioning every time it gets a little warm out. We're natural men. C'mon, roll down your window, smell the magnolias, smell the—whew!" A vile stench, half chemicals, half rotten meat, sloshed over the mint and invaded every cavity of his head. He closed

174

his window and flipped on the cold air. Too late. The smell was all over the car.

"It'll take a lot of magnolias to cover that smell!" Jake said. "What are you smiling about? Gloating is a low emotion, my friend, a low emotion."

The Grant house was near the LSU campus. He left the highway and worked his way through the neighborhoods, from time to time pulling over to study his map.

Built to keep the delta rains off, the houses seemed all roof, squatting like giant mushrooms on the suburban streets.

He took a wrong turn and found himself on campus. He was surprised to pass a fence lined with huge, sleek cattle—he hadn't known that LSU had an agricultural school. Winston was fascinated. Jake stopped the car a moment so he could get a good look. "See what cajun food will do?" Jake said. "Or maybe they got so fat because they've all got tenure."

The Grant house was a beauty, a virtual mansion with a columned porch, set among rolling hills. There were three big yellow trucks lined up in front. Several men were loading wooden platforms, light stands, power tools, cables, and a small generator. It was as if a film company had been using the house for location shooting and were now packing up to leave.

Winston sidled up as close as he dared and stood watching the men work.

Gimlet needn't have worried—Brasswater was long gone. The place seemed almost deserted. Jake recognized an agent from last week's meeting getting into a car and ran after him.

"Havermeyer, wait!"

"What are you doing here?" Havermeyer started the car, hardly looking at him, wanting to be away.

"You guys finished already?" Jake said. "That was fast."

Havermeyer looked puzzled. "Didn't anybody tell you?"

"What?"

"The forensic report came back this morning. No homemade silencer dirt in any of the wounds."

"Oh."

"You wasted a trip."

"Mind if I go inside anyway? Now that I'm here?"

"It's up to the local cops now. We've bailed."

"Where are they?"

"They're coming, they're coming. I'd stay and introduce you, but I'm late for something already."

Havermeyer drove off, followed by one of the yellow trucks.

Jake noticed that an old man was watching him intently from across the street. When Jake caught his eye, the man looked away and began industriously fiddling with the plastic shield on his bird feeder. He looked well along in his seventies.

Jake strolled across the road. "That ought to keep those pesky squirrels out."

"I hope so. This feeder is supposed to be squirrel-proof, but they climb it like it was . . ." His voice broke, then he quickly cleared his throat. ". . . a stepladder."

"Sad day, isn't it?" Jake said, then walked up to the man and extended his hand. "I'm Detective Jake Harrow."

"Doc Campbell. Maybe I shouldn't call myself Doc anymore. I'm retired." He spoke in a soft, cultivated southern accent.

"*Doctor* is one of those titles you always keep, like *president*. You'll always be Doc Campbell."

"What a kind thing to say," the old man said. He looked at Jake and suddenly began to cry.

"They were like my family," he sobbed. "My own children are long gone. My wife died five years ago. The Grants saw I was a lonely old man and took me in. The kids were always helping me with the yard work. They had me to dinner every Monday and Thursday night, without fail. We were always in and out of each other's houses. They didn't do it from obligation or guilt; they did it from joy—from sheer joy." He controlled himself. "I'm sorry. What you must think of me." He dabbed his eyes.

"You've suffered a terrible loss. They must have been exceptional people."

"Nobody around here knew how exceptional. People called them 'tree huggers,' and made fun of them for going on marches and blocking construction sites. But they stood up for what they believed in. Even converted an old troglodyte like me."

"They were Greens?"

"Endangered species were their big passion. Bill made speeches about preserving wetland habitats that raised some hackles. Talking about wetlands in the delta is like talking about rope in the house of a hanged man. We've pushed the river around for a hundred years, and now the river is pushing back, silting and flooding and shifting its bed. When you have oilmen, politicians, and real estate developers locked in mortal combat with the Army Corps of Engineers, the last thing people wanted was some professor sticking up for alligators. Some of our good legislators demanded he be fired. But he had tenure, and anyway, it's not the fifties anymore—they can't boss LSU around that easily these days. Of course, the one they really hated was Juleth."

"Juleth? Not *Judith*."

"Common mistake. She was named for the Rosenbergs—speaking of the fifties—the atomic spies who were executed back then? *Julius* plus *Ethel: Jul-eth*. Her folks were old-line Communists. Radicalism was in her genes, I suppose. She just switched from downtrodden workers to downtrodden animals. Dolphins were what got her started. It broke her heart that they get caught in tuna nets. Before they moved here, she once actually went out on one of those boats that interfere with the fishermen."

"She had courage."

"The courage of great kindness. She couldn't stand to see animals suffer. Not even an old lost dog like me." He dabbed his eyes again. "I'm getting maudlin; I'd better go inside. Thank you for listening to me, Detective. I shall miss those dear people."

"I know you will."

Doc Campbell studied him. "You're not like the other policemen who were here. I noticed, sir, that when I had my shameful little fit, there were tears in your eyes too. Why?"

Jake smiled. "I once knew some people like the Grants."

Jake took Winston by the hand and walked into the house. The few people still loading the trucks paid them no attention.

The living room was at the back of the house. It looked out on a wide lawn fringed by shallow woods that effectively screened out the neighbors.

Hung over the mantel like an ancestral portrait was a large painting of a condor, glancing down beady-eyed as if he were about to leave the family out of his will.

There was a small black burn mark on the beige couch where a bullet had entered and a round dent in the white plaster wall where Geraldine's skull had been smashed. Geraldine herself was long gone, of course; there was only a small chalk outline on the floor, a ghost's ghost.

He could feel Winston tensing up. He gripped the boy's hand reassuringly, wondering if bringing him here was such a hot idea after all. He was already having nightmares, did he need a new set?

A grouping of framed photographs ornamented a shelf above the couch. Bill was plump and already balding. Juleth looked like a beauty-contest winner, taller than her husband and elegantly slim.

In one picture, obviously taken by a professional portrait photographer, she sat with her arms around a boy about Winston's age—Lincoln—flanked by a bigger girl in a private-school blazer—Rosa—and Geraldine in a lacy pink dress. Dad William stood behind them, leaning out slightly to flash his Phi Beta Kappa key, smiling too broadly for a formal picture, delighted to have founded his dynasty.

Jake and Winston climbed the curving staircase, past framed photographs of lemurs, gorillas, and lion-tailed macaques.

Another outline had been chalked on the floor at the top of the stairs—Rosa. When Winston saw it, he jerked back and would have gone back down the stairs if Jake hadn't picked him up and carried him into Lincoln's room.

Lincoln's taste in endangered species had run to lizards. On the back of his door was a big head-shot poster of a tuatara, looking furious at the prospect of extinction. Crocs and caimans grinned from book covers. A stuffed komodo dragon guarded a telescope, chemistry set, and set of magnets for doing experiments.

His bed had already been stripped. A big bloodstain marked the headboard, a smaller one splotched the bare mattress.

Winston, who had been hanging back, suddenly darted forward and dove under the bed. Jake dropped to one knee to see what had attracted his eye.

On the far side of the bed, dangling down from the mattress, was a child's sing-along microphone, like the one on Winston's cassette player—except this one was shaped like a microphone, not like a banana. Winston tugged at it, trying to pull down the player.

As Jake came up he saw that the bed actually had two mattresses. Lincoln had wedged his cassette player between them, probably to hide it from his parents so he could listen after lights-out.

Winston yanked it free, and the machine, a more expensive and high-tech version of his own, tumbled into his hands.

"Hey, I didn't bring you down here to listen to tapes," Jake said.

Too late. Winston punched buttons; the tape Donald-Ducked backward. "The Big Rock Candy Mountain" boomed out from under the bed.

Winston clapped it to his ear and scrunched his eyes shut, safe at last in his own universe. Jake didn't have the heart to take it away. He left the room, thinking: *Look on the bright side. Maybe now he'll be obsessed with two songs.*

The master bedroom had been pretty thoroughly cleaned up. Bill's chalk outline was near the door—he hadn't died sitting in a chair like the other dads. The bed had been stripped, and the frame partly dismantled. There was no evidence of Juleth's final agony.

The adjoining bathroom had not been cleared out. Jake peered sadly at bars of soap in the shape and color of the blue whale, the green turtle, the white rhino. In the mirrored cabinet were cosmetics made from carrots, cucumbers, and pineapples.

Jake jumped, startled by a terrible flat scream, like a tortured animal. He ran into the hall. *CRASH!*—a window breaking. Lincoln's room. A series of short, piercing yelps, like the ones Winston made after he sketched the silencer.

He burst into Lincoln's room. Winston was rolling on the floor, biting his hands, eyes blind with terror. The tape player was nowhere to be seen. The big bottom pane of one of the dormer windows had been broken. But there was no glass on the floor. Jake rushed to him and yanked his bloody hands away from his mouth.

"It's okay, it's okay. We're gonna leave; we're gonna leave; we're leaving right now. Calm down. Calm down. Atta guy."

Slowly the thrashing stopped, the eyes came back into focus. Jake scooped him up and carried him down to the front lawn.

The last yellow truck was being loaded. The driver agreed to watch Winston. Jake went back into the house and left by the back door. He walked around the far side of the house to a point directly below the broken window. The tape player lay right where he expected to find it, in a flower bed, surrounded by shards of glass.

Lincoln's player was a high-tech little machine, with a brushed-steel case, able to record as well as play.

"The Big Rock Candy Mountain" was the last song on the side. Jake kept the volume low. This song had brought on Winston's seizure. He was on the other side of the house, but fear has sensitive hearing.

> In the Big Rock Candy Mountain, boys,
> The cops have wooden legs.
> The bulldogs all have rubber teeth,
> And the hens lay soft boiled eggs.
> The boxcars are all empty there,
> And the sun shines every day.
> I'm bound to go where there ain't no snow,
> In the Big Rock Candy Mountain.
>
> Oh, the buzzin' of the bees in the cigarette trees,
> The soda water fountain,
> By the lemonade springs where the bluebird sings,
> In the Big Rock Candy Mountain.

The song ended. Puzzled, Jake stood with the player against his ear, listening to the blank tape roll with a faint electronic hiss. What was there about this song that could possibly trigger such an attack? Maybe it wasn't the song; maybe something in the room he spotted while—
Click.

A child's voice—strangled, gargling, fighting for breath, but quite distinct—said, "He's got the police clothes, but he's not . . ."

A moment of silence. With a soft snap, the tape ended.

·28·

Captain Cowen was just hanging up the phone; he waved Jake expansively into his office.

"Sit, sit—you're not a well man. I heard you went home sick yesterday."

Jake stayed on his feet. "Oh . . . right. Just a twenty-four-hour bug. I'm much better today. Listen, I've got some important news."

"In a minute. First I insist you sit down. You're definitely looking peaked. You must never trifle with your health."

As Jake reluctantly settled himself in a chair, Cowen said, "I'm afraid I'm going to have to cancel the party."

"What party?"

"Jake, Jake, you wound me. Here I go to all the trouble and expense of a departmental party, and you forget all about it."

"Oh, *that* party. Sure, I remember. Uh, what night was it exactly?"

"Tonight."

"Oops. I guess it did slip my mind. Sorry. What I wanted to tell you—"

Cowen coyly inspected his manicure. "Aren't you going to ask *why* I'm canceling?"

Jake was irked with Cowen's smug manner. "It probably conflicted with a police-dog retirement ceremony. I just found out the Bureau has been keeping a dad-slays case from us."

"The Grants? A dry hole. I'm canceling my party because I'm flying to Florida tonight."

"Fine, fine. Enjoy your trip. Doug—don't take Brasswater's word on the Grants. Look, I can't tell you how, but I'm pretty damn sure it's the same man who killed the other families. I'll tell you something else nobody knows. He dresses as a policeman. He—''

Cowen laced his hands behind his head, crossed his legs, and leaned back in his chair. "You can forget the Grants. Trust me. By the way, sick man, I hope you haven't unpacked from your secret trip to Baton Rouge."

Jake stared at him, momentarily derailed.

Cowen grinned, enjoying Jake's mystification. "Oh, didn't I tell you? You're coming with me to Florida tonight. You, me, and Meatball the Cat. Don't worry about the travel req. I'll have Treva do it for all three of us. Unless you want to keep on buying your own tickets."

"There's been a break in the case in Florida?"

"I'd say so, yes. About an hour ago, the Family Killer made a full confession to the Daytona police."

·29·

"Once in a generation it happens, if you are lucky. You begin to read a manuscript by a complete unknown and suddenly you are rapt, transfixed, overwhelmed by an authentic new voice. Such was my experience with the work of Sally Payden Harrow. But let me read her first chapter aloud and see if you, too, do not fall under her spell."

Humphry Shaw opened his briefcase and reverently withdrew the manuscript, dog-eared from much perusal. Lorenzo Segura's tiny living room—made even tinier by the floor-to-ceiling bookshelves and crammed with Goodwill Industries furniture—was hushed, almost reverent. The inner circle of literary kingmakers leaned forward to hear Shaw's voice intone her words. . . .

Sally turned into her street and set down her two bags of groceries for a momentary rest. She glanced at her watch.

Yipe! Tina's going to kill me. I swore she'd only have to watch Winston for an hour.

She scooped up the bags and began to trot. As she neared the house she saw Jake bustle out the front door, holding Winston with one hand and an overnight bag with the other, and walk rapidly toward their three-year-old red Mustang. He saw her and waved.

Oh, God. He's off someplace. He can't drive me to the party. Pray Tina is free.

Sally set down her bags on the sidewalk and ran after him.

"Where to now?"

"Florida, Daytona."

"Why? What's going on?"

Jake stowed Winston in the car and beckoned Sally away out of earshot.

"Sorry, hon, you weren't home. I'm late for a plane. I was going to call you from the airport. We've got a confession in the Family Killer case."

"Thank God!"

"If it's the right guy. We're checking him out tonight. That's why I'm taking Winston. Cowen, the Bureau, we're all going."

"When will you be back?"

Jake started toward the car. "Don't know—watch TV. Cowen is hoping to announce we caught the guy at a press conference tomorrow morning."

"I'll keep an eye peeled for you."

She ran around the car and kissed Jake as he started the motor and put the car in gear. "Good luck, honey-tiger."

Jake grinned. "Cowen's in seventh heaven—it looks like we're back in the poker game. There's a warrant out for the guy in New York. Murder one. Last December, maybe you saw it? A nurse named Megan Barker."

Sally stepped back and blinked. "Wasn't she—?"

But he was already rolling out of the driveway.

"A *kid!* You're bringing a kid along? Now? On this case?" Cowen bellowed. Half the people in the departure area looked up; Brasswater and his people watched with interest.

"My dad lives in Florida," Jake said. "He's been eager to see the boy."

"Your compassionate leave wasn't long enough? Now you want to scrounge vacation time?"

"Come on, Doug, you know me. It won't be a problem."

"The kid stays here!"

"It's too late."

"Call your wife to come get him."

"They're boarding the plane already."

"Leave him with—somebody—the airline people." Cowen gestured at the man and woman who were ripping tickets at the gate.

"I won't leave him with strangers," Jake said.

"Don't be silly." He bent over and addressed the boy directly. "You wouldn't mind waiting with those nice people, would you, son? Of course not."

Winston sidled behind Jake.

"If he stays, I stay," Jake said.

"I thought this case was a big deal to you. Seems I was wrong." Cowen turned and walked toward the gate. Without looking back, he called, "The department's not buying his ticket. Don't try to bury it in your gyp sheet."

"Why is he getting all bent out of shape?" Jake asked Gatto. "The kid's not going to run up into First Class and patty-cake in his caviar."

Gatto mimicked Jake's voice. " 'My dad lives in Florida. He's been eager to see the boy.' Is this the same Joe Harrow you're always telling me about?"

"I talk too much."

"You notice I don't. Not around Cowen. You owe me one."

Tina didn't answer her phone. She and Dave must have gone out.

A cab was out of the question. She would not put herself at the mercy of a strange man driving through unknown streets, taking her God knows where. Bo had raped her in a car.

That left the subway.

Fine. Millions rode it every day. So would she.

She showered and slipped into a party version of the slinky skirt, scarf, big hat outfit she had worn before—the one Shaw said made her look like a young Virginia Woolf.

Resolutely, Sally marched to the front door, turned off the hall light, took a deep breath, and put her hand on the knob. "Here we go, ready or not!"

She flicked the light back on, walked back down the hall, went into the dark living room, sat in a chair, sighed loudly, got up, and marched into the hall meaning to turn left toward the front door. Instead, she turned right and walked back to the kitchen, hit the light switch, put water on the stove for a cup of coffee, sat at the kitchen table, drummed her fingers on its Formica top, got up, turned off the burner, dumped the water in the sink, flipped off the light, walked back into the hall, started toward the front door, stopped in front of the hall mirror, studied her face for a moment, sighed loudly, went into the living room, turned on a lamp, and plopped down on the couch.

"Damn damn damn damn damn!"

She tried to stand up again, but her muscles wouldn't work. She sat paralyzed in her slinky party dress.

She fumbled in her purse, dragged out her compact, and looked at herself in the mirror.

"Once upon a time there was a woman named Sally who was smart enough to write a wonderful book and brave enough to get the finest writer in all the land to read it. He loved it and wanted to make her famous, but on the appointed night, she was too frightened to leave the house and seize her prize. And so she sat in the twilight and let life pass her by. Do I blame her? Of course not. I pity her. I excuse her. She is infinitely sad, infinitely pathetic. I feel nothing but sorrow for the poor beaten little thing who let her life slip away when all she had to do was reach out and take it. I am going to sit here for the next three hours, and study her weak, puling, self-pitying face."

She stood up, turned off the lamp, and began to walk. Across the living room, along the hall, click off the light, through the front door, down the walk, through the gate, and toward the subway station.

She descended into the subway, token ready.

After too long, the train came. She boarded the middle car, seeking safety in numbers, but it was nearly empty.

At the next stop, four loutish-looking boys got on and, with the whole car to choose from, sat opposite her. One of them brazenly looked her up and down. Nervously, she raised her eyes and began silently translating the Spanish-language ad for a fertility clinic above his head.

The train rattled on, steadily filling up. A huge homeless man in army fatigues shoved through from the next car and began a loud spiel. "Now, I know I'm a big guy, but I don't mean you no harm . . ." When he went by she gave him a quarter.

"God bless you," he said.

His words shamed her. *How can I be afraid of this poor devil? He's begging me, not threatening me. I'm the one with the power.*

The lout across the aisle continued to stare at her. She met his eyes and held them. After a moment, he colored slightly and looked away.

Just a punk kid. If I asked him what he was looking at, he'd probably pass out.

Chin high, she looked around boldly at the other passengers.

Ordinary people. Nothing to be afraid of. Everybody says New York is full of freaks. Well, where are they?

"THEY BURY THEM UNDER THE STREETS."

She jumped and looked around for the speaker but couldn't find him.

"CON ED, THE TELEPHONE COMPANY, THE WATER-MAIN CREWS—THEY ALL DO IT. THEY BURY THEM UNDER THE STREETS."

She still couldn't locate the voice, but it was getting closer by the second.

"THEY COVER THEM WITH STEEL PLATES." A thin man was crawling through the crowd on hands and knees, his pale arms and legs clearly visible through his rags. When he saw Sally, he veered toward her, as if he'd been talking only to her the whole time. "DON'T

186

YOU BELIEVE ME? I'LL SHOW YOU WHERE THEY'RE BURIED." He crawled straight at her like a dog.

Why me? Why did he have to pick on me?

She jumped up and backed away. "That's okay," she said. He crawled after her.

"That man is chasing me," she said in a loud voice, and looked around wildly. The other passengers deftly avoided her gaze, like waiters with too many tables.

"I'll SHOW YOU WHERE THEY'RE BURIED. THE CITY PUTS OUT A MAP." He paused to fumble in his rags. The train rolled into a station. The door opened. Sally backed onto the platform.

"THEY BURY THEM UNDER THE STREETS," her pursuer screamed, crashing full speed through a jungle of strap-hangers' legs. The doors slapped shut in his face, and his shouts were lost in the thunder of the departing train.

She had made it to Manhattan, but she was at the wrong station. Her stop was the one after this. No problem. Another train would come along in a few minutes.

She was alone on the dark, silent platform. Above her, a car honked faintly. *They bury them under the streets.* Her heart thumped in her chest.

She walked down the platform and stood beneath the orange rectangle. It marked the "safe" area in sight of the token booth, but it only made her feel like an easier target. If the clerk saw her being mugged, he'd probably make sure the door to his booth was locked and lie on the floor telling his beads.

Far off in the tunnel's blackness, she could hear water dripping. How could it be so quiet down here? With the tremendous racket the trains made, you should be able to hear them miles away. Had they decided to stop for the night?

The stench of urine assailed her nostrils, a stale and overpowering reek. Men. Uncontrolled, drunken brutes, waving their big penises around, pissing where they pleased. She breathed through her mouth. The train would carry her away from the stench. If it ever came.

Where's the goddamn train?

It's only one stop. Walk it.

She pushed through the turnstile and hurried to the exit stairs.

Oh, God! Halfway up, a young man waited, radiating anger, his eyes on her. He wore sneakers—what Jake called "felony shoes." She fumbled in her pocket for a quarter, ready to pay her tribute. As she neared him he said, with barely controlled fury, "I am making a nonviolent request for a token."

What did he mean—a *nonviolent* request? She had no token. She had prepared a quarter—but now that was wrong. She didn't know what to do, so she blundered past without giving him anything.

At the top of the stairs, she glanced back, half expecting to see him charging after her, but he wasn't even looking in her direction.

This damn city was like a mattress fire—it might smolder harmlessly for days or flare up next second and burn you to death. You never knew.

Where was she? She looked around, but every pole she saw bore an empty metal rectangle. Why were all the street signs missing? *Who steals street signs?*

She stumbled ahead, trying to get her bearings. The warm May night had lured people outside. The streets jumped with life.

Hawkers had turned the sidewalks into an outdoor bazaar, selling the unsalable. She could hardly squeeze past the spreads of filthy secondhand clothing, tattered back-date magazines, and junk watches falsely offered as stolen.

On one corner a string quartet sawed away, only the tiniest bit flat. On the next, a young man in a toga stood motionless on a pedestal, pretending to be a statue.

She felt unbearably conspicuous in her party outfit. It seemed to invite comments. As she passed, men in doorways made mouth sounds, wet air-kisses, nasty little slurs on her human value.

I can't stand this.

She broke into a run.

That really brought out the catcalls: "What's your hurry, babe?" "Don't run off, mama; I got what you need right here." Men lunged forward as if to bar her way, reached out their hands to grab her. She ran a nightmare gauntlet of grinning faces, pawing hands.

She began to sob. She had to get out of here. Go home. Even if it meant riding in a cab. She should never have tried to come alone.

She rushed into the street and waved her arms at the oncoming taxis. Off Duty. Off Duty. Off Duty. Was it sadism? Did they drive around all night with the Off Duty sign to torment desperate people?

Try the next avenue.

She dashed across the street, turned the corner and, by some alchemy understood only by experts in Manhattan real estate, found herself on a quiet street of well-kept apartment buildings.

She stumbled to the middle of the block, getting her breath. She felt rattled and confused; she needed to sit, rest, get her bearings. She slipped through an open gate into a vest-pocket park and sat on a bench beside a sweet-looking old lady feeding a small army of squirrels.

Gradually, her trembling subsided. The little old lady seemed to sense her distress and patted her knee. "Want to feed them too?" She handed Sally a slice of white bread.

For the first time Sally looked down at the mass of scrabbling creatures that surrounded them and noticed their hairless snaky tails and burning red eyes. Too terrified to raise her voice, she whispered, "These aren't squirrels!"

The woman smiled beatifically. "Don't be prejudiced, dear. Rats need love too."

She had expected Segura to live in a converted factory, with a loading platform and a fresco of furious graffiti. Instead, she found a brownstone on an elegant treelined street.

The important thing was—she was here! She had beaten her phobia! Braved the subway and the street on her own, stayed the course in spite of maniacs, lechers, and rats. She suddenly felt powerful and free—she could do anything!

She rang the bell. A red-jacketed butler admitted her, after carefully scrutinizing her invitation. He strode ahead of her through Segura's elegantly furnished brownstone, past prudently locked doors, to a large living room, uproarious with a hundred conversations. This was not the "little get-together" of her fantasy; french doors had been flung open, and guests spilled out into a backyard where spotlighted trees distracted the eye from the building walls rising on three sides. A team of virile young waiters in green iridescent shirts and black leather pants flowed suavely among the crowd with trays of drinks and hors d'oeuvres.

Shaw was in the center of the room, holding forth to a circle of worshippers. She pushed through the satellite circles and stood as close as she could, hoping to catch some literary insights before making her move.

He was discoursing on the difficulty of finding a really good tailor in New York. She listened for a bit, then edged forward until she caught his eye.

His eyebrows hopped in recognition. "She's come—my greatest convert. Virginia Woolf, the policeman's wife. Our Lady of the Precincts." He kissed the air on both sides of her face with great élan, his breath strong enough to strip shellac. "Darling Virginia, you are radiant. The bloom's on your berry!"

His pun brought the house down. Sally stepped back abashed, but he clasped her hands and held her.

"Don't leave before we chat," he said quietly.

"Then you liked it?"

"Liked what?"

"You know. My book."

"Your . . . book." He stared at her blankly. "Oh, yes, your *book*."

Sally's skin burned and froze. "You did read it?"

"Yes, of course," he said heartily, looking away. ". . . ah, quickly, though. I'll need to study it more thoroughly before I can comment."

"Surely you can tell me *something*."

"I'd rather wait until my thoughts have crystallized." He smiled vaguely and looked around as if trying to find someone else to talk to, but his circle of listeners had drifted away.

"Is it good? Am I on the right track?" Their hands had reversed position; she was holding on to him now.

"I'll read it next week and drop you a note."

She fought back tears. She had endured insults, risked being mugged, slogged through living rats to get his comments. She couldn't leave with nothing. "Just tell me if you liked it," she pleaded.

"I see someone I must have a word with. Please excuse me."

She tightened her grip on his wrist. "You promised to critique my story at this party, *tonight*."

"You're becoming a bore, my dear."

"Why won't you tell me *anything*?"

He gave her an exasperated look. "Why won't I tell you anything? Perhaps because five minutes after you handed me your manuscript I filed it in a trash can. Happy?"

She released her grip and stepped away from him, but he followed, angry that she had forced the admission from him. "If I read every dog's dinner people dump on me, I wouldn't have time for my own work."

"*But why offer to read it then?*"

"I always do that. Ink-stained wretches like you won't take no for an answer."

Sally turned pale and nodded her head vigorously several times. "I see, I see. Thank you for telling me that."

"You're quite welcome."

"Now I've got something to tell you. Speaking as a policeman's wife."

"Perhaps some other time." He started to turn away.

"Mel Haney is the Family Murderer," she said.

·30·

Jake's flight had a stopover in Atlanta. The terminating passengers gathered up their things and deplaned. The Daytona passengers sat for forty-five minutes without air-conditioning, sweating and wondering why new passengers weren't boarding.

Equipment problems. Everybody off. Not to worry. Don't leave the lounge area. Another airplane is being readied in the hangar. When? Soon. How soon? Watch the monitor.

They ate soggy sandwiches wrapped in plastic and washed them down with canned soda. Word came their airplane was on its way from the hangar. Time passed. Word came that their airplane had gone back to the hangar. Nothing serious. Watch the monitor. Problem with the hydraulic system. A businessman sitting near Jake groaned and muttered, "It's always the damn hydraulic system. Let's go, let's go. Who needs ailerons?"

Cowen churned back and forth in the departure area mumbling, "Megan Barker is a New York case," like a mantra. The FBI contingent sat as far from the police as possible, Brasswater reading and rereading a thin sheaf of papers, occasionally darting suspicious glances at Cowen. As the clock advanced, the promised departure time receded like a mirage—first one, then two, then three hours.

Winston sat in a row of seats opposite Jake, tired but alert. He looked so cute that several adults had moved to sit near him, stealing glances, smiling, and trying to catch his eye.

Finally a plump middle-aged white woman in a flowered dress spoke to him directly. "And what's *your* name?"

Winston looked down shyly.

"Don't you want to tell me what your name is?"

191

"He's Winston," Jake supplied.

The woman looked aggrieved. "You should allow Winston a chance to speak for himself. Some children just need time and a bit of persistence. I know about shy little ones. I'm a schoolteacher. Winston, would you like to tell me how old you are? Of course you would; you're a big boy."

He put his hand over his mouth.

"I know you can do it. Come, come."

A black daddy traveling with his own family had been watching with growing irritation. "Excuse me, madam," he said in a Jamaican accent. "With a name like Winston, you must speak to him with the proper island lilt. You must say, 'How old you now, boy?' "

Winston didn't look up.

"I bet you eight—why you act like four? Tell me that, boy?"

Winston scrunched down in his chair.

A second black man took Winston's part. "Don't bully him. Perhaps the boy is from Haiti and speaks the Angel's Tongue." To Winston he said, "*Est-ce que ou ce Haitien?*" He gestured toward the Jamaican. "*Ou vle moin semin bouch li?*"

Winston put his head against his chest and covered it with his arms. Jake stepped across the aisle and took him by the hand.

"Time for a walk."

Winston jumped up, giving Jake a relieved look.

"What a scaredy-cat," the Jamaican man said.

"Don't say such things," the Haitian warned him.

"He should have counseling. We're doing so much with learning disabilities these days," the woman said in a peevish voice.

Jake smiled at the three of them. "Sorry folks, Winston doesn't understand a word you say. He's here from Cameroon to play in the chess championships."

They looked at Winston with respect bordering on awe.

The woman said, "Well now, I *thought* he looked exceptionally bright."

As Jake and Winston strolled off, she followed them.

"Excuse me? What is the language of Cameroon?"

"They speak Camera," Jake said.

Finally they took off, Cowen clenching a champagne glass in First Class, everybody else—including Brasswater—in Coach. Harrow and Gatto bracketed Winston. The weather had soured. Rain streaked crazily down the windows, lightning lit the boiling clouds around them. The plane dropped, bucked, rattled. Jake, wedged against the window, put a steadying hand on Winston's shoulder and glanced down: the kid was smiling gleefully, thrilled by the ride. When the plane climbed above the storm to reveal a vast moonlit plateau of rolling thunderheads, he climbed all over Jake to look out the window until Jake swapped seats.

They reached the Daytona police station after one A.M. Lieutenant Teavers in charge. He tried to tell them Haney was asleep in his cell, but a passing detective revealed he was back in interrogation—strange since Haney had confessed more than six hours ago.

Cowen wanted to look at the written confession.

"Not available," Teavers told him.

Yelling, threats.

Although it was the wee hours of the morning, Winston was wide-awake, nervously watching the angry men. Jake took his hand and wandered off. They mounted a flight of stairs, walked along a hall, rounded a corner, came to a cop at a desk between two doors. The cop lowered his copy of *Popular Mechanics*.

"Help you?"

"New York," Jake said, showing his ID. It didn't do much good.

The cop jerked his thumb in the direction of the far door. "Sorry. Our people are working with him now. Nobody else gets in."

"Understood. Teavers said I could watch."

"What about the kid? We don't allow kids in observation."

Jake winked as if he didn't want to talk in front of the child. "Teavers said if he was quiet, he could watch a couple minutes. Look what a good boy he's being—he hasn't said a word since we got here."

The cop looked uncertain. "Nobody mentioned kids. Is he a witness?"

"Maybe you better call the lieutenant," Jake said.

The cop picked up the telephone receiver and punched some buttons. "Who's this? Oh, Danny. You on the desk now? Yeah. Listen, I need to talk to Teavers, put him on, will you?" He waited, drumming on his metal desk-top with a pencil. "Hello, Lieutenant?"

Jake circled his thumb and forefinger in the okay sign. "Thanks, I appreciate it." He yanked open the near door, stepped into the observation room, and closed the door behind him.

The room was dark and small, hardly more than a walk-in closet. One wall had a big window of one-way glass, giving a full view of the interrogation room. A coffee urn hissed tiredly. The trash can blossomed with stained paper plates. The air reeked of coleslaw. Two men hunkered on chairs, watching the interrogation. Neither looked around.

Something peculiar was happening on the other side of the glass. The interrogator was a heavyset southern-sheriff type. His white shirt

193

showed big gray half-moons of sweat under the arms. He stood with his arms folded defensively, hands gripping biceps, like an employee getting chewed out by the boss. Haney, ferret-faced and smaller than Jake had expected, sat at the table, yelling and pointing his finger. His voice squawked from the ceiling speaker in low-fidelity.

"I gave you the list; I gave you the sequence. That was the deal! Now you're leaking the story all over the fucking place."

"It's not us," the heavyset man said doggedly. "We're playing it like you said."

Tensely, Jake lifted Winston so he could look through the window. He hated to do it to the poor kid. In two seconds he could be screaming and biting his hands. But Winston watched the two men the way he had watched the storm out the airplane window: fascinated, but without fear.

"Do you see Mr. Bad News?" Jake whispered.

Winston shook his head.

The door to the observation room opened behind them. "Let's go, New York," the hall cop said. "Teavers never gave you permission to come in here."

"Close the fucking door," one of the watching men said tiredly, without taking his eyes off the window.

Jake whispered to Winston. "The one in the chair. You're sure that's not Mr. Bad News?"

The hall cop came inside and closed the door. He put his hand on Jake's shoulder and said, "Move it."

The boy did something that was rare for him. He turned his head and looked Jake in the eye. He shook his head emphatically *no*.

Jake set him on his feet and whispered in his ear, "Thanks, pal."

They went with the hall cop.

From the speaker, Haney's voice quacked, "Listen, Farington, if I find out you're selling my ass to some local reporter for brownie points, I'll scream 'coercion' so fast your head will spin. That confession will be toilet pa—"

The closing door cut off his words.

"I'm sorry there ain't more chairs—I didn't know you-all were gonna be such a big group." Lieutenant Teavers opened and closed his eyes a few times, trying to jump-start his brain. It was now nearly two in the morning.

Teavers was not only tired, he was mightily pissed off. The brass had all run like rabbits, leaving him in charge. Haney was driving the public relations people crazy, New York detectives were barging in where they weren't supposed to be, and this Captain Cowen was all over him like bird dirt on the town cannon.

Now he had to face a room full of heavy hitters from the FBI and the New York Police Department. What if he came on too strong and they went over his head to complain? Or what if he was too accommodating and got into hot water with his own people? The potential for disaster was enormous.

They flooded into a closet-size conference room that had been hastily equipped with metal folding chairs. The blinds were clamped down against the dull darkness outside, and the fluorescent ceiling lights buzzed evilly. Brasswater marched to the front and seized the center seat. Cowen eased in beside him and hunched forward tensely, like a one-punch fighter looking to unload. Jake sat in the middle of the room, and Meatball Gatto plunked himself down by the door, leaving the windowsills for the slower members of the FBI.

Teavers gulped muddy coffee from a paper cup and began without ceremony, hoping to get the meeting over with quickly. He told the assembled group that Haney had kidnapped a girl out of the parking lot of a Daytona high school and taken her to a cabin in the woods, where he had evidently raped her and then clubbed her to death with a chunk of wood. A search party had found the girl a few hours later and stumbled over Haney sleeping on the ground nearby. He had been in custody awhile before they were able to identify him. While being questioned by the police, he had seemed confused at first, and unwilling to talk, but suddenly had confessed the murder in the woods and had gone on to confess the family murders without a break.

"Did he ask for a lawyer at any time?"

Teavers glared at him. "We didn't blow it, if that's what you're asking. Daytona ain't New York, but it ain't the sticks neither."

"I never said it was," Brasswater said evenly.

"Our boy is one of your jailhouse lawyers. When we Mirandized him, he kept saying that he could defend himself; he didn't need no 'legal cripples' to do it for him."

"Did he mention anything about a partner—a second man involved in the family killings?" Brasswater asked.

"No."

"You're sure? No attempt to spread the blame? No comments that might indicate he had help?"

"Nothing that I'm aware of."

Brasswater took the failure of the Bureau's two-man theory as a personal affront. "Have you done any independent checking of his story?" he asked belligerently.

"He told us where he's been living—a rooming house here in the Daytona area. It checks out."

"That's only the last five days," Brasswater said. Cowen's head jerked up. How did Brasswater know that? Had he been given information the NYPD hadn't?

"Where was he on Monday night?" Jake asked. That was when the Grants were murdered.

Teavers fussed over his notes, having trouble concentrating with everybody looking at him. "At the rooming house. He watched TV with the landlady until after midnight. The Jay Leno. She corroborates that."

Brasswater stayed on the attack. "What about before that? How did he get to Daytona? Plane? Bus? Car? Where did he stay in Skokie? Beals? Los Angeles? Washington? How did he get around? What did he use for money?"

"We don't know. He confessed and then clammed up."

Brasswater reached into his jacket and pulled out the dog-eared sheaf of paper he'd been poring over in the Atlanta airport. "I've been going over this confession for the last three hours—"

Cowen jumped up. "You refused to let me see that, Teavers. How come you faxed it to the Bureau?"

"Not my call," Teavers said.

Brasswater punched at the confession with his index finger. "Are you telling me that everything Haney said about these murders is in here?"

Teavers tried to make it a virtue. "Everything the man said."

"Then we have a problem," Brasswater said. "There's nothing in here that wasn't in the newspapers. Not a single new detail. This confession could have come straight from our own press release."

"Hold on here!" Teavers was getting upset. The Daytona cops had landed the world-record trophy bass, and now this Bureau biggie was trying to throw it back. "You're talking like Haney is one of these nut cases who confess to big murders to get attention. We caught this boy in the woods with a murdered girl. We know he committed at least one other murder in New York—"

"None of which changes the fact we only have his word he's the Family Killer. There's no independent corroboration. Not a shred of it."

Jake stood up. "Maybe I can save us all some time. Let me talk to him."

"Why you?" Teavers asked. Now these bastards were even implying they could have done the interrogation better. As if we hadn't got a complete confession out of the guy!

196

"He's Jake Harrow—the brother of one of the victims," Cowen said loudly. "He knows all kinds of stuff about the house and family that wasn't in the papers." This was what Cowen had been hunting for: a way to project his department into the middle of things—and pay Brasswater back for not sharing the confession with him.

"I thought Teavers said Haney's not talking anyway—"

"Jake might set him off," Cowen said. "Could shake the guy up to be confronted by a member of a victim's family. Jake even looks like his brother!"

Brasswater was getting heated. "Frankly, I don't see the value of sending in someone so emotionally involved."

Cowen shrugged. "What have we got to lose? We've got a signed confession. Haney's not talking anyway. Why not give it a shot?"

"Damn it, he could blow the whole case!" Brasswater shouted.

"What are you suggesting?" Cowen asked quietly. "That my man would lose control with someone he was interrogating?"

Brasswater realized he had overstepped himself. Part of his brief was to be seen as cooperating with his opposite number from the police department. Especially here in Florida, with local police in the room. He turned to Teavers. "He's your prisoner."

Teavers glared. The last thing he needed tonight was to be left holding one of Brasswater's hot potatoes. He lobbed it back. "If you-all got no objection, then we don't neither," he said.

The interrogation room was an all-white sterile little cubicle, lit brightly as a Baskin-Robbins. In the middle of the room was a rectangular table with a Formica top and steel legs, bolted to the floor so it couldn't be used as a weapon. On the table was a vintage reel-to-reel tape recorder with a standing microphone. The mike fed both the recorder and the speaker in the observation room behind the big one-way mirror on the far wall.

When Jake came in, Haney looked up sharply, his eyes bloodshot but alert under the fluorescent lights.

"Why am I back here in interrogation? I told them, I won't answer any more questions."

Jake closed the door and leaned against it, arms crossed. He stood motionless, without speaking or shifting his weight, and stared at Haney with slitted eyes for a good two minutes.

Haney met his gaze without apparent difficulty at first, but finally looked down.

"What's with you people? I confessed once already. I'm all confessed out."

"You don't know who I am?"

Haney raised his eyes again and cocked his head, looking at Jake with new interest.

"Oh, yeah. You're Roger Harrow's brother. The New York cop. Sorry I didn't recognize you when you came in—I've never seen a Harrow with clothes on."

Jake didn't move. He just stood in the doorway and continued staring at Haney.

The only sound was the faint squeak of the tape reels, turning steadily, recording only the hum of the lights.

After a while Haney turned his chair around and faced the other way. "This is my good side."

Jake didn't seem to hear. He continued to stare.

"Are you in love?" Haney asked. "I'd let you suck my cock, but I'm pledged to a Phi Delt at Vassar."

Another minute passed.

Jake's silence was so complete that Haney's words seemed to crumble to dust in the air as if they had never been spoken.

Haney sighed. "I know, I know—you want to beat me to a pulp. And, gollyoscars—were it up to me, I'd say, be my guest. I'd even tell you when I was tender in front so you could turn me around and do the back. But those old party-poopers behind the one-way glass just won't—"

"Why should I want to beat you to a pulp?" Jake asked quietly. He really seemed puzzled.

Haney stood up. "It certainly has been charming to meet you, but it's a school night, and I've—"

"Why should I want to beat you to a pulp?" Jake asked again.

"I told you, I've answered all the—"

"Why should I want to beat you to a pulp?"

Haney gave a put-upon sigh. "Let's see. Roger, Amanda, Jill, and Alexander. That's four reasons right there. Now, that's it; I'm going to bed."

Jake grinned, but only his mouth moved. "If you really slaughtered my relatives, I've got no beef with you. On the contrary. I like a guy who makes a clean breast."

"That's keen. Let's mingle blood and build a tree house."

"You think I'm kidding. I'm not kidding. If you're telling the truth, that's fine. I'm happy to leave your punishment to the criminal justice system."

"That's big of you."

"What I can't abide is a liar."

198

"I don't know what game you're playing here, but—"

"No game. I don't believe you killed my relatives. But you confessed to it. So the real killer is getting away. Because of you. That makes me grouchy."

"I confess to the crime of the century, I put my head on the block, and you don't believe me? You're the one with the burden of the argument."

"Everything in your confession is public knowledge. It's all in the newspapers. You haven't done the homework; you've just cribbed from the trot."

"Not only did I confess, I confessed in Florida—a state with the death penalty. Even you ought to give me the benefit of a doubt."

"Tell me one thing that's not in the papers."

"If you want additional details to masturbate to, you're just going to have to wait. I've got to save something for the Broadway musical."

"What was on Jill's ceiling?"

"A mirror. She was expecting me, the little tramp."

Jake chuckled at Haney's wit. He put his hand in his pocket and brought out a Kennedy half-dollar, which he began to flip and catch George Raft style.

"You can't tell me because you don't know. You're a lying little bastard."

Haney shrugged. "But enough about me. Let's hear about you. What's it like being a dickhead?"

"Not bad—we get into the movies for half-price. Oops!" Jake flipped the half-dollar high in the air and made no attempt to catch it. It landed on the floor by Haney's chair.

Before Haney could move, Jake bounded forward and dropped to one knee beside him. He gripped the leg of the chair in his left hand and lifted it, with Haney still in it, straight up into the air, while feeling around on the floor for his coin with his right hand.

Haney's head almost bumped the ceiling. He clamped the chair seat with both hands and held on, his face suddenly pale.

On the other side of the one-way mirror, Teavers's jaw dropped. "He's pressing the perpetrator! He can't do that! Can he?"

"Where *is* that pesky coin?" Jake's voice boomed hollowly through the ceiling speakers in the darkened observation room. Holding Haney high above him like a flag, he knelt on one knee apparently feeling around for his coin, although the table hid his movements.

Brasswater grabbed Cowen's arm. "May I ask you exactly what the fuck your man is trying to pull?"

Cowen shook off the hand. "Give him a chance. He likes to improvise."

Inside the room, Jake's right hand raked the electric cord of the tape recorder toward him and deftly wrapped it around his right shoe.

"Ah, here we go," Jake said. Gently, slowly, as if Haney were a Ming vase, he set the chair down, still using only one hand. In the process, he rotated Haney's chair ninety degrees so his back was to the wall.

As soon as the chair was securely on the floor, Haney got gingerly to his feet. "Very impressive, Hercules. Fuck you. You can't intimidate me." His voice shook. In spite of his bravado, he had been unnerved by his little flight.

"I didn't touch you," Jake said truthfully. He towered over Haney, only inches away.

Forgetting that it was the microphone that broadcast his voice to the observation room, Haney shouted directly at the mirror. "This man is trying to physically intimidate me! He's violating my rights!"

"Sit down," Jake said.

Haney sat. He was pale and sweating.

Without moving his feet, Jake reached over, dragged a second chair behind him, and sat on it, facing Haney so that their knees touched. The two men were wedged between the table and the wall. Jake's broad back was to the one-way glass, blocking the observation room's view of Haney almost entirely.

"The truth is, Mel, I don't give a shit about your rights. I'll do anything to solve this case. I don't even care if I go to jail myself. You with me?"

In the observation room, Brasswater said, "C'mon, c'mon, he's over the line. That's a flat-out threat he just made. It's on the tape."

"Two minutes," Cowen said.

Brasswater turned on Teavers. "Are you going to let your suspect be threatened like that?"

"Harrow don't work for me. I'm not giving him no orders."

The lines of authority were hopelessly snarled. Meanwhile Harrow was ripping up the rule book. Cowen would never allow an interrogator to act like this in New York, but down here Harrow was his only shot.

In the next room Harrow was saying, "Give me one detail of the murders that wasn't in the papers. Or else admit your confession is a lie. One or the other."

"I wouldn't give you the sweat off my balls if you were dying of thirst."

Jake slipped his hand in his pocket and pulled out the steak knife from Roger's kitchen, which he had been carrying around for three weeks. At the same instant, he jerked his right foot, yanking the tape-recorder power cord out of its wall socket.

With his left hand he clamped Haney's belt buckle, pinning him to the chair. With his right he gently scraped the serrated knife blade up and down Haney's fly.

"Answer me in ten seconds, or I slice off your cock. One thousand one . . ."

"He's got a knife. Help! Help me!" Haney shouted.

"They can't hear you; I killed the mike," Jake said. "One thousand three—can't see you either, I'm in the way—one thousand five . . ."

The chair-lifting had worked. Haney was paralyzed by his awareness of Jake's superior strength. He didn't even try to fight back but merely trembled in Jake's grasp like a doomed rabbit.

Jake whetted the knife more forcefully on the front of Haney's pants. With each down stroke, he could feel the blade bump over the ridge of the glans—this was a circumcised penis.

"One thousand eight, one thousand nine . . ."

Haney's eyes rolled in his head, showing white. He opened his mouth, but words wouldn't come. Foam geysered from the corners of his mouth and drooled down his chin. He was limp as a doll, he seemed to be falling apart.

"One thousand ten." Jake jerked the knife back to his sternum for its first stab.

"S-s-s-silencers-s-s-s," Haney hissed.

Jake sat like a statue with his raised knife.

"What? *What did you say?"*

The door opened behind him. Over the roaring in his ears, he heard Cowen's voice. "Something's wrong with the sound. We're not getting our feed in the other room."

"*Silencers!"* Haney screamed. "I used silencers when I shot the dads. Made them myself. That wasn't in the papers!"

Spots appeared in Jake's vision, spreading like miniature smoke bombs. Haney began to babble about PVC tubing, fiberglass, and resin, but for a moment Jake couldn't see or hear him.

Now there more voices behind him. The men from the observation booth were boiling into the room, talking excitedly.

Haney whispered, "Jake, the knife! *Put away the knife!"*

Instinctively, Jake slipped the steak knife back into his pocket.

Just in time. Cops and FBI men were all around him, slapping him on the back and pumping his hand as if he had just sprinted ninety yards for a touchdown.

As Jake left the room Haney lolled in his chair, hands laced behind his head, a grin on his face. "We simply must do this again sometime; you're even more fun than your relatives."

Cowen was ecstatic. "You did it, you did it! You nailed it down. Brasswater wanted to stop you. I said, 'No way.' I knew you'd come through. What the hell did you say to him at the end there? We couldn't hear; their cheesy speaker went dead."

"I threatened him with castration."

"All right, keep your tricks to yourself. The important thing is you got it."

Even Brasswater reluctantly shook Jake's hand in congratulations. Only Teavers was angry—why had the silencer clue been withheld from the Daytona cops—even after they captured Haney? Didn't the Bureau trust them to keep a secret? Or was it so the big New York guys could come down and grandstand?

"Stop grousing," Brasswater told him. "At least now we know you caught the right man."

·31·

Around five A.M., Jake tucked Winston into bed in a nearby motel. The boy was too sleepy to eat the mints on the pillows.

Jake sat in a chair and tried to catnap, but he was too shook up.

He was going crazy, chasing shadows. He had absolutely convinced himself the Grants had been murdered by the Family Killer on the basis of a disturbed child's tantrum and a fugitive whisper on a tape. Because of one success—the silencer drawing—he had turned little Winston into his Delphic Oracle. And now, face to face with the Family Killer, the boy didn't even react, didn't have the foggiest notion who was on the other side of the glass. And he, Jake Harrow, detective, streetwise smart guy with all the medals and plaques, had been so totally, uncritically convinced he'd damn near knifed a man who had already confessed.

Gradually, he fought himself calm. He'd been lucky. No real harm had been done. For whatever psycho reasons of his own, Haney hadn't made an issue of it. And if he tried to later, who'd believe him? His confession still stood, stronger than ever. Whatever happened to Haney, he would kill no more families.

Jake decided that the most constructive thing for him to do was give Winston back to Mrs. Appleby just as fast as possible.

He took a cab back to the police station to change his flight and watch Cowen's press conference.

A lot had changed in the short time Jake had been gone. His cab couldn't get anywhere near the station due to gridlock. He had to walk the last two blocks.

They had come with the dawn, like sharks in a feeding frenzy. Television crews and newspaper photographers, criminal rights lawyers and political activists, death-row groupies and just plain gawkers.

The television people had been promised a scoop of national importance, and they had put out the word. The Daytona police HQ was rapidly becoming a zoo.

As Jake walked through the parking lot he saw a young woman in red short-shorts jump out of a battered Camaro with signature plates that read "Li'l Cat."

In another car he recognized the famous lawyer Marion Thurber, lightning rod to a thousand left-wing causes. As Thurber lumbered out of his car Aztec fertility charms and hammered silver peace symbols clanked in his chest hair. With his mahogany tan and flowing white hair, he looked like an Old Testament prophet.

Jake could hardly push through the crush in front of the building. Inside the door, Meatball Gatto was grinning with contemptuous amusement at the crowd. As Jake slipped past him he remarked, "I'll say one thing for mass murder—it's a great way to meet ladies."

A very bleary Lieutenant Teavers manned the front desk. He was shouting at a tall rabbity man as Jake came up.

"No! No way! I don't care what he told you at midnight; this is morning, and he don't want to see you."

"But it's imperative—a matter of life or death! I demand my rights!"

"Demand away," Teavers said, and turned to Jake as a way to cut off the conversation. "You need something?"

"I'm going to reroute my flight home through Chicago. Any idea which airline?"

"You think I'm a fool?" the rabbity man yelled. "I know why the TV crews are here."

Teavers tried to ignore him. "We got one of them universal airline schedules back here somewhere." He began to dig through a big paper-crammed drawer.

The man yelled, "You're going to announce to the world that Mel Haney is the Family Killer!"

Teavers jerked upright. "Pipe down! You know that ain't official yet."

"*Yet!* There, you just admitted it. You're going to pin all these murders on Mel."

"Hey! Did he tell you we were pinning anything on him?"

"Well, no."

"All right, then. It was his idea to confess. We didn't even mention the damn murders to him."

"That's why it's so important that I see him now. He's got to repudiate that confession before the news conference."

204

"Well you're not seeing him, and that's that. And you watch your big mouth around reporters, or you might just never see him again, understand?" Teavers went back to rummaging in the drawer, and produced a torn and grease-stained schedule, which he pushed into Jake's hand. "Looks like February is the latest we got. It'll give you an idea."

Jake took it without looking at it. He had turned to the tall man with the pale pink skin and the watery eyes. "Excuse me, I didn't know Haney had a lawyer."

"I'm just a friend."

"Oh." Jake nodded, his interest fading. He flipped through the airline schedule. "You really don't believe his confession? You must think your buddy has a death wish."

"Death wish? Please! Can't you see what he's doing? The police already have him for Megan Barker and a Daytona teenager. But he knows that two murders are no big deal these days, so he's upping the ante, jumping into double digits, bringing in all the bigtime lawyers and the media. There's a thousand people out there, falling all over themselves to love-bomb a mass murderer. He's on his way to becoming America's Sweetheart. The more people he says he killed, the safer he is. He'll be too famous to fry. His biggest worry now is who'll play him in the made-for-TV movie."

Jake started to grin. "So he's trying to beat the rap on two murders by confessing to eighteen more? Whoa! Now there's a plausible theory."

"All right! I have no idea what goes on in his twisted little mind. But he simply could not have done those family murders. The papers described them as masterly jobs, carefully planned to look like suicides. Mel Haney is simply not capable of that kind of forethought."

"You don't think he's smart enough?"

"Intellectually he's brilliant, but emotionally he's a child, a creature of impulse. He lives in the moment; he doesn't plan—especially where violence is concerned. He's spent most of his life behind bars, don't forget. He never learned to control his outbursts; the state did it for him."

"Maybe we should let Haney out and put the state in prison." Jake was tiring of this gasbag and his theories.

"Look, whatever the reason, Mel Haney is an extraordinarily incompetent man. He can't use an electric can-opener or a toilet plunger. He can't even empty a pencil sharpener!"

"Maybe not, but the families weren't killed with a pencil." Jake turned away rather pointedly. "Yo! Teavers! You got a phone I can use?"

"Of course they weren't killed with a pencil. But what about those homemade silencers?"

"Maybe he had help," Jake said over his shoulder.

"He told me he constructed them all by himself."

Jake looked at him sharply. "He talked to you about the silencers?"

"He said he learned to make them in prison shop, but that's the lie of all time. He could no more—"

"When did you have this conversation?"

"When I arrived—a little after midnight. I begged him to admit his confession was a tissue of lies, but the little weasel absolutely stone-walled me."

"Who mentioned silencers first—you or him?" Jake asked.

"Oh, I did. I said, 'What's this bull about making your own silencers? You couldn't put my pencil sharpener back—' "

Teavers clapped a phone on the end of the counter and yelled, "Dial nine to get out."

"Lieutenant, would you come here a second?" Jake said.

Teavers took his time walking from the end of the counter. "What do you want now, towels? Ice water?"

"When did this guy see Haney?"

"Don't blame me for that. That was before the brass hit the silk. I hadn't taken over yet."

"But it was before we got here?"

Teavers squinted tiredly down at the sign-in sheet. "Twelve-fourteen. You gonna use that phone or not?"

Jake wheeled toward the tall rabbity man. "Who told you about the silencers?"

"Some policeman's wife."

"What was her name?"

Teavers yelled, "Watch what you say about this department!"

"No, no. It was in New York. Her name escapes me, but—I don't know if this will mean anything to you gentlemen—she was a dead ringer for Virginia Woolf."

Jake found Cowen in the men's room, dabbing the skin under his eyes with ointment to shrink the bags. He was smiling, excited. National exposure! The big time!

"Haney's not the killer," Jake said.

"Too early in the morning for jokes."

Jake told him what he had just learned from Shaw.

The captain didn't even stop dabbing. "You still haven't told me how Shaw beat us down here. Which I find especially peculiar since you say he left hours after we did, and I happen to know we were on the last flight."

"There were some CEOs at the party. One of them lent him a corporate jet. He must have passed us while we were stir-frying our piles in the Atlanta airport."

"So your little Sally was at a party in Greenwich Village with Humphry Shaw and a pride of CEOs. Guess it wasn't her bowling night, huh? You knew she was going to this shindig?"

"She told me about it, yeah. A while ago. It had sort of slipped my mind."

"When the cat's away . . ."

"Shaw had a manuscript of hers. He was going to critique it."

"Yeah, sure, whatever you want to believe, champ. Hey, she's your wife. None of my business. Pardon my face."

"C'mon, c'mon. You can bust my chops *after* you cancel the press conference."

Finished with his eyes, Cowen went to work on his hair, carefully patting it into shape, forming it lovingly with his hands, strand by strand, as if he knew each one by name.

"I'm in political thicket, here. No last-minute brain waves, okay? I just cut a sweetheart deal with the Effing B.I. Brasswater has stepped aside and let me be the spokesman for both groups. I can't change our agreed-upon position because of something Sally told Humpy and Humpy told Haney."

"Not even if we have the wrong man?"

"Jake, you're a hero, the man who got Haney to mention the silencer. Why are you trying to destroy that?"

"Haney made a monkey out of me. The bastard was *acting*."

"The silencer's not all we've got on him. He signed a full confession, don't forget."

"The real killer's still out there. He killed the Grants. He wears a policeman's uniform to confuse his victims. I've got a child's voice on tape, saying—"

Cowen glanced at his watch. "The dogs bark, but the caravan moves on. I can't wet-nurse you any longer—it's show time."

The television crew had set up in a hallway, if *set* is the right word for something so mobile: all the equipment was hand-held and belt-powered and backpacked—they were like a roving band of outlaw news-gatherers, always ready to flick on, focus in, and seize the fleeting moment.

The interview was conducted by a young black woman—obviously a rising star—who had been flown down from Atlanta for this job. It was being carried live by CNN.

Jake watched from the side as Cowen told a waiting world how the police had made the capture and gotten a confession. No mention of the Daytona PD. A viewer might be pardoned for thinking that Cowen's men had done it all. He went on to explain how a New York City detective, a member of the New York City Police Department, and close personal associate of Captain Douglas Cowen of the NYPD, had verified the confession by cleverly tricking Haney into mentioning the silencer, which he could not have known about unless he was the Family Killer.

Cowen was flying, cooking, having a ball. This was what he had been born to do. He had never met a camera he didn't like, but this one he loved, and the camera loved him back—it was a torrid affair.

But the interviewer knew more than Cowen thought she did. Suddenly she and the crew were moving. Past Cowen, straight to Jake.

". . . the man himself. Tell us, Detective Harrow, exactly how you got Haney to incriminate himself."

"I don't think he did."

"Be careful!" Cowen shouted from behind the camera.

"I don't understand. Are you saying Mel Haney didn't really confess?"

"He confessed all right. The question is—"

"That's enough, Harrow." Cowen was at Jake's side now.

"Captain, are you trying to muzzle this man?"

"His own relatives were killed. He's under a strain." Cowen grabbed Jake's arm and began to pull him away.

Too late. The reporter smelled NEWS; she strode right after Jake, her tech gang flowing with her, her microphone tracking his mouth like a heat-seeking missile. "Are you charging that Mel Haney is being railroaded?"

"He's railroading *himself*. He's lying!"

"Jake, I order you—"

"Then you think he's innocent—"

"Another family was killed on Monday. The Grants. In Baton Rouge. Haney couldn't have done it. He was in Florida."

Cowen's eyes began to dance crazily. Everything he had worked to build up was being torn to pieces—and by one of his own men. He panicked. "Shut up! Don't say any more! Gatto, help me!" Cowen flung himself at Jake and tried to wrestle him down.

Jake shouted, "Don't let them suppress the truth! Listen! The real killer wears a policeman's uniform so when people wake up, they won't scream or—"

Meatball Gatto crashed down on him like a restaurant air-conditioner falling off its ceiling mounts. Jake slammed face first into the tiled floor, dazed, every bit of wind knocked out of him.

"An historic first in American television!" the interviewer shouted delightedly, her voice rising above the general hubbub. "We are witnessing a police cover-up—live—and it looks like—Get away from him! Billy, get that on camera. The police are trying to unhook our equipment. Billy, don't let—Stop that! Let go!"

Humphry Shaw's voice boomed, "Mel Haney is an innocent man! His confession is false. Harrow has information to prove it's false. I can confirm—*squeeeeeeee!*" Feedback buried his words.

"Bastards killed the feed!" a technician shouted.

Captain Cowen's outraged voice thundered in Jake's ear. "You're suspended, you son of a bitch! I'm lifting your badge. I'll see you at the hearing!" Jake had humiliated him on national TV; he was almost crying. "I'll finish you, you crazy bastard. I swear to God, I'll finish you!"

· 32 ·

That afternoon in Princeton, a worried Sally dragged two big suitcases through the door of her old room.

Too distracted to notice the lump under the blanket, she heaved one of the suitcases on the bed. There were pitiful squeals as one of Nan's long-haired dachshunds scrambled up to the pillow and glared at her reproachfully.

"Aw, aw, I'm sorry, Ponty. I didn't mean it."

Nan, who had been lurking in the hall, seething with curiosity, took the opportunity to burst into the room and hoist the dog into her arms. "How many times has Mummy told Ponty? You snooze in a people bed, you get cwushed. Did Ponty listen? Hm? Did he?" To Sally she said, "It's not your fault, dear. Experience is a hard school, but Pontormo will learn in no other."

Sally didn't smile. She snapped open the suitcase and began to toss underwear into a drawer.

Nan hovered around, holding the dog, pretending to help with her free hand. "I didn't see Jake on TV this morning," she said after a minute, "but several of my friends did and called me, quite upset. They wondered if the poor man is . . . under some kind of strain."

"I suppose he is."

"Well of course, he's got this terrible case. But is there something else bothering him?"

Sally shrugged listlessly as she dumped an armload of cosmetic jars and bottles into a drawer and closed it without bothering to arrange them.

Nan stroked the dachshund, her eyes on Sally.

"There's nothing you want to tell me?"

211

"About what?"

"We all make mistakes, dear."

Sally paused over the suitcase and raised her head. "Please, Nan, don't start on me now. I'm just not up to it."

"I think I have a right to know why you're here."

"I don't know why myself."

"You don't. I see. And Jake? Does he know? Or are you both in the dark?"

"Jake asked me to move out for a while."

"This was Jake's idea?"

"Entirely."

"He must have a reason. What have you been doing?"

"You immediately jump to the conclusion I've been doing something!"

"What am I supposed to think?"

"You're not supposed to think anything. He didn't throw me out; he asked me to move out for a while. I haven't even had a chance to talk about it with him."

"He left you a note?"

"It was done through a third party."

"A lawyer?"

"Jake's friend Gimlet, the man who drove me here. It's as big a mystery to me as to you. When I learn what's happening, you'll be the first to know, okay?"

"I don't understand why you can't confide in your own mother," Nan said. "You might find I know a thing or two about holding a marriage together."

"I don't need doormat lessons!" Sally shouted. Pontormo began to yap excitedly. "Maybe you think I didn't hear you in the old days, on the phone all night about dachshunds, chasing the time zones west, yakking to California about the soy content of puppy chow at one in the morning, waiting for Popsy to wander in all flushed and tousled from screwing some little graduate student."

Nan listened to the whole speech with intense interest, nodding as if in agreement. "You poor dear," she said. "Things between you and Jake must be worse than I thought."

The engine's obbligato dropped a full octave, which startled Humphry Shaw awake. He scratched himself blearily and looked out the window as the jet rolled gently into a long arcing turn.

"Teterboro already?" he shouted at the back of the pilot's head. They were alone on the plane.

The pilot's name was Dexter. He was a freckle-faced youth who looked more like a bellboy than a pilot to Shaw. Dexter turned and grinned. "You were snoring before we got out of Florida. Heavy night, huh?"

Shaw clucked with irritation at the familiarity and turned to the window without answering. Far below, another corporate jet soared into his field of view like a white dove flushed by hunters. They were passing Teterboro, preparatory to their final approach.

In the afternoon sunlight, the airport looked semirural—rather like Lord's cricket ground, Shaw thought. Busy too—the approach road behind the hangars and the terminal was choked with cars. A large crowd waited in front of the terminal building; from this distance it pulsed on the tarmac like a great amoeba. He found it strangely beautiful.

Dexter sounded worried. Shaw couldn't make out the words, but between the usual tech chatter about compass readings and wind speeds, there was an anxious note of questioning.

Dexter turned and shouted, "Something's going on down there— some kind of demonstration—they're waving signs. Those Nintendo jockeys in the tower haven't a clue—they just keep telling me to land."

"It's not dangerous, is it?"

"Just a second." Dexter returned to the controls, lining up the plane for its final approach. Over his shoulder he shouted, "Anytime you get crowds next to runways, it's dangerous. Especially angry crowds."

"Maybe we shouldn't land." Shaw's voice rose in panic.

The pilot's hand swung back, gripping a pair of binoculars. "Do me a favor and try to read those signs."

Shaw took the binoculars but leaned forward and shouted in Dexter's ear, "I said maybe we shouldn't land! You're going in for a landing."

"I'll fly the plane; you read the signs!" Dexter shouted with such authority in his voice that Shaw snapped to the window instantly and focused the binoculars on the distant crowd. The lenses were powerful, the signs large and getting steadily closer, but Shaw was fighting vibration and shifting angles. Words and pictures darted in out of his visual field with maddening rapidity. Even when he acquired an image, he was squinting at a jiggling blur.

Shaw could perform an action only if he could explain it in words. "It's like snipping neck hairs in a mirror," he mumbled. "I've got to think in reverse. I'm traveling forward and down. So the glasses must pan back and tilt up." It worked. He acquired a big poster and held it, squinting fiercely. It was a face, roughly done, but familiar.

Below it, crudely lettered: HANEY'S WHORE.

"It's me! They're after *me*."

Like a bird hypnotized by a snake, he pressed his eyes into the binoculars. He saw a hangman's noose, effigies of children splattered with red paint, a cartoon of himself as puppet master, with Haney as puppet, wielding a bloody knife.

"You people are crazy," Shaw whispered. "I was only on TV a *second*. When I said Haney was innocent, I didn't mean *innocent* innocent, I meant—" The crowd charged the runway as if to stop the plane with their bare hands.

Shaw flung down the binoculars and shouted, "They'll kill me! Pull up! Pull up!"

Thump! The plane's wheels touched down.

Shaw buried his face in his hands and shouted hysterically, "I'm dead! I'm finished. God help me!"

He felt no roll. The motor whined with fresh power. He opened his eyes. They were airborne again, lifting rapidly.

Dexter turned with a grin that was pure Norman Rockwell and said, "That's what's called your basic 'touch-and-go.' "

Around five o'clock Sally happened to be in the front of the house when the doorbell rang. She opened the door to find Winston standing there and Jake walking rapidly away from her toward the red Mustang, its motor idling. She pushed Winston into the house and ran down the steps as Jake got into the car. When he spotted her he hastily applied himself to the gearshift.

"Wait! Please wait!" Sally rapped desperately on the closed side window. He glared at her but reluctantly shifted back to neutral and lowered the window.

"Are you all right? What's going on?" she asked.

"Later. Not now," he said.

"Talk to me, please!"

"I'm under the gun."

She opened the door and got into the car. "Drop me at Princeton Junction and I'll get a cab back."

"You have to get out of the car." His voice rasped, his eyes burned in their dark circles. She could see he was wired—no sleep, no food, running on black coffee and rage—but she was too upset to stop.

"Don't do this to me! I turn on the TV this morning and watch men jump on you like you shot the President. I go into shock. The phone rings off the hook with people saying they saw you go crazy on television. Then Gimlet's at the door telling me to pack, you want me to stay in Princeton. Why? Gimlet says, can't talk, Jake will explain everything. I've spent the whole day worrying and getting more and more upset. You can't just drop off Winston without saying a word to me."

"Calm down. Everything's going to be fine. I'm pressed for time now, that's all. Don't worry about me. I haven't gone crazy."

"Please, honey, I'm on your side, remember. Don't hide behind that tough-guy image. If you freaked out at the press conference, so be it. I can live with that. Just tell me."

"No, no. That was an act."

"An *act?* How? I don't understand."

"I set the thing up. I cued the TV interviewer she'd get a juicy controversy if she questioned me."

"Captain Cowen sure wasn't acting!"

"It's okay. I'll handle him when the time comes. Everything's under control."

"But why would you put on an act like that? Who were you trying to fool?"

"I really can't tell you any more."

Sally's eyes shifted rapidly in thought. "Okay. You think Haney's not the right man. You think the real killer is still out there. You did your act for *his* benefit, didn't you? But why show your hand? Why tip him off you're still chasing him?" She paused, frowning, then suddenly put her hand over her mouth. "Oh, God! You're setting a trap for the killer! You're trying to get him to come after *you!*"

"Sally, stop. You're letting your imagination run away—"

She raced on. "That's why you went out of your way to reveal that you knew about the Grants and the policeman's uniform! You want the killer to think you're closing in on him, you might catch him any day. Unless he kills you first."

"You're wrong."

She slapped the dashboard. "I'm right. The trap's at our *home.* That's why you stashed Winston and me in Princeton—out of harm's way. You figure he'll try to kill you tonight. That's why you're in such a hurry—bait can't be late."

He stared at the windshield. "Let's hope the killer's not as smart as you are."

"It's not fair! Why do you have to risk your life? Aren't there any other cops in the world?"

"Millions. They all think Haney did it."

"But how long can Haney's confession last? Once the FBI starts checking it out—"

"Meanwhile the real killer is doing a family every three weeks. And the gaps are getting shorter."

"But why do *you* have to be the goat tethered in the clearing?"

"Don't tell me how to do my job."

"It's not your job. Cowen didn't order you to do it. You chose to do it all on your own. You're not a cop here; you're just a private citizen with a carry permit—Mr. Jake Harrow, the man I sleep with."

"I've got to do this, whether you like it or not."

"Fine. I'll go with you." She reached up and attached her seat belt.

"What's the point?"

"Having me there will make your trap more plausible. He'll see me through the window, bustling around, singing, cooking dinner. He can kill us both over the gazpacho."

"Get out of the car."

"If you can choose, I can choose."

"If I don't do this, no one will. *There's nobody else.*"

"Why? Who appointed you to risk your life?"

"You did."

"Meaning what?"

Jake turned off the ignition and looked her in the eye. "I'm forced to work alone because of you."

"I don't believe this. How can you blame *me?*"

"You told Shaw about the silencer."

She turned bright red. "Oh, my God. What happened?"

"Shaw told Haney, and Haney used it to convince everybody he's the killer."

"Can't you explain to people how he found out?"

"I did, but it was too late. They're a mile down the track with Haney."

"Jake, I'm so sorry! Shaw told me he threw my manuscript in the trash without even looking at it. I wanted to hit back. I told him Haney had confessed to the family murders. I spat out everything I knew to convince him."

"Including the silencers."

"I ruined your case."

"You did, yes. I was madder than hell when Shaw told me about it, but it's water under the bridge."

"How can I ever make up for this?"

"By walking back up those porch steps and letting me get on with it."

"Yes, yes, of course." She unbuckled her seat belt, her eyes on Jake. "If you're killed, it's my fault. I'll never forgive myself."

"Damn it, stop that! You made a bad mistake, but you're not the killer."

"That's why you didn't want to talk to me, isn't it? If you were killed, you didn't want me to blame myself. You were trying to protect me from everything—even my own mistake."

"I tried, but you were too smart for me. Sorry."

She put her arms around him and kissed him. "Please don't die."

"Have you ever known me to die? I got too many cool moves to die."

She kissed him again, pulling and biting on his lower lip, darting her tongue against his.

"This is crazy," he said.

"It is," she said. "With your tight schedule we don't have time to go into the house and get undressed and get into bed and all."

She slid down his shirt-front, kissing the buttons, until she was on her knees in front of him, crouching under the dash, her head in his lap, her fingers deftly unzipping him.

"Uh, Sally. We *are* parked in your parents' driveway. If they come out—" He stopped talking and fell back on the seat, his eyes filming over with pleasure, as her silky-smooth mouth flowed over and engulfed him.

·33·

Jake guided his red Mustang through the streets of Queens. He hadn't slept in thirty-six hours, but his hands were white on the wheel. He hadn't eaten since the previous night, but he wasn't hungry. Anyway, an empty stomach was better for emergency surgery—doctors might be cutting him open an hour from now, stanching severed arteries, probing for bullet fragments.

As he neared his house he spotted a small unmarked van parked on an intersecting street. That would be Gimlet's control center.

Sharpshooters—friends of his from the department—lay flat on nearby roofs. They had the house covered front and back. Inside, Jake would be on his own. Everybody had radios, but the rule was radio silence unless they had an absolutely certain sighting. No status reports—they didn't want to scare their quarry off.

It was now completely dark. He hoped the killer wouldn't risk a long-range shot in low-light conditions. He wanted to force him to move in close.

He parked in front of the house, his heart hammering. The short walk from car to house was the worst part. He was exposed, and there wasn't much he could do about it. He slammed the car door and started around the car for the gate, fighting the instinct to run. He tried to move normally, in spite of the stiff body armor he wore under his jacket. The temptation to duck his head was strong—one bullet there could finish him.

Come on, man. Do the stroll. Eyes front. Don't check the bushes, don't check the roofs.

Take your time fumbling for the keys. Pray you're not in the cross

219

hairs. If he has to make his own silencers, maybe he doesn't own a night scope. You hope.

He unlocked the front door. So far, so good. Still alive.

Gimlet's team had watched the house all day. But the killer might somehow have slipped inside anyway, might be waiting in the hall shadows to gun him down.

Open door. Step inside. Close door.

Wait for the bullet to smash into your brain.

·34·

It was past midnight when the Electra nosed slowly into the treelined parking lot. There were only six other cars strewn haphazardly on the broken asphalt. A single naked light bulb dangled from a tree.

Shaw stepped out of the rented car and nearly fell down. God, he was stiff! He had driven all the way from Westchester Airport up here to Blithedale in northern Vermont. Except for a few roadside urinations, he had stopped only once for a sandwich, which he had bought furtively from a vending machine and eaten in the car, fearful of being recognized. That had been hours ago. His teeth crunched on road grit. He hopped from foot to foot to restore his circulation.

Blithedale was a writers' colony, a real get-on-with-it place, a velvet-lined Siberia. No telephones, no TVs, no radios—best of all, no human contact if you didn't want it. They would deliver your meals to the front step of your cabin and tiptoe away.

He could hibernate up here until the ever-fickle public found a new whipping boy. Glory be to God for the world's short memory. He would never complain about it again.

He found the narrow path up the hill. He saw no lights anywhere. The writers in residence had long ago turned in. Clouds hid the moon. The spring woods were profoundly dark. The paths of Blithedale writhed over the hills like a spider web, constantly branching. He tried to hurry, his flashlight jabbing at the gloom, making shadows scurry along the ground.

In his haste, he overshot his turn and had to backtrack. He paused at a Swiss chalet, puzzled, swept the light around, nodded, took the left fork, climbed past a rustic cabin, and turned into a secluded lane that wound up to the door of an A-frame.

They hide the key in a phony rock by the door. Mail-order magic. Pray the last person remembered to leave it. Ah, yes.

The key rattled in the old spring lock. Shaw stepped inside. He reached for the light switch; something hard dug into the small of his back.

"Hold it right there, dead man."

Shaw screamed, "Don't shoot!"

"*Shhhh!* Hand back your flashlight."

Shaw did so, whispering, "I swear to you—I've had absolutely no contact with Haney since December. Whatever he's done, I didn't help him."

"Flat on your back." The flashlight beam picked out the bed.

Shaw lay down. "I'm not trying to get him off again. I think he should be punished for murdering Megan Barker and the child in Florida. The TV transmission was cut off the air before I could explain myself."

The other man produced four lengths of clothesline from his jacket and rapidly tied Shaw's hands and feet to the four corners of the bed frame, spread-eagling him.

"Too tight! You're cutting off my circulation!"

The other man sat in a wooden chair opposite him. He clicked off the flashlight.

They were in darkness, except for some sky-shine through the big living room window. Shaw peered through the black. He was just able to make out the faint glint of the gun barrel in the man's lap. Why was it so enormous? He couldn't take his eyes off it.

"How did Harrow know I killed the Grants?"

"Oh, my Christ!"

"What did I do wrong?" Lamb asked quietly. "Did I leave something behind? Was it the *way* I did something—a telltale technique? How am I signing my name?"

"I don't know."

"How did Harrow find out about the policeman's uniform?"

"I don't know that either. Why should I? I'm not privy to his secrets."

"You're working closely with him."

"I'm not! I've only met him once, for a couple of minutes in Florida. I swear to you."

"That's a lie. You know him socially."

"No."

"You invited him to your party."

"Oh, wait, wait, this is all a misunderstanding. Really. Let me explain. His wife, you see, his wife—what's her name—?"

"Don't play dumb."

"I can't think of her name—I called her Virginia Woolf, and that's
what stuck in my mind. She fancies herself a writer. She asked me to
read something she'd written, and in a weak moment I invited her to
the party. Otherwise I've never had any contact with her or with Harrow.
I've never socialized with these people, I'm not helping them, and I
certainly don't know any of their inside information."

"And yet on television you said Harrow had information proving
Haney was innocent. How come the FBI wasn't privy to Harrow's information, but you were?"

"That's what confused you. I understand now. All I meant by that
—it's complicated—I told Harrow that Haney learned about the silencer
from me. Ironically, I learned about it from his wife. She showed up
at the party hell-bent to hear my critique of her manuscript—"

"Stop feeding me these lies about wives and manuscripts! You think
I'm one of your half-wit readers? You and Harrow did a brother act on
the morning news. You were helping him bait his trap."

"What trap? I don't know about any trap."

"You don't know anything, do you? You'll be happy to hear it almost
worked. You and Harrow should both get Oscars; you really had me
going. I drove to Harrow's neighborhood like a maniac, on fire to kill
him before he could tell the FBI what he knew. I was in such a hurry,
I almost didn't listen to the recording in my window reader. I would
have been a dead man if I hadn't started wondering why Gimlet was
rushing Harrow's wife out to Princeton to stay with her parents. They
didn't want her around when I showed up to kill Harrow and walked
into a hail of bullets."

"I don't know anyone named *Gimlet*. Harrow never told me he was
setting a trap."

"Keep it down."

"Yes, sure. I swear to God—"

"You don't keep a steam iron here, do you?"

"What? No. You've got this whole thing backwards. I don't know
anything. When I said Harrow had information, I was talking about
what he learned from *me*, which was only that I was the one who told
Haney about the silencer. Look, I know it sounds complicated, but I
can explain—"

"Stop worrying about it, Humpty. Everything's going to be just fine."
Lamb seemed to lose interest. He cast the flashlight beam around the
room. "Ah, pipes. You smoke a pipe."

"When I'm working, yes. Could you *please* do something about these
ropes?"

"Where's your pipe lighter?"

223

"In the desk drawer. No, the far one. I think you've dislocated my left shoulder."

"Got it. And a can of lighter fluid, almost full. We're in business."

Lamb flicked on the lighter. The flame spurted high, looking unnaturally large against the gloom. In its glow, Shaw could see that Lamb's pants bulged with an erection. He snapped the lighter lid down, walked to the bed, and began ripping up a pillowcase.

"What's that for?"

"A gag."

"No, no, please. I'll be quiet. I—"

Lamb gagged him and flicked on the pipe lighter again.

"You can't be quiet. I'm going to scorch the skin off your testicles and sear your prick to a charred stump. Then burn out your eyeballs, one at a time. I think you'd be well advised to tell me what Harrow knows about me, Humpty. While you've still got a tongue."

·35·

Killing Humphry Shaw had been a mistake, Lamb knew that now. A large risk for no result. The man had known nothing.

Even the act of killing itself hadn't helped. Instead of affording relief, it had stimulated him. His craving was becoming unbearable, seeping through the fear, undermining the foundations of his control like rising water.

The fire in the A-frame had fooled the local police, who came to the conclusion Shaw must have fallen asleep smoking his pipe. The media espoused three theories of his death:

1. Suicide due to guilt over Haney being the Family Killer.
2. Fatal accident due to unconscious guilt over Haney being the Family Killer.
3. What goes around comes around.

Lamb would have been amused, but he kept worrying about Harrow. Harrow wouldn't be fooled. How would he react? What would he do now? Lamb would have liked to download the window reader, but he was afraid to get even that close. The trap was almost certainly still in place. Harrow might know what he looked like—might know his car, might know—it was too dangerous to make the approach.

All that weekend, he felt like a leopard obsessively pacing an undersized cage. He had to have more information. After his morning class, he made the two-hour drive from Wren College to Queens.

As his gray Prelude drifted slowly past the mouth of Harrow's street he stared in the direction of the house, but saw no suspicious activity.

What did he expect? He was three blocks away—if the watchers were still there, they weren't about to advertise the fact.

He was tempted to turn and drive by but decided against it. As he passed the box elder he tapped the button under the dash and saw the small indicator light pulse red. The window reader was still in place.

The tape mechanism whirred as the computer chip fed its contents to audiotape. The window reader had recorded something. Thank God!

Lamb usually waited until he was cruising on the Grand Central to listen to these tapes. Today, as soon as the cassette had rewound, he shoved it into the tape deck.

A computer-generated voice said, "Saturday, May seventeenth. Five thirty-two P.M."

Slam!

"[inaudible] play bodyguard all summer for you." Gimlet was talking. "You know that. But they need a reason. Not some bullshit."

"What about you?" Harrow had come into the house with him. "Can I at least count on you?"

"I said bullshit."

"You want anything? A beer? Can I make you a cheese sandwich?"

"No, nothing. I'll eat at home. If Marge hasn't put the chain up."

"It's a morning."

"It's a day. By the time we get back from Connecticut."

"I should pay my respects anyway. Shaw took the hit for me."

"You can't be sure it was a hit. Nobody can be sure what happened to the guy—he was too badly burned. They had to identify him through his dental records."

"Come on—I set a trap on television by saying I know something, and he blunders on acting like he knows it too. That night his cabin burns down, and he's charred enough to obliterate all signs of torture. You think that's coincidence?"

"Stranger things have happened. Anyway, why would he come to the funeral? When has he ever come back to gloat? Or maybe you spotted him at Roger's grave, weeping into a pillow?"

"Shaw was a celebrity."

"So our boy will show up to get his autograph?"

"I already cut a deal to dress up as a chauffeur and drive one of the hearses. I'll need *some* backup, for God's sake."

"If he shows."

"I've got a hunch he will."

"You had a hunch he'd show here."

"So he waxed Shaw instead. I was half-right."

"Half something."

"What's your problem?"

"You're dancing to the dog whistle. I can't hear the tune."

"Then do it as a straight favor, okay?"

"Damn, I'd love to, but that's the day I'm getting my hat blocked."

A chair scraped the floor. Footsteps.

"You were my partner."

"You called that marker last night, remember?"

A door opened and closed with a soft *Clump.*

CRASH! The rattle and clink of dancing glassware. Harrow had walloped the kitchen table.

"Shit!"

Silence. The indicator light winked out.

And stayed out.

·36·

"Pontormo! Pontormooooo! Where, in God's name, is that dog hiding? Pontormo, baby, come to Mamma! He always does this the day of a show, he knows it drives me wild. PONTORMO!"

"Shut up, Nan!" Sally shouted. "I'm trying to concentrate!" Sally glared at the blank piece of paper in the typewriter. How was she supposed to get any writing done with her mother bellowing like a moose for its lost calf?

Maybe she should do a story about her relationship to Nan. Mother and grown-up daughter trapped in a house together fight furiously as they always have until they gain new respect for each other as they finally see that although they seem totally different, they are actually the same person? Symbolized by a little cherry-wood escritoire that the mother got on her wedding day from *her* mother, with three drawers, one above the other like the three generations, and they polish it together and in that simple domestic chore the daughter comes to realize how each fits into her own place in a larger structure . . . *Yech!* Puke! Break my thumbs! Stop me before I kill more!

"Sally, dear."

Nan was standing in the doorway of her room. Her voice was a velvet-wrapped razor. "Would you come out here, please? I want you to see this."

Sally followed her down the hall to Winston's closet. He was hugging and petting something that looked like a kielbasa with hair. The kielbasa was licking his face with a joy not shared by Nan. Indignantly, she scooped Pontormo into her arms.

"I didn't spend all morning shampooing and combing this dog, so this, this—*individual* could mop the closet floor with him."

229

"He looks all right to me."

"Everything looks all right to you. Unfortunately, you're not a show judge. He's all mussed up, aren't you Ponty! Ponty says, 'Dat's wight. I a muss.' "

"A little muss is good. He looks *vivant*. It's quite becoming."

"If you're going to stay here, you've got to keep that boy out of mischief."

"What mischief? He was petting your pooch."

"This pooch isn't for petting; this pooch is for showing! You keep that dim-witted brat away from him."

"Don't you call him a dimwit!"

"Why not? He's autistic. He doesn't understand words."

"He's not autistic; he doesn't choose to speak."

"Who had the bright idea to name him for a great speaker like Churchill? This one is more like Coolidge. Silent Cal."

"You should be ashamed of yourself!" Sally said. "How can you say such things right in front of him?"

"Oh, poo! He has no idea in God's green earth what I'm talking about."

"Yes he does. He's looking right at you."

"He's looking at Pontormo. Pontormo is the one who understands me."

Sally's eyes blazed. "That is such—wait, watch this: Winston, do you want pizza now?"

Winston nodded gravely.

"He knows what *pizza* means," she said triumphantly. "Isn't *pizza* a word?"

Nan held out her hand to the dog. "Ponty here knows some words too, don't you, boy. Shake, Pontormo. Shake."

The dog put his paw in her hand. They shook.

"You are disgusting!" Sally shouted. "How can you compare this child's mind to a dog's?"

"I'm not. I'm merely pointing out that reacting to words isn't the same as using language."

Sally glared venomously at her. "Stay there. Don't move." She got the telephone from her bedroom. The wire was just long enough to reach Winston's closet.

"What's he going to do with that?" Nan asked. "Call his broker?"

"Where's the number for the pizza parlor?"

"On the bulletin board in the kitchen. Don't tell me he's going to order pizza?"

"No, but I bet he can dial the phone. He's watched me do it often enough."

"Don't be ridiculous. He won't even know what you want him to do."

"Five dollars?"

"You're being utterly silly."

"Chickening out, mother dear? Afraid he might do it?"

"All right," Nan said. "I'll see your five and raise it to the price of a large pizza. At least we'll have some lunch out of this nonsense."

"You're on," Sally said. "Back in a mo. Hold the phone."

A minute later she bounded back up the stairs and rattled off the number to Winston. "All you do is press the right buttons in the right order."

"If he knows what a number is. Or a button."

Winston tapped Nan's knee gently with the receiver. Surprised, she took it, unable to believe he had dialed it in so short a time.

"Post-Graduate Pizza, please hold."

"Well?" Sally asked.

"Some autistic kids are good at numbers," Nan said slowly. "He must be one of those."

Sally smiled. "Winston, the lady just bought us a pizza. Sausage and peppers, right?"

·37·

Humphry Shaw was buried—not in the plain New England churchyard his writing style suggested—but in a large nondenominational cemetery outside Stamford, Connecticut. It was called Angel's Rest, and it already held two generations of Shaws.

Julian Lamb lounged easily at the wheel of a nondescript brown rental car and watched from across the highway as Shaw's funeral procession rolled endlessly through the big stone gates.

The funeral had been billed as "just for the family." Lamb saw what that meant when the deceased was a famous author who had been married four times. Ex-wives, their current husbands, relatives, everybody's children, literary friends, literary foes, editors, former editors, agents, former agents, magazine people, friends from the small town where he had lived—on and on they came, a multitude. Good. Harrow would have a lot of faces to peer at and wonder about.

Lamb waited a few minutes to let the big crowd arrange itself at the grave and for the minister to launch into his prayers. He wanted all the attention focused on the burial.

He rolled down the window on the passenger side. He drew a large automatic fitted with a commercial silencer from under his jacket and placed it on the seat beside him. This silencer was even larger than the one he had used on the Grants—longer and heavier than the gun. His shot would be no louder than the click of a dead-bolt lock.

Lamb was using a "safety slug"—so called because it would not penetrate through one person and hit another. Instead, it would expand, tumble, and fragment within the human body, causing enormous damage to flesh and bone.

He started the engine of his car. The cemetery was ringed by a busy

233

four-lane highway. He had to wait for a break in the traffic before he could gun his rented iron across the road, glide through the gates, and cruise slowly, like a late and timid mourner, down the one-lane cemetery blacktop toward the big crowd at the grave.

Organ music filled the air from concealed speakers, endless, lugubrious, a Muzak of death, sweetened with cathedral echoes that made no acoustic sense outdoors. Shaw would have hated it, Lamb thought, but no one had asked him.

His eyes raced along the line of parked limousines on the right side of the blacktop. In one of the cars nearest the grave, he spotted a silhouette in a chauffeur's cap. That would be Harrow. He had slid across to the passenger side of the front seat and was turned toward the grave, studying the crowd.

It was a classic—the car-to-car shot. Usually done at a traffic light just as it turns green.

Lamb had done it before—in Cairo. He had been more worried about the insane traffic than the hit itself.

Everything was dropping neatly into place. The driver's window on Harrow's limo was open. There would be no sound of shattering glass. Harrow was almost certainly wearing body armor, but it didn't matter. He was neatly framed for a head shot by the car window.

In a few more seconds, whisper to a stop beside him, windows lined up. Chances are he won't even hear you. You will raise the gun in one smooth practiced motion.

Assassination is like stage farce. You should rehearse it with a metronome and do it to the beat.

If the rhythm's right, you can't miss. Don't push. Your only enemy is haste.

You will put one bullet in his brain. Verify the hit. Place the gun back on the seat, wait until your right hand is on the wheel, then ease your foot down on the accelerator.

Nice and slow, around the little loop, and head for the entrance.

You will have at least ten seconds before the first scream from the crowd; as much as a minute before anybody puts together what happened—if they do at all. You may be so far away by then that nobody will make the connection. Your license plates are carefully obscured with mud. The traffic is heavy but moving fast. The only awkward bit might be getting on the highway. Don't rush it.

Lamb's car crept along at a walking pace, silent as a cloud. He was at the rear of Harrow's limo now, glimpsing Harrow's back through two thicknesses of black glass.

Lamb eased to a silent stop. Windows aligned. Harrow didn't turn. The gun swept up, his finger squeezed, the gun went *chunk!*

BOOM! Harrow's head exploded with a loud report. Tufts of hair flew in every direction. The body flopped out the window, suddenly slack. Lamb froze, his rhythm broken, the gun still held high.

A dummy! He had shot a dummy! It was a trap! He flung the gun down and stamped on the gas. His tires screamed as he slalomed around the traffic circle.

Far up the road, near the entrance, he saw another car erupt from an innocent clump of trees and barrel directly toward him.

Boom!
Harrow was in the middle of the crowd when he heard the signal charge in the dummy go off. He had disguised himself as a mourner, with glasses, a brush mustache, and some gray in his hair.

As he wheeled he saw a brown car leave the blacktop and bounce off among the gravestones. A second car roared after the first one— Gimlet in hot pursuit.

The crowd surged away from the explosion. Several people fell, others tumbled over them, shouting and screaming. Jake bulled through the crush, fighting his way to the limousine.

He wrenched open the door, dived over the wreckage of the dummy, fired up the engine, and roared off over the wet grass.

Gimlet glanced in his rearview mirror and saw Jake's limo coming up fast behind him, the big car wallowing from side to side, fishtailing through the narrow rows between the graves, banging loudly into headstones. The brown car was ahead and to the right, racing for some trees in the far corner of the cemetery.

They had him! The cemetery was surrounded by a high wall of smooth masonry. Impossible to climb. The only exit was at the front, and now he and Jake were bearing down from either side, cutting off the angles.

The brown car turned sideways and slammed to a stop among the trees.

Gimlet swung his own car broadside and stopped. He kept his motor running, in case the brown car should suddenly start up again and make a run for it. Jake skidded the limo to a stop about twenty yards behind him and bent down, fumbling for something under the seat.

Gimlet jumped out the driver's side and, with his car as a shield, aimed his pistol at the brown car.

"Come out with your hands up! Move! *Move!*" Gimlet yelled. His voice was shaking with rage. When the killer blew the head off the dummy, the man thought he was murdering Jake.

Silence. Gimlet could see no movement around the killer's car. He must still be inside.

As he raised his gun to fire a warning shot, Gimlet heard a tremendous roar to his right. Holy shit! Jake had an Uzi! He was standing straddle-legged behind the limo, the submachine gun braced on the roof, blazing away full auto.

Gimlet shouted, "Stop! Stop!" at the top of his lungs, but Jake just rocked and rolled, aiming below the window line of the killer's car, hosing it down with hundreds of bullets. The side windows exploded instantly—not from direct hits, but from the shock to the doors below them. The windshield blew out, spewing nuggets of safety glass into the trees. The hood popped open a few inches and swayed crazily. The trunk lid snapped open. The car swayed and slumped like a kneeling drunk as one by one the tires went flat. Puffs of chalk dust kicked up from the wall beyond as the high-velocity slugs ripped all the way through the car and out the other side, penetrating two doors and anything in between.

On and on he went, pumping in clip after clip, his face red, the gun bucking and jerking in his hands, seemingly intent on reducing the car to an oil slick.

Gimlet crouched low and raced across the open space between his car and the limo.

In a hairbreadth pause between clips, he shouted, "*Are you fucken crazy?*" directly into Jake's ear.

It was like trying to distract a lion during a kill. Jake didn't hear; he was in a trance. He pounded another clip into his Uzi and slammed it down on the roof of the limo ready to cook off more rounds.

"Jake, *stop!*" Gimlet grabbed at the gun barrel. "Ow! *Fuck!*" The metal was red-hot, he jerked his hand away, elbowing Jake in the chest. Jake grunted and stepped back, noticing him for the first time.

Gimlet shouted, "Hold it! Hold it! That's enough!" Jake squinted at the ruin of the brown car and slowly took his finger off the trigger.

Without warning, he yelled, "Let's go!" and took off at a run.

Gimlet yelled, "Wait!" But Jake was halfway to the brown car, clutching the Uzi carelessly by its barrel, apparently impervious to the blistering hot metal.

Gimlet raced after him over the wet grass to the smoking wreck.

"Empty!" Jake shouted. "The bastard's gone!"

They looked around wildly. He wasn't in the trees, wasn't under the car.

Barely concealed by the width of a small tree: a rope ladder dangled from the wall.

Jake swarmed up the ladder.

"I don't see him!" he shouted at the top.

He swung his legs over the wall and disappeared, dropping to the ground on the far side.

Gimlet climbed after him, pausing only at the top to pull his gun out of his belt before he levered himself above the wall.

He was looking down on a busy four-lane highway. Across it was a marshy field, flat and open, with no place to hide.

He looked wildly around, a feeling of sick fury growing in him. The view was clear for a quarter of a mile in any direction. Where was the killer? There hadn't been time to get away!

Jake was on the narrow grassy margin below him, also looking around in bewilderment, unsure of which way to run.

A green car was passing on the far side of the highway. Gimlet's eye caught a sudden movement by the driver.

"Jake! Look out!"

Chunk! like the closing of a dead-bolt lock, *skreek!* as the car peeled rubber. By the time Gimlet got his pistol up and leveled, the car had already hurtled forty yards down the road. As he aimed it changed lanes and tucked into traffic, making a following shot impossible.

Jake sprawled facedown in the grass, not moving, the Uzi strapped uselessly across his back.

His hair sparkled with blood.

·38·

"*Another* trap? You deliberately lured the killer there to shoot Jake?" Sally shouted.

"We were sort of hoping it would go the other way," Gimlet said.

Sally had been shopping with her mother in Princeton that morning; she hadn't gotten the word that Jake had been shot until after lunch. She felt blindsided; her knees had buckled. Jake shot other people, but nobody was allowed to shoot Jake.

It had taken several hours for Nan to drive from Princeton to the hospital in Stamford. They had stopped numerous times along the way to make frantic phone calls ahead inquiring about Jake's condition. The long tense drive, the snippets of news, now good, now not so good, had left her nerves in rags.

Now she stood with Nan and Gimlet in the main downstairs hallway outside the gift shop, talking to the exhausted, but still sharp-tongued surgeon. Dr. Simon and his team had labored over Jake for four hours in the OR. He'd required two blood transfusions. He wasn't out of the woods yet, but Simon was cautiously optimistic.

"This is your fault, Richard Gimmler," Sally said bitterly.

"It was Jake's idea, you know that. It always is."

"You helped him! You egged him on!"

Dr. Simon raised a restraining hand. "Mrs. Harrow, there's a very good chance Detective Gimmler saved your husband's life. His warning shout caused Jake to look up and take the bullet in the neck rather than the head."

Sally looked stricken. "I'm sorry. I didn't mean . . ."

Gimlet shrugged, embarrassed. "We're all a little shook up here."

"When can I see him?" Sally asked the doctor.

239

"Not for some hours. I want him in post-op until we're sure that wound is going to behave itself. I don't want some sobbing intern hunting for the right-sized catheter to transfuse him at four A.M., if you follow me." He stalked off.

"Just because he's a good surgeon, that's no excuse for rudeness," Nan said. She wandered into the gift shop.

Sally took Gimlet's hand. "Thank you for saving his life."

"I don't know if I did or not. You know how it is on the close calls —somebody always makes up a good story."

"Thanks for trying to save his life."

"Okay, I'll take that."

After a heavy moment Sally said, "So. How did you lure the killer to the funeral?"

"We staged a scene in your house saying that Jake would be at the funeral, dressed as chauffeur, no backup—a sitting duck."

"The killer is bugging our house?"

"So it seems."

"How long has that been going on?"

"God only knows. I've been over it with state-of-the-art equipment —couldn't find zip. Jake figured there must be one because of what happened on the first trap. See, he pretended to freak out on television and implied he knew stuff. Then Shaw grabbed the microphone and gave the impression he might be in on it too. The killer must have been fooled, or he wouldn't have killed anybody. But why go after Shaw? His bug must have warned him off Jake's house."

"*The Silencer murdered Humphry Shaw?*" Sally turned pale.

"What's the matter?"

"It's my fault. If I hadn't blabbed about Haney's arrest, Shaw would still be alive."

Gimlet shrugged. "At least now Shaw can send a letter of apology to Megan Barker. By gopher."

His tough-guy joke fell flat. In a horrified voice, Sally said, "I'll never talk about this damn case again. To anybody."

"Mrs. Harrow? You can see him now."

It was past midnight. Nan was asleep on a bench in the hall. Sally left her there and followed the nurse.

Jake had just been moved from post-op to his private room. Standing outside the door was a man in an orderly's uniform. Sally had already been told about him—he was actually a Stamford cop, part of Jake's armed guard.

The nurse ushered Sally into the room. There was a second nurse, a middle-aged woman, sitting in a chair watching Jake and knitting a sweater. She smiled sympathetically at Sally.

Jake was lying back on the pillow, eyes closed. Tubes ran into his neck from the wall behind his bed. *Tubes.*

What do you say to a man with tubes running into his neck? You say, "Jake? Darling? It's me, Sally. I'm here, darling." You say, "The doctor says you're going to be all right." You say, "I love you."

The pale stranger in the bed didn't react. Not an eyelid flutter, not even the tiniest of smiles. He looked like one of those brain-dead people kept alive by machines; it didn't seem possible that he would ever wake up.

The fluorescent lights buzzed in her ears like biting flies. The knitting needles went clack! clack! The puke-green hospital walls closed in on her.

Her protector. Her wall against the world. Pale as an albino, with tubes running into his neck.

Jake would live, but Mr. Cool Moves was dead.

·39·

Boom!

Julian Lamb resisted the temptation to floor the accelerator. Harrow's friends might be watching; there was danger, even half a mile away. Merely speeding up right after an explosion might cause some alert citizen to note his license number.

He continued slowly along the neighborhood street. No one looked out a window or came out on a porch. It was a muggy May morning in Queens; the neighbors probably thought they had heard the first Fourth-of-July cherry bomb.

They had actually heard a large chunk of C-4 that Lamb had wired up for just such a contingency. Although too cautious to get close enough for a visual inspection, Lamb could tell from the noise that the explosion must have blown away the entire top half of a big box elder tree—and vaporized the window reader that had been trained on Jake Harrow's house.

His magnificent laser window-reader! It was a CIA special, irreplaceable on the open market at any price. The risks he had taken to hold on to it! And now Harrow had forced him to destroy it!

Not that there was any point in retrieving it. He had been fooled, tricked, *raped!* Harrow and his sidekick had been playing to him the other day—performing for his benefit. They had used his own bug against him—fed him false information—led him into a trap. They had almost killed him! He could still hear the bullets slamming into the wall just below his feet as he scampered up the rope ladder.

No more bugs. He couldn't trust them; he would never know when he was being spoon-fed more lies. His ears had been stopped, his eyes poked out. His edge had been his little listening post. Without electronic surveillance, he had no way of keeping tabs on what Harrow was doing.

Lamb was on the Grand Central Parkway now, miles from Harrow's house. He had blown up the window reader and gotten away cleanly. But instead of relaxing, he grew more and more tense. All bets were off. Harrow wasn't going to die; the news had come over the radio this morning—he was no longer critical; he was out of danger. Soon he would be back on the trail.

Damn him! How could he have possibly found out about the window-reader? And the Grants? And the policeman's uniform?

What was Harrow's source?

·40·

"The great motor mouth is silent at last!"

It was Friday afternoon. Jake had a visitor: Captain Cowen.

He placed his gift, a large basket of fruit, on the table by the hospital bed.

Jake was awake and alert, but the bullet had nicked his vocal cords; it would be some time before he could speak. He wrote on his pad and flipped the sheet to Cowen: PEEL BANANAS BEFORE PUT IN I.V.

Cowen chuckled expansively at his own gaffe. "Ooops! Guess it's kind of hard to eat with your laryngitis. Well, you can use this stuff to bribe the nurses to rub your back. Listen, I don't want you to worry about somebody taking another shot at you. The Stamford police are all over this hospital like a flasher's raincoat. You're well protected. I want you to relax while you're here. Don't worry about a thing. Just concentrate on getting well."

The better to deliver his reassurances, he plumped himself down heartily on the bed. When he saw Jake's grimace of pain, he jumped up again.

"Sorry about that." He pulled up a chair to the bed and settled himself for a good chat. "By the way, don't worry about your departmental hearing. It won't even be rescheduled until you're feeling better."

Jake stared at him in disbelief. He scrawled: "STILL ON?"

"I'm afraid so. The commissioner is furious about your fighting with me on TV. Says you embarrassed the whole department."

STILL SUSPENDED?

Cowen displayed the tiniest of gaps between thumb and forefinger. "You're that close to getting booted out."

Jake drew a big ? on the pad.

Cowen shrugged. "You think taking a slug gives you a plenary indulgence?"

PROVES I WAS RIGHT.

"Says who?"

Jake pointed to his neck.

SILENCER'S BULLET.

"Detective Gimmler states categorically that neither of you got more than a distant glimpse of the guy. You can't even be sure the guy who shot you was the same one you chased."

Jake tried to shake his head in disbelief, winced, thought better of it.

WHO SHOT ME? HANEY?

"Wouldn't that have simplified things! Unfortunately, Haney is still in his cell in Florida. I tell you, Brasswater is absolutely determined he's the Silencer. He's obsessed. The less he finds, the harder he looks. My hands are tied, you know that. I have to wait until he's played out the last inch of line."

Under WHO SHOT ME? Jake crossed out HANEY? and printed SHAW?

"Ever the wit!" Cowen said merrily. "Actually, I'm glad you brought that question up. I've given it quite a bit of thought."

HERE COME DE FUDGE.

Cowen laughed enthusiastically, his eyes frigid. He took a press release from his inside jacket pocket and handed it to Jake. "See what you think."

The release was a fantasy about a grudge-bearing parolee (unnamed) from an unrelated case who had tried to kill Jake Harrow at Angel's Rest. Jake read half of it, wadded it up, and shied it over the end of the bed.

Cowen retrieved it without the slightest embarrassment and lovingly smoothed out the paper. "Just denying it was the Silencer—that's not enough. You always need a competing story for the media, something with a little meat on its bones. So we improvised. But something close to that might be true. You've put away some pretty rabid squirrels in your time."

Jake glared.

"I hear you. Uh, see you, anyway. Maybe Haney isn't the guy. Maybe we're wrong and you're right. As soon as that bandage is off your neck, we'd like your help. We need you back on the team again, instead of running a sideshow off on your own. We're offering to drop all the charges against you, quash the hearing, reinstate you clean as a whistle."

IF I SIGN OFF.

Cowen handed him the press release again. "Just give me your John Hancock. Anywhere there on the bottom."

Jake wadded it up. This time he flung it at Cowen, who caught it deftly and began smoothing it again.

"I don't need your signature; I can send this to the newspapers anyway. Can't you see I'm trying to help you?"

HELP OR GAG?

Cowen vigorously polished one of his own gift apples on his sleeve and took a vicious bite. "All right. You don't want to sign the release. Will you at least give me your word you won't contradict it?"

LIES HELP SILENCER.

"I'm not asking you to lie. All you have to do is stay away from reporters."

TILL NEXT FAMILY BUTCHERED.

"You think you're the wrath of God, don't you. You're out of control, Jake, you know that? You're not a cop anymore; you're some kind of super-stroke running amok with an Uzi. You ate that car at the cemetery; I saw the pictures. You must have pumped a thousand rounds into it. What was that, Jake?"

WARNING SHOTS.

Cowen flung the rest of the apple into the tall hospital wastebasket and stalked out of the room.

Twenty minutes later, in the hospital parking lot, Captain Cowen slipped into the backseat of a car: not a police cruiser courtesy of the NYPD, but a stretch limousine courtesy of wife Eden. It was Friday; he was not going back to the city.

As the chauffeur back-and-forthed out of the parking space, Cowen phoned the head of public relations back at the precinct. He punched the buttons without looking, squinting up at the sun-baked wall of the hospital with narrowed eyes, trying to pick out Jake's room.

"Harry, my boy, listen closely." He took the crumpled press release out of his pocket, held it to the mouthpiece, and began tearing it up. "Hear that ripping sound? Yeah, it's your masterpiece. Lean muscular prose, that wasn't the problem. Uh huh. He wiped his fundament with it. Because he's wacked, Harry. There is no pea in his whistle; his nightstick has lost its thong. I know he won all those medals. God gives talent to the wrong people, haven't I always said that?"

The press release reduced to confetti on the floor of the car, Cowen settled back on the luxurious goatskin-leather cushions for the long ride to the summer house in East Hampton.

"Just stop. I tap-danced my little heart out; you would have been proud of me. . . . Yes, he read it, the crazy prick wasn't buy— Yeah . . . yeah. . . . Will you shut your big public-relations mouth. Jesus! You're worse than he is, you know that? We hire the handicapped— the mentally handicapped. Yes, I want you to do a new one. Today would be nice—when the hell did you think, Arbor Day? What's your problem—someone else using the pencil? Didn't you have deadlines on the Rock Window *Times-Picayune* or whatever it was you claim you were a reporter for? Or is your résumé as full of shit as the rest of your writing?

"Stop bitching and listen—this will take some crafting on your part. I need a spin on the events at the funeral that leaves the door open to arrest Harrow later on. No, no. Don't point any fingers now, just muddy the waters. Mysterious shoot-out, time sequence unclear—ideally, the kind of open structure where we can drop something in later that pins the tail on the donkey. *Rashomon* it up. Maybe work the insanity angle in the graphics. Headless dummy, car full of holes, inset picture of Harrow. Don't overdo it. I don't want to make it our version versus Harrow's version; I want an official version with some air in it.

"What? Because I'm playing for time, nitwit. We can't arrest him while he's front-page stuff; you want to see him on Channel Five being dragged across the hospital parking lot, handcuffed to his I.V. tower? You're supposed to be explaining this to *me*—do I have to do every-body's job in this zoo? As long as he can't talk, he's no threat. Mean-while, no phone, no reporters, we peek at his mail. Yeah, the doctor says at least ten days, maybe two weeks. By that time this story will be on page thirty-seven below the ship arrivals. That's when we arrest him.

"Uh huh. Welcome aboard. I know his being wounded makes it tricky; that's why I need your head on this one. Uh huh. Interesting. Hmm. Time! You're getting carried away. We can't get into moving wounds around; this isn't the Kennedy assassination. Give me something I can write on the back of an envelope.

"Oh, and anything you can do to make it seem like it wasn't the Silencer at the funeral—Yeah, that's right, calling him the Family Killer helps; Harrow isn't a family, he's a cop, brilliant. Jesus, maybe I should ask Harrow to write it, he'd at least give me something with a little pizzazz.

"Yeah. Yeah. Uh huh. Stop with the reasons why you can't do it, and just fucking do it, all right? That's why they call it *work*, Harry. That's why *we* pay *you*, not the other way around. Yeah. Uh huh. In the time you spent whining you could have already finished the thing.

"Listen to me. I'm on Ninety-five in Stamford. I'll call you again just before I get off the eastern end of the L.I.E., and you better have a decent draft for me. That's right. Or in four weeks, you'll have been gone two. Bye-bye."

He leaned forward and carefully made himself a martini on the back-seat bar. He mumbled to himself, "Duck, Harrow."

·41·

The newspaper stories were teasers, small inside-page items, no byline.

Saturday: "Police would say nothing about the events at Shaw's funeral except that they were 'under investigation.'"

Monday: "Police would not confirm or deny persistent rumors that cocaine was found in the dummy at Angel's Rest."

Wednesday: "Police had no comment on allegations that a bag of cocaine seized in a bust had disappeared from a certain precinct on the West Side of Manhattan and turned up in the pockets of a mourner at Shaw's funeral."

Jake sat in his hospital bed and read the stories with growing rage and fear. Day by day, innuendo by innuendo, Cowen was setting him up. He was going to be arrested, charged with drug dealing. He'd be so busy trying to stay out of jail, he'd have no time for anything else, let alone the Silencer case. The only question was—when would they come for him? How much time did he have left?

He got the answer from Officer Decker of the Stamford police.

Decker was the cop/orderly who guarded Jake's door on the evening shift, a big rangy guy with a hanging lower lip. The assignment was driving him stir crazy—he was up and down, up and down, all evening, bounding around the ward like a hyperactive Great Dane, groping the nurses, yakking with any patient who wasn't comatose and a few who were. He was a kidder, a yeller, a compulsive joker who never noticed that he was the only one laughing.

One night he charged into Jake's room, switched off the overhead fluorescent, cocked the bedside lampshade so Jake was sitting in a pool of light, and went into a war-movie German accent. "So, Amerikaner, you do not vish to talk. Let me remind you, ve haf vays of making you

251

talk!" He fell to his knees, hands clasped in prayer, and switched to Ronald Colman "I say—do talk, there's a good chap. I beg of you. I've got to get out of here—I'm going mad, do you hear me, mad."

So that's it, Jake thought. *The penny drops as soon as my voice comes back.*

He took a noisy breath and moved his mouth as if desperately trying to form words. No sound came out. Decker laughed so hard he drooled.

Enjoy yourself, my friend, Jake thought. *You're going to be working here a while yet.*

· 42 ·

"*Hey! Honeybunch!* My guests are arrivin'. Why ain't you dressed?"
Popsy Payden made a great point of dropping his g's and saying "ain't"
like the English country squire he wasn't.

He had burst into her room without knocking, his plump, baby-
smooth face rosy with cocktails. Through the open door Sally heard
the roar of an academic dinner party, rising steadily in volume like a
747 revving for takeoff.

Almost two weeks had passed since Jake was shot. Sally was still
living in Princeton. She couldn't stay in the Queens house—the killer
might still be bugging it. She floated in a limbo of driving to Stamford
to visit Jake, writing in her old bedroom, and taking care of Winston,
with whom she held long and fascinating—if one-sided—conversations.

Sally crawled out from under the sheet. She had been catnapping in
her jeans and top. She sat on the edge of the bed with her face in her
hands. "Sorry, I just can't face it. I'll take a sandwich here in the room
and catch up on my reading."

"You ain't hiding your pretty nose in a book," Popsy boomed. "You're
comin' downstairs, young lady. And you better get a move on." A
lifetime of riding high on inherited money, laying down the law to
students, and generally throwing his weight around had given him the
habit of command.

"I just got back from the hospital—I'm wiped out." She didn't tell
him she had spent a tense day smuggling a cellular phone into the
hospital. She and Gimlet were the only ones who knew that Jake's voice
had returned.

253

"Pshaw, honeybunch. A party is the best thing for you. Lift you out of the dumps."

"Popsy, ple-*ease*." Where did that princess whine in her voice come from? she wondered. She sounded sixteen. Living at home will do that to you.

"Come on, dumplin', everybody wants to meet you."

"Don't fib. I've got nothing to say to them."

"Then do it for your old dad. I've been really lookin' forward to this dinner party."

Sally found that hard to believe. Popsy gave or attended a dinner party two hundred nights a year. He was one of those people who couldn't abide being alone. And to him, being with Nan counted as being alone.

"Tomorrow night, I'll spend the whole evening with you." Her concessions had started.

"That's much too long for an old dad to wait for his sweetie."

Damn it! she thought. *Doesn't anything get to him?*

"When I was growing up, you were able to survive without me for quite long periods," she blurted. It was a bit more than she had meant to say.

"Anyone would think you weren't livin' in my house and eatin' my food, all for free. All I'm askin' is a little hostess duty."

"You want me to sing for my supper?"

"Duck with oranges."

"How can you be so insensitive! My husband—who, by the way, is also your son-in-law—was shot almost to death. But all you can think about is some party."

He turned a shade pinker, but he didn't back away. Instead he came at her, still smiling, until his face filled her visual field like a great slab of medium rare roast beef. He reeked of an industrial-strength musk clearly designed to spread-eagle females with one whiff. She almost gagged; he smelled like a yak in heat.

"Now dumplin'," he said evenly. "You brought up Jake, not me. But I do read the papers from time to time. I'd be nice to your old Popsy if I were you. You might just need him the next few months."

Two weeks ago, Sally would have told him what he could do with his duck. Now a frightened little voice inside her whispered that she'd better watch her step. Poor Jake might be arrested any day; he was reduced to hiding behind silence, almost like Winston. Her parents were all she had.

"All right, all right, I'll be down in ten minutes."

As soon as she said the words, Sally felt really bad—as if she were one of those female graduate students Popsy was always bullying into bed in exchange for a little guidance on their thesis from its ultimate judge.

"That's my best gal." He moved to the door and then turned back, still smiling. "Wear that white dress of yours. You know I always like you in white."

Ten minutes later Sally came down the big center staircase, wearing the white dress.

She walked through the living room, past the portrait of Nan she had always hated. The painted likeness of her mother stared straight ahead, as full of fake innocence as Doris Day in a sixties sex comedy, deliberately blind to Popsy's flaws and peccadillos.

As she entered the living room Popsy was bellowing, "I've got forty acres up north of here—land ain't worth shucks." The academics listened agog, their booze-brightened faces floating like asteroids in Popsy's gravitational field, secretly thrilled by all the things they pretended to be above, and would joke about afterward—the servants, the finger bowls, the first editions, and family portraits—the whole air of bourgeois magnificence.

Popsy met Sally's eyes as she came in and raised his glass in a silent salute.

He hadn't been lying when he said these people were eager to meet her; she was soon the center of a large circle. The fastidious bookworms wanted to know what kind of ammunition Jake had used in his Uzi. Steel-jacketed? Armor-piercing? Had Jake been wearing a Kevlar vest? One layer or two? Yes, she visited him regularly in the hospital. And do you discuss the case? What—he couldn't speak? Communicated by writing? A bullet nicked his vocal cord, you say? They pumped her for specifics about the wounds as if he were St. Sebastian.

The medical update on Jake was only foreplay. They weren't on a condolence call; they lusted for the inside story: Is it true what we read in the papers—that the shoot-out at the funeral had nothing to do with the Silencer? That there was *cocaine* in the dummy?

Not again! she thought. As if Popsy's veiled threats weren't enough. Was this their idea of academic research—rummaging through the tabloids for dirt on Jake?

She was sorely tempted to denounce Cowen's phony news leaks, his vicious frame-up of her husband. But Jake had told her not to talk about it. He wanted to hunker down in the hospital, play for time, try to come up with leads with his cellular phone. All he cared about was solving the case. He wasn't interested in clearing his name. It was maddening!

Well, somebody had to stand up for him. Popsy was one thing, but she couldn't let these stack-crawling twerps insinuate Jake pushed drugs at society funerals.

She opened her mouth—and closed it again. The last time she lost her cool at a party, she had blabbed the silencer secret to Humphry Shaw. Which led to Shaw's murder. Which led to Shaw's funeral. Which led to Jake getting shot.

"I can't discuss the case," she said. "I'm sure you understand." The professors took that for the coquetry of the insider; it inflamed them more. Had Jake been undercover? Why are the police refusing all comment? Why all the mystery?

"No more, no more, *not another word*," she half shouted. They tightened the circle, closing in on her, attacking her with questions like court reporters hounding a Mafia don.

Mercifully, dinner was announced. Her inquisitors greedily chugged the last of their drinks and looked around furtively for places to park the empties.

Dinner was the usual big production, a sit-down meal for twenty-six, with hired servants, endless courses, and glasses for both red and white wine. Nan presided at one end, with her foot on a button that tinkled bells in the kitchen; Popsy sat at the other, ready to propose a series of toasts typed on cards in his pocket.

As she took her chair she noticed one of the professors from the circle was on her left, and she turned to the man on her right.

He smiled. "What were those people badgering you about?"

"An unsolved crime I vowed never to talk about."

"You'll be pleased to know I have no interest in crimes, solved or unsolved."

"That's good, because one more question about it, and I'm eating at Burger King."

He laughed. "I could see you were suffering."

She leaned toward him and whispered, "I hope you know how to be rude if the man to my right tries to chat about the stopping power of ammunition."

"I'll fight back with irregular Sanskrit verb forms. In a conversation, nothing has more stopping power than that."

She gave him a grateful smile and read his place card.

"Thank you, Dean Orpington."

He winked. "Don't tell anyone—I'm not Orpington. He's my boss. He wangled an invitation and then couldn't make it at the last minute. I'm just filling in."

Sally had never heard anyone say a good word for Wren College, and Middle Eastern languages were not exactly her greatest interest, but Professor Lamb turned out to be a lot of fun. He made Wren sound hilariously mediocre—a Brigadoon of the ninth-rate. They laughed together over a professor from Butte, Montana, who when drunk shouted things like "Unhand me, varlet" at the campus police. And a student who showed up on the wrong day and went through an entire hour of Hebrew irregular verbs under the impression she was mastering Medieval Persian.

He told her he was spending the summer in Princeton to pursue his research in its specialized libraries. He had rented a basement apartment. "I'm surviving, but just barely," he said. "Luckily the owners are in Europe for June, so I've got the run of the whole house. That's all that's saved me from terminal mildew. There's an underground river running through my living room, complete with rocks and ferns. Professor Reuter—that's my landlord—is a marine biologist. He thinks everything should be underwater."

"Reuter? The big black house behind our woodlot?"

"That's right. We're practically neighbors."

She asked him about his research.

"Right now I'm doing a paper on false etymologies," he said. "Typical academic stuff—dry as dust to the nonspecialist, I'm afraid."

"False etymologies? Sounds like you're debunking the dictionary."

"*Dictionaries?* Oh, God." He rolled his eyes. "Dictionary etymologies are a joke. No, no, I'm talking about serious scholars. Even they can be seduced by plausibility."

"Can you give me an example?"

"You know Dionysus?"

"Wasn't he the Greek party god?"

"That's right, the wine-bearer to Zeus." They both smiled as a waiter filled her glass as if on cue. "In Greek his name is spelled like this." He took out a ballpoint pen and printed *Dio nysos* on one of Nan's expensive linen napkins. "*Dio* means Zeus. And *oinos* is wine, as in *oenology.*"

"So *Dio-nysos* was literally *Zeus's Juicer?*"

"Obvious, isn't it. Or so generations of classical scholars thought."

"But it's wrong, right?"

"Dionysus is an ancient name, probably not even Greek. The god was borrowed from Asian religions."

"That's fascinating."

"It pays the rent."

"Publish or perish, right?"

Lamb smiled as if she had made a joke. "Something like that."

Sally hadn't had a pleasant conversation since leaving Queens. Under Lamb's unwavering gaze, she gained confidence, blossomed. She decided that Popsy had been right after all: she was enjoying the party hugely.

Lamb began to talk about his latest project at Wren—a literary magazine. Apparently some foundation had given them a vast grant earmarked for that alone. He wasn't sure why the dean had saddled him with it—maybe he was the only faculty member who was literate.

They didn't have a name for it yet. Did she have any ideas? Something with the word *Wren* in it.

Sally giggled. "How about *Wormy Words for Wrens?*"

Lamb frowned. "This is serious. This magazine could put Wren on the map."

Sally thought he was joking. "The masochist's map—who else would read the output of creative writing courses?"

Too late, she saw she had offended him. He explained sharply that it was nothing like that. They would solicit work from all over—name authors. So little short fiction was being published that magazines like this had become quite important. They had a respectable sale in college towns and quality bookstores; they went into hundreds of libraries; they were read by all kinds of people—including literary agents and big-time editors—they were a place to launch careers.

Sally stopped giggling and mentioned that she herself was a writer. She had been writing a novel of true crime—actually more a study of good and evil.

He turned with sudden hunger to his slice of duck. "I don't know. Action stories—even literary ones—aren't exactly—we're more concerned with subjective experience."

Sally leaned in front of him, her elbow almost on his plate. "I'm so *interested* to hear you say that, because I've come to the same conclusion myself. I've put the action book away and begun work on a short story that's much more subjective. It's completely different from anything I've done before. A real departure."

"I see." He twisted his body away from her, as if about to join the conversation on his far side.

She put a pleading hand on his shoulder. "I was wondering if you —would you consider it for your magazine?"

"Yes, of course. Send it to me in care of—"

"The story is upstairs in my desk. I can give it to you now."

He gave her an irritated look, and she was certain he would refuse. But to her surprise, he said, "Oh, I suppose so."

Sally jumped up from her chair. "You're going to like it. It's called *Silent Seer*. It explores the inner life of a boy who witnesses a multiple murder."

·43·

"Time for your Dalmane," the nurse told Jake.

Under her watchful eye, he popped the capsule into his mouth, and followed it with the water in the plastic cup. As soon as she left, he spat the pill into the bedside drawer with the others.

He peeked through the curtain and frowned. The ugly thing was still parked outside his room: black and shiny, the size of a 1965 Volkswagen: Decker's shoe. Decker's foot was doubtless inside. The rest of Decker was probably there too. Shit.

Jake glared at the ceiling of the dim room and waited helplessly, soothed by the sounds of a great healing institution. Television sets boomed from other rooms, bells and buzzers went off at random, ominously matter-of-fact voices paged doctors, carts crash-banged through the halls like the battle wagons of class warfare.

He could feel the hard angular shape of the cellular phone under his mattress. With each passing minute it bulked larger—like the pea that kept the princess awake in the fairy tale.

How could an energy trip like Decker just squat there on his butt? Didn't he know there were nurses to paw, patients' beds to short-sheet? Maybe one of the staff had slipped him a Dalmane to keep him out of their hair.

Finally, Decker spoke. "Yo! Helen. Lemme help you with that!" Hands at the ready, the grope-meister fired out of his chair and stampeded down the hall.

Lamb was so eager to learn what was in Sally's story, he read it sitting in his car in the Paydens' driveway after the party.

At first he was confused. Who was this little black boy she called

261

Manley, this silent seer who had witnessed a family murder and sketched a silencer?

Then he read how much the boy liked "He's Got the Whole World in His Hands."

That was the song that had driven Lamb crazy on the window-reader tapes! The manuscript rattled in his hand from his excitement. Manley was *Winston!* He wasn't Jake and Sally's son—Roger and Mandy had adopted him. He had witnessed the murders in Skokie, he had seen Lamb's face, but somehow Harrow had kept his very existence out of the newspapers.

Lamb put his head back and laughed in sheer triumph. Fantastic! He had wangled his way into this party to pump Sally for information as a last resort, a poor substitute for the electronic surveillance he feared to use. Lo and behold—she turns out to be a better than the window reader! How often had he listened to window-reader tapes of her or Jake rattling on to the boy without realizing who he was, or what he knew! Sally had delivered the inside story on a plate, thinly disguised as pretentious literature.

Winston was Harrow's secret weapon!

Thank you, Sally Harrow.

"R-R-R-R-Rattlers!" Chuell Vaughn's voice fluttered in Jake's ear.

"Detective Jake Harrow here. Remember me?"

"You called me before, right?"

"That's right."

"You're not the same guy that got in a scuffle with a police honcho down in Daytona are you?"

"The same."

"What's the matter with your voice?"

"I got a bullet stuck in my throat."

"At some funeral, right?"

"You're following the case."

"Somewhat. The Denver papers ran a picture of that car where you installed the Uzi air-conditioning. I'd say you left somebody with beau-coup body work."

Jake got off a bark of a laugh. "Hertz wasn't too happy."

Vaughn laughed too, then fell silent with embarrassment. "Uh, listen man, I want to apologize for coming on so salty to you when you called a couple of weeks ago. I thought you were just some chalk-walkin' cop. I had no idea you were a pistolero like us."

"It's okay. Maybe you can help me."

"Shoot. Get it?"

Jake forced a polite laugh. "Tell me why the Rattlers kicked out Lyle Sturluson."

"Oh, man . . ."

"Did he stop believing in the cause? Turn into a liberal?"

"It's really *necessary* that you know?"

"If he did something illegal, you have my word I won't—"

"Not illegal. Worse."

"What? Buying beers for Ringo's coyote? Tell me."

"Whenever we were up in the mountains on maneuvers, every day he would walk the three miles to the nearest phone to make a call. He said it was to his family, but some of the Rattlers didn't believe him. I believed him myself; some didn't. The guys were getting suspicious that maybe he was an informer or something.

"So to clear things up, one day I got down to the phone ahead of him. The booth was on the wall of a filling station, so I went into the crapper where you could hear real good through the wall, and sat on the pot and waited.

"After about an hour, I'm sitting there, flies buzzing around me, I hear his voice through the wall."

Vaughn stopped talking.

"Was he informing to the FBI?" Jake prompted.

"No, man, he was talking to his family, just like he said."

"So? What was he saying that was so bad?"

"It wasn't *what* he was saying . . . See, first I thought he was talking some foreign language. His people are from Iceland, and they've got a pretty strange lingo up there—like they're always clearing their throat? I could hear that Iceland accent. But then I could hear he was using mostly English words."

"He was speaking English with an Icelandic accent?"

Vaughn could barely force the answer out, so distasteful did he find it.

"No, man, he was talking baby talk."

"What kind of baby talk?"

"How can I explain it? Him and his family had cooked up a baby talk out of English and Icelandic and—you know—*goo goo* and *dah dah* and like that."

"What did it sound like?"

"Like a little girl googlin' to her wetsy doll. Damn it, Harrow, I'm a grown man. I told you about it, but I'm not going to talk it for you. After I realized what I was hearin', I damn near smashed through the wall. I told Sturluson, 'You better start hitchhiking, asshole. You ain't riding back to Beals with us.' I told him, 'We're Rattlers, not prattlers.' I said—''

"Hey, Harrow. Letterman is awarding the Silencer a *medal* for fighting noise pollution!" Decker charged into the room and made for the TV. "This you gotta—''

Jake started to shove the phone under the sheet, then stopped. It was too late. Decker had seen it.

"Why you sneaky fucker! You can talk."

Jake shook his head and pointed vaguely at the phone. Vaughn was talking loudly on the other end, unaware in his fury that Jake was no longer listening.

Decker frowned. "You gonna tell me that's the Weather?"

Jake nodded and extended the handset. Decker came around the side of the bed to take it, but as he reached, Jake jerked the handset away.

"Hey! Gimme that!" Decker yelled, and reached after it, off balance. Beneath the covers, Jake had clamped his free hand around the base unit, making a gladiator fist. As Decker lunged across him Jake slammed it into his jaw. Decker's head whiplashed; his feet left the floor; he crashed to the foot of the bed, bounced off the railing, and collapsed, his face in the blanket, his knees on the linoleum.

Jake sprang up, closed the door, dragged Decker up to the pillow, and pulled the blanket over him. He took a week's worth of Dalmane from his drawer, pulverized it in a glass of water, and dribbled it down Decker's throat.

He was snoring by the time Jake had gotten dressed.

Carrying the cellular phone and the FBI briefing book, Jake eased open the door, waited until the coast was clear, and walked quickly out of the ward.

·44·

Crash!

Winston opened his eyes and stared into darkness, confused between dream and wakefulness. The sound that had startled him awake still echoed in his ears. Had the Constable come for him at last?

Ca-rack! Thunder crashed. Rain drummed on the roof. Only a storm. He was safe.

It was long past midnight. On the second floor of the big Princeton house, everyone else was asleep: Popsy and Nan together in the master bedroom, Aunt Sally across the hall.

He yawned and turned on his side.

Bam-boom! More thunder. And then, downstairs, at the back of the house, as if trying to hide beneath the thunder, a click, a thump, soft footsteps.

He remembered those careful, muffled sounds. He had heard them before, in the house in Skokie.

The first night in this house, he had worked out what he would do when the Constable came for him. There was no place to stand over the back door like at Uncle Jake's, but there was a porch railing leading to a garage roof with a raised edge. When he lay flat on that roof, not even the Constable would be able to see him from the ground. Almost every night in the last two weeks, after everyone else was asleep, he had practiced slipping out of the house and hiding on that roof. It had seemed such an easy game, but now his heart was pounding like he'd run a mile, and he hadn't even started yet.

He crawled forward on his hands and knees. He knew the closet door creaked, so he had carefully left it open wide enough to slip by without moving it.

It was absolutely black in the hall—no night light like Skokie. He straightened up, listening. Far away, he thought he could hear the Constable edging across the kitchen.

His own bare feet made no sound on the carpet. As if he were playing giant step, he walked by memory: step, step, big step over the creaky board, step, step, step. He reached the stairs.

Below, the kitchen door sighed. He didn't have much time. He turned around and started down backward, too quickly to feel for the quiet spot on each stair. Thunder crashed. The heavy static of falling rain covered the faint sounds of his descent.

Over the sounds of the storm, he could catch tense breathing nearby. Then came a squeak like a baby mouse: the floor by the telephone table in the hall. The Constable was only a few feet away. The carriage lamp by the front driveway splashed a faint light through the living room window. Anything more than two feet high was faintly outlined. Winston hugged the stairs, staying low until he was lying on his face on the carpet in the front hall. He rolled to the shadowed wall, as the Constable stepped around the base of the staircase, less than a yard away.

The Constable put his hand on the banister but did not go up. He waited. Had he heard something? In the faint light, his police badge glinted.

Winston held his breath. One stab of bright lightning and the Constable would see him.

The man started up the stairs. Winston lay flat, not moving a finger, until he was all the way to the top. *Stay still!* The Constable paused, listening. Then he started along the hall. Winston crawled through the shadows by the base of the stairs, rose to his feet in the dark hallway, and eased toward the rear of the house.

Step, step, big step over the mouse board by the telephone table. The kitchen door always made a noise, like a sigh. There was no way to stop it. Winston waited with his hand on the door, hoping for thunder. None came. He heard the closet door squeak upstairs and felt sharp panic. The Constable had gone straight to his hiding place; the Constable would know he was running away! He pushed quickly into the dark kitchen and darted to the rear door, quicker than he had practiced.

The back door had two latches. One unlocked one way, one the other. He flung his hand up, twisted a handle, reached above it for the other, slapped wood, realized he had turned the top handle instead of the bottom one, turned it back, turned the bottom one, tugged at the door, realized the door had been unlocked when he started. In his confusion he had locked it! He panicked and began twisting the handles wildly, rattling the door.

Behind him, the thump of running footsteps on the stairs. The Constable must have heard him!

He forced himself to think, finally got it right. He yanked the door open. To his right was the porch railing—his escape route to the garage roof. But there was no time! The Constable was running down the hall.

Beyond the lawn was the dark wall of woods behind the house. They were his only hope.

He ran headlong into the storm, racing across the wide backyard. The soggy loam of the flower beds sucked at his feet. Half-blinded by the drenching rain, his clothes already sopping wet, he tore helter-skelter into the thick bushes.

Sharp branches slashed his face and raked his head; he hardly felt them. He glanced over his shoulder; outlined against the dim whiteness of the house, a shadow darted in pursuit. Lightning exploded all around him like a huge flashbulb, revealing open pathways to his right, thick bushes to his left.

Thunder *crashed!* Winston screamed. The sole of his right foot had come down full on what felt like a spike. He stumbled wildly ahead, pinwheeling his arms to keep his balance, trying to run and limp at the same time. He lost his footing and sprawled full length. As his face thumped the ground a fierce pain exploded in his left cheek, just below his eye.

Stunned, unable to rise, he scrambled on all fours into the thicket he had seen to his left. He crawled to a little open spot deep within and crouched low, partially hidden by the trunk of a small tree. He clawed at his face, found the top of a thorn sticking out of the skin, and yanked it out. A warm trickle of blood slid down his cheek. An intense needle of pain pierced to the back of his head, hitting him so hard he got dizzy and almost passed out. He clutched the tree to steady himself.

Suddenly he was dazzled by a big light, first swinging from side to side, then pointing straight at him. The Constable had a flashlight— the brightest he had ever seen! The beam sliced right through the curtain of rain and protecting branches to shine in his face. For a moment he stared directly into it, hypnotized, unable to believe it had found him so quickly.

A low distant *clunk!* Something smacked into the small tree in front of him, spattering his face with wood chips. The Constable was shooting at him!

Run! Run! Run!

Winston scrambled free of the bushes and sprinted wildly away, deeper into the woods. The pain in his injured foot mushroomed at every step, but he slammed down on it with full weight, too terrified to limp.

His eyes were still dazzled by the flashlight. All he could see was a big yellow circle. He charged through brambles, bounced off saplings, tripped over vines, slid and skidded on mud.

His whole body was one big hurt. Every step brought new cuts, new pain, but he knew that if he paused even for a moment, the flashlight would find him again.

And then a bullet.

The big yellow circle in his eyes faded, became transparent. Now he could see the real flashlight beam all around him, relentlessly seeking him, close as ever, sparkling in the wet leaves, leaping angrily from tree to tree, trying to trap him again in its web of light.

Fear, cold and terrible, choked him. It was just like in the dream. He had never run this hard in his life, but he wasn't gaining, he wasn't getting away! His strength was nearly gone. His legs were like dead logs; he could hardly lift his feet clear of the rough ground. He gasped for air, he tore his lungs out, he still couldn't get enough.

Lightning blazed, slapping his eyes with a glimpse of a calcium world. A clearing lay directly ahead—with a shed in it. It was his last chance.

The rain suddenly bucketed down on him more heavily; he was running through tall grass; he had broken into the clearing. The lightning flash had shown him an overhanging tree behind the shed. In his desperate haste he almost ran full tilt into it. The tree looked too big around to shin up, but he threw his arms and legs wide and flung himself on it. The bark was so slippery his hands could hardly grip it. The tiny footholds broke off against his shoving, pushing feet. He clung to the tree so tightly his shirt snagged on the branch stumps and ripped half off him. With all his remaining strength, he bucked, heaved, and scrambled upward.

His flailing right hand banged against the big branch that overhung the shed. He worked his fingers over it, but the branch was too fat, and when he tried to pull himself up, the hand started to slip off. He let go of the tree with his other hand and swiped wildly upward, over the branch, catching his sliding right hand and pinning it to the branch. He released his legs and dangled, gritting his teeth with the effort of holding on.

Over the top of the shed he saw the flashlight beam explode from the woods, riding on the rain like a searchlight. He kicked back and forth, to make his body swing, and hand-over-handed along the branch, changing grips each time he swung forward.

He dropped to the roof and lay flat, hugging the rough tar paper to make himself as small as possible. Unlike the garage, this roof had no raised edge to hide him from the ground. It also sloped a bit from front to back so that he lay in a sluice of rainwater.

He had trouble catching his breath. He saw colors again, not from the flashlight, but from the effort of running and climbing the tree.

Through the rumble of the rain on the tar paper, he heard running footsteps approach the shed and the rattle of the unlocked door being yanked open. The top of his head only a foot or so under Winston's stomach, the Constable overturned benches and flung around something that sounded like a big metal tub.

Winston's own breathing thundered in his ears. He put his hand over his mouth, trying to still it, but that made him so dizzy he was afraid he'd slide off the roof, so he did his best to breathe quietly by opening his mouth very wide and taking big slow gulps of air.

Thunder went *bang! Slam!* went the shed door. The Constable was outside now, circling the shed, painting it with his flashlight beam. Winston spread his arms and legs and pushed his face into the tar paper, trying to make himself as flat as possible.

The rainwater in front of him suddenly sparked faintly with reflections. He twisted his head and looked behind him. The trunk of the tree blazed with light from below. He heard scraping sounds—the Constable was climbing the tree! In a moment he would be high enough to see over the edge!

Winston wriggled up to the front of the roof, swung his body over, hung by his hands for a second, and dropped to the ground. From his right foot, a terrible shock of pain tore through the whole leg, his knee buckled, and he collapsed sideways in the mud. It hurt so badly he couldn't get his throat open to breathe.

Behind him he heard heavy scraping sounds on the tar paper. The Constable was on the roof.

Get up! Run!

Somehow he scrambled to his feet and pelted into the tall grass, dashing straight down the clearing away from the shed. There was no place to go, no place to hide. All he could do was drive his body on through darkness and rain and wet grass, rasping and sobbing for air, running blindly from the death that was always so close behind him.

But where were the footsteps? Where was the light? Could he be getting away?

Lightning flared, a huge bolt that turned the field to white noon. He flung himself down instantly, twisting to look back as he fell.

For a split instant, he saw the Constable standing on the roof of the shed, like a colossal statue, surveying the clearing.

Had the lightning flash given him away? He didn't know. Sobbing with effort and pain, he scrambled up and raced on.

Suddenly he saw his own shadow, big and undefined, wavering on the ground ahead. The flashlight had found him. The Constable was going to shoot!

Ahead—exposed by the flashlight—a trench cut across the clearing. Winston veered toward it, dove head first, tumbled over the bank, and landed on his stomach in four inches of running water.

Splat! Something whistled through the grass above his head and threw mud in his face—as if someone had narrowly missed him with a large rock.

He ducked low and splashed along the trench. The beam lit up the grass on the far side of the trench, but sailed helplessly above him, too high to touch his racing figure. Winston heard running footsteps behind him. The Constable would be in the trench himself in a few seconds, shining his all-seeing light along it.

The trench had taken him into the woods on the far side of the clearing; the undergrowth looked like a solid wall above him. Lungs burning, he clawed his way up the bank, and darted into the under-brush, ducking under creepers, and wriggling through small stands of trees.

No matter how fast he ran, the Constable ran faster. Already out of the trench, he smashed through the thickets, charging like a bear, closer and closer. His flashlight beam seemed to be everywhere now, lighting up the trees like a fire.

The thrashing sound of his pursuer was louder every second. The Constable was about to catch him!

Desperate with fear, he veered to his left into a particularly thick clump of bushes. For an instant the light was off him. He stumbled ahead, his right foot caught under something; he crashed forward, exhausted, onto a big old circle of wood. As he rolled off, he could tell by the sound there was a shallow space underneath it. He shoved his legs under the wooden circle, levered it up, and wriggled underneath.

To his surprise, the earth was dry here. He slid downward a few feet and settled onto what he thought was the bottom but was only a dense netting of roots and leaves. It gave way under him.

He plunged into darkness.

·45·

"Sal-lee. Sal-lee. Wake up."

Like a scuba diver following her own bubbles to the surface, she swam upward from the abyss of delta sleep and finally opened her eyes. Someone was bending over her in the dark room.

"Jake?"

"Shh. It's four in the morning. I don't want to wake up your parents."

"Honey—your wound." She put out her hand in the dark and gently touched the bandage on his neck.

"The last stitches came out yesterday. Almost healed."

"Why are you here?" she whispered. "What's happening?"

"Decker caught me talking on the cellular phone, and I had to bop him."

Sally sat up in the bed. "You assaulted a policeman?"

"It was either that or let them tie me up with phony charges."

"Jake, what are you going to *do*?"

"Try to solve the case, what else?"

"But they'll be looking for you—the police."

"I'll have to make sure they don't find me."

"But doesn't that make it worse? Becoming a fugitive from justice? Isn't that like an admission of guilt?"

"I'm the only one who's looking for the Silencer. If Cowen shuts me down, nobody will be."

"But how can you look for him if you're on the run yourself?"

"I'll think of something."

"No doubt about that." There was fatigue in her voice beyond the fact that it was four A.M. She snapped on the bedside lamp. "What do you want me to do about Winston?"

271

"Hold on to him a little longer."

"We'd better give him back pretty soon, or I won't want to. I'm getting awfully attached to the little guy."

"It's not really fair to him either, but he's given me just about every break I got on this case. He might come up with more stuff I can use."

"Anything else?"

"I need a chunk of money, and I can't risk using the cash machines. I don't want to leave a spoor for Cowen to follow."

"I'll go to the bank first thing tomorrow."

"They may be watching you by that time. Don't you have any money in the house?"

"Maybe a hundred in my purse . . . wait. Popsy's egg money. He keeps a couple thousand in cash on top of a beam in the basement for emergencies." Sally got out of bed and began to pull on her clothes.

"Great. And I'll need a car. I can't use the Mustang, and I can't rent under my own name. Do you have a friend who could rent one for me?"

"Take Popsy's station car. He never uses it."

"I better not. If he reports it stolen—"

"He won't. I'll take care of him. The keys are under the floor mat on the driver's side."

"You're terrific, honey."

"Jake, will we ever go back to our old life? Will this ever be over?"

He looked at her.

She raised her hand as if to fend off his answer. "Never mind. I know. You have to do this."

"I wish I didn't."

"Me too. I'll get your money."

She disappeared into the hall.

He noticed he was still wearing his hospital bracelet. He took it off, started to toss it in the waste basket, caught himself, and put it in his pocket. It wouldn't do for someone to find it in Sally's bedroom. She was right—he was a fugitive.

He had to start thinking like one.

When Sally came up the stairs with the money, she saw Jake running toward her in the faint spill of light from her room.

"Where's Winston?" he whispered urgently.

"He's not in the closet?"

"His cassette player is there, but not him."

"Have you checked the bathroom?"

"Yes. Could he be in your parents' room?"

"Unlikely. Nan isn't very nice to him. Maybe he got hungry."

"I got in through the kitchen door. I didn't see him."

For the next ten minutes, they searched the house as quietly as they could. They wound up in the living room.

"He's got to be in the house someplace," Sally said.

"The kitchen door was unlocked when I came in."

"Maybe Popsy forgot to lock it. Or maybe Winston was practicing those escape methods you taught him."

"In the middle of a rainstorm?"

"Wait a minute. Jake! Maybe he heard *you* come in, got scared, and made a run for it."

"Oh, God, you're right. I better have a look outside."

Jake took a flashlight and went out the back door. The rain had stopped. He studied the lock. No obvious signs of forcing. He ran the beam around the top of the door. No lintel. But there was a porch railing. He climbed on it and worked his way along, holding on to the side jambs, and calling Winston's name. His shoes overhung the narrow ledge, slipping and sliding on the wet wood.

This is all I need, he thought. *One misstep and I'm back in the hospital.*

The garage roof would have been a perfect hiding place, but the boy wasn't on it. "Why aren't you here?" Jake said quietly. "What happened?"

Jake crossed the lawn and ran his light over the flower bed. Was that the print of a small bare foot, there in the mud? Or his imagination? He thought he saw two toe marks full of water, but he couldn't be sure. The rain had been too heavy. He pushed into the shrubbery.

The lot was overgrown, the night dark, the bushes and trees heavy with water. He moved slowly, calling and scanning methodically with his flashlight beam. He crossed a clearing and trudged through more undergrowth, until he saw ahead of him the back of a large house. He was approaching the next subdivision. Pointless to continue—if Winston had left the woodlot, he could be anywhere in the wide world. If he was still *in* the wide world. Jake turned back and crisscrossed the woodlot for an hour. The edge of the sky began to lift; dawn was approaching.

In the faint light, he spotted a garden shed that he'd missed earlier at the far end of the clearing and trotted over to it through the wet grass.

He swept his flashlight over the inside of the shed.

The wheelbarrow had been flipped over and lay atop a ruptured bag of fertilizer. The wooden benches on each side had been upended.

Jake staggered back, his mouth wide in a soundless shout.

Winston hadn't run away by mistake. He must have hidden in this shed. And here is where the Silencer cornered him and dragged him away to his death.

Jake circled the shed, desperate for a sign that the boy had gotten out, run away. At the back, his eye fell on the tree trunk. Long black scrape marks scored the bark, raw-looking in the sullen dawn light. The branches overhung the roof of the shed. *Why would the Silencer go up there unless he was chasing Winston?* Maybe he didn't catch him in the shed after all.

Heedless of his clothes, Jake shinned up the rough, wet tree and swung himself onto the roof. Muddy smears marked where a large man had scrambled up to the crown. The oncoming daylight was brighter up here and showed colors. His eye was caught by a patch of pink in the center of the roof. Someone had bled there, shielding the blood from the rain long enough to stain the tar paper.

He was swept by gusts of conflicting emotions. The blood showed Winston had been hurt—maybe badly hurt. But it also showed that he had been alive, hiding, trying to escape.

He clambered back down the tree, fell to his hands and knees, and crawled around the house, studying the ground. He found more blood directly in front of the shed, tiny brown specks clinging to the undersides of blades of grass.

He crawled in widening semicircles, trying to pick up a trail. His flashlight beam was now washed away in the morning light; he stuffed it into his belt. The sun broke through the clouds for a moment, brightening the clearing, making colors more vivid. Even so, he picked up only a few more specks of blood.

Anguished and muddy, Jake finally stood up. What small trail he had lead directly away from the shed, down the middle of the clearing. Jake tramped it, head down, eyes intently sweeping the grass.

"I'm sorry, kid; you gotta bleed for me. Just a little, just a drop to show the way."

He jumped a trench, crossed the rest of the clearing, and shouldered through the brush, until he once more came in sight of the big black house in the next subdivision.

Fighting back despair, he turned around and started back. He hadn't seen blood anywhere except right around the shed. Was that where Winston's run had ended?

A few minutes later he let out a whoop. He had spotted a small smear of red on the rocks in the trench, saved from last night's rain by the overhanging bank. It was only visible from the far side of the trench, that's why he'd missed it on the way out.

He darted back and forth, trying to pick out which direction Winston had gone. Damn, it was frustrating! There was no trail on either side of the trench, and if he'd run inside it, he would have been in several inches of water, washing away all signs of his passage.

On one side of the clearing, where the trench plunged into woods, he picked up a track—not of Winston, but of what looked ominously like a large man. Someone had rampaged straight through the nearly impenetrable undergrowth, cutting a track of snapped saplings and trampled bushes.

Even with his predecessor having blazed the trail for him, Jake could hardly follow, so thick were the nettles and vines.

"Winston. Winn-stonn!" he called, trying to keep his voice steady. "Where are you? It's your unca Jake. All clear. You can come out now. Where-OW! Damn it!" A thorn had gone right through his trousers and punctured the skin of his thigh.

As he paused, gingerly pulling the thorny vine off his leg, a voice said; "So."

It wrapped around him like mist, without source or direction.

"Winston?"

Jake stopped pulling at the thorn, stopped breathing. He looked wildly around at the few trees above him. *"Where are you?"*

Again, from the sky, the trees, the empty air, floated that small "So."

Jake shouted, *"Talk to me! Talk to me! I can't find you if you won't talk to me!"*

"I is here here."

Low and to the left.

Jake moved quietly toward the voice, almost tiptoeing into a dense clump of bushes, begrudging every branch crackle and leaf rustle.

"I'm coming. Keep talking."

He skirted a rotting circle of wood and pressed on, stepping quietly, leading with his arms to fend off the branches. The brush thinned slightly, and he found himself in a low stand of young trees.

"Where are you? Keep talking!"

"You did go past," called a hollow voice behind him.

Jake spun around and raced full tilt back into the bushes. The voice seemed so close, but he couldn't tell where it was coming from. "Don't stop now!" he yelled. "Where? Say where you are!"

"Down the ground. I is down the ground!"

The old circle of wood! Arms flailing, Jake thrashed toward it. He squatted low, shoved his hands under the lip, and heaved. Ancient cast-iron fasteners released mushy wood. The entire circle flipped over and crashed into the bushes, revealing an abandoned well. For the first time in perhaps fifty years, motes of morning sunlight danced on the forgotten masonry.

Winston was about twelve feet down, standing on the dry floor, looking up and blinking at the sudden light with a frightened expression on his face.

"Good morning, Mr. Churchill—how do you want your eggs?"

"The Constable did chase mé."

"That's terrible. You must have been scared to death."

"He did shoot at me with his big gun."

"We should flush him down the toilet with the other Constable, what do you say?"

Winston nodded, his eyes darting worriedly.

"He's gone," Jake said gently. "It's safe to come out."

"You is sure sure?"

"Sure sure."

Winston nodded politely, not entirely convinced. Then he said shyly, "I certain starve down this hole. Thanks, Uncle Jake."

Jake said, "Knock it off, chatterbox. Can't you see the field mice are still sleeping?"

· 46 ·

Jake had gotten some rope and a bucket from the shed and hoisted Winston from the well. Fortunately, he hadn't broken anything in the fall.

"Did you know you were bleeding last night?"

"I did step on something sharp sharp."

"Let me see. I take a morbid interest in such things."

The boy leaned against a tree and raised his leg high to display the wound.

Jake knelt and took the foot in his hand to inspect it closely. "Rule three," Jake said. "Never dance on a bear trap."

Jake gently wiped away the dried blood and found a circular hole in the white skin of the arch, with a thick blue line of thorn vectoring deep into the flesh.

He pincered the tip of the thorn in his fingernails and looked off into the bushes. "Is that a fox?" As Winston followed the direction of his gaze, Jake drew out the thorn in one swift motion. The boy winced but didn't cry out.

Jake said, "I did that for a lion once, and he became my best pal." The wound oozed a single drop of blood and then stopped bleeding. He bandaged it temporarily with his handkerchief.

"You shouldn't walk on that foot right now. Better hitch a ride. Up you go." He set Winston on his shoulders and started back to the house.

"Ouch!" Winston's leg was abrading the side of Jake's neck where he himself was bandaged. "Why are you twisting around like that?"

"I is watching sharp for the Constable."

"Can you do it without moving around so much? I wouldn't want to give away our position with screams of pain."

277

Winston settled down, and Jake began to walk.

"You know, Winst, I've been thinking. You and I are in the same boat. You got the Constable chasing you, and I've got the New York police force chasing me. Maybe we should blow this burg, take a little car trip to someplace far away where nobody knows us. What d'ya say, kid? Ready to go?"

Winston bounced on his shoulder with the force of his conviction. "I is ready like anything."

"Ouch! It's a deal then. We hit the road for parts unknown in Popsy's car."

Winston clearly did not like this last piece of information. "You go tell Popsy where we going?"

"I'm not telling a living soul. Or Popsy either."

"It his car," he pointed out worriedly. "He go ask to know."

"We'll be gone by the time he wakes up."

"You go steal it?"

"No, no. Aunt Sally said we can take it."

"You go tell Aunt Sally where we going?"

"Watch my lips. Well, I guess you can't see them from up there. Watch my hairline. I'm not telling anybody. I'm not even telling you. In fact, our destination is so super secret, I'm not even telling me. I'm putting sealed orders in the glove compartment, which I can't open until we're out of New Jersey. And I promise to drive blindfolded. Okay?"

"Okay."

"You're satisfied?"

"I is satisfied."

"Good."

They moved along in silence for a little while through the early morning woods.

In a quiet, insistent voice, Winston said, "Ain't nobody know, nobody does tell the Constable."

At the house, Sally packed up Winston's few possessions, while Jake washed and properly bandaged his foot. The Payden medicine cabinet was plentifully stocked with Telfa pads, peroxide, and bacitracin. Jake stuffed his pockets. He could use them to dress his neck wound too.

No time for breakfast—Nan's clock radio was set for three minutes to seven. With less than a minute to spare, Jake and Winston eased down the driveway in Popsy's green Eldorado—built, as Popsy liked to say, "before they ruined the Cadillac." It was at the awkward age, too old to be impressive, too young for the classic-car rally. Popsy called it his station car, but since he rarely went to the station, and since he drove a Mercedes and Nan a Volvo, it bid fair to last forever.

As he drove slowly through the quiet residential streets Jake said, "There's something I've always wanted to ask you. What does *dead sea* mean?"

Winston flashed him a look of sheer terror. "I isn't know," he said in a strangled voice.

"Simmer down. I didn't mean to scare you. It's just that you say 'dead sea' in your sleep sometimes. Only you say it like this, 'dead sea.'" Jake came as close as he could to the bizarre baritone the boy used.

Winston started at the sound. "The Constable did say that."

"Did he say anything else?"

"He did speak many voices."

"What did he say?"

"Dead Sea."

"Besides that."

"I ain't understand." He looked like he was about to jump out of his skin with fear.

"If you think of anything else he said, you tell me, okay?"

The boy nodded, looking so worried that Jake reached under the car seat and drew out the little cassette player that he had planned to save for the highway. "Hey, cheer down. Look what I saved out for you. How about a medley of your favorite hit?"

Winston politely set the cassette on the car seat without playing it, loosened his seat belt, and wriggled around until he was kneeling on the front seat and looking out the back window.

"You've got a point there," Jake said. "Before we commit ourselves to the highway, we better cruise around here for a while and see if we can spot him tailing us."

Winston nodded gravely, his eye on the road behind.

"You're wasting yourself there, Hawkeye. I got the back covered pretty good. Sit down on the seat for a second."

Winston got down very, very slowly, watching out the back as long as he could.

"Okay, now," Jake said. "Your job—if you really want to help."

"I does," the boy said fervently.

"Good. Your job is to watch out the right side. Look way over to the next street running parallel to us. Keep your eyes peeled; sometimes you can see through between two houses. People don't always follow from behind; sometimes they'll follow from a street that's going the same way. What you're looking for is a car you've seen before. They can be tricky. If they can guess where you're going, they get ahead of you and wait. We have to be ready for anything. You with me?"

"I is with you." His eyes were already riveted to the window on the right.

They drove aimlessly through the outskirts of Princeton for about twenty minutes. Winston thought he had twice spotted the same blue Volvo.

The second time, Jake pulled over to let it pass. "I'm telling you, that looks like a different car to me. And it's not acting like a follow car. C'mon, everyone in Princeton has a Volvo. Nan has a Volvo. What do you say? Shall we head for the highway?"

Too embarrassed to meet Jake's eyes, Winston stared at the dashboard and shook his head.

Jake groaned. "The problem is, we could drive around like this all day."

"Let we be sure sure."

"Sorry, old bean, but I think the time has come for me to pull rank. We're heading out, because I'm the grownup."

"He did chase me."

Jake gave the boy a surprised look. He drove in silence for a minute.

"I forgot that. Sorry."

He drove into the more commercial area, not far from the university. They were in moderate traffic on a shopping street.

"I'm afraid there's only one way to be sure he doesn't follow us out of town. We are about to do what John Dillinger called, 'Losing the Blues.' You belted in pretty tight? Better put the cassette player on the floor; it's going to wind up there anyway. The words turn signal have lost all meaning for me."

He slammed the wheel hard left and roared up the alley between two stores. "Watch your mirror! Pray for Popsy's shocks!" Jake wheeled left behind the buildings and jounced across a loading area, snaking between parked trucks. Winston held on for dear life, one hand on Jake's pants belt, the other on his own shoulder strap, his eyes rock-steady on the right-hand mirror. They squealed through an areaway, crossed a back street, jumped a curb into the rear of a restaurant parking lot, empty at this time of day.

"Caution," Jake said. "Do not attempt these maneuvers yourself. Professional stunt driver." He fired right, fishtailed up a rutted drive, and turned the wrong way onto a one-way street. He ripped off a hundred wrong-way yards past neat white clapboard homes, stomped the brakes, whipped into a private driveway, and drove directly into the open garage beside a Nissan Sentra.

"Let's watch," Jake said.

Nothing went by for a good two minutes. Then a truck.

"See any Volvos, blue or otherwise?" Jake asked.

Winston shook his head.

"Are we clean?"

"I ain't know yet."

Jake lolled back in his seat, eyes on the rearview mirror. "We'll hang out here till you're sure."

They sat for ten minutes. Winston got out of the car, went down to the street, and looked intently in all directions, then came back.

"We is clean."

Jake made an okay circle with forefinger and thumb. "If you say so, partner."

A man in a banker's gray suit came out of the house, opened the door of the Sentra, threw his briefcase on the seat, hung his jacket over the rear right door, climbed behind the wheel, saw the other car in his garage, blinked, rolled down the side window on the passenger side, tapped his horn to get Jake's attention, waited until Jake had rolled down his window, and asked, "What are you doing here?"

"I'll take it," Jake said brightly.

"Take *what?*"

"The garage. Oh, not for me. It's a replacement garage for one I broke. You gift wrap?"

The man looked puzzled. "You've got the wrong place."

"You're not having a garage sale? Damn that *Penny-Saver!*"

The mailbox said *Reuter.*

The great black house backed on a hillside, four stories tall, almost threatening against the morning sky. A flagstone stairway toiled fifteen feet from driveway to front door. The basement apartment had its own entrance and high greenhouse windows that displayed the leafy upper branches of potted trees.

Inside, beneath the trees, a small underground stream with a white gravel bed flowed in a lazy S from wall to wall, gurgling noisily, sounding more like a storm drain than a babbling brook. Rocks. Lily pads. Fronds. Beside it on the tile floor, a glass coffee table, surrounded by beach chairs.

Julian Lamb slumped in one of the chairs, still dressed in a soaking wet policeman's uniform, his shoes caked with mud, his gun and flashlight on the floor by his hand.

For the hundredth time he visualized the closet at the Payden house, every detail blazing in the glare of his halogen flashlight—a child's cassette player, a water turn-off valve, a pillow still dented, a blanket thrown back, a pair of sneakers grinning like twin idiots, the small mattress *empty!* He remembered staring at it, stunned, uncomprehending, like a man opening a safe to find his life savings gone. He had put his hand on the mattress and felt the warmth whisper, *He was here only a minute ago.*

And then, faint and far away, the rattle of the kitchen door.

How did he get by me?

Did he know I was coming? Was he warned? Did he recognize the policeman's uniform? I wore it for the neighbors; I wasn't worrying about him.

And the sheer *speed* of him! Reading Sally's story, Lamb had envisaged a torpid little black mushroom rooted in the back of a closet. This kid had melted away in the underbrush like a startled sable. He had spotted the boy *twice* in the woodlot—and he had escaped both times. It was unbelievable! A six-year-old had done what trained terrorists had never been able to do—evade him, outsmart him, beat him!

He knew now that his big mistake wasn't the homemade silencers: it was missing Winston that first time at the Roger Harrows'.

Winston had seen him twice now. Winston was the source of Harrow's inside knowledge, the worst danger.

Before Harrow got out of the hospital, the boy had to be killed.

And not for pleasure. This was Red Queen all over again.

Winston was no longer a victim.

He had become a target.

·47·

He's got the whole world in His hands,
He's got the whole world in His hands,
He's got the whole world in His hands,
He's got the whole world in His hands.

By one that afternoon, they were rolling west on the Pennsylvania Turnpike. Winston had been playing "He's Got the Whole World in His Hands" steadily since Princeton. Once more he stopped the player at the end of the song.

Jake groaned. "I can hear you rewinding the baby boom-box, guy. I have this wild hunch you're going to play 'He's Got the Whole World in His Hands' again? Am I right?"

The boy nodded.

"This trip is turning into Hands Across America," Jake said. "You got something against 'Skip to My Lou'?"

Winston shrugged. 'The Whole World' go do me."

Jake broke up. "That's a mercy. I'm fresh out of other planets."

He's got the little bitty babies in His hands,
He's got the little bitty babies in His hands,
He's got the little bitty babies in His hands,
He's got the whole world in His hands.

The turnpike restaurant didn't offer pizza. Winston settled for a burger plate. Jake had one too. It tasted wonderful after the hospital food. He ate so ravenously, he didn't notice they were being watched from another booth.

Winston had a mammoth hot fudge sundae for dessert. He was stuffed to the gills, but it tasted too good to leave. Jake finished his coffee, paid the bill, and waited. The kid's jaws were struggling along in first gear; it looked like he would be there awhile.

"Hang in there," Jake said, standing up. "I'll go gas up the car while I'm waiting and maybe macramé a couch."

He fueled the car and then walked to the row of pay phones in the lobby of the restaurant. He noticed he was moving slower than usual, just dragging along—he hated what he was about to do: phone "Aunt" Freezie, the woman Joe had moved in with after his wife's death.

He could have called her from the car on the cellular phone, but he didn't want Winston listening—he was too embarrassed.

He could still see her in his mind's eye: a pale sweet-natured woman with wisps of hair sticking out of her babushka, always worried about something. He remembered listening in sullen silence as she talked about how much she had to offer his father: by which she meant the big house and the annuity she had inherited when her parents died, and her willingness to take care of his boys. How he had resented that! No one could replace his mother!

Once Roger had pointed out to him that they had come to live with Aunt Freezie practically from the funeral. Joe and Freezie must have known each other pretty well before their mother died. Jake asked him what he meant, and Roger made the mistake of telling him. Jake had burst into tears and punched him so hard, Roger never mentioned it again.

Jake still cringed to remember a prank he'd played around the time she and Joe broke up. He had lashed the rear bumper of his dad's old blue Chevy to the supports of her garage. His dad had tried to drive away and pulled the whole garage down.

Strange how the limited ideas of childhood can linger. Because of his chagrin over her garage, he had not once called or written her in all these years. He had never talked about her, not even with Roger. Sally had never heard of her. Neither had Gimlet nor Gatto nor anyone he knew from his single days in New York.

Which made her house the perfect place for him to stash Winston for a while. But it did not make this phone call easy. C'mon, he thought, *what are you getting all tense about? You probably won't even reach her. It's been twenty years. She's most likely moved, or gotten married with kids of her own. Maybe she's dead, or living in St. Louis with a gandy dancer.*

He hunched over the end phone in the row to get as much privacy as possible, took a deep breath, and lifted the receiver.

Winston finally could eat no more. He pushed away the fluted glass and looked up. Four middle-aged black women stared down at him.

Their leader seemed to be a gray-haired woman in brown slacks. She pointed at the glass. "Did you eat all that?"

He nodded.

"My what a big boy. I bet you like ice cream."

He nodded.

"What's your name?"

"Winston."

"Where's your mamma, Winston? Do you know?"

"She dead."

"See that?" another of the women said. "I told you we should mind our business."

"Be quiet, Marletta. We're not breaking any laws," said the tallest of them.

"I'm sorry to hear that Winston," said the gray-haired lady. "What about your daddy?"

"Stop beating around the bush," said the tall one who had silenced Marletta. She leaned over Winston. "Are you supposed to be with that man? The one who was here before?"

Winston nodded.

"You're sure of that? We're trying to help you."

"I is sure sure," he said in a small voice.

"What's he doing with you? Why are you two together? We're your friends, Winston. You can tell us."

"Do you know your home address? Just tell us that," said the woman with the gray hair.

"Has he told you where he's taking you?" asked the tall one.

Winston took a deep breath and said in a loud voice, "He go take me to play in the chess championship."

The tall woman recoiled as if stung. "Why didn't you tell us sooner?"

"I is from Cameroon," he said grandly, as if that explained everything.

"Can we please leave before that man gets back," Marletta said.

It was too late. Jake was approaching fast, with a big grin. "Winston, you devil. I turn my back two minutes, and you're surrounded by women. Let's go, let's go. That sundae has cost us a thousand miles."

To the women he said, "Sorry to break up the love feast. He's quite a charmer, isn't he."

"And so intelligent," the tall one said. "Imagine playing championship chess at his age."

Jake and Winston looked at each other.

"Some of the older grand masters are terrified of him," Jake said. "They never know what kind of crazy stuff he'll come up with."

"We got every kind of music here," the store manager said. "What you looking for?"

"Tell you the truth, I don't know," Jake said. He was staring in confusion at a large display of tapes in a five-and-dime outside Wheeling, West Virginia. Winston was waiting for him in the car, listening to "He's Got the Whole World in His Hands."

"We got country-western, gospel, bluegrass, polkas, operas, rock and roll—you name it, we stock it."

Jake snapped his fingers. "You know what he might like? Reggae. Do you have any reggae?"

"Comin' up." The manager dug deep into the back of a drawer and brought out a tape of Scott Joplin.

Jake covered his mouth as if he suddenly needed to cough. After a moment he said, "Not *ragtime*, *reggae*. You know, West Indian music. From the islands?"

"Don't get much call for that here in Wheeling. I had a steel band playing Beethoven's Fifth Symphony, but it sold out. Lemme think here. Island music. Hold on, hold on, I got just the thing. You're gonna love this."

Five minutes later on the highway, Winston was listening to his new tape.

"DAY-O, DAY-AY-AY-O . . ."

When the music finished, Jake said, "What do you think, Winst? Pretty good, huh. Island music. Like back on Trinidad."

Winston nodded. "I did hear it before."

"It was the only West Indian music they had."

"I did like it," Winston said, as he took the Belafonte cassette out and put back the two Gitt brothers. "Thank you."

"Things could be worse," Jake said. "If your favorite song was 'Kung Fu Fightin',' I'd be in a jar at Johns Hopkins."

Three-fifty-nine P.M. No "Whole World in His Hands." Winston was thrilled to turn it off for a chance to dial the cellular phone, a piece of equipment that fascinated him like nothing else—perhaps because he already knew how to dial it. Jake, his eyes on the highway, recited the number of a public phone in downtown Manhattan and put out his hand for the receiver like a surgeon reaching for a scalpel.

Half a ring. Gimlet's voice crackled, "Dr Pepper."

Jake gave Winston a crisp "mission accomplished" nod; the boy's face lit up.

"You heard what happened at the hospital," Jake said.

"Yeah. Where are you now?"

"Ohio. Moving west."

"Maintain that heading."

"Anything in the papers?"

"Nothing."

"I had no choice—Decker caught me talking on the phone. I hope this doesn't get you in hot water."

"Actually, it may work out good. Treva tells me Cowen talked the Stamford cops into sitting on the assault charge. No dope story in the papers this morning either. I think he's scared to accuse you—you might just break the Silencer case the same day. He'd have to drop the charges or prosecute his own hero cop for dope dealing. You put him in a no-win situation by flying the coop."

"I love it."

"I'm rather fond of it myself. I was also at Angel's Rest, remember? Cowen was planning to promote me to an instant drug-lord too."

"I've been worrying about that. I never thought—"

"I knew I was taking a chance. But do me a favor. Don't come back to New York without a new head or at least a sex-change. Quite a few people have an eye out for you. Even Meatball was sliming around my office, inquiring casually if I'd heard from his partner, subtle as an elephant's prick."

"Helping me out has really done wonders for your career."

"Yep. But I've been back-rooming to cover both our asses. You know the black TV reporter—Trask Walkins?"

"Wait a minute. Trask Walkins. Why do I think he's a good guy?"

"He had to hire bodyguards after he did that story about stun-gun torture in a Brooklyn precinct. He's not in anybody's pocket."

"You've contacted him?"

"I've had two meetings, plus two phone conversations, since Thursday. Lucky I had his ear *before* you booked. Nobody ever buys a story after the fact."

"He's on our side?"

"He's on nobody's side, but his mind is open. When you get something, he'll listen. So Jake, my advice to you is—get something."

"I got him. Winston."

"You've had him for weeks."

"Yeah. But he saw our friend again last night. And he's broken radio silence. Think you can get an Identi-Kit to me?"

"Give me the address. Slowly, I'm etching it into my flesh."

> He's got the gamblin' man in His ha-ands,
> He-ees got the gamblin' ma-an in His haaands,
> He-ees gah-aht the ga-amblin' maaan . . .

Late in the day, the Gitts lost their git-up-and-go. Their pitch began to wow, their timbre to shiver. Winston punched the "off" button and looked mournfully at Jake.

"It does need batteries."

"We can't go looking for them now."

"Why for not?"

"I want to make Cincinnati before we stop."

"Why for we must?"

"Come on, guy. We can't stop now. We're on the lam."

"Okay." Winston looked more and more mournful.

"Maybe they'll have some at the motel where we stop."

The boy nodded.

"I'm sorry, Winst, but that's the way the mop flops."

"You is right."

"Thanks for seeing it my way."

"The two of we is running like lambs."

They drove in silence for several minutes, Jake looking straight ahead, Winston staring at his dead cassette player.

Jake got off the highway to look for batteries.

> He's got you and me, brother, in His hands,
> He's got you and me, sister, in His hands,
> He's got you and me, brother, in His hands,
> He's got the whole world in His hands.

"I'm starting to feel like he's got my whole neck in His hands!"

Night had fallen. They rolled through southern Ohio on a battered four-lane highway.

"Hey—look what's under the dashboard—a flashlight. Why don't you take a break and play with that for a while? Blind oncoming drivers, cause a nine-car pileup, something to soothe my nerves."

The boy yanked out the flashlight and began shining it around the inside of the car.

"Not in here, Luke Skywalker."

Winston pointed it out the window, nearly straight up, and watched fascinated as it winked over treetops and utility wires.

The Gitt brothers kept right on singing.

"Oh, no. The 'Whole World' light show."

Winston smiled. The idea seemed to tickle him.

"Hold on, hold on here," Jake said. "This car has a radio. Maybe I can find something really good, like 'Disco Duck.' "

Jake scanned with the car radio until he heard a man with a hard-hitting backwoods accent intone, "Having trouble reading telephone books, newspapers, and the Bible? You need glasses, my friend. For five dollars plus postage and handling, we will rush you a fine quality pair of glasses by return mail, satisfaction guaranteed. Write *Glasses*, post-office box . . ."

"Listen to this, Winston! We've got the real thing here."

The announcer twanged, "And now, number three on the Hoe-down Countdown . . . that latest hit from the brothers Gitt . . ."

Jake pounded the wheel in glee. "I don't believe it! The Gitts! They made the big time! They're stars!"

The Gitt Brothers, so heavily doubled and reverbed they sounded like an octet, launched into something called, "When A Honky-Tonk Trucker." Jake joined in lustily, making up his own words when he couldn't predict them:

"When a honky-tonk trucker takes off his ring,
He'll swear that he loves you, but it don't mean a thing."

Winston looked down from his light show just long enough to turn up "He's Got the Whole World in His Hands."

Jake cranked up the radio volume and sang louder himself:

"That little white line on his finger so tan
Lines your highway to heartbreak with another gal's man."

Popsy's Eldorado flowed on through the big American night, a four-hundred horsepower king-size mattress. Winston's flashlight probed skyward like the searchlight at a Hollywood premiere. Jake and the Gitts flung their voices out the window like jubilant drunks strewing pocket change, the words glancing off signposts and trees and telephone poles to get lost forever in the grass.

· 48 ·

It was a bright Monday morning on Nassau Street in Princeton.

Lamb leaned back in the doorway of a bookstore and waited for Sally to emerge from the bakery down the block.

Despite his desperate need to find out what had happened to Winston, he was jittery about the encounter. He wasn't worried about her, but about himself. The other night at dinner he had become dangerously excited. She had been close beside him for hours, talking, laughing, moving her body, brushing against him. The longer he had looked at her, the more beautiful she had become. He had found it nearly impossible to wrench his eyes off her. After two glasses of wine, his window-reader tapes of her making love with her husband had begun to play in his mind. As she had spoken earnestly about literature in his ear, she had screamed "OH HONEY-TIGER! OOOOH SO GOOD!" in his head.

He must be careful to avoid being alone with her in secluded places. Why test himself? He could not afford to lose control. She was ideally placed to tell him what he desperately needed to know—without his having to ask her. Her very schedule, her comings and goings, would reveal when Harrow left the hospital—and could be killed. She had given him a story about Winston—a vague and disguised diary, but a diary nonetheless. Best of all, she was *unexpected*. Harrow would never think to plant disinformation with his own wife!

He spotted her in the glass well of the bakery's revolving door, swung his green book bag over his shoulder, and began walking ahead of her as if he'd come out of the bookstore.

"Professor Lamb! *Professor Lamb!*"

He turned and feigned a startled look, then smiled in recognition as she ran up to him clutching her bag of croissants.

"Mrs. Harrow. We *are* well-met. I've been meaning to call your mother to thank her for the delightful evening. Perhaps you can convey my appreciation to her." He winked at her. "Tell her how much Dean Orpington enjoyed himself."

"I shall tell her, your Dean-ness." She shifted from foot to foot, groping for a way to continue the conversation, obviously afraid to ask him if he had gotten around to her story. "Uh, so, have you caught any fish in your living room?"

"I'm settling in, thanks."

"How is your research going?"

He shrugged. "The usual academic forced labor. Bailing the ocean with a teaspoon." He decided he'd teased her enough. "Listen, it's important we talk about *Silent Seer.*"

"You've read it already?" She seemed more scared than pleased.

"I dipped into it on Saturday night after the party, frankly expecting, well, at best—intelligent mimicry of current literary fashion, shall we say? You surprised me. It kept me awake a good part of the night."

"You liked it?" she asked, not ready to believe good news.

"What a tour de force—viewing everything through the eyes of a wordless child! He's so utterly alone. I loved your technique of naming only him and describing the adults only as they impinge on him— sometimes you can barely tell whether they're men or women."

He was thinking, *The damn thing drove me crazy! Half the time I couldn't tell what was going on. She obviously wants to write about Winston without writing about the case.*

"And you think it's okay that I never describe the murders? I was a little afraid the reader would have no idea what was going on."

"That's wonderfully eerie. The business with the drawing game and the tape recorder—Is it therapy? Is the boy insane? But then when someone lifts him up to look through the glass at a man in another room—without words, without explanations—you know that's a suspect in a murder."

"That's exactly what I was trying to do. I'm so glad it all worked for you."

"It's incredibly powerful. I don't know when a piece of prose has moved me so strongly."

"Thank you. That's great! Wow!" She blushed; she smiled; the sun rose in her face.

I did that! he thought, and wanted to kiss her.

He paused, letting her savor the moment, hating to spoil her pleasure.

Then he hit her with the four-letter word. "Of course, it needs . . . work."

The Lord giveth and the Lord taketh away. Her smile rheostated down to dim. "How much work?"

He extracted her manuscript from his briefcase. Every page was densely interlineated with his handwritten comments.

She winced. "I thought you liked it."

"As I said, you're trying for a tour de force. Naturally you didn't quite bring it off on the first try."

She tapped her fingernail on the title of one of the sections:

RIVERMOUTH

Lamb had circled it and written "Where is this?" in the margin.

In an aggrieved tone, she said, "Just a minute ago, you told me the vagueness was wonderfully eerie."

"It is. But your story is mostly physical description, and it's very hard to appreciate it without an anchor in reality."

"Isn't it clear this is somewhere in the south, near water?"

"You need the actual place name—the specific city or town. The reader must believe there's something real behind the kaleidoscope of colors and smells and tactile sensations that flood over the boy."

"You think it's really that important?"

"Essential."

"Okay, I'll think about it. You've given me lots to think about. There's more criticism here than story."

"These aren't criticisms; they're editorial suggestions on how to make it better."

"*Editorial?* As in magazine editor?"

"You think I went to this much trouble for my health?"

She brightened up. "You mean if I can satisfy these comments, you'll publish my story?"

"I'll lead the issue with it."

She pumped his hand, delightedly. "It's a deal."

"One small problem. Orpington called me last night. He wants the material for the first issue in his hands by the weekend."

"But the magazine doesn't even have a name yet."

"Orpington should have read the grant proposal more closely. Turns out it's contingent on a panel of writers passing on the first issue. Orpington assures me it's pro forma—but I find it worrying. Your story could be our best ammo—if you can bring out its full potential."

She turned the pages of the manuscript dubiously. "I'll do my best. A week's not much time."

"I feel bad putting so much pressure on you. Any way I can help?"

"You could erase half these comments. No, seriously—it would be terrific if you'd glance over what I'm doing as I go along. I'd hate to find out on Friday I'm on the wrong track."

"How often are you talking about?"

"Ideally, every day."

"When will you visit your husband?"

"I don't think it'll slow his progress if I don't go to the hospital this week."

"I suppose I can work you into my schedule."

"You're living right near me. I could come over in the afternoons."

"No! That wouldn't work. I'd rather meet in Princeton in the mornings. How about that place on the corner?" He pointed to a waffle-and-ice-cream restaurant called The Hole in the Wall.

"That's fine with me. I'll be working day and night anyway."

"Then it's settled."

"If I'm going to have this by Saturday, we'd better get started now. C'mon, I'll buy."

Lamb smiled. "No, no. Never dangle a participle, split an infinitive, or pick up a check with an editor at the table. I'll make a writer out of you yet."

As he waited for the two mugs of cappuccino at the counter he watched Sally weave her way through the potted ferns to a butcher-block table by the window, admiring her legs in her tight jeans.

Thank God, we're in a public place.

Lamb went through the story page by page, line by line, playing at literary critic. It came naturally to him after grading the papers of his students. As Orpington was fond of saying, "Every class at Wren is a class in writing." Lamb had had plenty of practice teaching coherence and flow of ideas—not to mention grammar and spelling.

All he needed to do here was change his vocabulary slightly. He discussed imagery, emotional transitions, narrative logic. He challenged her on details she had simply tossed in without thinking—did they *work*, did they strengthen the total impression?

When her eyes started to glaze, he leaned back and asked, "Do you have children?"

"No. Why do you ask?" She knew of course, but she needed a compliment right about now.

"The little boy—Manley—perfect name—he's a terrific character. So accurately observed. I was wondering who he's based on?"

"You don't think I'm creative enough to have made him up?"

"Most writers start with a real person—sometimes several—when they create a character. Did you do that with Manley?"

"What difference does it make? Doesn't the story have to stand on its own?"

"It's just that Manley is so lovable, you naturally want to know if there's a real boy like him somewhere."

She smiled at him. "Ah ha! So the flinty editor has a soft spot after all. Okay, I'll confess. Yes, Virginia, there is a Santa Claus. Manley exists—with a different name, of course."

Lamb laughed. "You caught me. I do find him a very engaging character. I keep wanting to know more about him."

"Okay, I'll drop in more details."

"You'll have to do better than that. I suspect readers will want to know much more. Twice as much."

"Really? Wow! I don't know how I can do that."

"It might help to return to the source. Will you be seeing the real Manley soon?"

"I doubt I'll see him before the deadline."

"That's unfortunate. It would help the story so much—"

"There's a chance I'll talk to him on the phone."

Lamb's cup shook, splashing cappuccino on the cuff of his shirt. "I thought he didn't—I mean Manley doesn't talk. Isn't he like Manley?"

"He didn't used to talk, but he does now. But maybe Manley shouldn't. Doesn't that change the character too much?"

"No, no! It makes him more interesting. In fact, why don't you call him up today and see if you can get some dialogue?"

"I don't know where he is."

"Couldn't you find out?"

"It's complicated," she said and looked away.

Damn it! She won't discuss anything even vaguely related to the case.

He forced a smile. "Just a thought. I've already given you more than enough to do for one day. I hope you don't feel too bruised and battered."

She shook her head. "The truth? When you first showed me the manuscript with all those corrections I thought—'Overkill! He's dropped a brick on my spider web.' Was there *anything* you liked on those pages? How about the watermark?

"But when we started going over it, I realized—hey! I'm working with an editor on my story! He's ripping into it because he's serious about it. Yeah, it hurts—growth often does. This isn't one of my kitchen fantasies where success falls in my lap. This is reality; this is being a writer."

Lamb stood up. "That's the attitude."

"Tomorrow, same time, same station?"

He gave her the thumbs up sign. "Don't worry—we'll lick this thing."

Lamb turned and headed for the door, relieved that he no longer had to hide his agitation.

Winston starts talking and immediately disappears! Who's got him now? Who's he talking to!

Sally followed him with her eyes as he strode away, suddenly struck by how handsome he was. She smiled to herself. The women at Whatchamacallit College must all have mad crushes on him.

·49·

No "He's Got the Whole World in His Hands" played this morning.

Winston hung in his safety belts, out like a light, sleeping off a second stack of flapjacks.

They had spent the previous night in a motel outside Cincinnati. Now it was midmorning, and Popsy's Eldorado rolled along a two-lane blacktop in Indiana.

A sign announced they were entering Grissom, population 7,500, an old prairie town of white balloon houses on streets named after trees and presidents. Actually, it was no longer really a town, just a place to live, its identity drained away by shopping malls and industrial parks beyond its limits.

Jake shook the boy. "Almost there! Wake up! I want to show you something. On our right? That's Grissom Lake. That's where I saved my brother from drowning."

Winston squinted at it sleepily. It didn't look big enough to drown someone. They passed a pocket handkerchief of sand signposted "Town Beach." Nobody was there.

"The lake looks smaller than I remember it," Jake said. "You think it could have shrunk? But then everything around here looks smaller. I haven't been back since I was your age—around the time of the Spanish-American war.

"Now it can be told. We're going to stay with a very nice lady named Aunt Freezie. I stayed with her when I was a kid, and I enjoyed it a lot. So will you."

Winston looked dubious. "Popsy does know where she live?"

"Sheesh! Are you still chewing about that?"

"Time go come they talk together."

297

"Oh! It's the *aunt* that's bothering you. She's not really my aunt; I just called her that when I lived there. Popsy never heard of her, and she never heard of Popsy. Okay?"

"Okay," he said, still dubious.

New houses had crammed the remaining vacant lots on Willow Street, but Aunt Freezie's surprised him by being just like the place that occasionally turned up in a mournful, anxious dream, right down to the metal swan on the lawn and crab apple tree in the side yard. The tall white house was wrapped in porches and protected on three sides by a hollow square of bushes, fully seven feet tall, and several bushes thick. When in leaf, as it was now, the big green wall had provided lots of neat hiding places when he was a kid. He could crawl from end to end without showing himself. Roger had called it the jungle.

Apparently, Aunt Freezie's annuity didn't stretch as far as it once had. She had told him on the phone that she now "helped out" in the kitchen of a local manufacturing plant. Still, her schedule was flexible. She'd be home when they arrived.

She'd been keeping an eye out for them. Before they were halfway up the walk, she came out the front door and watched them climb the porch steps with a strange expression on her face.

"Look at you," she said.

"Look at you. You look great." Jake was immensely pleased by her appearance. He had been expecting a crabbed and beaten woman. Freezie had bloomed. Her hair, no longer wispy, was fashionably frosted and cut. She had lost her sallow complexion and nervous manner, and appeared confident and at ease.

She kissed his cheek. "You're better looking than your dad was at your age, and that's going some. And you must be Winston Churchill. I'm pleased to meet you."

She held out her hand. Winston shook it, too shy to speak.

Jake brought in the bags. Freezie lived alone in the big house—there was plenty of room. She still slept in her old room. She couldn't bear to use the room her parents had slept in when they were alive. She put Jake in there and gave Winston the guest room.

They had lunch, spaghetti-tuna hotdish. Winston had recovered magnificently from his indiscretion with the flapjacks and acquitted himself well.

After lunch, Freezie said, "He'll be all right in the house. Let's stroll around the neighborhood."

As soon as they were outside, she asked, "What is this?"

"I told you, I can't talk about it right now."

"You must have been married to adopt this child. Are you still?"

"Yes."

"To a black woman?"

"White."

She absorbed that information poker-faced.

"Why are you here without her? Did something happen to her?"

"Nothing happened to her. Nothing's wrong between us."

"Does she know you're here?"

Jake ambled along, hands behind his back, looking around at the old town with great interest, not a care in the world. "I can't talk about it."

"Just a minute here. The child is hers too. You can't even promise me she knows his whereabouts?"

"She's in total agreement with what I'm doing."

"Will you do me a favor? Call her right now and let me talk to her. You don't have to let me see the number."

"I can't do that."

"Why not?"

"For all kinds of very good reasons."

"You drop out of the blue after all these years with a little boy that I'm supposed to look after for several weeks, and you won't reassure me on any point at all?"

"I know it's a lot. But you've got to trust me."

"You sounded like your father just then."

"You know how to hurt a guy."

"I'm serious. This smells like one of his stunts."

"It's not."

"You won't tell me anything about yourself? Where you live, what kind of work you do?"

"It's better for us both if I don't."

"I could call Joe and ask him."

"You won't do that."

She looked away. "When did you get so smart?"

"Rather than lie to you, I decided not to tell you anything," Jake said. "When you get the whole story you'll see I was right."

"Will you at least stay a few days until the boy settles in?"

"I plan to do that."

"Thank you for filling me in on your plan. You've got one hell of a nerve, Jake Harrow."

They walked along in silence, Aunt Freezie casting covert glances at Jake, Jake checking out the town.

"How's Roger these days?"

"I told you the boy is legally adopted, and he's mine. That's all I can say."

"You won't even talk about Roger? You're afraid you'll say something that reveals where Roger is and I'll call him up?"

"I don't want to play twenty questions."

"I only ask you because I always worried about Roger. He was a sensitive boy. I always wondered if he was strong enough to handle the rough and tumble of life."

Jake shrugged without answering.

"Jake, please, I'm not fishing. Just tell me in a general way. Did Roger ever marry?"

"Yes."

"Any children?"

"Yes."

"He's doing all right? He has a good life?"

"You don't have to worry about Roger."

"That's wonderful," she said with a radiant smile. "It's a load off my mind to know he turned out well."

"He did."

"You looked sad just then," she said.

"What? Oh, I was just wondering if you ever worried about me?"

"You? No, Jake, can't say that I did. You were such a little dickens."

"That time I wrecked your garage?"

She started to laugh. "When you tied your dad's Chevrolet to the garage, you mean? I remember hearing this terrible crash and running out, and there was the garage roof lying on top of my Dodge at a funny angle like a graduation mortarboard and the outside wall flat in my pansy bed, and all I could think was a twister must have touched down out of a clear blue sky. Then I heard somebody laughing, and my eye traveled along the driveway to the beam, the rope, Joe's car, and Joe, standing there laughing and laughing.

"I'll never forget him, the way he looked right then. He had on his good gray slacks and a white shirt—good-bye clothes. But he'd spoiled the effect with a bright red cap—one of those awful ones with the bill in front.

"He said, 'This is Feisty's work.' He always called you *Feisty*. He said, 'This ain't Roger; he ain't up to this. Little Feisty done this all by himself. Look—he even buried the rope under the gravel so I wouldn't see it!' And he laughed some more. Finally, he wiped his eyes and said, 'I'm sorry, I shouldn't be laughing at a time like this. I'll pay you for it when I can.'

"I said, 'Never mind, Joe. I know Jake didn't mean to wreck the garage.'

"That embarrassed him, and he told me I was a good woman and

300

kissed me on the cheek. I remember Roger, pale and worried, craning his head around like a little giraffe, his eyes all red from crying, watching Joe untie the rope, trying to figure out what had happened. Joe said, 'Back in the car, Roger; we're still going.' And he drove away, and I never saw him again."

"You left out one thing," Jake said. "Before he got in the car. He peered around at the trees and the house and the bushes—he knew I was somewhere close, watching. He yelled, 'Nice going, Feisty! My hat's off to you,' and tossed his cap in the air—way up, high as the house. The breeze floated it over the bushes into Ridstrom's yard. He didn't even look for it, just drove away."

Aunt Freezie looked away. "Did he? I'd forgotten that."

"I hid out in the bushes all day, afraid you'd kick me out for wrecking your garage. You weren't mad—you didn't spank me—you didn't even mention it. I could never forgive myself for that stupid prank. My whole life I've wondered—why? Why did I do it?"

She put her hand on his shoulder. "You didn't want your dad to leave. You were trying to make him stay with a length of rope. You loved that man. You'd sit by the living room window watching out for him every afternoon. I always knew when he was home, I'd hear you yell 'Mighty Joe, Mighty Joe,' and then the door would SLAM! as you ran full tilt to meet him."

Aunt Freezie put her fists in a boxing pose. "He'd say, 'Come on, Feisty, lead with the left, follow up with the right. Let's see the old uppercut, Feisty. Straighten 'em up with a jab, then get 'em in the solar plexus. Come on, Feisty.' " She dropped her hands and laughed. "He loved the sound of *solar plexus*."

Jake smiled wistfully. "One night he came home with a pair of boxing gloves for me—huge things—bigger than my head! I went wild."

"That's right. He had his own pair, and the two of you would box from one end of the backyard to the other, those long summer evenings, laughing and laughing. God, you could laugh! The two of you. I could hear you laughing for blocks. I think it was the happiest sound I ever heard in my life. You were always his favorite."

Jake shrugged. "He loved both his boys—as long as he didn't have something better to do. After we left here, he turned into a guest-star parent. He would drop out of our lives for months, then suddenly show up drunk at three A.M. on the hottest night of the summer, lugging an electric fan. In his mind that fan made everything all right and canceled out the missed months. He'd sit on the end of Roger's bunk for hours, raving on endlessly about how much he loved his boys. I used to wonder why, if he loved us so much, he wouldn't let us sleep?"

301

"No use being mad at Joe," Freezie said. "He's a slender reed."

"I always thought he was pretty strong. He's done exactly what he wanted his whole life, and to hell with anyone else."

"He never did what he wanted, not really," Freezie said. "Somewhere deep down, he was broken, afraid to live. If he found he really loved something, he felt overwhelmed and had to run."

Jake looked into her face, full of hard-won compassion for the man who had walked out on her so long ago. He put his arm around her and gave her a hug. "If you can forgive the old flat-leaver, I guess I can too."

She pushed his arm away. "Forgive and forget," she said.

After that Freezie talked in a general way of her job at the plant, her church work, her friends. She asked Jake what kind of boy Winston was. He'd had a bad scare, but he'd soon be all right, Jake said, and then began telling stories about things the boy had said and done, but always vague as to where and who else was there: people in an airport, women in a restaurant, some people somewhere who didn't think he could dial a phone. She noticed that when he talked about the boy, he glowed.

As they walked up her driveway an express delivery van nosed in behind them. The smiling young driver in the crisp uniform bore a parcel about the size of an attaché case.

"Are you Freda Rugan?"

"Yes, but I didn't order anything."

"It's for me," Jake said. "I took the liberty."

She signed the receipt. "Now, maybe you'll do me a favor."

"Name it."

"My back step has been broken for two years."

"Where do you keep your tools?"

She left Jake to his task and went in search of Winston. She found him in the upstairs hall, walking slowly back and forth, an intent expression on his face, as if he were searching for loose floorboards.

"Come into the living room with me; I want to get to know you a little better."

He followed obediently. She sat on the couch, and he took the farthest chair.

"So, Winston, did you and your dad have a nice trip?"

He nodded.

"You like it here in Grissom?"

He nodded.

"Miss your mama?"

He shook his head.

"What a brave boy. Can you tell me your full name?"

He mumbled something.

"Could you say that just a little louder. I couldn't quite hear."

"Winston Churchill Harrow."

"That's very good. Now, can you tell me your address?"

"It a secret."

"Your address is a secret? But surely you can tell me."

Shyly but stubbornly, he shook his head.

"Can you tell me the name of the town where you live? Surely that's not a secret."

He nodded doggedly. "It a secret."

In the next few minutes she learned that everything was a secret, from his mother's name to which states they had driven through to get here. Jake had primed him well, she thought.

"Excuse me a minute," she said. Catching the anger in her voice, she went on, "I'll be right back. And I promise not to ask you any more questions. How's that?"

He looked relieved.

She went out to the driveway and had a look at the Eldorado.

New Jersey plates.

Winston was sitting right where she had left him. He hadn't even changed his upright posture. Why was he so rigid? It was more than Jake's priming, she thought. This boy was frightened. Her heart went out to him. She had to help him.

"You getting hungry?" she asked.

He nodded, relaxing slightly.

"Jake says you like pizza. Is that true?"

He nodded again and began swinging his foot.

"We have a pizza parlor right here in Grissom; did Jake tell you?"

"We did pass it."

"So you were the one who told him!"

"I did make sure he ain't miss it."

She laughed. "You sly devil."

"I is sometime sly," he said. What a nice smile he had.

"What do you think? Should we order some pizza now?"

He nodded enthusiastically, bouncing in the chair.

"What's your favorite?"

"Sausage and peppers."

She centered the telephone on the coffee table in front of her, "Sausage and peppers it is." She picked up the receiver and then replaced it.

"Wait a minute. Jake told me you're the pizza dialer at home."

He smiled proudly. "That is true true."

"Would you dial pizza for me?"

He nodded eagerly.

She patted the sofa cushion. "Come sit by me, then."

He darted around the end of the coffee table and plumped down beside her. He grabbed the telephone receiver and poised his finger over the buttons.

"Dial nice and slow," she said. "I want to see how you do it."

He looked up at her, puzzled. "I go need the number."

"Same as always," she said. "Pizza parlors are the same all over the country so people can order it anywhere."

She watched him punch the buttons.

"Wait! What are we doing? We haven't asked Jake what he wants." She replaced the receiver. "Would you go ask him please?"

Winston raced off. She took a pencil stub from her pocket and wrote the telephone number he had dialed in the margin of a newspaper, tore it off, and stuffed it in her pocket.

After dinner, Jake and Winston sat at the same living room coffee table. Jake set the express package he had received earlier in front of them.

"You think the Constable is the strongest guy in the world, don't you?"

Winston nodded. He had been looking relaxed and cheerful after the pizza. Now his face froze with apprehension.

"Well he is pretty strong, that's true. But if two good guys like you and me really stick together and help each other, we can whip him. What do you say?"

"I ain't know."

"Me neither," Jake said. He shrugged. "But I'm gonna try anyway. It's a dirty job, but somebody's got to do it. I've got no chance at all without your help. Will you help me fight him?"

The boy looked nervously at his thin arms. "If we does wait a year, I go be some bigger."

"I'm not just talking about a fistfight. There's lots of ways to fight. Remember in Princeton how you helped me shake him off? We beat him that time. I couldn't have done it without your help."

The boy brightened at the memory. "We did lose the blues."

"You know why? Because we're a team. See, in a team, each member has something special to give that nobody else has, and when you put

all those special things together, the team gets stronger than anybody
—even old what's-his-name in the fake uniform. Understand?''

"We go stick together.''

"Attaguy! Now, remember I said we each have something special to
give? Like, I'm all grown up and big, so I'll take care of the fistfights,
okay?''

Winston nodded judiciously. "What does I do?''

"It's like this. Nobody knows what Mr. C. looks like, so nobody knows
who to fight. The police don't know, the FBI doesn't know, the army
doesn't know. If we knew what he looked like, hundreds of guys would
be chasing him. You're the world's only expert on what he looks like.
Will you give that special knowledge to the team?''

He gave a doubtful little nod.

"I knew we could count on you. See this package here? Know what's
inside? Our old pal the Identi-Kit. With all those funny noses and
mustaches and stuff, remember? Do I have your permission to unwrap
it?''

He nodded.

"You're not going to toss it out the window again?''

He shook his head.

"Good deal." Jake unwrapped the Identi-Kit. "Now, let's see if you
can show me the Constable, or a reasonable facsimile thereof.''

Winston leaned forward grimly. "I go try.''

New Jersey had three area codes.

She tried 201 and got an out-of-service recording.

She tried 908 and got a plumbing supplier.

She tried 609.

"Post-Graduate Pizza, please hold.''

Freezie tapped her pencil stub on the counter top nervously. Jake
and Winston were playing some kind of game in the living room, but
there was always the chance they'd want a glass of water. With her
luck . . .

"Yes, what can we do you for?''

"This is an emergency," she said. "What town have I reached,
please?''

"Princeton.''

"I'm calling from Mercy Hospital in Trenton. There's been a terrible
car accident, and we're trying to locate a woman. Someone told us she
was one of your regular take-out customers.''

"I'll help any way I can.''

"Thank you so much. The only name we have is Harrow."

"Hold on, the delivery man is just going out. Jamal, wait a minute. We got a hospital emergency. You deliver to a Mrs. Harrow? No? You're sure. He says no. Sorry."

"We may have the wrong name. She's a white woman with an adopted black boy about five years old."

"Jamal, come back! Somebody grab him! Jamal, where you going? Just a second. How about a white woman with a black boy about five? Yes. No, doesn't have to be Harrow. You want to tell her? Just a second, I'll put him on."

Jamal came on the line. "You from the hospital?"

"Yes."

"Okay, there's a white woman with a black kid about five. They order up a pie almost every day. The name is Payden. P-A-Y-D-E-N. You want me to look up the address? I got the book here."

"Just give me the phone number."

He read off the number. "What happened to her? Nothing bad, I hope."

"That remains to be seen," Aunt Freezie said.

At ten o'clock that evening, Jake unceremoniously yanked open the door of the hall closet.

"What are you doing in there?"

The boy blinked up at him guiltily. "I ain't know."

"Aunt Freezie went to a lot of trouble to fix up the guest room just for you. You've got a nice soft bed, where you can stretch out and be comfortable."

"Closet go do me."

"You slept in a bed at the motel."

"We was going quick sharp."

"This hurts my feelings. Why do you think I drove you a thousand miles? So you wouldn't have to sleep in a closet."

"Princeton a long way from Skokie. He did find me."

Jake studied him for a moment, then stepped back. "You sure picked a narrow one this time. Couldn't you find a bigger closet in the house?"

"It were in the hall."

"You don't want to be trapped in a bedroom when the Constable comes?"

Winston nodded.

"I don't think we can wedge a mattress in there. Let me see what I can scrounge for you." He walked away.

Winston waited. He could hear Jake and Aunt Freezie talking quietly downstairs. He strained his ears but couldn't quite make out the words.

Jake came back carrying sofa cushions. "Gotta roust you out of there for just a second. She claims there are clean sheets on the top shelf, but I don't—Oh, yeah, here we go." He reached up and yanked the sheet off the shelf, dragging something with it that fell to the floor. Jake picked it up. The old baseball cap proclaimed "ST. LOUIS CARDI-NALS" in flourishing white script on its red cloth. Jake turned it around in his hand for a moment and then carefully placed it back on the top shelf.

The boy stood in the hall and watched Jake make up his bed.

"Aunt Freezie is mad like anything?"

Jake dropped into a squat so they were both the same height. In a low voice he said, "She wanted to drown you in the lake, but I squared it with her."

"I is sorry," he said in a miserable little voice.

"It's okay, nobody's mad. You sleep where you want. But you're giving yourself lumbago for nothing. The Constable isn't going to find you in Grissom, Indiana, for God's sake."

·50·

When Sally walked into The Hole in the Wall the next morning, Lamb was already waiting impatiently at a back table.

He pretended to be so engrossed in his Arabic newspaper that he didn't notice her get a cup of coffee and came to the table.

"Good morning, Professor Lamb."

He nodded without looking up.

"I figured out why I've had so much trouble working more material about Manley into the story," she said brightly as she sat down. "I kept trying to pad out existing sections, especially *Baton Rouge*, without adding any new action. So I've written a whole new section. At the end he takes a long car journey to a new place."

Yesterday she didn't know where Winston had been taken. Now she does. She's in contact with the people who are hiding him. She's a gold mine.

She pushed the manuscript pages toward him. With elaborate unconcern, he finished the article he was reading and turned his attention to her work.

"Grissom, Indiana," he read aloud. "See how much better it is when you use the real place name?"

"You were absolutely right," she said. "It makes things much more specific."

It didn't. The car ride seen through the little boy's eyes was even vaguer than usual. No names, no road signs, no clear descriptions of people. A man was driving. Who? Nobody else on the trip. He devoured her airy prose, hungry for facts, like a starving man gobbling cotton candy:

309

Wind whoosh. Motor moan. The boy looked out through glass. Beyond the glass, metal. Sun splash. Light leap. Green the metal. Green the color shadows on the glass before him.

Got it. The car is green. What else, for God's sake?
A two-day trip, ending in Grissom. Another house, another closet. A woman. The driver's wife? Couldn't tell. No details at all.
I could spend the rest of my life driving around Grissom, waiting for Winston to come out on a porch. How can I get more information without making her suspicious?
"It's going in the right direction, but it's not there yet," he told her carefully. "I'm not quite sure what to tell you. . . ."
"Oh, I just showed it to you for concept," Sally said with a smile. "I was going to rewrite it anyway. I was pretty upset when I wrote it."
"I'm sorry. Has Jake taken a turn for the worse?"
"No, no. It's Nan. I think all these years of Popsy's philandering have finally affected her mind."
"What's she doing?"
"You don't want to hear this."
"Go ahead. You've got to tell somebody."
"Well, yesterday evening, I was talking on the phone in the kitchen, and she must have been listening out in the hall. When I hung up, she burst in all raddled and wild-eyed. 'Who were you talking to?' I told her it was none of her business. 'It was a *man*, wasn't it!' I said that as a matter of fact it was a woman. 'Don't lie to me. I heard his name. I heard you call him *Reuben!*' I'd been talking to a woman whose last name is *Rugan*. How that's for paranoia—she twisted it into a man's name."
"Couldn't you just tell her who it was?"
"Nan never heard of her."
"Why didn't you call this Rugan woman back and let your mother talk to her?"
Sally looked away, suddenly uncomfortable. "I don't want to discuss—that's not the point. I shouldn't have to make long-distance phone calls to prove I'm not cheating on my husband."
"Of course not. No wonder you were upset."
She wrote the new section after the long-distance call from the Rugan woman. That call must have told her Winston's in Grissom.
"Thanks for listening," Sally said. "I'm over it now."
"Good." He gathered up his newspapers. "So you'll jump on that rewrite immediately."
She looked startled. "You mean *now*, this minute?"

"The sooner you start the better."

"But I've got changes in the other sections to show you."

He stood up. "I'll look at everything next time."

"You're leaving?"

"I've got to run."

"Will I see you tomorrow?"

"Tomorrow's a problem. I've got meetings most of the day. I'll see you Thursday." He walked briskly toward the door.

"Julian, wait!"

He was already out of the shop. She rushed after him, but when she reached the sidewalk, he was gone.

Startled, she looked around and spotted him two blocks away. He hadn't been kidding when he said he had to run—he was sprinting full tilt along the sidewalk.

The back steps were only the beginning. Aunt Freezie had apparently been saving up odd jobs since the day Joe left. At the moment, Jake was down on the living room floor, converting an old-style phone connection to modular, while she kibitzed.

"Do you see your brother much these days?" she asked.

Jake gave her a wary glance, "I stayed at his place a few months ago."

"You don't live near each other."

"No," he said. The word *live* in her question made him feel like a liar.

"That's too bad. You were so close as boys."

"Red to red, green to green." Jake was talking to the wires, not her.

"You even had your own language."

"We had a few code words. I wouldn't call it a language."

"I would. You jabbered away in it to beat the band. The two of you would sit at the dinner table and one would say something like, 'Gauge tire pressure.' And the other would say, 'Lugnut.' He'd eat for a while and then say, 'Danger of a blowout.' And then you both would look at Joe and me, and try to keep a straight face."

Jake smiled rather wanly. "So we did. It was more Roger's thing than mine. He was really into it."

"I always thought it was Roger's way of winning you away from Joe. Everybody was competing for you, Jake."

"Just kick that screwdriver toward me. Thank . . . you."

"You had your own names for everything. *Toothpaste* meant 'shut up!' 'School' was the *rat farm*. 'Homework' was *rat farming*. I was *Tigibbet*, short for *flibbertigibbet*, and your dad was *The Youngster*. Short for *Mighty Joe Young*—the gorilla in the movies. It used to worry

311

me. I talked to the school psychologist about it—remember her, Miss Pope? The one all the big boys had a crush on? She said private languages like yours—with enough vocabulary to hold conversations—were extremely rare except for identical twins."

Jake stood up, his eye still on the 42A Block. "That's done. If the language was so secret, how come you know all about it?"

"Because years after you left, I found a notebook with the whole language written up in Roger's handwriting. I'll show it to you."

"You know, I'd really rather not talk about Roger."

"This isn't about Roger *now*. It's about the two of you as children. Please look. I've always wanted to show it to one of you."

"All right."

"Come into the alcove."

Gently, as befits a relic of another time, Aunt Freezie lifted the battered and stained old notebook from the drawer of her writing desk.

MAPLE LEAF
150 Sheets
3 Subject Dividers

"Here it is, *Webster's Unabridged*," she said. "You boys had hundreds of words.

"Here's the page on food names. Take a look." She handed him the notebook:

Meat: Tires
Vegetables: Any wild animal, esp. Crocodile, Hippopotamus or
    Rhinoceros.
Salad: Venus (fr. Venus's flytrap)
Potatoes: Clouds

Jake looked up from the page. "Amazing. I'd forgotten most of this."

"Some words you used all the time aren't in there, like *jamjar* and *rinsewater*. What did they mean?"

"You were supposed to wonder about that. They didn't mean anything. We just threw them in to confuse things."

"What was *lugnut*? You used that every other sentence."

"Ah ha, *lugnut*. That had two meanings. First it meant 'Roger.' *Lugnut* was Roger's secret name."

"And also . . . ?"

"And also—'I read you.' Pilots say *Roger*, so we said *Lugnut*. It's coming back now. My God!" He paged through the notebook and

312

laughed delightedly. "That's right, 'going to the toilet' was *sky diving*, 'lies' were *rimshots*, 'playing hooky' was *dressing warm*. My God!''

She asked, "What on earth was *worm furniture*? You were always saying it, but it's not in the book either."

"*Worm furniture*. Wait a minute. *Worm furniture* was whatever we wanted at the time. If Roger was 'dressing warm' in the fall, *worm furniture* was a football. In the spring it might be his fielder's mitt. I always knew. He'd pretend to leave for school and sneak around to the side of the house, and I'd toss it out the window to him."

"Telepathy. No wonder I never figured it out."

He started to laugh. "I remember, you'd be standing right there in our room, and Rog would say, 'I'm really gonna *dress warm* today. Where's the *worm furniture*?' He got such a kick out of fooling you— it was the best part of playing hooky."

She sniffed. "I wasn't completely fooled, young man. By the time your dad took Roger away, I'd figured out quite a bit of it. I never let on; I didn't want to spoil your fun. And, of course, the day Roger left, you stopped speaking it."

He strode briskly but without haste down the crowded concourse. Clean-shaven; dark suit neatly cut; regulation tan trench coat of the American business class over his arm: the everybody nobody would remember.

Beneath his calm facade Lamb was boiling. Without benefit of his usual meticulous planning, things were already going wrong. After his reckless drive from Princeton, he'd run into a traffic jam at LaGuardia itself and narrowly missed a direct flight to Indianapolis. Instead, he would have to fly to Cincinnati and wait ninety minutes for a puddle-jumper.

Trying to be careful and look bored at the same time, he floated his carry-on bag into the rolling maw of the X-ray. The bag contained a bomb.

The X-ray missed it. So did the array of chemical sensors buried under the moving belt. He lifted it gently before the next suitcase could bump it and walked rapidly to his gate.

He much preferred a gun, but he had no time to mail weapons ahead; he'd been forced to opt for Trans-RDX, an explosive that could pass undetected under the most sophisticated electronic eyes and noses. Trans-RDX was a little-known cousin of RDX, the active ingredient in C-4. A little dab'll do ya—his bomb was a wafer no bigger than a poker chip. Unfortunately, the same molecular twist that made it fifty times more powerful than RDX also made it fifty times more impact-sensitive—far worse even than PETN. If it went off while he was carrying the bag, there wouldn't be enough left of him to bury. He hated being near the stuff: in Princeton, he kept a small supply buried by a tree stump well away from the house. Security forces weren't looking for it because terrorists never used it—even fanatics didn't want to be killed by a speed-bump.

Crowhurst had taught him how to insert the deadly wafer into a raw egg through the shell, tamp it into the yolk with a paper clip, and reseal the shell with Super Glue. The contents of the egg masked its shape under X-ray and insulated it from vibration—Crowhurst swore you could drop the egg off a ten-story building without detonation.

The New York–Cincinnati flight eased forward and started its takeoff run. The egg rode with him in a brown paper bag with a sprout sandwich and an apple as part of his "allergy" lunch.

He stared unseeing at Manhattan Island spread out grandly below him in the noonday sun and promised himself he would not fail again.

·51·

Jake repaired two faucets, a ceiling fixture, and the sump pump and then went for a stroll around Grissom Lake with Aunt Freezie.

She pointed at a spot in the lake. "That's where the old pier was. It's gone now, thank God; the town finally took it down. What a hazard! Your poor brother tripped over a loose board and fell into twelve feet of water. He couldn't swim a stroke. He was yelling and thrashing. You swam right to him. Do you remember what happened next?"

"I told him to hold on to my shoulder, and I towed him to shore."

"You said, 'Roger, hold on to my shoulder?' Like that?"

He skipped a stone. It spanked the calm water once, twice, three times, leaving three sets of concentric ripples. "Here we go again. Enough about Roger."

"But you've got it all wrong."

"Okay, I've got it wrong. *He* saved *me*. Give me a break."

"Poor Roger was out of his mind with terror. I could hear you shouting, '*Float!* I'll tow you! *Float!*' You knew he was an expert floater; he played shark with you in the shallow water. When you tried to get hold of him, he clutched at you and started to drag you under with him. The two of you wrestled around for several minutes. You kept screaming at him to float, but Roger was struggling so hard you couldn't tow him. I ran out on the pier with a rope and tried to cast it to you, but you were getting farther away every minute. I couldn't swim any better than Roger; I was getting frantic.

"Suddenly, I heard you say, in a quiet voice, not yelling, 'Roger. *Dead Sea.*' He stopped struggling immediately, and you towed him all the way to the shallows."

Jake's head whipped around. "I said *what?*"

315

"*Dead Sea* meant 'float.' You boys heard the Dead Sea is so salty, people can't sink if they try. When he heard you speaking to him in your own private language, it finally got through to him."

"*Dead Sea was part of our private language*? You're sure? I didn't see it in the notebook."

"It's there somewhere. Why, what's the matter? You suddenly look all wild."

"We've got to go back to the house. *Now.*"

"Take it easy, I'll find it in a minute." She paged rapidly through the notebook, trying not to tear the fragile pages from the coiled wire that bound them together. "Here. My goodness, I'm so out of breath I can hardly see straight. '*Dead Sea*: float. Also cool it, stop arguing, or do as you're told.' "

"Let me see." Jake snatched the book away from her and stared at his brother's neatly rounded handwriting. " 'Do as you're told.' That's what he was telling them. But how did he *know*?"

"How did *who* know?" she asked, but he was already halfway out of the room.

Jake's first call was to Baton Rouge. Doc Campbell sounded upset by the question.

"My goodness, how did you hear about that? You really need to know about that little language of theirs?"

"It's important; I can't go into why."

"Very well. It started from a tape Juleth brought home—supposed to be like a Berlitz lesson on Dolphin language. They were wild about it —they started making up their own words and bringing in other endangered species like the mountain gorilla and the bald eagle. It had its own alphabet of grunts and twitters and a vocabulary of fifteen-hundred words."

"Tell me, was it common knowledge around there? Did they talk about it with the neighbors?"

"Never. It was their little secret. Or maybe big secret. They took an oath—even Lincoln, the six-year-old."

"But you knew."

"I was in their house so much, a bit of it had to leak out. But I never spoke it with them. It was their private world. I didn't want to intrude—I felt it was too intimate—they were pleased I kept out of it. Part of being a good guest is knowing when to be hard-of-hearing."

"Did they ever write anything down?—a dictionary."

Silence on the other end. Finally Doc Campbell sighed. "Well now,

I was afraid you'd ask that." He sighed again. "You absolutely need this?"

"It's vital."

"Then I have a confession to make. The next night after it happened—before you got down there? The FBI had the place sealed up, but they left at midnight. I had a key. I wanted a memento. Foolish, I suppose."

"You loved those people."

"I took their little handwritten dictionary. To remember them by. They called the language 'Dolphone.' "

"Dolphin?"

"Dolphone. Like *Anglophone* for 'English-speaker'? On the cover of the dictionary it says—please don't laugh; I know it's silly but they didn't mind being silly—it says: 'Dolphone: The Endangered Speechies.' "

Learning about the Giles language was somewhat tougher. Morton had been a set designer, Audrey a psychoanalyst: the FBI listing of relatives, friends, colleagues, and business acquaintances looked like the LA phone book. But nobody knew anything about a family language, not even the Mexican woman who had been their full-time maid.

After thirty-two phone calls, Jake was about to give up, when a jogging buddy of Morton's said, "Ever hear of Grace Boudreaux? She's a theatrical producer, avant-garde, multimedia kind of stuff. Morty did a lot of her sets. She was tight with the family. She might know."

It took Jake forty minutes to track down where Grace Boudreaux was working that day—a go-go palace on Sunset that rented as a rehearsal space.

"It's about time you people called me. I tried to tell the cops last winter Morty didn't kill his family. He was an artist. He built a miniature country in his basement, with towns and castles and mountains. You should see the dolls he made. Incredible. Terrible loss to me personally and professionally—he knew how to realize my visions far better than I did. He'd never hurt a fly. He cried when they buried the pussycat."

Jake asked her about the family language.

"How disappointing. I thought I was the only one outside the family who knew of its existence. It was their version of King Arthur talk. Morty used to tell the girls stories about days of old when knights were bold, and it just evolved from there. Norse endings, Gaelic verb forms—I don't know why they were so shy about it; it sounded like it was very cute and fanciful."

"They spoke it with you?"

317

"Never. I found out about it by mistake. Francine—the four-year-old—used to call me something and giggle and cover her mouth. I thought she was saying 'Auntie,' which frankly did not thrill me, so I confronted them on it. Turned out they called me 'Argante,' who was the fairy queen who nursed King Arthur. Just so I wouldn't feel they were making fun of me, they confessed they had names for everybody and everything, and told me a little about the language—what I just told you—but *Argante* is the only word I ever heard them say. They had an iron-clad rule: only at home when no one else is there. They wouldn't speak it in a restaurant when the waiter wasn't around—none of that."

"Did they write any of it down?"

"A dictionary? I never saw one. Anyhow, you're late. You know how home buyers react to a house where a family was murdered. Nobody wants the Amityville Horror. The relatives came on like Lady Macbeth—out out, damned spot. If there was ever a dictionary, it probably got burned up with Morty's dolls. What a waste."

The man with the scraggly beard in the ratty bomber jacket raced through the Indianapolis airport, cradling his carry-on bag in his arms like a sleeping child.

A line! At the car rental counter! Damn it, he thought. He should have rented the car *first*, then changed into the disguise.

He slowed to a walk and took his place at the end, trying to hold down his harsh breathing. He did not set his bag down on the floor—somebody might kick it.

The customer at the counter had asked for directions and was having trouble understanding them. The young woman from the rental company was being endlessly helpful and midwestern, penning circles and crosses on his map, loading him with landmarks, and warning him about places he might make a wrong turn.

"No, Booth Tarkington isn't a tollbooth; it's the name of the exit . . . no sir, there's no place called Tarkington . . . a songwriter—I think he wrote 'Down Home in Indiana.' "

Lamb yearned to charge the counter shouting, "Emergency! Emergency! I must have my car now!" But of course that would make him memorable. It might even draw close scrutiny to his disguise. All he could do was fidget, as the line edged slowly forward.

"You have a reservation, sir?" The Booth Tarkington expert in her crisp blazer was looking with faint disgust at his old bomber jacket.

"I reserved this morning; they said no problem." He pushed the credit card and driver's license at her.

She tapped computer buttons. "Ah, here you are, Mr. Halliburton."

While she wrote up his contract, Lamb studied one of her maps.

"All set, sir," she said, handing him the key. "Need any help with directions?"

"I'm cool," Lamb said.

He had already memorized the route to Grissom.

Four o'clock that afternoon. Detective Richard Gimmler stood on the sidewalk in downtown Manhattan beside a pay phone. He didn't expect it to ring, but it did.

"Dr Pepper," he said.

"Looks like we've got a caucasian male, regular features, no distinguishing marks, no glasses, brown hair, probably around six-one or -two, athletic build. Age is a problem, I'd put him twenty-five to thirty-five. Face is still generalized; I'll try to sharpen it up today."

"What do you plan to do with it? Stat it down to wallet size and carry it with you always?"

"They're going to have to listen now. I've got a hell of a lead. Three of the families on the FBI list shared a certain quirk. The Grants have it too. I've struck out so far on the Leiths, but I bet they had it—they were the first and the trail is pretty cold. But at least four of them had a secret family language."

"Don't most families have pet names and stuff?"

"Oh, sure, every family coins a few words. But I'm talking about whole languages where people can hold long conversations outsiders can't understand."

"This helps to nail our buddy?"

"A private language! Think what that means. You don't declare it on a tax return. It's not part of your credit rating. There's no directory of families with one, no club, no newsletters. Private languages are secrets. They're like the family's own code, not to be revealed to outsiders. I only found out this morning my brother's family used one. And yet our friend located four, and probably five such families, all in different parts of the country. *How did he do that?*"

"Maybe he drives around the country in an RV, planting microphones in people's houses."

"Or maybe he's a guy whose job is bugging hundreds of people, and he's cherry-picking the special kind he likes."

"Except who would bug those families? None of them had real money; no R and D people with technical secrets; not an inside trader in the bunch. My rule is—if I can't find a million-dollar art object in the house to plant my bug in—I leave. This ain't a player."

"Mandy was in the Green party. Somebody could have thought she was a security risk. Ditto Juleth Grant with her Commie parents—especially when she and her husband fought city hall and the refineries to save rare reptiles. Sturluson, the survivalist—you know how they watch those guys. Audrey Giles was a psychoanalyst with a Hollywood practice. Hasn't it always been vital to the national interest to monitor the bedroom high jinks of the stars? They weren't interested in the Gileses—Audrey's practice was a window on her clients. And if Leith proves out—well, he was an accountant with a lot of political clients. Another window."

"You think the guy works for my 'Uncle.' "

"Works or worked, yeah. Rogue agent."

"Agent is a leap. Could be anyone with access. A file clerk, code breaker, hot runner. Or even a complete outsider, bribing a light-fingered secretary. Or how about a computer hacker? Thought of that? If the worms crawl in, they might crawl out—with dossiers."

"Look how he kills. Look how he covers his tracks. He's a trained pro."

"Mm. That's a point. So what's your next step?"

"I need a meeting with Brasswater. Neutral ground. Can you set me up?"

"Hey, what have I been telling you? They'll collar your ass."

"But maybe I can convince him first."

"To do what?"

"Find out if the federal government had these families under surveillance at any time. See if the same agent was on all the cases."

"You been wasting time chasing crooks when you should have been listening-up at the watercooler, my man. Brasswater is FBI. At the very best, all he can do is check out the Bureau. Now, suppose our rogue agent is CIA? Or DEA? Or DIA? Or NSA? Or Treasury? Or army intelligence? Or naval intelligence? You think those folks are going to let a Bureau guy run barefoot through their bag-job files?"

"What would you suggest?"

"Talk to Trask Walkins."

"A local TV crime reporter?"

"Local TV my ass. He's on a network O and O in New York City. And this story starts his hibachi. I don't have to call him anymore; he calls me. He's hot to expose the PD for planting those coke stories about you. When you tell him the Silencer is CIA, he'll go ballistic."

"But that'll tip off the bad guy to run for it. And it'll lead to a cover-up—the intelligence community will set their shredders on turbo."

"All kinds of things could happen. It's a quick way to get your idea out in public, where everybody has to deal with it. You got a shot at catching the guy. Isn't that better than jerking off in an Indiana cornfield?"

There was long pause at Jake's end. Finally he said, "Is there a top?"

"Of what?"

"The system. Intelligence."

"Yeah, the President. Commander-and-Chief. If you call him up, better have a Rubik's Cube to solve while you wait."

"I'm asking you for some of that watercooler wisdom. Is there one leader for all the alphabet soup? DEA, DIA, BVD, and all the rest? Or do they each report separately to the President?"

"The DCI. The director of central intelligence. He is both head of the CIA, which is only one part of the intelligence apparatus, and also, miraculously, head of the entire intelligence community. Plus, he teaches on the side. Now, shall I explain how a bill becomes a law?"

"He's the guy I'll talk to."

"You're not serious."

"You convinced me; I've got to get above the petty politics."

"You'll never get the director on the phone. And while you're on hold, they'll trace your call and send the local cops to arrest you."

"I'll go to Washington and walk into his office at the CIA."

"You're nuts. Nobody does that."

"Sell, sell, sell."

The big overhead turnpike sign didn't bother to mention it, but Lamb knew he had reached the Grissom turnoff. He cut the wheel for the exit ramp and set his jaw grimly—the country roads ahead would be bumpy, and he was only too aware of what was hidden in the carry-on bag he had placed so carefully in the trunk of the car.

·52·

"You're going *now?*" Aunt Freezie was upset to find Jake packing up his suitcase.

"Something's come up."

"Why not at least wait for morning? It'll be dark in a few hours; you'll have to stop anyway."

"I'm driving straight through."

"What about the boy?"

"If things work out the way I hope, I may be able to take him off your hands in a few days. I'm making better progress than I expected."

"You can't take him with you?"

"I'll be working day and night. He'd just be in the way."

"I thought you were at least going to stay a few days until he got used to the place."

"It's a little soon, I know, but he'll be fine in a day or so. He's a smart kid—he understands things when they're explained to him."

"Here's your chance," she said, with a slight head-point to the bedroom door.

Winston sidled uncertainly into the room.

"I'll be down the hall," Freezie said. On her way out, she gave Winston's shoulder a reassuring pat.

"We is leaving Aunt Freezie's?" His eyes searched Jake's face as if his whole future were written there.

Jake found he couldn't quite meet his eyes, so he looked him in the eyebrows.

"I'm taking a little trip. You get to stay here and relax, you lucky dog."

The boy clutched the sides of his head in shock. "Let we go together!"

"No, this time I have to go alone. That's how it has to be, okay?"

"Why for?"

"Because I'm going back to the East to catch the Constable. You don't want to see him again, do you?"

"You go need my help."

"Absolutely, your help is vital, but see—you already helped me. That picture you made of the Constable? I'm going to use that to catch him. I'm going to show it to a lot of people who might know where he is, so we can track him down and arrest him."

"Let we go together. I isn't play 'The Whole World.' "

Jake smiled and blinked rapidly. "I love traveling with you, 'Whole World' and all. But I need you to stay here."

"Isn't we a team?"

"We're a great team. But teams can't always work in the same place. Right now there are two jobs to do. To do both, the team has to split up. My job is go east and arrest the Constable. Your job is hold the fort here."

Winston's eyes brimmed. "You said—*we go stick together.*"

"Easy does it, easy does it. What can we do about this?"

He stroked his chin for a moment. "I think I see your problem. You're worried that while I'm back east, the Constable might sneak out here and catch you all by your lonesome. That's why you want to stick so close to me. Sure. So what can we do about that?"

Winston watched him with grieving, expectant eyes.

"Okay, okay, I got it. Whew! This is a big one. This is heavy duty. Stay right there; don't move."

He went downstairs to the desk where he had been working and got his cellular phone. On the way back he looked into Freezie's room. She was stretched out on her bed, arms folded behind her head.

Without opening her eyes, she asked, "So is he going with you, or are you staying here with him?"

"All right, he's taking it harder than I thought, but I've got a little gift for him that will soften the blow."

She blinked just long enough to see what he was holding. "What's he going to do with that gizmo?"

"Trust me, he'll love it. Kid's a phone freak."

"How about you? Don't you need it?"

"I'll fall off that bridge when I come to it," Jake said. "I've got a major problem here."

Winston raised his head as Jake came back into the room. He was not crying, but there were tear tracks on his cheeks.

"Summer Santa is here! Remember this baby? Sure you do. Now you can be the first kid on the block with your very own cellular phone. I'm giving it to you, no strings attached. You can keep it right there in the closet with you, ready to go at all times."

Winston hardly glanced at the phone. His eyes stayed on Jake's face.

Jake squatted down in front of him. "You want me to stick around in case the Constable comes. But having this phone is actually *better* than having me. Say while I'm out east, you heard the Constable come into the house. Just dial 911—three numbers, you can do it in the dark—and you've got the police. And that's a whole town full of cops, not just me. How's that for terrific?"

Jake held out the case. "Take it. Go ahead, it's yours. I'm not going to ask for it back."

Winston took it.

"Okay, let me check you out on the entire unit. Can you show me the aerial?"

Winston stepped back as if to study the instrument and suddenly raced out the door and down the hall, the cellular phone cradled under one arm like a football.

Slam! The door to the bathroom.

Flush!

Jake jumped up. "Not again!"

As he ran up to the bathroom door it popped open. Winston shot past him and fled down the stairs.

The phone was at the bottom of the toilet; it's aerial wedged into the outlet hole.

"Damnit! I thought we were past this," Jake shouted in disgust. He heard the outside door slam.

Aunt Freezie came running into the bathroom and saw what was in the toilet. "Maybe it still works." She bent down to retrieve it.

"Leave it!" Jake snapped. "There's only one person who's going to dirty his hand in that toilet." He bolted down the hall and ran out of the house.

Winston was nowhere to be seen.

"You come back here! I want you here right now! *Winston!*"

Jake circled the house calling angrily without result. He went back upstairs.

Aunt Freezie was waiting in the hall. "He'll be back," she said. "After you leave."

"Sure, sure, he'll get over it. All it'll take is a hundred reps of 'He's Got the Whole World in His Hands.' "

"No Jake. His whole world is leaving in a green Cadillac."

"I'm sorry, I can't spend any more time worrying about his feelings.

325

I have work to do." He went to the master bedroom and got his suitcase. "You don't know how much good you're doing by taking care of him. When I can explain things, you'll see how important your help was."

"I'm certainly looking forward to that. Take care of yourself, Jake."

He kissed her. "When that little slam-dunker shows up, make him remove the phone from the toilet himself and explain to him that he has no right to destroy valuable property like that—even if it's his own. I won't ask you to spank him, but that's what he really needs."

"He needs his dad."

"He needs his dad to spank him. He ruined a perfectly good cellular telephone."

"You once ruined a perfectly good garage."

Jake cocked his head and looked at her. "Good-bye, Aunt Freezie."

He went downstairs to the car, stowed his suitcase in the trunk and slowly backed the green Cadillac out of the yard. The high bushes loomed on his right, the house on his left, the new garage directly in front of him with Freezie's black car hunkered inside. The garage caught his eye. Funny—he couldn't see any difference from the one he had wrecked.

He backed all the way to the sidewalk, then braked. The garage had the same white clapboards, same blue doors, even the same pansy bed on the yard-side wall.

He turned off the motor, got out of the car, and stood, hands on hips. He sighed. He threw his head back and looked up at the sky, late-afternoon cobalt blue. He could see the top of the house in the corner of his eye—the old chimney still sitting there, out of a job since gas heat, the louvered attic window, the emphatic black line of the roof gutter. Planes and peaks and angles of green tile. It had looked tremendously high to him when he was a little boy.

"Nope," he said. He walked slowly up the driveway, looking at the sky. Nothing but blue. Nothing but blue. Nothing but blue.

He was almost at the garage when he saw a bright red baseball cap sail up past the roof gutter and climb into the blue, higher than the house, the louvered attic window to the right of it, the disused chimney to the left. The breeze caught it and fluttered it a moment, like the flag of a country that never was, and then spun it over his head and away.

In his mind a long-lost voice whispered low so no one would hear, "So long, Mighty Joe."

He must have been just about here. Maybe a tad lower and further back. He stepped to the edge of the driveway and parted the branches.

Winston crouched in the little open spot between two bushes as if he were in his closet. His eyes were wide and sorrowful.

Jake put out his hand. Winston ducked back, afraid he would be hit. When he raised his head again, Jake's hand was still there, waiting for him to take it. After a moment's hesitation, he reached out his own hand and was lifted gently to his feet.

"Come on, Feisty," Jake said. "We've got a long way to go."

·53·

To his relief, Lamb found only one Rugan in the Grissom phone book. He drove slowly past the address on Willow Street. The big house was not falling to pieces, but it wasn't what you might call "aggressively maintained." Phrases such as *shabby genteel* and *seen better days* came to his mind.

Her mailbox almost defiantly proclaimed "Miss Freda Rugan." The shadowy driver of Sally's story was clearly not her husband. Nor was the green car in evidence—just an old black Plymouth.

He smiled. This was no safe house. Winston wasn't living with the Grissom chief of police. It was beginning to look as if Harrow's little helpers—Sally, Gimlet, whoever—had merely stashed the boy out of harm's way with somebody's maiden aunt. They were waiting until Harrow got out of the hospital. There was no real security to worry about. He could concentrate on Winston himself.

He watched the house from several vantage points through the evening. A middle-aged woman moved around inside—that was all. By ten-thirty the only light was in a second-floor bedroom. At eleven-thirty it went out.

At one in the morning, he reparked his rental car out of sight in a subdivision behind the house. No police uniform—Winston was on to that. He stayed with his aging hippie look.

He swaddled his Trans-RDX egg in a pocket handkerchief and buttoned it into the side pocket of his bomber jacket.

He walked up someone's driveway and around the outside of their garage. If they had a dog, better to find out going in than coming out. They didn't.

329

Shining his flashlight low, he pushed through some shrubbery, and breached the high hedge behind the Rugan house.

The telephone wire drooped above him. He crossed the lawn to the outside service box on the wall and hacked through the bridle with a pocketknife.

He attached tiny unobtrusive motion sensors low to the ground on the garage edge, the birdbath, and the crab apple tree. He dragged the metal lawn swan several feet, so it lined up with the garage and the tree, and attached a fourth one, completing the circuit. If Winston slipped out of the house, these sensors would pinpoint his position.

The lock on the back door was strictly cheeseball. He shoved his pocketknife between the door and the jamb, stabbed into the soft metal of the latch, forced it back against its spring, and opened the door. Quicker than a key. Quieter too.

He darted into the house, flashlight blazing, almost hoping Winston would try to slip by. He saw no steak knives, so he took a bread knife, a nice one, sturdy and serrated, the steak knife's big brother. He moved swiftly to the stairs and eased up them, playing his scorching halogen beam all around.

He knew Winston always insisted on the second-floor hall closet; it was one of the few clear facts in Sally's story. He tiptoed to the door and pulled it open.

Startled by the light, the empty closet spit in his face. *Gone again, gone again,* it jeered. *Worse than before. You don't even rate the sneakers this time. Not even a cassette player!*

The pillow was smooth, the cushions cold. More than gone. Long gone.

He burst into Freda Rugan's bedroom and drilled the big light into her face, making her open her eyes, gasp, go blind. "Who are you?"

"Where's Winston?"

"You have no business here. Get out!" she said, fearful and defiant. She sat up in her blue gown with the high, white lace collar and pushed back at his flashlight beam, squinting behind her hand, trying to see him.

"I asked you where Winston is."

"This is my house. I'll call the police!"

He moved closer to the bed and turned the flashlight beam on the bread knife in his hand. "I know it's your house. It's your knife too. Is it sharp enough to cut you open? What do you think? Speaking as its owner."

Her eyes were wide, jerking back and forth between his shadowed face and the gleaming knife. "Put that down! Get away!"

"Tell me where Winston is, or I'll slash you until you do."

"I don't know where he is. Be careful with that knife!"

"His bed is in your closet."

"I left it there. I do my laundry Thursday."

"If he's not here, who took him away?"

"I don't know."

"*You don't know who took him?* Freda Rugan! That just has to be a lie. I'm going to have to hurt you for that." He raised the knife.

In his left ear a tiny loudspeaker emitted a tone . . . silence . . . higher tone . . . silence . . . even higher tone. Somebody—or something—was moving across the back of the house. The pitch of the signals located it one-third of the way from the garage to the birdbath, moving toward the birdbath.

As he was about to dash across the hall and look out a back window, a second set of beeps, two octaves higher, began to chord with the first. He darted to her bedroom window in time to see a policeman stalking across the front lawn with his gun drawn.

On a silver mailbox across Willow Street, red and blue light pulsed swiftly as a bird's heart: roof-light reflections of a cruiser parked out of his sight.

"*Help! Help!*" Freda Rugan jumped out of bed and rushed for the door.

In a leap he caught her, grabbed her hair with one hand, and dragged her to the bed, still yelling.

"Shut up!" He brandished the knife in her face.

"*Help!*"

He parked the knife in his belt, flung her on the bed, snatched a towel from her bedside table, and jammed it over her mouth.

As he lifted the towel he saw what was hidden under it: a cellular phone, its leather case dull with moisture. He stared at it, hardly able to believe his eyes.

She must have heard me come in and called the cops. That's why they parked out of sight. They've got the place surrounded. I'm trapped.

Freda Rugan struggled furiously, trying to free her mouth from the towel. He dropped his knee on her stomach with his full weight, yanked the bread knife from his belt, and slit her throat.

She bucked wildly, lifting him completely off the floor, making muffled whoops of pain like a woman in labor. Her arterial blood warmed his hand through the towel.

Her struggles weakened, her head flopped back, small blood bubbles formed at her throat wound. She made a noise like a long sigh.

Hurry up and die, damn you.

331

Her hands and feet were still jerking spasmodically when he darted to the window and raised it as far as it would go. The tiny beeps in his ear told him one cop was at the front of the house on the driveway side. He knelt by the sill, leaned out cautiously, and spotted the man with his back to him, looking around the corner of the house.

Freda Rugan sprawled motionless now, with staring eyes and grinning throat. Lamb cradled her warm body in his arms, carried her to the window, and threw her out. She hit the ground with a thump, landing on her left side, and actually seemed to curl up and make herself comfortable on the grass.

The cop had already disappeared around the side of the house, but he heard the noise and came back. He stood gaping at the light blue shape for several seconds with a puzzlement close to awe. He clearly had no idea how it got there. He walked wide of it, peering out, trying to see around the far side of the house.

He shined his flashlight on it, blinked, and staggered slightly. He dropped to one knee and grabbed a wrist, trying to find a pulse. He yelled as if he'd been wounded, "George! Come here quick! George! George!"

A moment later George galloped around the far side of the house, yelling, "What?"

"It's Miz Rugan. She's dead."

"My Lord."

George ran over to look.

The two men were too intent on her dead body to notice the poker-chip-size wafer skimming down from the window above them. It landed near George's shoe, hitting the ground edge-on. The impact, hardly more than a finger-snap of force, was enough to set off a detonating shock wave in Trans-RDX. One thirty-thousandth of a second later, the wafer exploded.

After throwing it, Lamb had rolled under the bed. Even with his ears covered, the blast was painful. The floor swayed under him like a ship in heavy seas. Plaster rained down from the ceiling and popped off the walls in jigsaw pieces.

He scrambled to his feet, his right hand yellow with egg yolk. The room was littered with broken glass. Plaster dust billowed in choking clouds. He looked out the window. Part of the facade had fallen on the lawn, covering the spot where Freda Rugan and the two cops had been. A chain reaction of collapse continued to rack the old house like the aftershock of an earthquake. All around him beams cracked, walls buckled, ceilings crashed down.

Sprinting down the stairs, he heard the ominous roar of fire.

·54·

Naked, Sally's body seemed to glow. Her beauty excited him, almost stunned him.

She frightened him too. Sexually mature—yet no one's mother. Not a prostitute like Tanaba. Sally was near the right age, the right background, for him. The woman he should want to meet, know, and marry. The woman he always stayed away from—even in fantasy.

Lamb began to undress.

Excitement and fear, he trembled with both. He had never come at a woman like this—quietly, vulnerably, as an equal. He had always been the master, the feared one, the monster from hell. The women had been bound and gagged. Voiceless and helpless.

To approach a woman without the power of life and death over her—to submit himself to her judgment, to her human scrutiny—was terrifying. But it was also, unexpectedly, alive with possibilities. Moment by moment, he was taking the risk. He was no longer locked into his ancient script, screaming and shouting but always knowing the end. He was with an equal, and they were improvising.

As he pulled off his underpants, he covered his flaccid penis with his hand, as if it were a promise he couldn't fulfill.

Sally watched him from the bed, a little smile on her face. She seemed to understand his feelings exactly—to be far ahead of him. When he got into bed, she waited for him to take her in his arms. She cuddled up to him without urgency. She seemed happy just to be in his embrace.

They lay like that for a while. Lamb began to relax. He stroked her back. She pressed closer to him, skin to skin, pillowing him in cool softness. The touch of a woman's body, all up and down the length of him, was a revelation, like stepping into an earthly paradise.

333

"Umm, you're so nice," Sally said. "Such a honey-tiger."

Honey-tiger. Lamb knew those words. He had them on tape. She called Jake *honey-tiger* during lovemaking. It was her secret little phrase of love. *She was saying it to him!*

Tears started in his eyes. "I like that," he said. "Call me that again."

"What? *Honey-tiger?* Well, you are, you know. You are my honey-tiger."

"Would you—would you do something for your honey-tiger?"

"Ummm. What's that?"

"Would you give me your wedding ring?"

She held up her hands so he could see her wiggle off her wedding ring.

Lamb's penis was erect. He rolled over to face her. She took his hand and slid her ring on his little finger.

"My only honey-tiger," she said.

With growing eagerness, he put his arms around her. Her legs clasped one of his, her breasts flowed and pressed against his chest, her belly cradled his erection in a feather-soft groove. He had never felt anything like it.

Her mouth opened to his kisses, her hands flowed over him, gently pleasuring him. He stroked her back and thighs, his hands instinctively moving over the landscape of her body. They lolled together for a time like that, stroking and touching and kissing each other, until his skin rang with pleasure at every heartbeat like a bell.

The act that had been impossible for him all his life was now easy. He mounted her and felt her soft hand guide his penis into her vagina.

Could it be? Had she *healed* him? Could he change his life, get off his murderous treadmill?

They moved together now, faster, more urgently, intent on each other's pleasure and their own—no leader, no follower, dancers lost in the dance.

They were wrapped in each other, mouth to mouth. She moaned into him, opening and clinging, locking and releasing. He gathered her up, lifted her almost vertical from the soaking sheets. He felt her bear down to give birth to her orgasm.

"Oh, my honey-tiger," Lamb said. "Mine, all *mine.*"

Together! They were one flesh. The blood was roaring in his ears.

"Sir, *sir*—shall I help you with that?"

Lamb opened his eyes. The young flight attendant raised his seat back to its upright and locked position with swift impatience. The plane was landing at LaGuardia.

He had slept all the way from Indianapolis. The midmorning dazzle hurt his eyes. He rubbed them, wondering: *Could I really do it? Make love to her like a normal man?*

Like Jake?

What the hell was the director doing?

Cal Ordway froze in the doorway, startled at what he saw in the room.

Just as he was leaving for the day, from out of the blue, the director had summoned him here: Level five, E-section at Langley, an inside conference room; workaday, cheap reproductions on the walls, a coffee urn on the table to the back. The door was color-coded green, proclaiming it to be only moderately resistant to electronic bugging.

Three men already sat at the table: Pritchard, Sylvere, and Rance. Together with Ordway, they constituted the Liar's Club, the club that never met. Each of them ran a deniable operation, sealed off not only from the Company—and from congressional oversight—but from each other. They were careful never to visit each other's offices, talk in the hall, appear at the same restaurants or parties. Once Ordway had played through Sylvere's foursome at Burning Tree; neither man had nodded.

For the director to bring them together like this was a violation of a taboo. It bespoke desperate haste, networks compromised, lives at risk.

Ordway took his place at the table. He sensed immediately that the others were as confused as he was. Nobody knew where to look, so they stared uneasily at the walls and ceiling.

"Good afternoon, gentlemen." The director bustled in. No apology for the hour. He was in shirt-sleeves, wearing his trademark red suspenders, red tie, and red socks: flares to show his flair. The red said: *I may come out of Analysis and not Operations, but I'm no gray little paper-pusher.*

He made a swift circuit of the table, handing each man a folder, and then sat back, arms behind his head, feet on the table, showing them his red socks while they—in the jargon—*read in.*

The folders were stuffed with newspaper clippings. Oh, yes, the Silencer killings. Ordway was vaguely familiar with them. Tabloid fodder, along with smoky fires and gangland shootings. What did this have to do with the Game of Nations?

The director looked around the table, his raised eyebrows asking if they were ready. They were.

"We had a walk-in this morning, saying he could prove the Silencer was a rogue agent and demanding to see me. Of course that wasn't possible, so he ended up telling his theory to the public relations people. He had evidence that three of the four murdered families on the FBI list had elaborate secret languages. And he had one more thing. He's convinced the killer murdered a fifth family—one the Bureau checked out and rejected. Name of Grant. He can prove they also had a secret language. Who else but a surveilling agent could locate four families like that? That was his argument.

"He had a boy with him who he claimed witnessed one of the family killings. The boy had made an Identi-Kit composite, which the walk-in wanted to run through the personnel computer files, trying for a match."

The director took his feet off the table and leaned forward. "Our walk-in also claims that after Haney was in custody, the real killer tried to kill both him and the boy. But he has no proof of that.

"So far pretty thin, but he's quite a persuasive fellow, our walk-in, and he somehow got the PR people to call the FBI and ask them to search Leith's effects for evidence of a secret language.

"Leith was murdered back in January, but he was an accountant with a lot of political bigwigs for clients. All his stuff was impounded by the DC cops—his clients had to get a court order to get their own tax records. Of course, none of the pols complained—they didn't want their private finances lying around for everybody to look at.

"Midmorning, two junior agents go to a storage warehouse out in Arlington and trash-dive in Leith's papers. Lo and behold, they come up with a beautifully desktop-printed and hand-bound dictionary in their teeth. The Leiths had a family language called 'Righteous.' It's a mixture of Gullah, old-time southern Blacklish, Sotho, and nursery words."

Sylvere started digging through the clippings in his folder. "Where did I get the idea the Leiths were white?"

"Lily white," the director said. "Albert Leith was from an old southern family. According to the dedication in the front of the dictionary, he learned Righteous as a boy from a black woman who worked for his family. He calls her 'my true mother.'

"Righteous made it five-for-five for Harrow's family language theory. That's when the PR people took their careers in their hands and yanked me out of a meeting with the DNC. In the last hour, I've talked to the heads of the other services. They've pledged to search their files—all of them. Including the unredacted ones. I want you to do the same. The names of the members of all five families are on a sheet in those folders. If our walk-in is right, most or all of them were under surveillance at one time or another by the same agent. As soon as you leave this meeting, you are to go wherever you keep your soft files and look for those names. If even one shows up—in any connection—I want to know about it. I'll need your answer by midnight."

Ordway ran his eyes over the names of the murdered families. None of them rang a bell.

Rance glared at the director. "You're aware that we can't delegate this search to anyone. We don't share material this sensitive. We'll have to do it ourselves."

"Sorry to spoil your evening," the director said.

"Was the Identi-Kit picture ever run through the computer?" Ordway asked.

The director smiled blandly. "Like a turd through a log flume. No match."

Ordway fought hard but unsuccessfully to keep the anger out of his voice. "You want us to take the family jewels out of the strongbox because of some nursery-gabble dictionary?"

"Care to see it? I could hardly get it back from our linguists, they were so fascinated." The director placed a large black box on the table. On the cover, in gold letters, was embossed the title:

RIGHTEOUS
BE
RIGHTEOUS

The four spy masters stared at it stonily.

The director was enjoying this. He stifled a grin. "The walk-in told me the Grants spoke a kind of Doctor Doolittle Esperanto made up of languages of animals that are becoming extinct. They called it—" He covered his mouth and looked down. "*Dolphone. The Endangered Speechies.*"

Pritchard said, "You wouldn't be twisting the tail of Operations, now would you?"

The director shrugged, openly smiling now. "Operations and Analysis—Scottish rite and York rite."

It was an old wheeze that the two sides of the Company were as similar as the two rites of Freemasonry. Sylvere mused, "Only people from Analysis ever say that. I wonder why?"

The director stood up. "I'd admire to sit here and chew the fat, but we've all got work to do."

No one else moved.

The director raised his eyebrows. "Come, come, gentlemen, you'd

337

better get a move on if you're going to dig up your basements by midnight."

"I want an explanation," Ordway said.

"Of what?"

"Why you whistled us all together like a brother act when you know it's part of our brief never to meet?"

"Don't tell me—I've committed a *gaffe*? Violated the sacred rules of trade-craft? A man of action like you should be the first to understand. There's not always time for these hoary old traditions in a crisis."

"Crisis? Because some walk-in has a bright idea?"

The director put his knuckles on the table and leaned toward him. "Calvin, Calvin. Maybe it's time you came in from the cold. A crisis today isn't about one-time pads and leaving the microfilm in the crotch of the old oak tree; it's about *budgets*. Who gets how much of that ever-shrinking pie. They're crazy for cuts on the Hill, and we're already having trouble justifying our reason for being. What if the walk-in is right? That means one of our own people is out there, insane, murdering moms and kids. And he's more likely to be caught every passing day —by somebody else. If that happens, we have no way to shut him up. What if he surrenders to a newspaper columnist or television station? Or takes hostages and demands to tell his story over the air? This isn't dirty tricks in some Third-World country Rand never mentioned to McNally; it's multiple murders right here in the U.S. of A. We trained this guy at taxpayer's expense to kill taxpayers. We become the guard dog that ate the baby. Think how that will play at appropriations time."

He walked to the door. "Midnight—no later. I'll be waiting."

Ordway had his home in Potomac Overlook, but he maintained a pied-à-terre in Georgetown—a big attic room in a mansion on M Street near Wisconsin—it was here he was now forced to spend the next few hours, strolling down memory lane.

He unlocked the door to the apartment and went in. Outside his dormer windows the trees were in leaf, and the white ghetto of the District's northwest quadrant glistened sleekly in the long June evening. For a moment he thought, *The hell with it, I'm not going to find anything.* Why not nip down to Nathan's Tavern for a pint of the best? The director will never know.

But no. He still had some discipline, even if nobody else did. If the director wanted a Chinese fire-drill through his old files, that was what he would get. With a sigh, he dragged the vacuum cleaner from the hall closet into the bathroom. He opened the shaving cabinet and moved a blade dispenser from one side of the shelf to the other, turning off a timer buried in the wall. The timer was set to degauss the data if the cabinet door was left open for more than thirty seconds. Any attempt to break through the wall would also erase the data as well as set off a very nasty explosion.

He took from his briefcase a specially built nozzle, which he attached to the vacuum cleaner and held flush with the razor-blade disposal slot in the back of the cabinet. He ran the vacuum for a while, then opened the bag. Inside were what looked like one hundred used razor blades. In fact, they were all data-encryption devices. Ninety-nine of them contained plausible but utterly false information. He sorted through them carefully, until he found the one with the correct pattern of edge nicks and slipped it into what looked like an ordinary VHS cassette, which he inserted in the VCR. He turned on the equipment and settled back in a chair, with a remote in his hand.

A list of names scrolled down the face of his television set.

He took the director's list from his pocket. *Okay, the first name is* Giles. He knew that of course it wouldn't be there.

What the hell—?

He stopped the scroll and squinted at the name on the screen. Then he tapped another button on the remote and accessed their file.

Los Angeles, California. Giles, Morton and Audrey. Three little girls.

Same family.

Surveilling agent: Evan Highland.

Damn it. The director would want a full report from him on this family, in person, probably around two A.M. Luckily, he wouldn't have to waste time tracking down the agent. Highland had been blown to quarks more than a year ago in Europe. Minnick had shown him the relics—a belt, shoelaces, bits of clothing. Thank God for small blessings.

Next name: *Grant.*

·55·

After their meeting at Langley on Wednesday, the director arranged for Jake and Winston to disappear to a safe house that, he told Jake, was used for only the highest-level defectors and diplomats, and was unknown even to the inner circle who were combing their files for evidence of the Silencer.

The director had promised an answer by Friday morning. There was nothing to do but wait.

Two agents escorted them to a parking garage, sat them in the back of a windowless van, and drove them for three-quarters of an hour. Jake had the impression they were going in circles, but couldn't be sure. When the van doors opened, they were in the cellar garage of an old stone house. Every window had a heavy ornamental grating, and all you saw when you looked out were walls and trees. From the tang in the air, Jake guessed they were somewhere near the Potomac.

Nobody actually said it, but it was clear they were to stay inside the house.

Jake and Winston sat side by side, alone at a table for fourteen, and were served a superb *coq au vin* by a taciturn staff of too many people, all of whom packed guns under their aprons. Jake worried the fare might be a bit too fancy for Winston, but he turned to it with a will. Even the waiter-assassin couldn't suppress a smile when the kid grabbed a hunk of bread and started to mop up the gravy.

They watched TV for a while, with two large men who never laughed at the jokes. Jake put Winston to bed, turned out the light, and stood in the doorway of the room.

"This is the life, huh? We're living in a safe house. What a great name for it. Nobody can get at us here. Right, Winst?"

"Where is you go sleep?"

"Right next door. Try it here, okay? If you don't like it, I'll have them put a cot in my room for you. See how long you can last."

Winston felt safe for several minutes by thinking about the big powerful men who were downstairs guarding them. They sure looked mean. They were almost scary the way they didn't talk or smile and were always looking around like they heard something you didn't.

Meanest of all was that big man who had driven them over. He seemed to hate everybody—*What if he was the Constable in disguise?* Maybe that was why he didn't talk much—he was afraid Winston would recognize his voice. That cot began to sound better and better.

He slipped out of bed and opened the door to the hall.

Directly across from him—How had he missed it before?—was the door to a linen closet!

Or maybe it wasn't a linen closet. Did a safe house have linen closets? Maybe it was full of guns and bombs. Maybe it was full of dead bodies hanging in a row like suits.

But they had lots of beds here. They must keep the sheets and pillowcases *somewhere*. He darted across the hall and yanked the door open.

Stacks and stacks of snowy white sheets glowed like ghosts in the dim light.

Feeling a little ashamed, he stepped quickly inside and closed the door behind him, leaving only the narrowest of cracks for fresh air.

He crawled under the bottom shelf, lay on his back, and wedged himself in sideways, his head on one wall, his feet on the other. Immediately, he felt safer. It was such a relief to be hidden away in his own little place. He began to feel sleepy.

He wiggled his right foot down the wall, looking for the best angle, until he felt the cold metal of the water turn-off valve. Stretching, already half asleep, he gave it a slight shove.

Silently, the back wall swung away from him like a door, spilling him on a floor behind the closet. He lay there blinking for several seconds, not quite sure he wasn't dreaming. The backs of the linen closet shelves loomed above his face, bulging with folded sheets like a ladder leaning on a cloud. He rolled over and clambered to his feet. He stood at the base of a flight of stairs that rose steeply to a door rimmed by light.

In the room above, a woman was groaning loudly. Was the Constable hurting her, like that night in Skokie?

No, the woman wasn't groaning from pain but from something just as fierce that she couldn't get enough of. He started up the stairs. Now he could hear a man groaning too, his groans getting quicker and louder, saying yes and no at the same time.

On the final step, Winston put his palm on the door and gently pushed it forward.

He entered something like a small movie theater. At the far end was a huge television screen, surrounded top and side by a dozen or so normal-size monitors, with motionless green pictures on them. Down front, only the backs of their heads visible, two men sat on a couch, watching in the half-light. The groaning man and woman were not in the room at all, only in the movie on the big middle screen. He wore cowboy boots, a big hat, and nothing else, and she was completely naked, her legs wrapped around him. In the movie it was bright noon, he had her over the hood of a truck, and they were both bouncing up and down, her teeth clacking together, and her neck all corded.

A strange metallic voice said, "Motion, sector one."

For an instant, Winston was aware that something was moving on one of the small monitors; abruptly it jumped to the big central screen, replacing the man and woman. In a black-rimmed mass of green, a huge-eyed bird flapped its wings, obviously flying upward, but also, somehow not moving—an owl. Something small and frantic and doomed struggled in its talons—a mouse.

One of the watchers down front said, "Fuckin Barney again. I swear he waits for the good parts."

Winston turned and slipped softly down the stairs, under the cloud ladder of sheets, through the closet door, and back to the bed he had left. It was still warm.

Twenty minutes later he opened his eyes to see a big silhouette standing in the doorway of his room, watching him. Jake. It seemed to him at that moment that Jake was like a sheltering mountain who would always be there.

"I is asleep," he said.

"You want the cot? It's okay."

Winston felt himself floating away on the warm sea of sleep.

"Bed go do me," he said.

Ordway paced his Georgetown attic. Should he tell the director what he had found? Do nothing, and hope for the best? Go after Highland by himself? No matter how he drew the decision tree, he saw himself dangling among the branches, hanged by the neck until dead.

He looked again at the Identi-Kit picture. Even in this rough approximation, it was clear Highland had changed his face beyond recognition—and just as clear that beneath the plastic surgery, this was the man he had mentored and brought along and trained.

Evan Highland was his agent, his creation, his creature. He would stick to Ordway like a tattoo.

Soft breezes bellied the diaphanous white curtains on his dormer windows. On the brick sidewalks below, prides of yuppies bayed for nightspots where they could be ripped off with that cool, Georgetown efficiency they so admired.

I tried to kill him.

Did that make things better or worse?

Worse. Failure is always worse. Highland had outsmarted him, successfully faked his own death. He was still alive, out there somewhere on the North American continent, using his elite training to butcher six-year-old girls and get away with it.

The digital clock flopped soundlessly.

Ten P.M.

He had until midnight to call the director and either tell him what he'd found or go for a cover-up.

It was so tempting to do nothing, drop the razor blade back into the slot and go home; hope that Highland was never caught. But if Highland's story ever became public, the director would scapegoat Ordway. He'd do the same thing in the director's shoes. Who could resist? It was too damn easy, Red Queen was designed to be deniable. He had thrust his own neck in the noose. He would end up in Marion, Illinois, tapping out chess moves with his tin plate to Edwin Wilson in the next cell.

But the FBI and the police were still hypnotized by Haney. What if the Company caught Highland? That was the more likely scenario—if they knew he was out there, if they had his name. Ordway had files on Highland—height, weight, blood type. Tomorrow morning a hundred CIA agents would be questioning his family, relatives, friends, searching his old haunts, armed with an Identi-Kit of his new face, and a boy who could identify him. Oh, yes, the Company would find him in short order. And then what?

In the old days the whole thing would have been kept secret; Highland would have been ground up for Fish-Meal Helper, no one the wiser. But today? No, this director wouldn't bury it. He'd go public—use it to consolidate his power.

That little humiliation in the meeting room—bringing all the Deniables together like clerks—that was the first shot in a war. This was just the stick he needed to beat Operations to death. Bury Highland? He'd call him the tip of the iceberg and dig for more. Show trials, public shriving, all his enemies demoted, disgraced, jailed. He'd work with his cabal on the Hill. Convene another Church Committee to study abuses. The hour has struck; the best disinfectant is sunlight; pass the bowl, it's Pontius Pilate time. Evan Highland on C-SPAN explaining how you grip the gun two-handed and shoot for the bridge of the nose, while senators squatted on the hypocrite high chairs and faked their squeals like wedding-night whores. "Are you telling me that it was the policy of this government to execute foreign nationals in their own countries? Without *due process of law?*"

"I was only following orders."

"Whose orders?"

"That man's, sir. Sitting right there. Calvin Ordway."

Ordway decided to tell the director he had found nothing.

He would go after Highland himself.

·56·

"How's Reuben?" Nan asked. She was leaning against the kitchen sink with her arms folded.

Sally was carefully pouring hot water into an individual filter, making herself a midmorning cup of coffee. She didn't look up. "Don't start that again; it's too depressing."

"You're not going to tell me how dear Reuben is?"

"I don't know any Reuben! How many times do I have to say it?"

"Well, Sibyl Ghilinhall saw you having breakfast with someone."

"So now you've got your friends spying on me. How charming. How adorable."

"You're the one who's conducting a public love affair."

"Have you any idea how insulting this is? It would never occur to Sibyl—or to you apparently—that I could be in a public place with a man for anything but an assignation. That man was Professor Lamb of Wren College. He's going to publish a story of mine in a new literary magazine. We were going over the manuscript. And we were only having coffee, not breakfast."

"Sibyl said you acted like you were on a date."

"Oh, and I'm supposed to answer for Sibyl's active fantasy life? She's the one you should be mad at for spreading malicious gossip."

"Princeton isn't New York City. People see things."

"I don't know why we're having this conversation. I'm a grown woman."

"You're also a married woman. And I'll thank you to behave like one as long as you're living in this house."

"I met him in this house."

"Met who?"

347

"Professor Lamb was at your dinner party on Saturday night."

"That doesn't give you permission to have an affair with him."

"I'm not having an affair with him, and I wouldn't need your permission if I were. I have a right to my own life."

Nan seemed to regard the statement as too silly to bother with. She dumped the paper filter full of Sally's coffee grounds in the compactor and frowned thoughtfully. "I don't remember inviting a Professor Lamb."

"Somebody else couldn't make it and gave him the invitation."

"Nobody spoke to me about it. Honestly, some people! We're not running a public restaurant . . . Lamb wasn't that young man on your right at the table, was he?"

"You dealt the place cards, Mommy dearest. We were sitting where you put us."

"Until you plastered yourself to him—you were practically on his lap. You never said a word to anyone else around you—I was watching. It was so rude."

"You're worse than Popsy. I thought I was a guest, not an entertainer."

"You may not be an entertainer, but you made quite a show of yourself. I tried to wigwag you little signals to control yourself, but you didn't pick them up. You were too busy crawling all over your new boyfriend like a drunken little tramp at a fraternity party."

"What's going on with you, Mother? I'm telling you I'm not having an affair. Professor Lamb is helping me with my short story. That's all, that's it. You want me to swear on the Bible?"

"I'd rather you opened the Bible and refreshed yourself on your marriage vow. Jake Harrow is your husband. Whatever is going on between you, however bad it may get, you still have an obligation to him to behave decently."

"You want to see the manuscript with Professor Lamb's suggestions on it? When you see how many there are, you'll realize we wouldn't have time for hanky-panky, even if we wanted it." She started out of the kitchen.

"Don't bother," Nan said. "I'm not interested in alibis and evidence and proofs."

Sally wheeled in rage. "Nothing I say, nothing I show you, will make a particle of difference, is that it? Are you God? Where do you get off being so sure."

"I'm not sure. This is only a warning. But if I hear any more scandal about you and this Professor Lamb, you are leaving this house. I will not have an unfaithful wife under my roof."

"Oh, but an unfaithful husband is just dandy."

Nan stared at her for several seconds. Then she turned to the sink and began to rinse cups, talking with her back to Sally. "I should have walked out on Popsy when I was young. Now it's too late; I like my life too much; I'm too comfortable. What's strange is—" She turned suddenly and looked Sally in the eye. "—it still *hurts*. I won't have you doing it too, not in my own home, right under my nose. If you're going to betray the trust of those who love you, you'll do it out of my sight. I have to live with Popsy's lies. But I'll be damned if I'll watch you become just like him!"

The wind on the Chesapeake shouted for sailors. Ordway heard, but could not heed.

He spent the day hunched in a swivel chair, stomach churning, fighting for his life, making one phone call after another, feverishly taking notes on yellow pads, with nothing to help him but his trusty old voice-stress analyzer.

He had loved that machine ever since it tipped him off that his first wife was cheating on him. He would never part with it.

The analyzer was from the Paleolithic era. He joked that it was the last coal-fired model ever built—a big upright job with a bank of LEDs: honest green, doubtful yellow, and whopper red. Ordway liked those big horsey lights—they showed whether the speaker was truthful or not, without subtleties or qualifications. What more could a machine do, anyway? The new analyzers were more sophisticated, miniaturized down to cigarette-pack size, but all they showed you were little black digits, plastered like soggy tea leaves on a gray magma.

He felt a terrible pressure to work quickly, to find Evan Highland before somebody else did. Every hour that passed was another hour away from last midnight, when he had begun to lie to the director.

His telephone numbers were all out of date. He had to call and wheedle and play games just to locate the people on his lists. And when he finally reached them, they didn't know squat.

The problem with his soft-filed information was that there were no teams of clerks to update it on a regular basis, as happened with the official files. Personnel information decays rapidly: the half-life of a telephone number is under twenty months. Even in backwaters like Selvage and Malcolm, people move, marry, change jobs, and die at a fearsome rate. But Ordway had to make do with what he had—he dared not ask anyone at the Company for help.

Walter Highland had long ago sold the house in Malcolm and was living in Atlanta with his third wife. He hadn't spoken to Evan in more than a decade. When Ordway mentioned the name, his father shouted,

"I got a notice he was dead. You mean he's not?" The idea that his son might still be alive seemed to spoil his morning.

Evan Highland's past had been scattered to the winds. His childhood friends now lived in Palo Alto and Little Rock and Rome. They hadn't kept up with each other, let alone Evan. His high school had been spun off into four high schools; the original building was now a community college.

By early afternoon, Ordway's left ear had been rubbed red and sore by the phone and a knot had drawn tight in the pit of his stomach. The personal stuff—family, childhood buddies, old girlfriends—that was where even the cleverest fugitives slipped up. No one can walk away from his past totally. By now, in searches like this, there was always something, a hint, a glimpse, a phone call in the middle of the night to hear a remembered voice.

We trained him too well, Ordway thought. *He left no tracks.*

He stared at his voice-stress analyzer as if it were a shortwave radio that picked up nothing but static on every frequency. Where was Evan Highland—outer space?

Wait a minute, he thought. *Damn my methodical mind!* He had missed an obvious link—the walk-in! The walk-in said Highland tried to kill him and the child witness. My God—as soon as the director was convinced there was no rogue agent, the walk-in would turn into a walk-out.

How long before Highland tried again?

Follow the walk-in.

When Highland finds him, I find Highland.

The driver of the van—the mean-looking one Winston suspected of being the Constable in disguise—watched from behind the wheel of the van as Jake and Winston boarded the elevator in the Langley parking garage. He parked the van in its numbered stall and took a different elevator to the surface. Barr Polowski had finished work for the day.

As he crossed the outside parking lot to his car somebody nearby called, "Barr my friend, come here a second!"

To his left—the black BMW with the roof rack. He bent and peered. Cal Ordway was sitting at the wheel, motioning him to get in the car. As Polowski slid in on the passenger seat he noticed Ordway was holding a crisp stack of new bills under the steering column.

"You know currency," Ordway said. "You think these hundreds are counterfeit?" He handed Polowski several.

Polowski squinted at them judiciously. "Excellent stock. High fiber content, correct colored-thread count. They might be legal tender."

"Last night's guest list at Chain Bridge?"

"Two. They were together. Man and a little boy. I took them over in the early evening; I just now drove them back. Red Suspenders wanted to see them."

"Sounds right." Ordway peeled off several more bills and handed them over. "Who's the guy?"

"A New York detective named Jake Harrow. Hero cop. Ton of medals."

Ordway's eyes widened. "Jake Harrow. I read about him. His brother's family was one of those killed. Now I understand why he won't take no for an answer. A man with a mission." He forked over another hundred. "What's the deal with the kid?"

"He's called Winston Churchill Harrow. The brother adopted him. Oh, and he's black. Almost forgot that. West Indian."

"It would be nice if I could locate Harrow's car." He gave Polowski the remaining bills and dusted his hands.

Polowski frowned, looking closely at the money. "Is this Franklin on here or Zsa Zsa Gabor?"

Ordway went into his jacket pocket and came out with another hundred. "That's the stack."

"Too bad. Franklin's still sporting cleavage."

Ordway took out his wallet, removed a hundred, and handed it over. "Leave me carfare."

Polowski watched him a moment, and then said, "You know that two thou you still got in your jacket? Toilet paper. Don't bother showing it to me. An old green Cadillac Eldorado. Visitor's Parking."

"Barr, you're better than a black-light reader."

"A pleasure, Mr. Ordway. Your money's always good with me."

Jake and Winston were told to wait in a conference room with their suitcases. Jake's heart sank. Yesterday he met with the director in his office. He remembered Cowen explaining that he never gave people bad news in his own office. If they got emotional, he wanted to be able to walk away.

The director bustled in. No shirt-sleeves this time—in fact, his jacket was buttoned. He seemed to be leaving for the day. He didn't sit.

"Sorry to switch times like this. Frankly, I thought it would take longer than it did to turn over every rock in the garden. I wanted to check out even the low-probability operations. The kind of people who are good at this work don't always pick up on the first ring, as I'm sure you appreciate."

"You're not going to tell me you didn't find anything?"

The director took an index card from his inside pocket and consulted it. "No files anywhere on Giles or Leith. Harrow—I'm sorry—your brother—and his wife, the Grants, and Lyle Sturluson cropped up here and there on old lists of possible subversives or troublemakers, but none of them was ever under surveillance."

"If you had found something, would you tell me?"

"Probably not. But we haven't."

"Somebody's covering up."

"That's always possible, but remember—every one of my senior people has now put his career on the line. You say the Silencer is still loose out there. If he's caught, and it turned out he actually did work for us—I doubt anyone would be crazy enough to take that kind of risk."

"Maybe one of them is involved."

"Maybe I'm the Silencer myself. There's always another scenario. I have now twisted the scrota of the entire top echelon of American intelligence for you. I'm afraid that's all she wrote."

"Did you get me here a day early because you didn't find anything —or because you did?"

"I told you immediately as a courtesy. I'd have let you cool your heels in the safe house until the Fourth of July if I'd known it would help you to feel secure. I thought you might have better things to do."

"Yeah—like going to the media. I still think someone is covering up. I warn you, I'm going to raise some hell."

He pumped Jake's hand warmly. "I want to thank you for your yeoman work on this. I enjoyed meeting you, I really did."

He bent down and shook hands with Winston. "You too, young man. Maybe when you're a little older, you'll think about a career in intelligence. Will you do that? Hm?"

Winston nodded gravely.

He straightened up and winked at Jake. "Plucky little chap. Safe home, detective. Someone will see you out."

Lost in calculation, Jake didn't bother to reply. They would have an early dinner in Washington; he'd call the TV station from the restaurant. The drive to New York should take four to five hours. With any luck he'd be spilling his guts to Trask Walkins before midnight.

Ordway sauntered through the visitors' parking lot.

An old green Cadillac Eldorado. Cop with a Cadillac—little status striving here? Bet he lives in the suburbs.

There it is. Ah ha! What did I say—Jersey plates! Nice old Caddy— well maintained. Hasn't been driven much, considering the vintage.

*He probably lives someplace close, like Fort Lee. Takes the bus to work,
that's why this old buggy is so clean.*

He strolled up behind the car and drew a small metal box from his
pocket: a high-powered transmitter with good strong magnets that clung
like epoxy. Not even New York's axle-eating potholes could jar this
baby loose.

Without breaking stride, he slapped it under the Cadillac's left rear
fender.

·57·

Cal Ordway arrowed north on the throughway in his black BMW. His direction finder beeped softly, as it copied a steady stream of pulses from the transmitter under Harrow's fender—it would alert him to any radical change in the speed of the vehicle ahead. Its field-strength meter automatically controlled his speed to keep him two miles behind Harrow's car. The right-left indicator needle floated lazily back and forth with the long, well-engineered curves of the highway—he could ignore it.

With Harrow locked in his electronic sights he could concentrate on finding Highland.

At his side was a laptop computer holding every scrap of information he had and loaded with an A/I expert program for sniffing out connections. He wore a telephone headset to keep his hands free. The computer dialed for him with a single keystroke. There was no need to take notes. All his calls were tape-recorded, so he could keyboard new information into the system when Harrow took rest stops. His voice-stress analyzer, hung under the dash on the passenger side on a gimbal, yawed toward him so he could check it at the flick of an eye.

He could pursue two quarries at once and drive with both hands on the wheel.

Highland had kept clear of his childhood connections. That left Harvard and the CIA.

There were a few CIA people Ordway could have called. Other scanners, agents, technicians whom Highland had known casually. Ordway avoided that. He didn't want word percolating back to the director that he was on the trail of someone who had once worked for him. He had taken enough risk with Polowski.

Ordway didn't bother trying Highland's Harvard friends. None of them would still be at their old numbers. No problem. Universities keep very good track of their graduates for fund-raising; he'd call Harvard itself in the morning and get the current addresses and phone numbers.

That left professors. Not a promising lot, but what the hell. He knew from years of experience that fugitives find it surprisingly hard to move to places they've never lived. Highland might have returned to Cambridge. One of his old professors might have spotted him strolling on Brattle Street. Or he might have written for a job reference. Sometimes the smartest ones do the dumbest things.

He'd find these people fast: unlike other head workers, professors stay put, nailed in place by tenure. This would be a little easier.

It wasn't. He'd forgotten how short the academic year had become. This was June. Most of the people on his list were already rusticating at their summer homes or boondoggling in Europe at conferences. He talked to a gaggle of renters and house sitters.

Of the few professors he did reach on the first try, none remembered Highland. They had all taught him as an undergraduate.

By now it was full night. The last Wilmington exit dropped away behind him. The computer screen was showing Professor Osbert Orpington of Harvard. The name was faintly familiar. The computer told him this was Highland's thesis adviser. Ordway tapped a button and listened to the phone number being speed-dialed in his ear. Out of service. The computer automatically looked up the current phone number of Orpington's Cambridge house. The new owner still had Orpington's number in northern New Jersey.

Beep Beep BEEP. He was closing rapidly with the green Cadillac. The field-strength meter kicked out of cruise control and turned the accelerator back to Ordway. The direction needle sliced right. The next highway sign proclaimed gas and food coming up. Harrow was taking a rest stop. Ordway tooled up the service road, parked in the furthest rank, got out of the car, and checked around. The lot was three-quarters full, mainly vans and RVs. He couldn't spot Harrow, but it hardly mattered. The important thing was that nobody was looking at him. He unzipped his fly and urinated on the asphalt.

"Typical BMW owner," he said and got back in the car.

He fast-forwarded his phone tape and keyboarded the new numbers. He ate a Granola bar and some trail-mix, washed down with bottled water.

BEEP BEEP BEEP. He hurriedly dumped the gain on his direction finder. The old green Cadillac rolled directly in front of him and headed out. Harrow must have been parked down the row.

"At least he didn't catch me splashing the boots."

Five minutes later, Ordway was back on the interstate, asking Orpington if he had heard anything from Evan Highland in the last year or so.

"Evan Highland? Hmmm. Oh, yes, I remember him. Bright student. He left academia to join the CIA. I haven't heard a peep out of him since."

Ordway had been using the voice-stress analyzer for a dozen years. It measured microtremors in the voice—changes too small for the human ear to pick up. But like any good biofeedback device, it had trained Ordway to the point where he hardly needed it. He heard instantly that Orpington was lying. For one thing, he was suddenly talking slower. And Ordway could hear the tension—a squall line crossing the voice. Still, he glanced at the machine to be sure the LEDs were flashing red.

They blazed like a taxi's brake lights in a panic stop.

BAM! BAM! BAM!

Lamb jumped to his feet.

Someone was pounding on his door—why hadn't he heard a car? He darted to the suitcase on the floor, unzipped the concealed compartment in the lid, and yanked out his silenced gun.

He bounded upstairs and peeked out the living room window.

Directly below him, he could see a blond head. Alone, unarmed, her fine-boned fist raised for another episode of pounding, it was Sally. She was carrying a familiar brown envelope—she had her manuscript with her.

What the hell is she doing here?

BAM! BAM! BAM! BAM!

Better not let her in. We'll be alone. What if I lose control?

BAM! BAM! BAM! BAM!

Too late, she knows I'm here—she's seen my car. I can't alienate her—not before I find out where Winston is.

Lamb dashed downstairs and ran to the door. Sally stood there in a Pendleton shirt and jeans, no makeup, hair flying, looking deliciously upset.

"I'm sorry to bug you, but can we go over the story changes now?" she said.

"I'm right in the middle of something."

"I can't meet tomorrow morning."

"I might have a free hour later in the day. What time would be good?"

"*I don't know,*" she shouted. "I'm sorry. I've got a problem."

"What's that?"

"Julian, *please. Now* is good for me. Can't we just do it *now?*"

Stop blocking the door like an idiot. Let her in. Too late for anything else.

"I guess you'd better come inside." He tried to sound light, but his words were leaden with reluctance. He stood aside to let her pass.

The underground stream was still swollen from the weekend's rain; its loud gurgling echoed hollowly in the tiled room, like an indoor swimming pool in the final stage of emptying.

"You weren't kidding. The River Styx." She had relaxed a bit after winning her point.

They crossed the absurd little bridge. He walked behind her, trying not to watch her body move in her tight jeans.

"Sit, sit. Would you like coffee?"

"That would be great."

He stepped into his little galley kitchen and took his time with the coffee machine. Without her to look at, he regained some of his control.

So far so good. Just don't let the pictures start in your head.

He came out of the kitchen, walking carefully so the coffee wouldn't slosh. The glass-top coffee table was piled high with newspapers in Arabic, Hebrew, and Greek. "Throw those on the floor," he said. He waited while she stacked them neatly.

He placed the two cups down on the table and sat in the beach chair across from her.

Don't stare at her legs.

"So what's this big problem?"

Sally took agitated little sips of the hot coffee. "After the Reuben episode, Nan must have sicced her kennel club bitches on me. One of them spotted us working on the story at The Hole in the Wall and told Nan we were pitching woo amid the prune danish."

"That's embarrassing," he said.

Nan's friend just assumed I'm Sally's lover. Does everybody who sees us think that? Yes. Of course they do. They think, "Look at him. He's got that beautiful girl; he owns her. She can't resist him; she does whatever he wants."

"Nan threatened to kick me out of the house if it happened again. I hate to burden you with my problems, but it would be a lousy time. There are reasons I can't go back to Queens yet. So with Jake out of the picture—still in the hospital and all—I have to play along with Nan's weirdness. She had a dog meeting tonight, so I could leave. I'll try not to take too much of your time."

"Let's get to work, then."

"I really appreciate this," she said.

Appreciate the ties that bind. The bonds that bind. The rope that restrains—but not too much. The jump rope. First you're roped, then you jump. Rope you and rape you.

She scooted her beach chair next to his and put her manuscript on the table. He turned toward her.

Her face divided in two—Sally on one side, Linlinma on the other —as neatly as if sliced by a razor.

One face—blond and blue-eyed on the right, red-haired and green-eyed on the left. The lips were a nearly perfect match, lusciously full on both sides. They began to speak in Sally's voice.

What's she talking about? Jabber, jabber, jabber. Tape her mouth, rape her mouth. Where's my clit-dicer, tit-slicer, my nipple-ripper-stripper? Where's my cat-coring little steak knife?

"There's something I need," he said, getting up. He was vaguely aware that his voice was thick, drugged sounding.

"Are you all right?"

"I'm fine. Keep talking, I'm listening." He walked into the kitchen, wrenched open a drawer, and fumbled for the knife.

It had been too damn easy, Ordway thought. A few vague threats, and the dean of Wren College had unraveled like a cheap suit.

"You talk like you hardly remember him, Osbert. That's very strange. Weren't you, in point of fact, his *thesis adviser*? Never mind who I am—let's just say, a government agent. Go ahead, hang up. We can do this the hard way: squad cars, court orders, subpoenas. We have documentary evidence that he contacted you. Yes, Osbert, recently. Quite recently. Perhaps you'd like to share with me the subject of your conversation? I see—a close personal friend of yours joins the CIA and shows up years later with a *new face*—and you want me to believe you don't remember what you talked about? Why are you protecting him? I'm going to forget you said that, Osbert. I'm going to give you another chance to answer. . . ."

A few more minutes of that, and Orpington had crumbled.

A faint insect rattle issued from Ordway's cellular fax; it spat out Julian Lamb's Wren personnel file the way a kid spits the bubble gum into Mama's hand. Orpington had probably run all the way to the administration building and broken a window with a brick to get it.

Too impatient to wait, Ordway swung into the emergency lane, stopped the BMW, and eagerly read the fax as it squeegeed out of the slot.

He called himself *Julian Lamb* these days; poor Orpington had already blown the gaff on that. Here was the list of the courses he taught, his purloined Social Security number, putative date and place of birth, hair color, credit data, medical records, registration and license-plate number of his Prelude.

Most important of all—here was Lamb's summer address: 109 Leacock, Princeton, New Jersey. How convenient. Ordway was nearing Philly.

He pulled up the Princeton street map on the computer and typed in 109 Leacock. The cursor pulsed at the address. He typed a bit more and got the best route from the turnpike. He zoomed the map up and down in size, getting a feel for the area.

More under-dash scrabbling—the frightened professor had delivered the whole nine yards. A current photograph of Julian Lamb dot-matrixed into his hand.

He laid it on the seat next to his presurgery photo and the Identi-Kit. Winston hadn't done badly. The Identi-Kit looked a lot more like Lamb than the old shot of Evan Highland did.

Now, that's what I call two-faced, Ordway thought. *He must have found a genius plastic surgeon. I ought to ask him for the name before I waste him.*

Ordway powered back into traffic. His field-strength meter showed Harrow was now almost ten miles ahead, about to drift out of range. He flipped it off and speeded up. Let Harrow and son go home to their suburb in north Jersey, he no longer needed them. With any luck, Highland or Lamb or whatever he called himself would be dead before midnight.

Ordway was nearing the Princeton turnoff when he passed the green Cadillac.

It was all he could do not to wave.

·58·

"We is being tailed."

"You're sure?"

"I is sure sure."

Jake thought, *Now he sees the Constable behind every windshield. Why did I mention going to the Payden house?*

Winston himself was the reason for the detour. Trask Walkins had offered to put them up indefinitely at his home in Ardsley. It had just occurred to Jake he'd probably be leaving Winston alone there with strangers for days at a time. He did not respond well to being abandoned. Better pick up Sally and bring her along.

"Maybe you're just imagining things."

"The car are red."

"So you keep telling me. How come I never see it?"

"You is steering."

"Sure, give me sensible answers. What do you care. Princeton exit coming up. Look sharp now. If he's back there, he's got to get off too."

There was a long line at the pay booth. Winston, who had been riveted to the right rearview mirror, suddenly pointed through the windshield.

"Look! He are paying!"

Jake caught a glimpse of a red hatchback in the headlights of the car behind it. Before he could get a good look, it moved on and his view was obscured by the booth.

"That car was in front of us, not behind."

"You did say they might."

"I did? When did I say that?"

"When we did lose the blues."

"Oh. So I did. No fair. I don't teach you these fine points of police

361

knowledge so you can use them to crush me like a grape. Anyway, that car we just saw was a hatchback. You didn't say anything about a hatchback."

"Ain't see no hunchback."

"*Hatchback.* You know what a hatchback is."

Winston shook his head.

"A hatchback is a car with a . . . hatch . . . in the back . . . What the hell is a hatchback? The rear window and the trunk lid are one piece. They're flat on the back."

"It were *red.*"

"Red is a popular color. My Mustang is red, remember. *I'm* not following us. There are twenty cars in this line. One of them is going to be red."

The boy gave him a defiant look and turned to watch the right mirror again. "I did see it before."

"Sorry, sorry. Don't mean to bust your chops. Okay? We're being followed from the front by a red hatchback. But from now on, try to notice some distinguishing marks, okay? A mole, a squint, a sixteen-valve overhead cam engine—something besides just color. Okay?"

"I go do my best," Winston said, his eyes on the right mirror.

As Ordway took his change from the tollbooth attendant he glanced in the driver's side mirror and nearly dropped the money.

Five cars back—*Harrow's Cadillac.*

Was Harrow following *him?* Had he somehow made him back there on the road—maybe at the rest stop when he passed so close?

Ordway followed the ramp to the bottom, made the turn toward Princeton, and coasted along at highway speed for about a mile. He pulled into a closed gas station and parked on the side where he judged Harrow wouldn't notice him—unless Harrow was following him.

He spread his arms wide and slapped a two-handed release on the dash. A tray with his gun, silencer, and holster popped out of the seat beneath him and banged against his calves. In one motion he shrugged off his jacket and belted on the holster. He twirled the silencer onto the gun, laid it in his lap, and slipped his arms back into the jacket. He was ready for whatever Harrow had in mind.

A moment later the green Cadillac sailed past and kept on going.

If he's not following me, what's he doing here? Don't tell me the Avenging Angel has somehow found out where Lamb is living?

It hardly seemed possible. Still . . .

He holstered the gun, slapped the switches on the direction finder, and drifted toward the street.

No cruise control or two-mile gap here—he had to stay just far enough back to be out of sight. Once Harrow left the car, he could disappear.

Ordway drove with jaws locked, leaning forward, cybernetic slave to the steady beep of his direction finder. If the beep got too soft, he eased down on the accelerator and tightened the gap. Too loud, he gently lifted his foot and let Harrow pull away.

It was impossible; it couldn't be! Street by street, turn by turn, Harrow was driving the most direct route to 109 Leacock—as if he'd leaned in the BMW's window outside Philly and copied it off the laptop.

What was he planning to do with Lamb? Bring him back in cuffs for the greater glory of the NYPD? Toss the corpse on the director's desk? Cut him up with a chain saw and sell the pieces to the Fox Network?

It hardly made any difference now. Harrow was the wild card. He had the secret. His next phone call could destroy Ordway's career, disgrace him, put him in jail. He was a greater danger than Lamb. Lamb didn't want to tell the world the truth.

Harrow had to be killed. His young witness too.

First.

Before Lamb.

Now.

Minutes earlier, as Ordway had driven away from the tollbooth, Winston had said, "We is being tailed by two."

"Another one?"

"This one are black."

"Where? Point him out to me."

Winston pointed at the booth ahead. "He did pay."

"Another car following from the front? Are we being tailed or convoyed?"

"We is being tailed."

"Yeah, but both cars in front? Who's watching our buttissimo."

"I did see him at the stop!" Winston shouted.

"Okay. Okay. A black car. Another hunchback?"

Winston shook his head. "It were regular."

"As distinct from what? High-octane? You've got to give me more."

Silence.

Jake paid his toll and drove down the ramp.

"Aunt Freezie's junker was black. Did it look like that?"

"It were more new."

"Well that sure hones it to the bone. Remember what I said to look for?"

"Extinguisher marks."

"Exactly—those helmet-shaped dents you get when you sideswipe a fire truck. *Distinguishing* marks! Things that set it apart from other cars. You say you saw it when we stopped back there on the highway. Okay, it's a regular black car. There are lots of them. Why did you remember that particular one?"

"It did have antlers."

"You mean *antennas*? Those wires that stick up—like on the cellular phone?"

Winston shook his head. "It did have antlers so." He put his hands on his head, with the knuckles sticking up.

"You don't mean there's a twelve-point buck strapped to the fender? *Antlers*? You're not talking about a roll bar? You said it was a regular—"

Winston punched him in the side. "There! He are there!"

"Ouch! Where? The black BMW? I don't—oh, *those* antlers! We non-poets call that a *luggage rack*. Anyway, that car is parked."

"He go watch our buttissimo."

Jake had to laugh. "No flies on you. You're right. Classic setup. Red hatchback in front, black BMW behind. Communicating by walkie-talkie, alternating exposure, minimizing risk."

"You go lose the blues?"

"You'd like another roller-coaster ride, wouldn't you. But we're almost to Popsy's house. I don't want to put any extinguisher marks on his Eldorado at this late date."

"You ain't believe me."

"Just an honest difference of opinion. Tell you what. Let's both keep a sharp eye out. If we—" At that moment he glanced in the rearview mirror and caught a glint of metal. Four blocks back, at the crest of a hill, a black car passed under a streetlight and kicked light from its luggage rack.

"Bad news, kid, you may be right." Winston gave him a terrified look and began to tighten his straps.

"Not yet. We're going to turn right and pass a big sports field. If you look diagonally across it—kitty-corner—that's it—you can see back to the traffic circle we just passed through. I'll slow down, we'll see if Antlers is still on our buttissimo."

Winston pulled himself up and twisted around to look back. They reached the sports field.

"He coming quick sharp!" Winston shouted. Startled, Jake stole a glance through the rear door window. The BMW shot across his field of vision, doing at least sixty on a residential street.

He stood on the gas pedal. "Strap down!"

That BMW will eat me alive. Got to lose him quick. Please, God, no firefight with the boy in the car.

They were near the Payden house; Jake had a general idea of the area. The next right was a long crescent that connected residential enclaves and looped back to the road he was on. Maybe a death trap, but it was the only way off the straightaway before the BMW turned onto it and could see them again.

Jake arced over into the left lane, eased up on the pedal, wrenched the wheel to the right, and floored it. The old Caddy heeled over, tires squealing, and flung itself into the mouth of the crescent street.

Now, do something! Quick—while you're out of sight!

He half stood, looking around wildly. He felt the slight drag of Winston's weight; his left hand was clamped to Jake's pants belt.

They raced past a series of short streets that dead-ended in turnarounds.

Why did I come in here? He's going to know it's the only place—

Beyond a turnaround, through a gap in the trees, Jake spotted moving headlights. Another road ran behind these houses.

He careened into a wide U-turn, peeled back to the spot where he saw the gap, and raced left on a narrow street past expensive, well-kept homes. Halfway around the loop at the bottom, he veered into a driveway.

Please, God, no fences, no stakes.

He drove across a lawn, churned through a flower bed, ripped through a low border of shrubs, and powered into the woods.

Someone had cleared out the trees back here—that's why he had seen through to the other road. He jounced through weeds and rocks, until he hit the dirt track made by the trucks, then bucked at high speed through a forest of stumps to the pavement beyond.

He turned left and drove off at fifty-five.

"All clear, Hawkeye. We dumped the chump."

"Red one isn't dump."

They tooled along past open fields for a few minutes. Jake said, "See all those lights about a mile ahead? Route One. You don't like Princeton? We're gone. Out of the area. Straight to Ardsley."

For the first time since they left DC, the boy smiled. "I is glad."

"I'm not giving Antlers a second—"

The black BMW jumped into his rearview mirror like a jackrabbit hopping up from behind a wall.

He stamped the gas pedal to the floor.

"He found us. *How in hell did he find us?*"

Acceleration shoved him into his seat. At eighty he felt Winston latch on to his belt again. At a hundred the game old Eldorado was still picking up speed. His perceptions changed: the sides of the road squeezed together in front of him; he was forced to straddle the center line.

Not fast enough.

Each glance in the mirror told him the BMW had chopped a major chunk off his lead.

The traffic light on Route 1 came at him like a wild pitch.

"Stay green," Jake ordered under his breath.

It blinked orange.

He leaned on the horn, pumped the brakes, and yanked the wheel left. Tires screaming, the two-ton automobile danced and skated through the turn, cut directly across the bow of an oncoming tractor-trailer, and smoked up the highway in the outside lane. Barely fifty yards ahead was a motel complex. He squealed into the lot without slowing down, raced to the rear, swung wide, and tucked into a parking slot between two other cars. He was behind the main building, out of sight of the highway.

"Out of the car—we can watch from back there."

Jake sprinted along the edge of the parking lot, then plunged into the weeds behind it, Winston right behind him. They ran low, dropped to all fours, then crawled to a point far enough south to give a view of the highway.

Winston crouched, Jake lay flat. The ground seemed dry, but dampness instantly seeped through his clothing at the elbows and the length of his legs—wherever his body touched the ground.

Winston clung to his arm with the tenacity of fear, watching the road intently.

"He are coming!"

The BMW flashed past in the heavy traffic, roof rack shining under the highway lights.

"That time we know he missed us," Jake said.

Winston tugged at Jake's arm. He was staring across the highway at the parking lot of a steak house. A red hatchback was just backing into the slot directly opposite them.

"I see it," Jake said. "There are hundreds of cars around here. One of them is bound to be red. We'll wait awhile to be on the safe side."

After another minute on the wet ground he said, "If I ever doubt you again, I swear I'll listen to 'Whole World in His Hands' ten times when you're not even there."

The BMW had just thrust into view at the far end of the lot.

As if on rails, the black car swung around the rear of the motel and made straight for the green Cadillac. There appeared to be only one man in the car. Area lights on stanchions played over his shadowy face as he drove toward them. As the car passed directly in front of their spot in the weeds, Jake could see the driver was steering with his left hand. His right was pointing a very large handgun out the passenger side window. The gun had a silencer on it.

The man wheeled slowly past the rear of the Eldorado, circled around in a big arc, and stopped in front of it. Apparently satisfied there was nobody inside, he stuffed the big gun under his jacket and drove rapidly back to the main motel building. Leaving the motor running, he jumped out of his car and ran inside.

Jake badly wanted to sprint down the line of parked cars to the BMW and crouch behind the fender, gun drawn, until the man came back to his car. But he couldn't leave Winston alone here in the weeds. Especially not with another hostile car out there. What if he himself were killed? The men who were following him knew that Winston was somewhere around the motel. He had to get the kid to safety. That was the first priority.

"Antlers went in the motel," he whispered. "If we can lose the red hatchback, we're home free."

Winston took off like a shot, racing through the weeds toward the Cadillac.

Ordway pelted up a flight of stairs and charged along a corridor.

Harrow had made him. No question after his fade in the crescent. The direction finder had clearly shown him turning right, somewhere near the middle. But where was the damn road? Nothing on the map. Ordway had wasted precious minutes driving back and forth, looking for it, and finally been forced to go all around Robin Hood's barn to catch up.

Now Harrow had ducked into this motel. He must be calling for help—calling the director—telling somebody else that Lamb is the Silencer. Stop him! Don't let him get to a phone.

Ordway burst through a pair of ornamental swinging doors into the lobby.

A mob scene! There must have been ten people at the desk alone and twenty more milling around the lobby. A red-faced man in a sport jacket was bellowing at the clerk about his guaranteed reservation.

Ordway forced himself to walk. *Where were the goddamn phones?* He circled the crowd at the desk. *There!* In a big alcove to the right of the desk, two long rows of booths.

He spotted Winston tugging at the door of the end booth on the right; Harrow must be inside.

He walked calmly to the end of the alcove and drew his gun. Winston stopped tugging at the door and stared at him, then quickly backed away in fear. Ordway wrenched open the door of the booth.

The man inside said, "Levon, what did I just tell—?" Then he saw the gun and froze.

He was black.

"I'll give you my money, just don't hurt the boy," he said quietly.

Ordway controlled his urge to shoot them both out of sheer frustration. Not only did he have the wrong people, he was stuck with them. If he walked away, this guy would holler bloody murder.

"Hang up," he said quietly.

The gun was a Colt .45 finished in stainless steel. Fitted with its huge silencer, it hypnotized its targets like a gleaming metal cobra. Eyes riveted on it, the man fumbled the telephone receiver into its cradle without looking back.

"Who're *you?*" Levon asked.

"Not *now*," the man said sharply.

Ordway pointed the gun at the boy, then back at the man. "I won't hurt Levon if you do as I say."

"I'm not carrying much cash, but I'm wearing a gold Rolex," the man said.

"Good. Synchronize it to mine."

Ordway showed him the face of his own gold Rolex.

The man did so and made a motion to remove his watch.

"Keep it," Ordway snapped. "You can't buy your way out of this. The only way to save the boy's life and your own is to do exactly as I say. Stop trying to think and focus on what you must do. I want you to call the weather number. Keep doing that and listening to it exactly twenty minutes. Call anyone else and I'll know. Leave the booth and I'll know. Then go up to your room without telling anyone about this. You never saw me. If you ever tell anybody about this, I'll know and I'll come back and kill you both. Understood?"

Levon asked, "Dad, is that a real gun?"

"I'll explain later," the man said in a quiet voice.

Ordway tapped the man's chest with the gun. "I asked if you understood."

"Listen to the telephone weather report for twenty minutes. Go up to my room. Never mention this to anybody."

"That's it. Start immediately."

Ordway watched the man turn smartly around and begin to dial. Then he backed away, holstered his gun, and walked out of the phone alcove. Levon followed. As he crossed the lobby he heard Levon telling the bell captain, "That man pointed a gun at my dad."

As he pushed through the swinging doors he heard the bell captain say, "I bet you like to play cops and robbers."

Nobody had come into the corridor. Ordway broke into a trot.

As he went out the back door he glanced down to the end of the lot. No green Eldorado.

He darted to his idling BMW and flicked on the field-strength meter. Harrow was eight miles north and counting. Almost at the end of his electronic tether. A few more minutes, and he would have slipped out of range.

Son of a bitch!

Ordway stood on the gas pedal. Tires screaming, his BMW hurtled in hot pursuit.

Ordway watched the speedometer climb past ninety. Traffic was heavy, he had to weave in and out. He was gaining steadily. Harrow was only four miles ahead. Then three.

He drew his Colt, unscrewed the silencer one-handed, and holstered it again.

No more vanishing acts. Kill him on the highway. Drift in behind him and blow his brains out. I'll be in front before he loses control. Then I'll swing by the wreck and put the kid out of his misery if he's not already dead.

Beep beep BEEP. Harrow was slowing down. The direction meter flickered, then began to slide over. His quarry had turned left. Ordway saw his chance to make up a lot of ground and pushed his speed into three digits.

He closed to two-and-a-half, two, one-and-a-half miles. The direction meter strained to the left. Where was the turn? A moment later the instruments told him he had gone past.

Another phantom road!

He had far outdistanced the last pod of cars he had passed; the road was relatively clear on both sides. He slammed on the brake. His tires screamed in torment. The BMW bucked and bounced but refused to fishtail—it drew two long lines of black rubber down the highway, straight as a ruler.

As the speedometer plummeted below twenty-five, he threw the gear to neutral, cut the wheel left, and jerked the hand brake while holding the release out with his left hand. The rear end fairly flew off line; the car spun one hundred eighty degrees, now sliding backward. He muscled the wheel straight and pumped the foot brake. For a millisecond, the car was actually motionless. He popped the hand brake, stamped on the gas, beelined into the opposite lane, and accelerated back up the highway—now going the other way. The acrid stench of fried rubber billowed through the car.

"You're not getting away, Harrow!"

As he neared the indicated turn again he braked and lifted up a few inches from his seat, squinting hard at the right side of the highway. There it was—a dirt road into the trees.

He cut the wheel hard right and bounced into the woods.

His quarry was straight ahead about a mile. Even with the missed turn, he had still made up most of the distance. He powered ahead, risking a broken axle in the big ruts, pushing to the limit.

Beep. Beep. BEEP. The field-strength meter showed he was closing rapidly. Harrow had slowed way down—he was only doing about ten miles per hour. The road must be petering out up ahead. He'd made a bad mistake taking that big Caddy into the woods.

The BMW was no off-road vehicle either. It wallowed in the deep ruts, swayed and jerked as it lost and gained traction. Its accurate road feel, usually such a pleasure, pummeled him until he felt his eyeballs would come loose.

The field-strength meter said he was still gaining rapidly.

Good, good. This time I'm going to get right on top of him. Climb up his tailpipe. No sudden disappearances.

He killed the headlights, leaving just the parks, but hardly slowed down. The road continued rough but straight. Harrow was dead ahead, maybe six hundred yards.

He dug the Colt out of its holster, held it against the steering wheel, and worked it into his left hand, driving and holding the big gun, ready to shoot out the driver's side window. He could shoot with either hand—it didn't matter to him; he kept himself checked out on both.

Beep. BEEP. BEEP. Closer, closer—he wondered how the Caddy could make headway at all. The road kept getting worse. It slanted up steeply like a hill directly in front of him. Harrow was three hundred yards dead ahead and doing ten miles per hour. Ordway gunned the engine.

The car bucked violently up the hill, reached a level place where the rear wheels suddenly grabbed full traction, and launched itself into nothingness.

It was airborne for an instant, then nosed over and dropped vertically.

It crashed on a steep embankment, mashing springs and shocks. It plunged downward, hit a low tree stump, flipped over, and rolled thirty feet to the bottom.

Jake heard the crash and stopped running. He put his hands on his knees and puffed for a minute, regaining his breath.

Then he tossed away the little transmitter he had pulled from the underside of his fender and, illuminating the path with a flashlight, jogged back the way he had come.

When he had peeled out of the motel lot, the red hatchback hadn't followed. Winston had been wrong on that one.

So how did the black BMW track them after he lost it at the crescent? How could it follow them into the motel parking lot and drive right up to them as if magnetized? He had begun to wonder if there might be an antenna in that roof rack. And a transmitter clinging to the underside of his own fender.

He trotted along a dirt road for some distance, then clambered down an embankment, and worked his way across the pit of a huge construction site, moving with more caution than he had allowed himself a few minutes earlier when he was doing his impression of a car.

The BMW was pitched on its roof. The driver hung upside down in his seat belt, an occasional drop of blood falling from the left side of his head where it had been smashed against the door. He was obviously dead.

The roof rack was crushed. In the flashlight beam, Jake could see where the two magnetic whip antennas on either side of the rack had been connected. The leads had been hidden under a chrome strip that had been knocked off in the fall.

He studied the corpse. An older man, expensive clothes, expensive haircut. Even bloody, dead, and upside-down, he looked like a corporate CEO. Not the Constable.

Worried about fire, he knelt, reached inside, and turned off the ignition. The car was loaded with sophisticated electronic equipment.

He searched the dead man's pockets, feeling queasy. He found three sets of ID. One set belonged to Calvin C. Ordway of the Central Intelligence Agency.

"I should have kept my big mouth shut with the director about going to the media, right, Calvin?"

The director had located the killer and decided on a cover-up. Jake and Winston were the only ones who could expose it, so he had sent Calvin here to kill them. He was going to bury the whole thing and let Mel Haney's wet dream become a miniseries. Why? Did the rogue agent have connections in the intelligence community who were protecting him? Were they planning to kill him, pay him off, promote him? Hard to know. One thing was clear—if they got to him before Jake did, he would disappear forever. There was no time left.

Winston had left the Cadillac where Jake had hidden it in the woods and was descending the embankment by sliding from root to root.

"Stay back," Jake shouted.

As respectfully as he could, he reached around the dangling corpse and took the evidence from the car: the audio tapes of his cellular phone conversations, the dossiers and faxes. The laptop had a hard disk; he took the whole computer.

"Sorry to act like a greedy nephew on the day of the funeral, but I need this stuff to convince Trask Walkins that I'm not blowing smoke. But I don't mean to monopolize the conversation—if you think of something jump right in."

Lying on the ceiling of the car were three pictures:

Winston's Identi-Kit of the Constable.

An Agent: Evan Highland. Address on the Greek Island of Spétsai. Supposed to have died in Europe some time ago.

A professor of languages from Wren College: Julian Lamb. For the summer, he was renting from a family named Reuter at 109 Leacock, Princeton. Jake recognized the street name and shined his flashlight on the little map someone had sketched below it.

"Wait a minute—isn't this the big black house on the other side of Popsy's woodlot? Don't tell me the Constable lives there!"

Highland and Lamb didn't look much alike—but oddly, they both resembled the Identi-Kit. Were they the two suspects? Was the director using the Identi-Kit as his guide?

The boy darted past him to the car and looked into the dead man's face.

"I told you to stay back," Jake said, running to him.

Winston shook his head grimly. "He are not the Constable."

"I know—I was trying to spare you," Jake said. "How about these two?" Jake held out the pictures of the two men.

Winston frowned as he looked from Highland to Lamb, Lamb to Highland.

He raised his hand and brought a finger down again and again like a pecking bird on the picture of Julian Lamb.

"He are he."

"You're sure?" Jake asked.

Winston continued hitting at the paper.

"Constable self!"

·59·

"Whoa! Guess my work's cut out for me. At least I know what I've got to do," Sally said.

Lamb's bed was snowed under with manuscript; they had been using it for a desk. Sally gathered up the pages. "I'm off. I'll stick the revisions in your mailbox tomorrow whenever I get a chance. I have to be careful—Nan has a thousand eyes."

"Bang on the door. Some of my meetings have been canceled. I'll probably be around. Want something to drink before you go?"

"A glass of cold water would be nice."

Lamb walked out into the dark living room and along the wall to the kitchen. He switched on the light and paused for a moment, shaking with excitement. He no longer wanted to kill Sally. Instead, he had become obsessed with the thought that after he killed Winston and Jake, she would be alone, vulnerable, needy. He'd close in on her, take her over emotionally, dominate her, make her forget that Jake had ever lived.

He took the steak knife from his jacket pocket and tossed it back into the drawer.

Jake raced fast and low along the back wall of the dark living room, the gurgling of the indoor stream covering his footsteps, his Beretta 9 mm thrust in front of him in a two-handed grip.

At the far end of the wall, light spilled from two open doors.

A man came out of the far one carrying a glass, the light full on him.

The face Winston had pointed to on the fax—Lamb Highland Silencer Constable. Dead Man.

Gotta get close. Point blank. Blow his brains out.

373

A familiar voice said, "The bed is all yours again."

She came out the near door, directly in front of him.

His life burned to the ground. His brain screamed in his skull. His perceptions splintered crazily like cracking ice. *Sally*—coming from the bed of the man he hated most in the world, the man he had sworn to kill?

Jake must have cried out. He saw Lamb turn in slow motion, a look of slight confusion on his face, and peer into the shadows that rushed along the wall.

Sally's eyes followed the direction of his gaze. "Jake!" Startled, she stepped toward him, blocking his shot at Lamb.

"Stand aside!" Jake shouted, his own voice sounding hollow and faint to him. He dimly saw Lamb race behind Sally into the bedroom. The image dwindled down a long narrow tunnel.

Close by his ear, Sally screamed, *"Stop! It's not what you think!"*

He raised his Beretta.

Her hand darted out of nowhere and snatched the gun. She flung it in a high trajectory across the indoor river. It plopped in the gravel of the far bank.

"Don't listen to Nan. She's gone crazy!"

Lamb bent over a suitcase, fumbling with the lid.

Zip!

Jake raced into the bedroom.

Zip Ziiiiip! Lamb had the false compartment in his suitcase lid open.

Jake sprinted the length of the room. He saw the tip of the silencer swing up. He hurdled the bed, flinging a pillow at the gun.

SHEW!

The bullet creased his right side like a wallop from a poker. The pillow exploded. Lamb had both hands on his gun, cocking it. Jake charged through the feather blizzard and punched him full in the face. He crashed backward against the wall. Jake grabbed his gun hand and pounded it on the radiator like a man killing a snake. The gun thumped on the floor.

Lamb smashed his fist into Jake's still-healing throat wound. He went "unh!" and stumbled back, spitting blood.

Lamb dove through the bedroom window in a shower of broken glass and raced into the night.

Jake scooped up Lamb's gun, twisted off the silencer, and vaulted through the window after him.

From the head of the driveway, Winston heard the crash of glass. A moment later he saw a dark figure race from behind the house and

374

plunge into the wooded strip at the side of the Reuter's property.

The Constable had gotten away! He was on the loose! Winston wheeled and ran.

Lamb blundered ahead in the profound darkness, until he half-crashed into a chain-link fence.

He fell to his knees and crawled along it, flailing blindly until he found his marker tree stump. He tore at the ground in front of it. His right hand throbbed painfully where Harrow had pounded it on the radiator.

What was that sound?

A song, faint and persistent, drifted to him from beyond the chain-link fence.

He's got the night and the day in His hands,

Winston! A hostage! Harrow won't dare shoot. I can lure him close enough for a throw.

He's got the sun and the moon in His hands,

His burrowing fingers scraped over a smooth surface. He snatched the egg and shoved it in his front shirt pocket.

The chain-link fence towered twelve feet. He climbed up it, levered himself over the top, and dropped to the ground beside a one-lane asphalt road. He raced toward the music.

He's got you and me, brother, in His hands,
He's got the whole world in His hands.

Ahead in the darkness—a big car parked by the fence, pointing away from him. The music came from inside. He wrenched open the passenger-side door; the dome light blazed.

HE'S GOT THE LITTLE BITTY BABIES IN HIS HANDS,

The car was empty. The cassette player was lying on the floor in the back, playing full blast.

HE'S GOT THE LITTLE BITTY BABIES . . .

375

Lamb stamped it into silence.

Behind him—distant footfalls—rapid, pounding.

Harrow.

Lamb darted into the impenetrable darkness by the fence and raced twenty yards in front of the car. He wheeled, snatched the egg from his pocket, crushed it in his hand, and gripped the wafer in his swollen fingers.

When he reaches the car, I throw.

Winston clapped his hands over his mouth to stifle an anguished cry. *By the time Jake got here, the Constable would be gone!*

He had to stop him! But then the Constable would know where he was and come after him! The thought made his whole body tremble. For a moment, his arms and legs wouldn't move.

Then he rolled from beneath the Cadillac, opened the driver's side door, and clambered onto the seat.

Lamb saw the dome light come on. In its aquarium glow, a small figure leaned against the wheel.

He came back to the car! I can still hold him hos—

The car's headlights hit him like a silent explosion, full high-beam. He staggered, floodlit in a blast of brightness, stunned and blinded.

Little bastard! I'll cut his heart out!

BLAM!

Harrow had seen him! He was shooting from somewhere up the road. Lamb whipped back his arm and skimmed the wafer like a Frisbee, hard as he could, at the distant spot where he had seen the muzzle flash.

Jake had a brief image of a huge fireball directly in front of him. The force of the explosion hurled him backward ten feet.

He sprawled on the asphalt, stunned.

The Cadillac rolled over like a Saint Bernard. A second fireball bloomed as the gas tank exploded with a roar, throwing the trunk lid thirty feet.

Red hot shrapnel rained down, clanking on the road and igniting small fires in the grass.

"No!" Jake shouted. "Please, God. No!"

Winston was in that car!

Black smoke billowed from the wreck. Lamb charged through it, brandishing a tire iron.

Jake looked around, slapping the asphalt with his hands. Where was his gun? He couldn't find his . . .

Lamb blotted out fire and sky, his tire iron whistling down toward Jake's head like a woodsman's ax.

Jake caught it with his right hand and screamed; the metal was red-hot. His hand jerked open involuntarily; the iron crashed through and clubbed him full on the chest—*THUMP*—like a dropped watermelon hitting concrete. The shock momentarily stopped his heart. He flopped back on the pavement. Lamb, his hands protected by scraps of upholstery leather, reared back for another blow.

"Dead sea," he said.

A small wiry figure ran up behind him and jumped on his back. Winston clamped his arm around Lamb's throat and choked him. Lamb took one hand off the tire iron, ripped Winston's arm loose, and flung him into the grass.

Lamb spun back to Jake and brought down the glowing hot tire iron again.

Jake ducked and twisted sideways, fending off the blow with his right arm. The iron skidded along it and slammed the side of his face. He heard a sizzle like bacon frying, smelled the stench of burning blood. The side of his head exploded with searing pain. He had been branded from mouth to cheekbone. His vision dimmed. He sprawled on his back, writhing helplessly in torment, his consciousness slipping away.

Lamb raised the tire iron again.

His head jerked grotesquely backward. Winston had jumped up and grabbed his hair.

He staggered, lost his balance, swayed for a moment, swiping back awkwardly with one hand. Winston twisted away from the punches, and clung fiercely.

The tire iron rang on the pavement. Lamb reached over his shoulders with both hands, lifted Winston high by the arms, pivoted, and hurled the boy over his head like a projectile. Winston crashed down on his back by the side of the road fifteen feet away and lay without moving.

"You're next," Lamb shouted as he scooped up the tire iron.

He wheeled back to Jake, who had stopped writhing and was struggling to get up. Lamb planted his feet and brought his weapon down full force at the skull of the man beneath him. Jake caught the searing bar with his left hand and held it.

"Winston!" he shouted. "By your foot—the gun!"

Lamb jerked the iron from side to side, desperate to free it, crucifying Jake's hand.

"Shoot!" Jake hollered. "Pull the trigger!"

Winston screamed, "I is scared to hit *you!*"

"*Shoot!*"

Lamb swiveled his head and caught a glimpse of a small figure standing in a shooter's crouch, arms extended, hands empty.

No gun.

Every cell in Lamb's brain screamed *TRICK!* as he plunged forward, and Jake surged up from the pavement, his left hand hauling on the red-hot bar, his right arcing up from his jacket pocket with Roger's steak knife. The blade ripped through Lamb's throat in a shower of blood, half decapitating him.

His tire iron clanked feebly on the asphalt. He collapsed, his face on top of Jake's, almost kissing. His eyes were wide with surprise, his body jerked and heaved as if he were making love.

The geyser of blood from his neck slackened and subsided. He stopped thrashing and became much heavier.

Jake shoved the corpse away and stood up. The pain from his burned left hand suddenly hit him, and he swayed, gritting his teeth.

In the distance, he could hear Sally calling his name.

In the flickering light of the burning car, Jake caught the glint of his gun barrel twenty yards further up by the roadside, where the force of Lamb's bomb had thrown it.

Winston stared hard at the Constable as if making sure he was dead.

Finally he looked up at Jake and said, "We did put a cool move on him."

Jake nodded. "So we did, Winston Churchill Harrow, so we did."